Life Number Nine

Also by Joe Heap

The Rules of Seeing
When the Music Stops

Life Number Nine

JOE HEAP

b

THE BOROUGH PRESS

The Borough Press
An imprint of HarperCollins*Publishers* Ltd
1 London Bridge Street
London SE1 9GF

www.harpercollins.co.uk

HarperCollins*Publishers*
Macken House,
39/40 Mayor Street Upper,
Dublin 1
D01 C9W8

First published by HarperCollins*Publishers* 2025
1

A catalogue record for this book is available from the British Library

Hardback ISBN: 978-0-00-847502-4
Trade Paperback ISBN: 978-0-00-847503-1

This novel is entirely a work of fiction.
The names, characters and incidents portrayed in it are
the work of the author's imagination. Any resemblance to
actual persons, living or dead, events or localities is
entirely coincidental.

Lyrics to 'Saturday Sun' by Nick Drake.
Reproduced with permission from Blue Raincoat Music

Typeset in Sabon by Palimpsest Book Production Ltd, Falkirk, Stirlingshire

Printed and Bound in the UK using 100% Renewable Electricity
at CPI Group (UK) Ltd

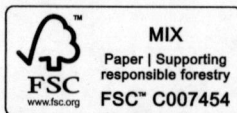

MIX
Paper | Supporting
responsible forestry
FSC
www.fsc.org
FSC™ C007454

This book contains FSC™ certified paper and other controlled sources
to ensure responsible forest management.

For more information visit: www.harpercollins.co.uk/green

To
Sue and Tim,

who stopped me becoming a tortured genius
by being wonderful parents.

Thanks for nothing, guys.

I dream of you, to wake: would that I might
Dream of you and not wake but slumber on;
Nor find with dreams the dear companion gone,
As, Summer ended, Summer birds take flight . . .

– Christina Rossetti

Little birdie, little birdie
Come and sing me your song.
I've a short time for to be here
And a long time to be gone.

– American Traditional

Someone, I tell you, will remember us,
even in another time.

– Sappho

Think about stories with reason and rhyme
Circling through your brain
And think about people in their season and time
Returning again and again . . .

– Nick Drake, 'Saturday Sun'

1

Let's get one thing straight – Earth doesn't go round in circles. She *spirals*. Watch her blue hips swinging her belt of sequinned satellites. The whole galaxy is diving into deep space, one thousand kilometres per second. You're never in the same place twice. Remember where you were for the worst moment of your life? You'll never stand on that spot again. It's back there, in the dark we left behind. Earth is corkscrewing into the night, a lonely helix dreaming of her double. Can't go back; got to go forwards.

Think of it like a spiralling seed.

Think of it like a swallow on the wing.

Think of it for a moment, this ball of rain and cloud you've lived on your whole life, going like a bullet from a gun without ever noticing.

With all this spatial uncertainty, you'd be forgiven for thinking we'll never locate our protagonists. Our X and Y. Two specks of dust on another speck of dust, circling a burning speck of dust which (though it seems super-massive from our point of view) is one among two hundred billion trillion, all racing hurry and scurry like Piccadilly Circus.

Zoom in.

Past the clutter of telecommunication satellites. Past noctilucent clouds. Past the soup of radio waves: pop songs, military manoeuvres, late-night call-ins. Past the ozone layer, still licking its wounds. Past passenger jets, fretting the sky with beams of silver. Past the city's dusky night-veil of pollution. Past phone masts, slate roofs, upper windows admitting no light, hoardings for English classes and Thai massages, pigeon-proof crowns of haloed street lamps . . .

Berwick Street.

Here he is – our Y, one half of our equation. Jem Adjaye, worrying at his phone. He's in a rush, like the universe. His Clarks desert boots follow where Virginia Woolf's espadrilles and William Blake's shabby hobnails trod before. He's on time for his reservation at a small plates bistro in Smith's Court, but would rather be early.

Jem doesn't go on dates. Not if he can avoid it. In this case, he couldn't avoid it – the match-up was arranged by his friend, Lucas. (*My best friend*, Jem tells himself. *Your only friend*, he replies). This time he's been matched with a senior solicitor with a spaniel who goes to doggy daycare. The spaniel, not the solicitor. Be polite but not over-eager. Rejections can be handled in the DMs.

Now we have one of our coordinates, hold on to Jem whilst we rummage around for the other. *Everything exists in relation to something else. Someone else. A frame of reference is necessary to calculate position and velocity.* We need to find the X to Jem's Y, and here she comes. Further down the street, Mika Zielińska maintains a steady speed in the direction of work.

Have you ever wondered how many times you met someone before you met them? How many times you passed a future lover in the street, sat in the same restaurant as a friend-to-be, rode the train with a not-yet-enemy? Or perhaps it was more remote. Did you laugh at the same joke on TV? Did you look up to the moon at the same moment? It must have happened. How entangled were your lives, before you tangled?

And before that? How many times did your mothers meet, or your mothers' mothers, or your great grandmothers' great grandmothers? Those were your lives too. You just forgot them, at the moment of birth. With each birth a forgetting, a splitting in half, but the truth remains: you were there.

The air pulses like dragonfly wings. A thousand sounds lapping and overlapping. People shout from stalls, music belches from nightclub doorways, rickshaw stereos doppler past. Other sounds go unheard – shivering electricity junctions, dyspeptic groans from the Tube below, pigeons burbling in the masonry. Each noise swamped by the rest, each adding its timbre to the whole.

He almost misses her.

A moment longer looking at his phone and Mika would have passed by. But he does look up, and for a moment he sees her looking back at him. Auburn hair held back with clips. A freckled nose, pierced on one side. That's all, and then she's gone. If Mika notices Jem, he leaves no impression on the soft paper of her memory.

They speed apart, our X and Y.

Mika summits the road, then stops. You'd be forgiven for thinking the shiver of destiny made her pause. But no – on the corner is a van, white with a blue-chequered band.

3

It looks almost like an ordinary police van, but Mika knows better. IMMIGRATION ENFORCEMENT, with *Home Office* in smaller, embarrassed type. She takes her phone out, crosses to the other side and continues. Within a minute she is in the kitchen, scrubbing up and buttoning whites.

Jem continues until he reaches a temporary crossing. Blue plastic barriers shield a tarmac abscess. *We're Fixing Pipes.* Jem glances down at the sedimentary layers exposed to Soho's neon lights. Coke bottle, clay pipe, flint axe, bone fragment of hippopotamus, river clay. Deep time. As he waits for the lights to change, three notifications shiver through his phone.

You there?

Don't do a runner.

I promised you weren't a knobhead.

Still looking at the screen, Jem steps forward. A speeding BMW 3 Series slams its brakes on too late. Six cylinders of turbo-diesel power the car into Jem's side. The impact is similar to a fall from a third-storey window. Jem is thrown over the bonnet; his head hits the windscreen, cracking the glass next to a plastic dancing hula-girl. The car stops. He rolls back and drops to the road. People shout or scream. A car door opens. The night fractures, makes an effort to put itself back together, falls apart again. Humpty Dumpty sat on a wall . . .

Jem is folded into a black envelope.

2

Some hours pass. A lot happens or nothing much happens, depending on your point of view. Frames of reference. Temporal resolution. There are sirens and flashing lights. There are shouted dinner orders and gouts of brandy-flame. In geological time, it is less than a millionth of a billionth of a second. Twenty-six mobile phones are lost on the Tube; fifty-three babies are born in the city's hospitals; seventeen cats kill eighteen rats (for one cat catches two).

After this stretch of nothing-and-everything it is 1 a.m., local time. Jem is a little way away, but let's stay in Soho for the time being. After work, and after-work drinks, Mika has returned to the restaurant with a singular purpose. She's going to break in.

'Right, I think I remember this . . . '

'You think?'

'If the alarm goes off, we walk away,' Mika shrugs.

'Briskly, yes?'

Mika is with her friend, Suzy, and their new colleague, Olly, who isn't sure why he's here at all. They work in the kitchen of SINE, which a critic for the *Guardian* likened to 'eating a bucket of oysters at a monster truck rally'. The restaurant is very popular, very expensive, and very loud. Mika is a sous-chef, acting head chef on the days when their boss is too hung over, which is every day. Suzy is a saucier and Olly a dishwasher. After work they went for a couple of drinks and plans were made.

'You know this is insane?' Olly looks at her. 'I'd feel better if you admitted this was insane.'

'Relax.'

'But—'

'Hush!' Suzy snaps at him. Her mouth flicks up at the corners like a cat, giving her a permanently smug look.

'It's fine,' Mika says soothingly. 'We work here. If we get caught, we say the security system wasn't on.'

'And if he asks why we're here?'

'I'll say I left something – my phone charger – and we were passing on our way to the Tube.'

There is no need to specify who 'he' is. Their boss, Michelin-starred James Conroy, is an alcoholic, a coke addict and a narcissist. None of these ingredients is hard to source in the catering industry, but whisked into one man-sized amuse bouche, they're something special. He'll say he's not easy to work with and laugh, as though laughing makes it okay. Add to this the fact that the restaurant, like most restaurants, has no HR department . . . well, sometimes you have to take matters into your own hands.

'Here we go.'

Mika punches a code into the keypad. She found the six numbers scrawled on an invoice for their seafood supplier. She holds her breath and presses the enter key. *Click*. A green light flashes six times; everything is quiet.

'Fuck . . . oh fuck.' Olly is hyperventilating. 'Why am I doing this?'

Mika is confident the answer has to do with getting into her pants, but it seems rude to point this out.

'Come on.'

'You're enjoying this!' Suzy shakes her head and uses her staff key to unlock the door.

Inside, everything is dark. The air smells of the food they prepared a couple of hours ago. Mika waits for the door to close, then hits the lights. The fluorescent strip lights rustle and blink like sleep-dishevelled angels. The kitchen is spotless, every surface wiped and every utensil in its place: Mika made sure of that.

'This way.' She walks to James's office, down a short corridor at the side of the kitchen.

All this started in the bar, when Suzy complained she couldn't go to her cousin's wedding. Out of holiday allowance. Her contract allows nineteen days of leave. Long-serving staff – and Mika – get twenty-three. Not a lot, but she had to haggle for it. Maybe it's because Mika knows she will be moving on soon; maybe she's just sick of their boss. In a couple of minutes, she had a plan. She turns the light on.

'Suzy, find your contract. They're in that drawer over there. The key's on a bit of Blu Tack under his desk. Olly, you're our lookout, yes?'

'Lookout for what?'

Oh, his face! Like a frightened, blond rabbit.

'Just go – nobody's going to show up.'

He walks back to the kitchen. Mika fires up James's computer. Two and a half billion transistors begin their dance of and/or/not. Mika knows the password because he gets her to do admin when he's 'not feeling well'. He'll sit in the corner with a Bloody Mary, dictating emails like a Fifties business executive. She cannot wait to get out of here. Another two months is all she needs.

'Found it.'

'Great – put it in the shredder.'

Doubt clouds Suzy's face.

'Maybe we shouldn't be doing this.'

'Suzy, tell me, have I ever let you down?'

'That time you—'

'It was a rhetorical question. Trust me now?'

Suzy takes a breath and puts the contract in the shredder. The grinding noise makes Mika's stomach flutter.

'Right, here's the file . . . '

She pulls up the template on James's computer. This plan wouldn't work if he emailed people their contracts, but he has a policy of not leaving electronic records. Paper can be misplaced.

'I'll just fill in your details . . . ' She types sloppily, correcting as she goes. 'Now we change the number nineteen to twenty-three . . . '

'You're sure he won't remember?'

'He's off his face twenty-four seven. He'll think he opened the wrong template and made your contract like the old ones. If he disagrees, there'll be no proof. Turn on the printer.'

They run off a couple of copies and Suzy signs both. It's only now that Mika realises she needs to forge James's signature. She's done it before, but she gets another contract out of the cabinet for reference.

'Now, where is it . . . '

'What?'

'His pen.'

'I've already got a pen.'

'No, he's got a fancy fountain pen. It's a present from when he got the Michelin star. He uses it to sign everything.'

She opens drawers, scanning the contents. An empty vodka bottle, scrunched-up bills and betting slips, nasal decongestant, a bag of hard toffees. Nestled at the bottom the pen is cap-off, bleeding ink into a spare shirt. She takes it and tries to write, but the nib has crusted over. She does her best squiggle. It's not perfect, but he's unlikely to scrutinise it. Mika is reaching for the stapler when Olly races in.

'There's someone!' he hisses.

'Who?' Suzy jumps up.

'Someone, I dunno. They're putting in the code!'

Mika staples the contracts together, shoves one in Suzy's hand and slots the other into the filing cabinet. There's no time to put everything back together. She sprints around the desk to where Suzy stands, struck mute. Mika grabs her by the shoulder.

'Quick!'

They run. As they pass the kitchen, she hears the lock click. It can only be James. She thought he had gone home. He must have been roaming Soho for hours, trying to score. Now he's back, impatient to sample his purchase before getting into a taxi. There's no time to cross the kitchen, to the locker room where they might be safer. Instead, she runs down the corridor to the walk-in refrigerator and yanks the handle.

'We're hiding? In there?'

'Get in!'

Olly and Suzy get into the fridge just as Mika hears

the door open. She follows them in and closes the door. The light is off. She can smell soft cheese, shellfish and cold, dead meat.

'I've just realised,' Olly rambles. 'It just became April Fool's Day, right? You got me! Ha ha.'

'Sorry,' Mika shakes her head. 'We're actually in trouble.'

There's a clunk as the door swings shut.

'Is it him?' Olly whispers.

'Who else is it going to be?' Suzy snaps.

'Oh, I don't know, maybe some more kitchen staff here to alter official paperwork.'

'Calm the fuck down.'

'I only just started here, now I'm getting fired . . . '

'You'll cope, Olly.'

'I need the toilet.'

'Can't you hold it?'

'I've *really* got to go.'

'There must be a bottle in here you could empty.'

'It's not a wee . . . '

'Fucking gross.'

'Hey,' Mika hisses. 'Will you both shutthefuckup?'

She gets her phone out and turns the light on, then regrets it when she sees their faces, lit from below like horror-movie victims-to-be. There are uneven footsteps in the kitchen. They echo off all the hard surfaces, then become smaller, more contained, as James moves into the corridor. He pauses. They look at each other. Mika starts to grin, then suppresses a giggle. Olly looks at her like she's lost her mind. The footsteps move on, towards James's office, then there's nothing, just their breath.

'What's he doing?' Suzy whispers.

'No clue.'

'Won't he be suspicious that the lights are on?'

'He probably thinks *he* left them on.'

'Are we trapped?' Olly shivers.

Mika can tell what he's thinking. This isn't the walk-in freezer, but they're dressed for mild weather. Hypothermia is a possibility.

'The door isn't locked,' she reassures him. For the first time she feels a little bad for dragging him along. 'Even if he locks it, there's that.'

Mika points to a red button by the door, though she wonders who would hear the alarm if it went off in the middle of the night.

'So, what do we do?'

She thinks.

'We wait. If we don't hear anything, I'll go out and talk to him, yes?'

'What?' Suzy hisses.

'Relax – I'll say I forgot something, like we planned. You can sneak out while I'm chatting.'

'What if he fires you?' Olly asks.

'There are other jobs.'

They wait another minute. There is no noise.

'Right. Get ready to run.'

She opens the fridge door. Even softly, it makes a click. She pauses, waiting for James to shout, but he doesn't. She edges down the corridor, shoes making little squeaks on the lino. At the office door she pauses. There is a sound from inside, very soft. She would never have heard it from the fridge. Snoring.

James is asleep in his chair, head back and mouth open. There is a bag of white powder and his platinum card on the desk. How drunk do you have to be to sleep through a line of coke? She tiptoes back to the fridge, where Suzy is trying to huddle closer to Olly. For warmth.

'Come on; quiet now.'

They tiptoe out. Through the back door, one by one. Warm air rushes over their skin like relief. She locks the door and arms the security system. It's only when they're halfway down the alley that they start to laugh. Suzy remembers the contract clasped in her hand and waves it in the air like a peace treaty.

'We did it!'

'You're going to your cousin's wedding.'

'I'm going to get so *drunk*!' she beams.

'You guys are mental.' Olly puts his arms around both their shoulders, grinning like a schoolboy who has skipped class.

They walk in the direction of the night buses, stopping at a newsagent to buy snacks.

'It's my dad's uncle's daughter who's getting married,' Suzy is explaining to Olly. 'They're all psychos on that side of the family, so it should be fun. There'll be a fight by the end. I never see them since my parents split up.'

'Oh, mine too,' Olly interrupts clumsily. 'My dad's on his third wife. How about you, Mika?'

'Am I on my third wife?'

'I mean, are your parents still together?'

Suzy tries to subtly kick him in the side of the leg, but misses. Mika pauses, feeling the heat rise to her cheeks.

'My mum died when I was little.'

'Oh . . . '

They walk in awkward silence for a minute before Suzy gets a call from her auntie and starts recounting the evening's events in Filipino.

'Sorry for bringing that up,' Olly says quietly.

'Don't be, it's fine.'

'I know it's really not the same thing, but my sister died when I was four. Car accident. She was five. We were practically twins.'

'I'm sorry.' Mika looks sideways, seeing him for the first time.

'Maybe it's just me, but I think a lot about how I would have been different. If she'd been around, you know? A different person.'

Mika thinks for a moment, then says:

'Where are you staying?'

'Out west with a relative, until I find somewhere more central . . . '

Mika exchanges a look with Suzy, who is still talking on the phone and frowns in puzzlement. She knows she shouldn't, but hell, she just bagged her four extra days of leave. Mika turns to Olly and raises an unsubtle eyebrow.

'It's late. You can sleep at mine if you like?'

Several miles away, a hospital bed is tumbling through space at one thousand kilometres per second. It always has been, along with the hospital and everyone in it, it's just that Jem is appreciating it for the first time. Poised between life and death, like a coin flipped in the air, his concussed brain serves up its first bona fide out-of-body experience. Hallucinations, hot and fresh!

He's aware of voices in stereo. As though heard through headphones, the voices are panned hard left and right, never meeting in the middle. They whisper, too low for him to make out. Still, he understands they are in a negotiation of sorts, not between either side, but with him, Jem. The negotiations between life and death have reached an impasse and he must arbitrate.

Advocating on the side of life he has doctors, nurses, the beleaguered and defunded forces of the NHS, and a steady drip-drip-drip of hydromorphone. He vaguely remembers the racket of being inside an MRI machine. Death's case for the prosecution: broken bones (how many?), internal bleeding (where?? how much???), and the sense that, if it doesn't happen today, won't it eventually? What's the difference of thirty, forty years, set against the fathomless depths of time? Be reasonable, Mr Adjaye, we haven't got all day.

It's all very entertaining, in a macabre sort of way.

Despite their petitions, Jem feels powerless to intercede. Surely the decision of his continued existence will be made for him, not by him. He is a disputed territory, a patch of land where either life or death may reside. Life's claim is subject to doubt, because life itself is nomadic. *Isn't it time you were moving on?* Death smirks.

He always imagined an out-of-body experience would be like viewing his reflection in a mirror, or floating above while his body lay beneath. He would see himself, clad in sugar-almond blue hospital pyjamas. He would see the wires connected to his chest and the snaking tubes, piercing his arms with metal fangs. But his body seems to have been done away with entirely. He cannot see, cannot taste, cannot feel.

All he can do is listen.

When he was more lucid (though is it not a flavour of lucidity, to know you are not lucid?) he overheard a conversation to the effect that the risk of death from this sort of crash is 50 per cent. It's official – his life is a coin tossed into the air, waiting to land.

The clamour of negotiation builds, though he still can't make out the words. Other noises join the chorus – beeps and trills of machinery, the clatter of steel, hurried footsteps. The sounds of the intensive care unit bleed into his brain and he struggles to hold on to the vision. Or rather, whatever a sound-based hallucination is called. An audition? That can't be right. He is auditioning for the role of Jem Adjaye and the director seems unimpressed.

There is one thing, apart from the noise. A smell, but not the sort of smell you would expect in a hospital. It's an outdoors smell, a middle-of-nowhere kind of smell, a wild, head-swimming smell. It reminds him of family holidays abroad, back when he used to go on family holidays. Back before . . .

But really, what is it? A syrupy smell. A kind of tree. Yes, a certain tree with a certain kind of fruit. The fruit is falling, fermenting in the heat. Big tree, big leaves. Five points, splayed out like green fingers . . .

A fig tree.

Why is there a fig tree in the hospital?

He is being prepped for surgery. Somewhere, nearby, people are washing their hands, putting on gloves, setting out the knives which will open him like ripe fruit. Like a ripe fig. Is he scared? Yes, he is scared. But it goes so far beyond that little word as to be something else altogether.

Fifty-fifty.

That's what he is. Alive and dead. A wave and a particle. A quantum superposition. At the beginning of his life and at the end. Sitting on the riverbank of the present, dipping his feet into eternity.

Was it a good life?

Jem isn't shocked to be asking the question. He has asked

himself many times before. Each time he decided that, yes, more or less, his was a good life. Certainly there were worse. But with the any-moment-now feeling of Death pulling out his cannula, Jem isn't so sure. He turns over the pieces of his life and finds old receipts, train tickets with faded destinations, loyalty coupons for coffee chains, bank statements, cashed cheques, Post-it-note grocery lists, small change, unused stamps. Is this what his thirty-two years amount to? Insufficient scraps. They cannot be stitched together to make the fabric of a human life, but they're all he has.

He thinks of Emily.

Well, yes, there is Emily. But she is not a scrap, not a fragment, not an artefact of his life. He cannot claim her existence to justify his own. She is not a part of his life. The thought twists inside him like a shard of broken bone. How long has he been dulling the pain of separation? Too long. He wants his daughter back; he knows there is no chance.

He thinks of his years working at the bank. Do they seem like a waste? Someone had to be doing that work, but did it need to be him? A single word keeps coming back to him:

Adventure.

It is a childish word. A juvenile idea. Life is not about having adventures; life is about getting on. Yet he cannot think of another word, another idea, that tastes so sweet. Like honey drizzled onto his tongue, straight from the jar. Golden. Jem wants to have an adventure. Just one. Standing at Death's open door, it's all he wants. One more adventure. If he gets out of this place, he will find one. He will be immature, inexperienced, irresponsible. Jem Adjaye says it

16

to himself, holy mantra, over and over in a voice no one can hear:

Let me out . . .

Let me have an adventure . . .

Let me have one *adventure . . .*

Let me . . .

A fresh wave of sedation hits, and Jem's conscious brain switches off. Somewhere across London, Mika rolls to the other side of her bed and slips into pleasantly exhausted sleep.

3

The tree hangs low with purple fruit;
    the jungle is a wall of green.

Mika steps into the clearing
    dressed in clothes of animal hide.

She rubs her belly's pregnant curve,
    and feels a gentle kick reply.

This morning she gathered cattail stems
    for roasting by the evening fire,

picked mushrooms from a glade she knows,
    and ran away from river pigs.

That was with her friends, but now
    she wants to spend some time alone.

Life Number Nine

Sometimes she likes to be alone.
    They tease her for it; she doesn't care.

The ground is thick with fallen figs,
    fermenting in the midday heat.

She sits her back against the tree.
    The figs are rolled in golden dust and

here and there the ants have gathered
    where the red is oozing out, but

Mika doesn't mind. She splits one;
    juices dribble down her wrists.

Does anything taste as good as this?
    This sun-warmed, not-quite-rotten fruit?

She closes her eyes to hold the taste,
    but footsteps open them again.

A human tread, and coming closer,
    She takes a fig in case she flees.

Jem finds the clearing, spotting Mika
    just as she is spotting him.

They eye each other for a moment,
    like wildcats, weighing up the fight;

not that Mika wants to fight but
    he is from the other tribe.

He hesitates and starts to turn,
    to walk a different jungle path.

Raising hands she signs to him:
    You can join me, if you want.

His people speak with hands, like hers,
    although their dialect makes her laugh.

Jem hesitates, then comes and sits.
    In the blue and purple shade.

She shows her treasure on the ground:
    You can try them; they are good.

She takes a fig and throws it to him;
    he catches it mid-air and eats.

She signs to him: *why are you here?*
    He frowns and signs: *why not?* She signs:

Aren't you too busy tending crops
    to take a long walk in the jungle?

He looks annoyed and shakes his head.
    I've done my work, and now I'm here.

He thinks, then signs with sticky fingers:
    This tree for us has many tales.

Oh, this is a special tree?
    She pats the trunk, then starts to giggle.

Life Number Nine

The sun-fermented fruit is going to
    her head; she's feeling mischievous.

He says nothing so she adds:
    Tell me a story of this tree.

Perhaps I will another time.
    Tell me, please; I want to know.

He shuffles closer, leaning back
    against the smooth trunk next to her.

Long ago, we found this place;
    our dead are buried in this grove.

Mika pouts at the fig she's eating,
    which looks too much like human flesh.

This was long ago, remember.
    They say this tree grew up above them.

They say no harm can find you here.
    They say the leaves are truly . . .

Truly what? I want to know
    all the story has to tell.

They say each leaf is truly a hand,
    that will tell your story after you're gone

and teach it to the other trees.
    Mika squints up at the leaves;

They do not look like hands to her.
  A chubby baby's hand, perhaps,

but keeps this to herself.
  They eat in silence, understanding –

a feast like this comes once a moon.
  It will not keep, so eat your fill.

Who is the father? Jem signs slowly,
  pointing to her belly's curve.

*I do not think there is one only –
  a baby is made by many fathers.*

*A little of what each man is best at –
  hunter, dancer, lover, cook.*

Oh . . . Jem looks a little bashful.
  She signs: *You think that idea strange?*

*No, it's just we don't believe that.
  One father per child – that's the rule.*

That's a man's idea, she grins.
  Men are fond of taking credit.

Jem starts to laugh; a gentle laugh
  and in a moment, she laughs too.

Mika's tribe is led by grandmothers;
  in Jem's, the patriarchs say what's right.

Life Number Nine

In her tribe they hunt for food,
    and move around with change of season;

in his, they grow and store the grain.
    and do not fear the winter's coming.

Mika doesn't understand
    tending a crop like a newborn child.

A bellyful is always nice, but
    is the trade-off fair for trudging

the same tracks and eating the same
    porridge, morning, noon and night?

I was surprised to see you here,
    Jem signs slowly as he chews.

Aren't your people going north?
    Following the deer for winter?

At the next full moon, perhaps;
    we are watching for the signs.

And will you be glad, when it's time to go?
    She catches a wistful look in his eye.

It is my favourite time of year,
    the moving times, following the deer.

They eat a minute more in silence;
    the figs around them all are gone.

Joe Heap

Jem lunges for one beyond his circle
  and finds that he has lost his balance.

The jungle colours break and ripple,
  like scenes reflected in a pool.

Well, he signs at length, *it was*
  good to sit, but I should go.

Crops to water? Mika mocks,
  her movements coming syrup-slow.

Water will not fetch itself,
  he smiles, *but what will you do now?*

Down to the river, catching frogs.
  I'm good at it, when I'm not drunk.

He laughs. *You look like someone who'd*
  Be good at catching frogs, I think.

She looks and sees him clearly now.
  You're handsome, she says, slurring signs,

I would like a handsome child.
  He smiles but does not understand.

She puts one hand upon his shoulder,
  kneads the muscle with her palm.

He smells the sweetness on her breath,
  and understands. He reaches out and—

Footsteps at the clearing's edge;
    at that moment, Jem smells smoke.

Mika looks and sees her friends,
    Pushing through the waxy leaves.

One has a bundle on her back,
    green leaves fastened tight with vines,

Breathing clouds of pale blue smoke,
    slow fire burning at its core.

The other two have sticks and bags;
    That can mean one thing only.

You found honey? Mika signs.
    Her friends reply, three-at-once:

Mika, it's huge! You've never seen—
    Come on; you're good at smoking out—

Did you sneak off with a boy?
    She turns to Jem, who's bashful again.

Do you want to come along?
    (Does she look hopeful that he might?)

Her friends' gazes are off-putting.
    No . . . I should be getting back.

Fine, she shrugs, a little hurt.
    I'll see you here again sometime?

When you're back from the north, I hope.
    She gets to her feet, unsteadily,

then lopes away towards her friends,
    who tease her now and blow him kisses.

Jem watches until she's out of sight,
    and listens to their footsteps fade

into the jungle's ceaseless sound.
    Above him the leaves are signing of

the meeting beneath their branches –
    A meeting of two tribes, two worlds –

told in couplets like hands together,
    working as one to make their meaning.

Jem listens to the rustling leaves,
    Rests his head against the tree

                   and dreams.

May

4

A month has passed. Sorry about that; should have warned you. Mind the gap. The Earth's inner core of crystalline iron has grown 0.04 millimetres. The last copy of an undiscovered poem by Sappho, written on third-century papyrus, has been destroyed in a fire at the home of a private collector in Ankara. Around the world, humans have spent 315 billion hours in REM sleep.

Mika knocks back a shot of flavoured vodka. Her jaw aches as the chemicals in the alcohol do a bad impersonation of sour cherries. A playlist of gay anthems thumps through a subwoofer.

'Stupid.' She turns to Suzy, who is doing the same. 'We spend all day making delicious food, then we come and drink this stuff. Tastes like gummy sweets left behind a radiator.'

Suzy's face contorts as the shot pinballs around her taste buds.

''S'cheap though.'

'Yeah.'

'You want another?'

Mika nods, turning to watch the room. They came with Olly, who is on the dancefloor, being chatted up by a man twice his age.

'Here – chin chin.'

They clink shot glasses. At least, they would clink if they weren't made of plastic. No glass allowed here; the edges of the bar and tables are covered in soft moulded plastic, like a crèche for alcoholic toddlers. They watch Olly across the dance floor, politely fielding questions. His floppy blond hair gives him the air of a golden retriever.

'Do you think he knows he's being hit on?' Suzy yells in her ear.

'I think he could be invited back for coffee and think the guy just wanted to show him his French press.'

'Is that what we're calling it?' Suzy dissolves into giggles, then catches herself against the bar. 'Oh jeez, I'm drunk already.'

'You're just tired. I'm going to the loo if you want a moment. Olly will survive.'

'Sure, let's go.'

The ladies' loos are quiet enough, stripping the music down to just the bass. It pounds against the walls of Mika's chest like a second heartbeat. They take neighbouring stalls.

'So, are you going to . . . you know . . . with Olly?' Suzy speaks across the great divide.

'I think it was a one-off.'

Olly is nice but not too bright. He's from a well-off background and could take over his dad's business one day. Mika coaxed the information out of him after a few beers. It's a drinks marketing company, a multimillion-pound racket, but Olly has a dream. He's going to be a chef. Mika, who has eaten one of his morning-after fried egg sandwiches, doubts it. But Olly's dad went to the same public school as James Conroy and arranged the job for him.

'Well, never say never,' Suzy says.

'Is that your motto?'

'Fuck off, Chef.' She laughs. 'Still though, I totally would, if he were interested.'

'I know.'

Silence, and Mika is worried that Suzy hasn't taken this ribbing in the spirit it was intended.

'You okay?'

'Yeah . . . shit, I've started. You don't have a tampon, do you?'

Mika rummages in her bag. 'I've a pad.'

'Lifesaver.'

They make the exchange under the stall and there's a lull in conversation. Two thoughts have been placed next to each other in Mika's mind. Mixed with the cheap booze, they make something volatile. She feels sick.

Her period is late.

Not by much, less than a week. She thinks back to that night with Olly. They had another drink when they got in, though she wouldn't say they were drunk. They used a condom, but she remembers his hands fumbling over it, tugging it into place when it didn't roll down.

'Shit.'

'Something wrong?'

'Oh, no . . . almost dropped my phone down the toilet.'

Mika steps out of the club, but Soho is just as noisy. Cars and buses rumbling past, mopeds weaving between them all, delivering pizzas and organ donations. People talking to each other, talking to their phones, talking to themselves. Somewhere a dog is barking.

Mika tries to shut it all out.

She needs to get home. She needs to go to the off-licence. She needs to buy a test. Tottenham Court Road is the nearest Tube station. The city air is too warm to sober her, but the act of walking makes everything a little sharper. This isn't a bad dream; she's awake in the real world. There are no fairy-tale obligations. She has options.

She walks past piles of noodles on heated metal plates, homeless people in doorways, a crowd of people waiting to enter a club. Inside the modern Tube building, footfalls bounce off the ceiling, raining back like unanswered prayers. She goes down the escalator to the Northern Line. There's internet down here now. She takes out her phone, pacing the platform, searching for several related things in quick succession – percentages, time frames, addresses. She doesn't linger on the details, glancing over the information. She's just checking it's all there.

Her train arrives and she rides north in an empty carriage. Taking out her tangled earbuds, she selects music on her phone. She should find something soothing but prefers stimulation. A synth bass pulses, faster than her heart. Perhaps she is trying to wake up; perhaps she knows that nothing will calm her down until she knows.

She gets off at Camden Town, hurries to the shop and buys a couple of pregnancy tests. Stashes them in her bag before leaving, as though someone she knows might see her. It's her village mentality coming out. After all these years, she's still not used to the anonymity of big cities. In that far-off land called home, the two hundred locals would know within an hour what she had bought.

She walks to her flat at the top of Parkway. On the weekends, a steady stream of families trudge this way to get their fill of exotic animals at the zoo. The air smells of weed and incense. Her flat is above Yanni's, the worst falafel shop in Camden. Mika doubts it would survive anywhere without so much unsuspecting foot traffic. She doesn't eat the food but always stops to chat. Tonight, she tries to slink past while Yanni serves a customer who is struggling to stand upright.

'Mika, how's it going?' Then, to the customer: 'You want sauce on that?'

'Hey Yanni. Got a throbbing headache.'

'The mayo stuff, what's that got in it?'

'Coriander. You want some aspirin? I think I have some back here.'

'Who, me?' The customer squints.

'No thanks – I think I just need to lie down in the dark.'

'I'll just have the spicy one then . . . '

'Might be a migraine; you should be careful. My cousin who worked at the furniture warehouse had migraines and he— Hey! Are you going to pay for that?'

'I dunno if I have enough for both, mate. Could you let me have it? I'm really thirsty.'

Mika takes the opportunity to slip away.

'Night, Yanni!'

'See you tomorrow, Mika!' Then back to the customer – 'Does this look like a charity? A soup kitchen? You want the drink, pay for it.'

'Mate, I have a medical condition . . . '

Mika closes the door behind her. Within a minute she is sat on her toilet, holding the plastic stick and waiting. How absurd, this ritual of finding out. She's no luddite, but she imagines there was a certain magic in the way women used to find out – the missed periods, the fatigue, the slow sense of knowing – which is lost when crouching to pee on a piece of injection-moulded plastic. She thinks of that night with Olly, April first, and hopes this is all a delayed joke, a cosmic Fool's Day gotcha.

It's not like she even wants to be a mother; the magic of the moment shouldn't matter. She has nothing against people who want kids, it's just that the idea of 'mother' seems hazy to her, and she can't see how she would ever transform into one. Mika tells people her mother died when she was little. Actually, her mother left when she was four years old, and never came back. She's dead now. Fell off a bicycle on Crete a couple of years ago; no helmet. Mika had been surprised to receive a sum of money in the will, a bad apology.

She has only pictures of her mother. No videos, no voice recordings, just silent, smiling faces. At the time, she mythologised her. She used to make up stories about why she had to leave – everything from her being a sorceress to a spy. In Mika's imagination she prowled like a tigress, hiding behind the daytime to meet her in dreams, Queen of the Night. Even now, to her adult mind, her mother is more symbolic than real.

The timer on her phone beeps and Mika looks at the stick. She gets up, chucks the test in the pedal bin and washes her hands. She goes through to the kitchen, takes out eggs and melts a little butter in the pan. She chops chives and parsley from her window box, beating them into the eggs with a little Parmesan. When the omelette is done, she shuffles it onto her favourite plate – the one with the apple blossoms around the edge – and eats at the one-person breakfast table, blowing on each bite.

Cells.

That's all it comes back to. Cells travelling down tunnels which are, to them, as big as cathedrals. Cathedrals made of their own kind. All those cells growing in cloudy nebulas, luminous clusters drifting through the warm darkness. Cells settling on pink, translucent folds of heaven. Cells wavering in an invisible breeze, like seed heads that might blow away again. Cells holding fast, setting down roots. Cells splitting into cells splitting into cells splitting into cells (one becomes two becomes four becomes eight becomes sixteen becomes . . .), until the splitting becomes too fast to see, becomes an explosion, becomes a city, becomes a time-lapse video of ice crystals forming on a dark window.

Every second of every minute, all over the world, the cymbal crash of sperm hitting egg, again and again, a fluttering cloud of potential winners, a brief struggle, then only one. Every moment the doors to one hundred million futures close as one springs open.

Taking out her phone she types a message to Suzy:

Hey – you make it home okay?

It's only a few seconds before a reply comes through.

Almost. U?

Yeah, all good. You doing anything tomorrow?

The wait is a little longer this time.

Was planning to sleep until the pm. I've got a lucid dreaming workshop at 2.

Mika doesn't know what a lucid dreaming workshop is, but Suzy is into New Age stuff.

Mind if I tag along?

Sure. U ok?

Yeah, I'm fine. Would just be nice to see you outside work time. I could buy you a coffee before?

Won't say no to that.

Mika closes her phone and gets up, puts the plate in the sink and goes to the window. She watches the wavering lights over Camden, smells the familiar perfume of stale beer, urine and smoke from the street below. She closes her eyes.

'Fuck.'

Bless you, Jem gives his benediction to a red post box as it lasers by. Bless you, traffic lights; bless you, bin lorry; bless you, graffiti tags. He's sitting in the passenger seat of his own car as London smears past, and he can't remember ever being so happy.

Lucas is driving him home. He's not included on the insurance, but Jem doesn't care. He's had his share of calamities for one year. Or two years, or three – perhaps the rest of his life will run smoothly! Since his moment of uncertainty between life and death, he cannot rid himself of magical thinking. Bless you, little chihuahua out for a walk. Bless you, fruit stall; bless you, shop selling vape sticks, and bless you, grubby, fog-eating London.

'How you doing there?'

'Fine, yeah. Hurts a bit when we bump up and down.'

'I'll make sure to hit every pothole I see.'

Lucas has been mock-angry since Jem woke up in the hospital. Mock-angry at him for stepping into the road. Mock-angry at him for almost dying. Mock-angry at him for standing up the date he arranged. It's just a front, Lucas's way of showing he cares. Jem is usually the same. Banter is the way they express themselves. Feelings are never stated – that would be too awkward.

Except now, Jem feels cracked open.

At first, he thought he was like a computer running in safe mode after a crash. At some point he would wake up and all his features would be reinstalled. Now he's starting to think this is the new him. Jem Adjaye V2. So, when Lucas says 'I'm waiting for you to be fully healed so I can kill you myself', Jem has to hold himself back from replying: 'I love you. I'm glad you're here.'

But he keeps it inside.

They speed up and slow down with the traffic on the Wandsworth Road towards Catford. The inside of the car is the closest thing Jem has come to quiet for a long time. The hybrid engine purrs. Inside this capsule, the noise of the city – horns, drills, planes – is muted. Jem fills his lungs with cool, conditioned air, trying to relax. Truth be told, he's nervous to meet his old life.

'Did you visit me much? Before I woke up?'

When he glances sideways to look at Lucas's face, his jaw is clenched. When he notices Jem looking, the muscles relax.

'Every day.'

'Sorry I don't remember.'

'I, uh . . . I read to you.'

This makes Jem laugh, but Lucas looks deadly serious.

'What did you read?'

'Some thriller that I found in the coffee room. Something about a deadly virus and there's only one man who can stop it in time . . . never did find out how it ended.'

'Thank you.'

Lucas shrugs.

'It's what you do, innit? Well, it's what they do in films. And the docs didn't stop me, so I figured it wasn't a bad idea.'

He goes quiet, and Jem doesn't press for more. He puts his head back and closes his eyes. Their silence is a comfortable thing. The next time he opens his eyes, Lucas is pulling into the car park by his block of flats, and Jem feels he might cry and whoop, a man sighting land after a sea voyage. The block is new and high spec, sandwiched between train lines and a sludgy river. The air quality here is so poor that residents are advised not to leave windows open, and each unit comes with its own air purifier. When Jem changed the filter for the first time, it was soot-black and sticky, like a honeycomb of treacle. Just as well he couldn't look at the inside of his own lungs.

Jem takes his time getting out of the car, while Lucas brings him a crutch and fetches his bag. After he woke up, Lucas brought a change of clothes to the hospital. Jem had asked to put them on straight away, eager to regain a scrap of his identity. When he finally got them on, however, there was clearly some mistake – these were the clothes of a larger man. They had to find a belt to hitch up his trousers. Ready to leave, he had caught his reflection in a shaving mirror. He looked like a teenager dressing in his father's clothes.

It takes him a long time to reach the lifts, and they stop several times. The doctor was satisfied with his recovery – he shows no signs of cognitive decline – but it doesn't change the fact that he's bone tired. Though he has barely left bed for weeks, he feels as though he has run several marathons in a row. His joints hurt. One leg is in plaster and aches more or less all the time.

The lift doors open on a blank hallway. Lucas goes ahead, opening his door and dumping the bag.

'Home at last.'

'Thanks.' Jem smiles at his friend, suddenly so tired, all his blessings spent. 'I'll be okay from here.'

Lucas hovers uncertainly. 'You sure? I can stay for a while, if you want. I got you the essentials this morning, but we could get a pizza . . . '

'I'm pretty tired. You should get back to the kids.'

'Okay. How long have you got off work?'

'Another three days, more if I need it. But I'd rather get back to it. Back to normal, you know?'

'Good, well . . . '

For a second Lucas hesitates, then nods. They say their standard goodbyes. Just as he's walking out the door, Jem asks:

'Did Emily visit me, before I woke up? I spoke to her on the phone, but it was as though she wasn't sure what happened.'

Lucas freezes. Jem knows that his mother and brothers visited him in the hospital, because he has seen them since waking up. But no one has mentioned his daughter or her mother.

'I told Sarah . . . '

'They didn't come?'

'She said she didn't want to put Emily through it,' Lucas shrugs, threading a fine line between what he wants to say and what is appropriate. 'I kept saying it was serious, you know. Especially early on. I said, I dunno, it might be illegal not to bring Emily. You had rights, even if you weren't awake. But she wouldn't listen. Said you were going to be fine and there was no point making a big drama out of it . . . '

He stops himself before his voice gets too loud; Jem nods.

'Thanks for letting me know. Anyway, it doesn't matter. I'll see her soon enough.'

Lucas nods, pats him briskly on the shoulder and turns away. Jem closes the door and waits until he can no longer hear his friend's footsteps in the hall. He limps across the room and crash-lands on the sofa. Then, when sitting becomes insufficiently restful, he lies down and pulls a bobbled blanket over himself. Closing his eyes, he can hear the burble of the fridge in the kitchen. Outside, the soft rumble of a train. The air purifier shifts down a gear in its cupboard.

This is the quietest place Jem has been for a month, and he feels himself expanding outwards. The sensation is so visceral, so Alice-in-Wonderland, he thinks he might be having another out-of-body experience. But he opens one eye and the real world is still there, looking back. He hadn't realised how small hospital had made him feel, how much the noise compressed him.

For a few moments, he is peaceful.

He opens his eyes. As he looks around, a note of discord creeps into his thoughts. Something about the room strikes him as odd. There's a thin layer of dust over the glass coffee table. Over everything. But no, it's not that. It's not that anything has changed. It's that everything is just the same. He sees his living room through fresh eyes. Solid, mid-range furniture in an assortment of greys. Walls painted a lighter grey. White highlights from the TV tables and standard lamp. It is very neat in here. No clutter. Clean lines. It looks like a showroom, and an uninspired one at that.

After he's stared at the room for five minutes (enough time for two hundred and ninety-eight weddings to be sanctified around the world) he takes out his phone and opens a folder of pictures of Emily. He picks one – her eating candy floss at a school fair – and looks at it for half a minute until the image is seared into his brain. He does this, sometimes, when he's about to call her. He hates talking to her on the phone – her disembodied voice is so inscrutable – but the pictures help. Right now, he only wants to tell her one thing, over and over, in the hope she will believe him.

'I love you,' he says to the picture. 'So much. And I'm going to do everything I can to see you more.'

He takes a deep breath, then dials Sarah's number. After a further nineteen you-may-kiss-the-brides, she picks up.

'Jem . . . '

'Hi, Sarah.'

'It's not time for your call. Emily isn't here right now . . . '

He feels the air knocked out of him; what once would have seemed a minor setback now seems a terrible blow. He cannot trust in tomorrow the way he did before the accident. Weakly, he says:

'No, no . . . just thought I'd check in.'

There is an awkward pause on the other end. At least, that's how he interprets it.

'How are you feeling?'

'A little beaten up, you know.'

'I can't *believe* you walked in front of a car.'

He has nothing to say to that, so changes the subject.

'How's Emily?'

'She's fine. Doing well at school.'

'Did you . . . ?'

'What?'

'When I called, it was like she didn't know.'

'I hadn't expected you to call.'

'But did you explain—?'

'No, I didn't. Does that make me a bad person, Jem?'

He isn't surprised by the anger in her tone, but he finds himself unable to rise to it in the way he used to.

'Of course not.' He clears his throat. 'She's had enough to worry about; I'm glad you didn't tell her. I just wondered . . . if she missed me. My monthly visit, I mean. The calls.'

'She . . . ' Sarah sounds wrong-footed. 'I told her that you were on holiday. She asked me why you hadn't told her in advance . . . '

'Ah.'

'I'm sorry.'

'It's fine, I . . . '

'Anyway,' Sarah seems to squeeze the sympathy out of her voice like wringing a wet rag. 'You'll want her to be at your mum's birthday?'

'Yes, I . . . '

'Fine, I'll put it on the calendar.'

With that, she hangs up. Jem puts the phone down and stares for a long time at the room, unfocussed, until all the shades of grey swim with colourful afterimages. Unbidden, that word comes back to him, like a bailiff at the door, wanting payment of a debt:

Adventure.

At length Jem gets himself up to sitting. There is one bit of clutter in the room, one area that has not been tamed into straight, monochrome lines. Pushed to one side of the doormat is a bright pile of junk mail. Taking up his crutch he hobbles over and stoops, awkwardly, to pick it up.

25% off all pizzas!

No.

Axford Furniture Warehouse Closing Down Sale is now—

No.

Mr Edjabe, are you happy with your smile?

He throws each leaflet to the floor, one by one, until there is only one left. It's a bad photocopy with a yin-yang symbol at the top:

Madame Gonzalez-Whippler

Invites You to Learn —

• Tantric Yoga • Meditation • Breath Techniques •
• Vipassana • Lucid Dreaming • Mindful Crochet •

Adventure into the Unknown!

(Nearest Station Dalston Junction)

There is a phone number and an email. Usually, this flyer would have been in the recycling before he'd read it. Now Jem holds it like a summons from a magical land. It says it right there: *adventure into the unknown!* It's not the adventure he had in mind, but there's no time to waste. He doesn't believe in next week the way he used to. Hobbling back to the safety of the sofa, he dials the number.

'Hello, is that . . . ah, great, hello. I was wondering if you had any classes coming up that I could join? The sooner the better. Well, maybe the lucid dreaming?'

Jem isn't sure why his eye is drawn to this one. He remembers having strange dreams in the hospital. One of them, when he was first going into surgery, was especially vivid, but he can't remember it now, only fragments of sensation – colour: green; taste: sweet; touch: soft. The voice on the phone is talking to him.

'Sorry, could you repeat that? Tomorrow. Yes, tomorrow is great. Let me get a pen . . . '

5

A night and a morning pass. The International Space Station orbits Earth nine and a half times. 449,166 babies are conceived. By the width of a strand of spiderweb, St Mark's Basilica sinks deeper into the Venetian lagoon. Today is the universe's 13.8 billionth birthday. A Tuesday.

At 1.56 p.m. Mika is sat in the hall of Dalston Community Centre, sipping coffee from a paper cup. There is a ring of ten chairs in the centre of the hall and, apart from the one occupied by Mika, three are already taken. It's clear the others know each other. Suzy woke late, so there was no pre-session coffee. She assures Mika she is on her way. Madame Gonzalez-Whippler hovers around the room, dispensing drinks and biscuits.

'Custard cream, dear?'

'Sorry?' Mika is knocked out of her reverie. She had been staring a loose polystyrene tile on the ceiling, wondering how much asbestos is in this old building. The older woman rattles the selection box under her chin and Mika accepts a ginger snap.

'You alright, love? You seem worried.'

Mika isn't sure whether Madame Gonzalez-Whippler is very perceptive or whether, if you go around saying 'you seem worried' to people, you're more often than not correct.

'It's nothing . . . just waiting to talk to my friend.'

The woman smiles kindly and rattles the biscuit tin again. Mika takes an additional Jammie Dodger to get Madame G-W off her case. More people arrive, filling up all but one seat next to Mika (where she has placed her bag) and one on the other side of the circle. Madame G-W starts rifling through a plastic folder, taking out worksheets. People quiet their conversations. Just as Mika thinks she's doing this alone, Suzy enters through the double doors at the back of the hall. Her black trainers squeak across the room like echolocating bats.

'Sorrysorrysorry . . . '

'It's fine, I just—'

'I think we're mostly here,' Madame G-W enunciates, 'so let's begin.'

The rest of the circle sit straighter; Mika grits her teeth. This rigmarole wasn't worth it for a quick chat.

'We're here today to learn about lucid dreaming. If you're not here to learn about lucid dreaming, you may have got the wrong date. Zumba is on a Friday!'

Polite laughter.

'I'm sure many of you know about lucid dreams already, and want to get on with how to have them. But let's have a quick intro for anyone new to this subject.'

She looks at Mika, who frowns.

'Lucid dreams are dreams in which the dreamer becomes aware that they are dreaming. Try saying that after a few glasses of Chardonnay! They might even gain control of the dream characters, the narrative, or the environment. They might choose to do something impossible such as flying, or something normally off-limits, such as sleeping with their next-door neighbour.'

This elicits a few titters; Mika looks at Suzy and widens her eyes just enough to convey 'what have you brought me to?'

'Lucid dreaming has been studied since ancient times, and both Indian Hindus and Tibetan Buddhists cultivated their ability to realise when they were—'

The double doors bang open again. Madame G-W stops to look, followed by the rest of the group. Mika turns as Jem enters on crutches, awkwardly manoeuvring through the doors that are trying to close on him.

There is a buzzing in the air.

At first, Mika thinks it must be a fluorescent bulb on the fritz. Jem hears it too. Or perhaps it's not a sound so much as a feeling. His body vibrates. He crosses the room as quickly as he can, forgetting how to use his crutches and almost tripping over himself. The journey here was difficult and he's looking forward to sitting down. Suddenly his eyes meet with those of the woman at the back who is peering round at him.

Auburn hair held back with clips.

A freckled nose.

It's not a memory, exactly, that Jem experiences. His memories from the night of the crash are splinters, too sharp to piece together. What he feels is recognition, followed by confusion – he has never met this person before in his life. He hobbles the last few feet to his chair, right next to Madame G-W, and lands heavily.

'Sorry I'm late.'

'Looks like you have good reason to be,' she quips. 'Don't worry, you've not missed anything. As I was saying, lucid dreaming goes back to ancient times, and we have a lovely example from the poet Zhuang Zhou . . . '

Jem tunes out, distracted by the woman on the other side of the circle. She is fat, has naturally flushed cheeks, and her button nose turns up at the end. Unbidden, Jem thinks the word 'soft' – for her hair, her body, the pronounced bow of her top lip – then quickly stops thinking it. His face feels hot. He catches her looking at him, then back at the tutor with a slight frown. He looks at his shoes. Well, one shoe, one ankle brace.

The thing about Jem which catches Mika's attention is his arms. He's wearing a chunky knit sweater, the colour of double cream, with a few threads loose, rolled to the elbow. His forearms and hands look strong; his fingers are knotted together. She has been with enough men and women to know what she likes. She knows what she finds sexy, and Jem fits into that broad category. But there's something earnest about him which almost makes her feel bad for thinking those thoughts. This, in turn, makes her resent him.

There's something else about him, but she struggles at first to put her finger on what it is. For some reason she still remembers the dream she had a month ago. It was unlike any dream before or since. She can still taste the figs, still feel the foliage whipping against her legs as she walked through the jungle, still smell the smoke from the green leaves. Above and beyond all that, she remembers what it felt like to be that other version of herself. To know so much about the forest, about the creatures living in it, about the others in her tribe. To think in a different rhythm, a different metre.

Looking again, she realises that the man across the circle is a ringer for the man in her dream. Grasping this, she forgets about it – the dream wasn't real, so she doesn't have to worry about it.

She tries again to focus on the lesson. She's paying fifteen pounds for it, after all. But all she can really think about is the conversation she wants to be having with Suzy. She hadn't questioned until now why she wants to talk to her. They have worked together for two years and, in that time, they've had fun. Mika would probably say they're best friends, except now she thinks about it, she's never shared anything like this with her before. Perhaps she just had nothing to share. But she has never told Suzy the truth about her mum, or talked about her childhood in any detail. In return, she doesn't really know anything about Suzy's life.

Still, Suzy is the best she's got.

The class goes on. Madame G-W hands out paper and gets them to note down anything they remember about last night's dreams. The tectonic plate under North America moves the continent further away from Europe and Africa by the length of a single bacterium. They break for tea and coffee, during which time Mika and Jem do not look at each other.

'So, I'm guessing you didn't just come for the class?' Suzy asks, to one side of the room.

'No, it's just . . . '

Now she comes to say it, Mika is unaccountably shy. It's not an emotion she's used to.

'I think I'm . . . '

At this moment Jem, who has taken a while to get up and cross the room, appears next to them.

'Sorry, I—'

Mika turns to him, frowning.

'Do you mind? This is a private conversation.'

Jem stands a little straighter with indignation.

'I only wanted a biscuit.'

'Can't you go around?' Mika says, more angrily than she intended. She's impatient to get back to Suzy, who looks both mortified and amused.

'It's actually quite hard to go around, at the moment,' Jem shakes his crutch.

'Here,' Mika grabs the biscuit tin and shoves it at him. 'Help yourself.'

Jem's eyes go wide. He doesn't actually call her rude, but says nothing more, and hobbles back toward the seats.

'Are you . . . okay?' Suzy asks, watching Jem go.

'I think I'm pregnant.'

'You *think*?'

'Well, no; I am pregnant. I did a test. Two tests. But I think it might be . . . actually I know it has to be—'

Suzy gasps so loudly that everyone else in the room, who had been chatting politely, turns to look. She claps one hand over her mouth and uses the other to turn Mika away from the room.

'Are you . . . you mean . . . ?'

'Yeah.'

'Olly?'

'Yep.'

'Shit.'

'Yes.'

Suzy thinks.

'Are you going to . . . keep it?'

'God, no.'

'Oh, okay.' Suzy does something between a sigh of relief and a huff. 'So this is just . . . '

'I needed to tell someone, okay?' Mika is aware of sounding defensive.

'No, of course, I just mean . . . are you sure?'

'You're not trying to talk me out of it, are you?'

'Isn't that what you want?'

'Like I said, I just wanted to tell you.'

Suzy shrugs. 'You can tell me anything. And if you've made your mind up, that's fine. But you came all this way. I'm just saying, it feels like you wanted more of a conversation.'

'I . . . '

'Okay everyone, let's get back in the circle!'

Mika stands for a moment more, her hard words jellifying. Caught in the contradiction of saying one thing and meaning another, she has no comeback. She feels vaguely ashamed as they shuffle back to their seats.

'So let's get down to the nitty-gritty, shall we?' Madame G-W says, clapping her hands together. 'Let's learn some techniques that will help you to go home and have a lucid dream tonight!'

In the second half of the session they talk about 'testing reality'. This is done by looking at clocks, turning light switches on and off, or trying to breathe while pinching your nose. Doing this regularly in real life, she tells them, will mean they do it while dreaming. In their dreams, they will notice that the time is eighty-five past six, that the light switch does nothing, or that they don't need to breathe. They talk about keeping a dream journal next to the bed, and how this will help them re-enter REM. They talk about dream signs and mnemonic induction, setting alarms and reciting mantras.

Jem takes a lot of notes. All this information is bewildering, but the more he listens, the more he wants a lucid dream. He remembers one he dreamt as a child, floating up to the ceiling of his primary school classroom. But lately? Nothing. Why is growing up like that? Why do we set solid, like clay drying in the sun? Jem is sick of it, sick of feeling like the magic of his life is in the past. Madame G-W talks about lucid dreaming as though it's something he can do every night. So, he's going to take notes, he's going to get it right, he's going to ace this test. His activities are limited, for the moment, by his bad leg. What better time to have adventures while sleeping?

Mika has checked out. She should have left before the second half. Maybe she should pretend to take a call? Part of her wants to stay and rebuke Suzy. Except what would she say? The answer to that question sinks below the horizon as she moves. They're about to do another exercise on photocopied worksheets when she stands up.

'Sorry, I've just got to . . . '

Madame G-W sees through her, without judgement.

'You're leaving.'

'I am, yeah.'

'Well, I hope you'll take something away from today's session. But I'll tell you the most useful thing now, which I usually save until the end – just thinking about lucid dreams makes people have them, without the other techniques.'

'That's . . . great to know.' Mika smiles weakly and turns to leave. Suzy doesn't follow after her. Jem watches, with an unaccountable tug of sadness, as she leaves the hall.

*

Time passes.

The session ends, the group disperses, a caretaker puts away the chairs. Night marches over London in an irregular procession, and all the grey-white streets turn smoky purple. There are not so many flocks of birds as once there were, but above Lambeth a murmuration of starlings wheel and whoop. Superorganism; one form, dreamed by thousands of minds. The gauzy fabric twists, wrings out, passes through itself. It tears in half and reforms – *ta dah!* Nobody watches for more than a few seconds except six-year-old Keira Abdullahi, transfixed on her sixth-floor balcony. Watching the formless forms break and return, like waves without a beach, new questions rise in her mind – how did we get here? Where are we going? What does it all mean? Is this all some huge accident? – until her mother calls her in for fish fingers, chips and peas.

Mika goes home. She ignores messages from Suzy. She will reply to them tomorrow. She makes arrangements, but for now there is nothing to do but pass the time before bed. She makes herself a grilled halloumi salad, watches a documentary about rainforests, considers drinking a beer and has water instead. What is wrong with her? She has always known the contents of her own mind, even when she didn't like what she found.

Jem goes home. It takes him longer, with all the hobbling and finding of lifts at stations that he hasn't needed since he was pushing a pram. At last he is back in his apartment, with the air purifier purring. Loneliness tightens around his chest. He orders Chinese and plays *Call of Duty* on his old PlayStation until it arrives. He eats the takeaway and three snack cakes from the cupboard and feels sick. He finds an empty book to be a dream journal and rereads his notes from the workshop while drinking lager in bed.

Around the world, unborn babies are waiting for life to begin. Babies in bathtubs, beneath the warm dome of their mother's stomach. Babies on buses and trains, feeling the motion of an unseen journey. Babies in cafés, conference rooms, sweat shops, each hearing the muffled words of a language they will one day know. Some are large, full-made, only waiting for the moment of their birth. Others are small, translucent, their hands little more than paddles, their eyes black dots, lungs which do not breathe, hands which feebly grasp the shining twist of umbilical cord. Lips, noses, ears – tomorrow's faces forming in the red-dark like photographs in a developing room.

Simultaneously, Mika and Jem turn the lights off and close their eyes. The first sign of synchronicity. One north, one south, entangled.

X and Y.

Nothing much happens for seven hours. Not to Mika and Jem, at least. They toss and turn but do not wake, in dreams which morning will not remember. Between them their hearts beat sixty-two thousand times, pumping three hundred thousand litres of blood. Colourful puffs of hormone cloud the underwater world of their bodies – melatonin, aldosterone, leptin, growth factor, insulin.

An hour before dawn, Mika is dreaming of being trapped at work. An angry customer chases her around the building, stabbing at her with knitting needles. Jem waits at a bus stop for his daughter to arrive. Instead of cars and lorries, huge caterpillars undulate down the road. Both of them dream ordinary, nonsense dreams.

And then, they don't.

6

Object(s) Type: Five tablets
Museum Number: K.3867
Findspot: Kouyunjik, North Iraq
Production date: c. 1700BC
Materials: Clay

Translation by A.J. Fitzsimmons

Tablet 1
She sits in a room with twenty others.
She sits in a room of baked brick
With two open windows allowing light.
The sky is a dome of lapis lazuli;
The sun is a disc of burnished copper.
Around her, a dozen women incline their heads,
Their shaven heads, bone styluses in hand,
Copying the records from wax tablets
Copying from wax onto soft river clay.
Jem looks down at her work.

She looks and for a moment is confused.
She blinks a few times before reading,
With no difficulty, what she has copied.
A debt of twenty pots of oil,
Of which fourteen have been collected.
Upon the death of the debtee,
The remaining pots shall be paid unto his first son . . .

'Jem, are you listening to me?'
A woman appears at her side.
Her head is shaven like the rest
But she wears a cap of braided hair
As a mark of her higher station.
This is the overseer; the others look sideways,
She bears the mark of Ishtar on her brow.
'Yes, I am sorry,' Jem replies.
'Go to the market; see if the beeswax man
Has for us the wax that he promised.'

Jem stands, head bowed, and walks.
She walks out into the courtyard,
Past the latrines, and ducks through a doorway
Onto the street beyond their cloister.
She stands aside while a cart
Pulled by two oxen makes its way,
Then carries on to the market.
Chickens peck at the dirt, dark feathers shining.
She passes doorways where bread is baking,
Others where copper is smelting.
Two men lead an auroch towards the abattoir . . .
[Some lines missing here]

Tablet 2

The market square is wide,
Centred around the city's largest well.
Though they come and go, Jem knows
The layout of the stalls by heart.
She smells her way through piles of produce:
Musty grains and yams, peppery cuts of meat,
Sweet fruits and fermented honey.
There are jungle birds and owls,
Monkeys and pangolins,
All tethered to heavy branches.
She passes a stall where a river dolphin
Is being butchered, the copper knife
Parting its pink-grey skin.
It is a day like any other.

There are many people here.
Some move respectfully out of her way;
Some people stride towards her
With the expectation she will let them pass.
Most pay her no notice at all.
Jem is neither the highest nor the lowest.
Though her clothes are plain,
They denote her position as a scribe.
Unlike every other profession, a scribe
Deals in the abstract.
Even priests must meet their congregation.
Jem does not handle the grain nor the oil,
The ideas of which she presses into river clay.
People regard her job as mysterious,
The tablets akin to magic seals.

She is about to continue,
To continue to the far side of the market,
To speak to Porus the beeswax man
About the beeswax they are owed,
When something slows her legs.
Perhaps she is already thinking of bees,
Wax cells filled with honey,
But suddenly she is wading through sweet syrup.
Someone nearby is making music.
A woman's voice rises above the din,
Accompanied by notes plucked from a lyre.
Jem follows the sound.
Does she follow the sound?
Better to say the silver hook
Which has hooked her by the ear
Pulls her through the teeming crowd,
Like a fish that doesn't struggle.

The woman sits and plays
With her back against the city well.
A headscarf casts her face in shadow.
Jem stands a little way off,
Crossing her hands in front of her.
All around, the market doesn't notice.
All around, the market is deaf to the music.
Hawkers and costermongers trundle their carts
Crying out what they have to buy:
Fish, bread, flasks of wine.
The regulars argue at their stalls.
The argument is always a variation
Of the argument around which the market was built:
How many apples are worth a bolt of cloth?

Life Number Nine

How many bolts of cloth are worth a pot of honey?
How many pots of honey are worth a week of labour?
The answers to these questions are ever-changing,
Because sometimes the apples are sour,
Sometimes there is no great demand for cloth,
Sometimes the honey is tainted
And may only be eaten by gurus and mystics.
This music, though . . . [partial line]

Jem knows of many kinds of music.
She has heard hymns and prayers in the temple.
She has heard them playing in taverns
To entertain the drinkers.
She knows nursery rhymes to lull children to sleep,
She knows tunes that you can hum
While doing work of no importance.
Each sort of music has its worth,
Depending on the time and place.
They can be compared to one another,
Like apples and cloth and honey.

This music, though, is different.

Jem thinks of times when she was young.
She thinks of stones they took from the river,
Soft shale they split with bigger rocks,
To see the sheen inside, like peacock feathers.
It was valuable to no one, and afterwards they threw
The pieces of broken rock back to the flood.
But for those moments, they shone in the sun
Showing off their strange colours.
This music has no worth, which makes it precious.

It shines in the sun for a moment and is gone.
The woman sings of heroes and animals,
Of gods turned into trees and clouds,
Of fools who became kings
And kings who became fools.
The lyre sings its own song,
Complementing these tales but not of them,
Singing of something else, something of the sky.
Jem listens and tastes wild figs.

Tablet 3
The music ends and Jem is still standing,
Hands crossed in front of her,
While the market carries on around.
The woman who was singing turns a peg,
Plucking the string to tune it.
Then she looks up, right at Jem.
'Good morning, can I help you?'
'I'm sorry; I have nothing to give.'
'No matter,' Mika shrugs. 'Come sit, if you like.'
Jem looks around; she should not dawdle here.
She could get into trouble,
If she were seen to be wasting time.
Her time, like all things in the market,
Has its value, which she has traded
For bread and beer.
But Porus the beeswax man likes to chatter,
And when the chatter is done
He takes his time over haggling.
Perhaps a minute here will not hurt.
She sits on the step next to the woman,
But does not rest against the well.

Mika sets the lyre by her side
And takes from her bag a piece of bread,
Wrapped in cloth, and shows it to Jem.
'Would you like a piece?'
'I shouldn't . . . '
'Please, be my guest.'
Jem accepts a piece of bread.
The bread is sweetened with condensed milk,
Flavoured with cardamom and orange peel.
'You remind me of someone,'
Mika says, looking at her sideways
From out of her headscarf.
'It's a beautiful lyre,' Jem says,
Because there is no reply to this;
A similar thought had come to her.
'Where did you get it?'
'I made it myself, with help.'
The stranger hands the lyre to Jem,
Who holds it awkwardly, like a newborn babe.
It is made from the shell of a turtle,
Black and yellow, highly polished,
With a stick frame supporting the strings.
'I've had this one for a year.
Musicians need to know how to mend
Or make a new instrument when the old one breaks.'
Jem can feel the lyre vibrating in her hands,
Like the purr of a housecat.
It responds to the woman's voice,
As though responding to its mistress.
'I liked your song,' Jem says quickly,
Handing back the instrument.
'I've never heard a song like that before.

Where did you go to learn it?'
'Here and there,' the stranger shrugs.
'I don't understand?' Jem frowns.
'I take pieces I find and put them together.
Like a recipe. Or like a blanket made from rags.
I place them together, just so, and make my own
stitches.
In the end, you have something new.'
She eats a little of the bread;
Jem watches the way she licks the crumbs,
Licks them from her fingers.
'Often, I hear songs but I don't speak the language.
So I learn the song, and make up my own words.'
'How far have you gone on your travels?'
'Everywhere from the Eastern Ocean
To the Kingdom of the Three Sovereigns
And back again,' the stranger says.
Jem thinks about this for a moment.
She has heard these names, of course.
Traders in the market boast
That their wares are from these places,
But so it always seemed – a boast.
In stories for children these names were shorthand
For 'as far east and as far west as you might go'.
Fairytale places, in other words.
Between them is several thousand miles,
Between them is the whole world.
'Surely that would take a lifetime?'
'Yes, that is my life,' says Mika.
'I was born on the road, trading with my parents
Until the time I was thirteen, mostly spices.
I was never good at that, as they were.

Now I play music, but it's the same life.
What is it that you do here?'
'Me?' Jem's cheek colours;
For suddenly her job seems a paltry thing.
'I am a scribe. I copy records, ledgers, edicts.'
She clears her throat, but the stranger only smiles.
'I can't write a thing. I always wondered
How it was done. Could you copy a song?'
'A song? Like yours?'
'Yes. I mean, they're here and gone.
They last as long as I breathe out,
Then vanish from the world forever.
Even a meal leaves a smear on the plate.'
She laughs, her eyes twinkling.
'I suppose, perhaps I could . . . ' Jem says,
But she isn't sure.
She could record the meanings of the words,
But not the words themselves.
Someone reading the record back
Would not say the rhymes and rhythms
The way they were intended.
As for the music itself . . .
[Some lines missing]

They sit in silence, watching the market.
Jem is about to say that she should leave,
Thank you for the song and the bread.
'I've always wondered what it would be like, to travel.'
Mika looks sideways at Jem, half-smiling.
'Have you ever left this town?'
Once again, Jem blushes.
It never seemed a thing to be ashamed of,

But the furthest she has been is the far riverbank.
Jem shakes her head; the stranger puts a hand on hers.
Her palm is soft but the fingers are calloused
From holding down the lyre's strings.
'It's nothing to be ashamed of.'
'I suppose I feel . . . ' Jem begins, but cannot finish.
The feeling is too embarrassing to admit.
It is the feeling of inexperience;
The feeling of being a child,
The feeling of standing outside the arena;
The feeling of innocence made inappropriate by age.
Why does she feel this now?
A few moments ago,
The time it would take to write a line of text,
She did not think or feel these things.
The song has changed her.
Or was it something else?
She says: 'What is it like?'
'Travelling? Or do you mean the world?'
'I suppose that I mean both.'
'Travelling is hard work, like everything else.
You're always looking for the next place to stay,
The next place to get food and drink.
You're always on the lookout for
Who might be friendly or unfriendly.
So it keeps your eyes sharp.'

Jem looks briefly into the stranger's eyes.
Her eyes are very blue.
She thinks of the deadening silence
Of the room in which she works
And the way that, even when copying texts

Of great complexity, she can lose
Minutes, hours, days to daydreaming.
'And the world?'
'The world . . . ' Mika smiles again.
'The world makes the effort worthwhile.'

They watch the market for a minute more,
And the stranger finishes her bread.
She seems relaxed, at ease,
Unaware of the turmoil in Jem's mind.
There is a resonance, too low to hear,
Like the lyre purring in her hands.
Jem's head has been set ringing
By the words of this stranger,
By her voice, by the way she sits
With her back so easy against the well,
By a look from her sharp eyes.
There is a memory she cannot grasp,
Which seems to come closer
With each moment in her company.
A memory of one person staying, one person leaving.
Jem opens her mouth to speak.
She is about to say: 'Let me come with you.'
She will say that scribes are always in demand,
That she can sell her skills on the road,
To people who need records.
Perhaps she could even teach the stranger
How to write herself.
Perhaps, together, they could find a way
To write the songs down together.

___

Joe Heap

A shadow falls over them.
'Took long enough, but I got us some.'
Jem looks up to see a man.
A man, dressed in desert robes,
Is standing over them, holding two clay cups.
He hands a cup to the woman.
It's hot spiced milk; Jem knows the stall it came from.
Under his arm, the man has a folded animal hide.
'You got something to mend the saddlebag?'
'Yes.' The man drinks from his cup
And wipes his mouth on his sleeve.
'Cost more than I would have liked,
But there should be some left over.
Who's your friend?'
'Oh, I . . . ' Jem stands hastily, brushing off crumbs,
Makes a formal bow to both of them,
Which seems foolish a moment later.
'I should be on my way.'
'You're sure?' the stranger says.
She is smiling, but is there disappointment?
Later, Jem will hope not,
For the thought will itch at her like a loose thread.
'My work . . . I am already late . . .
It was very nice to meet you.'
She turns and starts to walk
Towards where Porus waits with his gossip,
His haggling and his beeswax.
She does not look over her shoulder.

Tablet 4
[Some lines missing]
Time passes with the business of business,

And soon Jem walks back through the market,
A bundle of wax hugged to her breast.
She walks close to the well,
Expecting to hear the woman's voice
Raised in song, or to see her chatting with the man.
She has it in mind to say something.
That if they will wait to the end of the day—
But there is no one by the well.

She looks around the market square,
But there is no sign of the woman.
At last, she recalls the lost memory,
Though she is unsure what it means.
Sitting under a spreading tree,
Watching the woman walk away
In clouds of blue smoke . . .
[The rest of Tablet 4 is missing]

Tablet 5
Bearing her burden, Jem walks back.
Time settles into its old arrangement.
Her eyes, which for a blink grew sharp,
Start to dim again, like sunset.
When she arrives, she expects a scolding,
But today, for once, the overseer
Seems too drowsy to make fun of her.
She puts down the bundle of wax
And finds her way back to her desk.
There is her stylus and clay,
There are the water and pallets,
There are the records set out to be copied.
She takes the clay, wets it a little

And spreads it out on a pallet.
She picks up her stylus and hesitates.
Of fools who became kings
And kings who became fools . . .
She writes, but it is not the words
Of the document she is writing.
It is the stranger's song, or something like it.
Gods turned into trees and clouds . . .
Jem makes the marks for a couple of lines,
Then stares at them for a long time.
Then, she writes again:
Under a fig tree, with leaves like hands
To tell your story after you're gone . . .
Around her the work goes on,
Copying records to make other records,
Building a storehouse, piece by piece,
Which holds not wheat or barley
But knowledge about people's lives:
What they own, who they owe,
How much of their time they have promised
In exchange for bread to feed their children.

Turning the stylus around to its flat end,
Jem wipes out the marks she has made
With a few long strokes,
Sprinkles the clay with fresh water,
And starts again.

June

7

It's half past nine in the morning and ten million species are going about their business on Planet Earth. Humans are largely unaware of their fellow passengers. Many are too small to see, existing down in the sultry steerage of the soil, in blankets of decaying tree matter, in the briny oceans. The gorgeous, messy dance of life is a pass-the-parcel of energy received from the sun, cycled through photosynthesis, predation, decomposition and nutrient recycling. Take your partner by the hand, swing them round, do-si-do!

An alarm is sounding behind Jem.

'Could you stop there, sir?' The request is delivered with a degree of menace. What has he done to make this man angry? 'Sir—'

'Sorry, where is this?'

The security guard brushes the question off – it's not the one he was expecting. His hand grips Jem's shoulder, exerting enough pressure to focus his attention.

'Is that the shirt you were wearing when you came in, sir?'

Jem looks down. The shirt – blue flannel with a plaid pattern, thin yellow stripes – is unfamiliar. Who dressed him in it? He seems to be in a shopping centre. A desert of imitation marble stretches around him. He looks back to the shop which he (presumably) just walked out of. A few people are watching their exchange with thinly veiled amusement. Jem catches a woman's eye and she renews her examination of a pair of jeans.

'Can you come with me, sir?'

The hand steers Jem back to the shop. People glance his way. He tries to remember what happened before he heard the alarm, but his memory is a blank document.

'I think I've had a blackout—' he tells the guard, who has released Jem from his grip, but hovers over his shoulder. The guard says nothing. They pass through racks of brightly coloured dresses, through lingerie and handbags, to the muted colours of menswear. Jem wants to tell the security guard about his time in hospital, his out-of-body experience, and how things haven't been quite the same since. It's as though the elastic holding his soul to his body has been stretched, and occasionally his soul comes free, like the male genitalia coming loose from a pair of aged briefs. On reflection, Jem decides, this will definitely make him sound insane; he keeps quiet. A woman, presumably the manager, waits to greet them.

'Thank you, Asif.' She smiles at the guard. 'Now, Mr . . . '

'Adjaye . . . Jem, my name is Jem. I'm sorry, I—'

'Mr Adjaye, could we have a word in my office?'

'I'm so sorry. I haven't been myself . . . '

'Mrs Adams?' A young man appears, carrying a shirt and a flat box. The box has a clear plastic window and contains a sheet cake. The cake is iced white, with words piped in blue – HAPPY BIRTHDAY MUM!

'He left these in the changing room.' The young man offers them to the manager.

'Oh . . . ' she frowns, mentally changing track. 'Is this your shirt, sir?'

'Yes . . . it seems to be.'

'Sir?'

Jem looks at the cake and a memory stirs. 'The cake is for my mother. I was stopping off to find a new shirt before the party . . . '

'Are you okay?'

The young man gets Jem a chair, and he is encouraged to sit while a drink of water is fetched. Events blur for a few minutes, but he gathers he is no longer in trouble. He waits for them to let him go, hoping he will not be late for Emily.

'Oh, and a bucket of champagne!'

The waiter smiles with poorly disguised contempt. Olly turns back to Mika with the look of a puppy who has fetched a ball. She resists the urge to put her face in her hands. This isn't a place to order champagne, even if it's on the menu. That's why she chose it. But Olly has a habit of ordering champagne wherever he goes, and insists on footing the bill. It's sweet really, his refusal to pretend his bottle washer's wages are all he has to live on. Well, maybe not sweet to the other bottle washers.

'How have you been? Man, these breadsticks are so good! We should do breadsticks at SINE . . . '

He witters on, not waiting for Mika to reply. Olly isn't good at silence; it makes him uncomfortable. It's obvious that he thinks this is a date. Mika tried to pick somewhere that would shatter that illusion before it formed, but even the fluorescent strip lights of Bella Mamma haven't done the job. Olly smirks his confident, rich-boy smile. A violent urge rises in her, and she delivers the words like a slap.

'I'm pregnant.'

His hundred-watt confidence flickers.

'You're . . . oh, congratulations! Should I cancel the booze?'

'It's yours.'

Full blackout this time, just as the champagne arrives.

'Sir?' The waiter presents the bottle for inspection, hamming it up like an extra in a period drama who's been given a line.

'I . . . um . . . maybe we'll send it . . . '

'That's great, thank you.' Mika nods.

The bottle is uncorked into stained linen and Olly tastes the champagne.

'Yes, fine, thank you . . . ' he mumbles.

Mika accepts a glass and takes a large sip. It's vinegary and too cold, as though the bottle has been pressed against the back of the fridge. She remembers, for a moment, the taste of sun-warmed, half-rotten figs. In the different restaurants she has worked in, Mika has tasted the finest pudding wines – leftover Amontillados, Sauternes, and Muscats by the score – yet the taste in her dream was better than any of them. The waiter places the bucket on the table and sashays away, leaving Olly to make some laboured calculations.

'You're sure it's mine? We used, you know . . . '

'I'm sure, thank you. And yes, you should probably work on your condom technique.'

Long pause. She takes another sip.

'Are you going to keep it?'

Ah, clever boy.

'No, Olly, I'm not.'

'Oh.' A quick-change of emotions, like masks dropping away – relief, disappointment, relief again, then puzzlement. 'Then why are you . . . why are we . . . ?'

'Here? Because I thought it would be polite to tell you. I know that sounds strange.'

'No, no, of course . . . ' He nods and drains his glass. 'You don't want me to . . . '

'To what?'

'I don't know,' he flushes. 'To talk you out of it?'

'No, thank you. I've made my mind up. This is a . . . ' she pauses. What is this, after all? 'A courtesy call.'

'Oh, right . . . good.' Olly's face brightens, not to its usual luminosity, but as though someone has fired up an emergency generator.

'Though financially, you know . . . '

'Oh, yes, of course. No worries.'

Mika looks at him for a moment more. All the posh-boy masks have dropped away, and she sees the same person she glimpsed, that first night, when he told her about his sister. A damaged person, making the best he can out of the rest of his life. Their bruschetta arrive. Mika looks away, and they focus on eating quickly.

Her mind should be on the next steps, but instead it's back in her most recent dream. She's finding it hard to shake off. Every sensation was as real, perhaps more real, than her memories of yesterday. She remembers sitting by the well. She remembers singing songs, though when she tried to sing them in the shower, they sounded wrong.

Though that knowledge has faded, like all dreams fade upon waking, she still has the feeling of it – a whole other life.

Most of all, she remembers *her.*

Of course, she has no name to give her, or rather him. She – or he – was the man from the lucid dreaming class, the one she got angry with for wanting a biscuit. He wasn't really in her dream, she knows, however real it seemed. That's not possible. Yet she has an unaccountable urge to find him and make sure. To call up Madame Gonzalez-Whippler and ask for his contact details. But no – that's insane. She is not going to act like a crazy person because of one weird dream. (Two. Two weird dreams, if you count the fig tree. Which she doesn't, really.) She looks out of the window just as a child streaks past, trailing ribbons from a baton. Mika's thoughts tangle in the colours.

All over the world, children are growing.

Children are crawling over kitchen tiles. Children are shuffling over carpets. Children are climbing stairs on all fours while parents hold their breath. Children are standing, walking, running! Running down backstreets after their older siblings, running through battered playgrounds with the high-rise giants towering on all sides, running through dusty villages, chickens scattering as they go. Wind whooshing in their ears. Running downhill until they lose their footing and tumble to the grass, laughing.

Laughing, yes, because it's a funny business, growing up. You'd have to laugh or it would drive you mad. Feel sorry for the serious child, the 'old soul', the one who never cracks a smile. Theirs is a heavy burden.

Children are being swung round and round and asking

for more. Children are being thrown into the air, or balanced on one hand. Children are bouncing balls, blowing out candles, picking dandelions, solving puzzles, pushing siblings away. Children are hitting, children are crying, children are wobbling on bicycles, somersaulting into ball pits and swimming pools. Children are joining hands and dancing in a ring, children are paddling in the sea, children are on a roundabout, children are playing counting games, skipping games, rhyming games, children are making toys for themselves with paper and sticks.

Children are dressing up as doctors, firefighters, soldiers. Children are dressing up for church, for mosque, for synagogue. Children are waving flags that their parents gave them. Children are chanting 'stop the war' and children are chanting 'burn the gays'. Children are copying dance moves from the TV. Children are putting on makeup. Children are trying on fashions. Children are learning more from the way their father speaks to the lady on the checkout than they'll ever learn at school. Children are joining in the dance without knowing when it started.

About 16.9 kilometres away, Jem is sitting on his childhood bed. He is thinking of a face he saw in a dream. Suddenly the door opens and his mother comes in.

'Brought you some cake.'

She sits heavily by his side. The bed creaks alarmingly under the weight of both of them.

'Thanks.' He accepts a piece of the frosted cake he brought. 'Happy birthday, by the way.'

They bump paper plates.

Downstairs the family have assembled – Jem's three brothers, their wives and partners and seven children, ranging from a baby to a near-teenager – for a full-day affair. He's already thinking of excuses to slink out in an hour or so.

'Another year.'

'It's an achievement,' Jem says, and wonders why.

'About what happened in the kitchen . . . '

His mother trails off, inviting him to supply the details, but he frowns as though he doesn't know what she's talking about.

'With the banana glacé.'

'Oh,' he forces a smile. 'Made a mess, didn't it?'

The cut-glass trifle bowl, filled with his mother's favourite pudding, had been picked up by his nephew to put in the fridge. He made it halfway before it slipped out of his arms and fell to the tiles. A nebula of whipped cream, mashed bananas, candied fruit, almond flakes and glass shards burst over the floor. Jem supposes the noise wasn't actually that loud, but it seemed to him like a bomb going off. He wouldn't have been surprised if the windows had blown out. The next thing he knew, everybody was rushing in, lifting the children away from the mess, laughing and reprimanding and giving advice on the best way to clean it up. Jem had felt a hand on his shoulder – his mother's – and realised he had his hands clamped over his ears. He was in a semi-crouch, heart beating so hard he shook.

Jem says nothing; his mother changes tack.

'You wanted some air?'

'No . . . it's just a little busy down there.'

'You think I don't know? I shuffle round this house 364 days of the year, then suddenly—!'

'We visit more often than that, Mum.'

'Maybe *you* do.'

Jem takes no pride in being the diligent son. His mother

would rather he went out and made a success of himself than visit all the time. He has a bite of the cake. Usually he would enjoy it, but now it tastes oversweet and synthetic. He remembers the bread from the market, flavoured with cardamom and orange peel. He remembers the feeling of her hand on his. (Or should that be hers?)

Every time Jem thinks about the dream, he finds himself smiling. This should worry him. The fact that it doesn't worry him makes him worry. He is adept at this kind of meta-worrying, where his own anxiety or lack of anxiety becomes the basis of a new fear. His eldest brother got him a fridge magnet which read: 'the best way to stop worrying about something is to worry about something else.' Jem thought it was perfectly idiotic. Besides, his built-in fridge is non-magnetic.

Footsteps thump up the stairs outside; someone yells something about opening the champagne. They are safe here, in his childhood bedroom.

'Are you okay, Jem?'

No, he wants to say, I am not. I've been following the wrong track for years. I've lost the only things precious to me. I've been involved in a car crash which has left me with some kind of PTSD. I've been given a second chance at life but I don't know what to do with it and I'm terrified I'm already wasting it. I had the strangest dream and I half believe it was real. I'm afraid there's a crack in my brain and I'm starting to leak out of it. I'm afraid I might be going crazy.

'I'm fine, Mum.'

She sets down her plate on the bed, cake uneaten. 'You always worried as a child.' They look at each other briefly then look away, magnets repelling. 'You were worried about the cat running away in the night. You were worried about the people who moved in next door. You were worried about your father's smoking.'

'Yeah, and as it turned out—'

'Your brothers would play with fire and jump out of trees—'

'And I watched from in here, reading a book.'

His mother sighs.

'I just wish you would get out, take more risks. Nobody ever made a success of themselves by playing it safe.'

He puts his cake down on the bedside table, next to a *Thunderbirds* alarm clock which hasn't been wound for years.

'I don't need a lecture, Mum.'

'You've always worried that something bad would happen, and now it has.'

He nods, trying to placate her, to make her stop, but she's wrong. Something bad already happened, four years ago. Everything since then is an epilogue. For a moment he thinks he will say something. He would feel better, if he said it out loud. Who can he talk to, if not his own mother? He takes a breath and says—

Nothing.

She waits for a long time. Music starts up downstairs. She looks at his face to see if it will prompt anything, then picks up her plate and stands slowly. The bed groans with relief.

'I better get down, see what they've done to my kitchen.'

'Okay.'

'I'm sorry . . . ' She wrings her hands. 'That Emily didn't come.'

'It's fine.' He looks to the window. 'Sarah was apologetic

– one of those honest mix-ups where everyone had the wrong end of the stick.'

His mother harumphs. 'You're too forgiving.'

'I'll see Emily soon. It's fine.'

His mother says nothing and, when he looks back, she has gone. Jem watches silence settle like a fine layer of dust over his childhood. No thoughts pass through his mind, and then suddenly he is picking up his phone and scrolling back through his recent calls. Without knowing what he is going to say, he dials.

'Madame Gonzalez-Whippler speaking.'

'Oh, hello . . . '

'Can I help you?'

'I came to one of your classes the other day, about lucid dreaming. My name is Jem?'

'Oh yes, the note-taker. How's the leg?'

'A little better each day, thank you.'

There is silence between them for a moment, and Jem cannot think how to break it. He isn't sure why he called.

'Was it something about the class that you wanted to talk about?'

'Yes, well . . . I actually did have a lucid dream. Or something like one. On that first night.'

'Oh, well done! You were a very attentive student.'

'Yes, well . . . I suppose this sounds crazy, but I dreamt I was sharing the dream with someone else. Someone who was also in the class – she left early?'

'That doesn't sound crazy to me,' he hears her understanding smile down the line. 'Dreams are strange. It's just that, when we remember them clearly—'

'No, but—' he cuts her off. 'What I mean to say is, I think I really did share the dream with her.'

'Of course it may have seemed that way. And I'm very open to the possibility of—'

'I'm just saying, if you happened to have her number . . . '

He realises his misstep a second too late. There is silence, but Jem thinks if it were possible for chilly air to blow down the line, he would feel the breeze in his ear. When she speaks again, he tries to fend off her objections, one overlapping the other.

'She was a pretty girl—'

'I'm not trying to—'

'—and I don't doubt that she seemed *very* real in your dream—'

'I didn't mean it like—'

'—but that doesn't mean I'm going to forward her—'

'You could send her my number—?'

'—a stranger's unwanted attention—'

'I'm not . . . '

At last, he falters, and cannot restart his argument. Of course he is being absurd, and making a fool of himself. It was just a dream, and he's the weirdo for believing it was real.

'I'm sorry,' he says. 'You're right, of course.'

Madame G-W breathes out, air rumbling the receiver.

'If she gets in touch with me, I'll let you know, okay?'

'Thank you, I—'

Before he can say more, the line is dead.

Jem gets up to rejoin the party.

The morning is unexpectedly fresh. A westerly breeze, sky cloudless, and flocks of birds bursting from the squares like puffs of confetti. Mika has booked an early appointment in the hope she'll make her shift, despite what she read online. She can feign food poisoning down the phone if necessary. Her body clock, which sleeps until noon unless prodded by multiple alarms, decided to wake her at half five. Mika made breakfast but didn't eat. Her pregnancy has been undramatic, but her appetite comes and goes. She drank a peppermint tea, put on walking shoes and set out on foot. She likes long walks; they help her think.

The city looks good, the way places look good when you've decided to leave. She has worked in Paris and Barcelona, the Italian riviera, and a Michelin-starred bistro outside Aix-en-Provence. She has worked in the galleys of cruise ships around Scandinavia and spent six months in the kitchens of a Swiss ski resort. Along the way she's worked in kebab shops and pizza parlours, knowing it wouldn't be long before something better turned up. She wants to try for somewhere further afield this time – Melbourne, perhaps, or Cape Town.

The city is quiet, or as quiet as it ever is. She crosses Trafalgar Square, passing through holiday snaps (her left elbow, captured in the background of a honeymooning Japanese couple's selfie, will hang on a dining room wall in Osaka for the next twenty-six years, until their divorce). She stops for a can of lemonade on the same spot Canaletto bought a bag of roast chestnuts in 1746, after a morning sketching the Thames.

She walks with the unsettling feeling that someone is walking with her, or behind her, saying nothing. She's had this feeling since she first took the test, though she couldn't put her finger on it then. It's the feeling of being in a room with someone who's not talking. Sitting in that restaurant with Olly, she felt like there was a third person at the table. She doesn't want to put her headphones on and seem rude to her silent companion. She's being followed by silence, and she doesn't like it.

In St James's Park, she skirts the edge of the lake. It's alright, she reminds herself: there's more than an hour until the appointment. This is better than a café in Fitzrovia, with the dark suits stamping and steaming for their morning espresso like impatient horses.

She watches a moorhen preening itself. She watches two squirrels fighting over some prize, watches them spring apart as a jogger approaches. She watches seven geese fly east in formation, soundless save for a baleful honk. She wants to narrate each of these happenings to the silent presence accompanying her. But that would be crazy. At least, it would look crazy to a passer-by. She doesn't feel crazy.

Mika doesn't believe that the thing in her belly is a person. She doesn't believe it has feelings, much less feelings about its impending fate. It's a cluster of cells, without the capacity for thought or pain, and the decision to get rid of it is rightfully hers. What she does believe in is potential. The way something can be there and not there at the same time. The silence is the other half of a conversation she's having. The half that doesn't exist yet, but exists in negative.

Joggers pass by in ones and twos. The geese return and land on the lake with a clatter of wings. A helicopter appears, hovers like a dragonfly thinking of perching on a reed, then moves on, out of sight. The city goes on around her like a machine, like a plant, like a heart pumping blood, like a person, like a city. Mika hears the silence clearly, despite the noise. She doesn't get up from the bench. When she finally looks at the time, an hour has passed. She takes out her phone, finds the right number and dials.

'Hello? Madame Gonzalez-Whippler.'

'Ah, hello. I attended one of your classes the other day
. . . most of it. And there was this man there, with a crutch,
yes? This will sound crazy but I had a dream . . . '

'Oh,' Madame Gonzalez-Whippler says. 'Oh . . . '

8

Let's pull back for a moment and watch the Earth, forging into darkness. Another thing to get straight – the Moon appears to orbit Earth, though in truth they go around each other, circling an invisible centre point some 1700km below the earth's surface. The same thing happens with Earth and the Sun. Even in these unequal relationships – star to planet, planet to moon – their attraction is enough to cause the larger partner to wobble on its axis. To cause a little uncertainty. When binary stars are formed, the attraction is more equal. Sometimes they may exchange mass, a bridge of burning fire stretched between them, blurring the line between one and the other.

Round and round they go; where they stop, nobody knows.

Jem is sitting in a window booth at Hoban's, arms propped on the pink Formica table. His crutch is propped against the window. Outside, the colours of Soho are running in the rain. Reds, greens and yellows turn blue, black and purple. Inside, everything is heat and steam and noise from the kitchen. Jem is sweating, but it's not the humidity. Every few seconds he checks his phone again, as though a new message might have appeared without the screen lighting up to announce it.

'Can I get you something?'

Jem jumps. A girl in a too-large apron has materialised from the steam of the espresso machine. She peers out from a mass of dark hair.

'I'm just waiting for someone.'

'So I see. A coffee, maybe?'

'Sure. Flat white.'

'You got it.'

'No, wait!' Jem stops her as she turns. Coffee is only going to make him more nervous. The girl turns slowly on her heel.

'Problem?'

'Do you have decaf?'

'Absolutely not.'

'Herbal teas?'

'We've got green tea, orange blossom, chamomile, jasmine, ginger, tomato mint, awabancha, hibiscus, rhubarb and custard, mint choc rooibos, kukicha, yerba mate, strawberry shortcake and Earl Grey.'

He watches her face to see if she's mocking him, and her face replies, unequivocally – 'yep'.

'I'll have a green tea.'

'*Excellent* choice.'

He reopens his messages. From three days ago, three out of the blue from someone not in his contacts:

Got your number from woman at lucid dreaming thing.
She said you'd already been in touch so guess I'm not

losing my mind. Or I'm not the only one. Mass hysteria?

Anyway, we should meet up. Off work tomorrow if you want to grab coffee.

Oh – my name is Mika.

He hadn't known what to say except yes. She suggested the time and place. Now it's five minutes past the time she gave and he has been here for fifteen. He circled the block a couple of times before that. He's not sure what he expects to happen. He hopes she turns up. He hopes she doesn't. The girl returns with his tea. She's turning back to the kitchen when she yells:

'Mika! It's you!'

'Tamara!'

He cranes around to see the person who is now hugging the waitress and feels his stomach swoop like a trapdoor opened under him. It's her. It's the woman from the class. The woman from the dream. It's her, dressed in T-shirt and jeans instead of desert robes. She isn't paying him any attention.

'How's Kenny?'

'Dad's in the kitchen,' the waitress says, as though this is enough of an answer. 'You want something? I'll tell him you're here.'

'Beggar's Banquet, and an apple juice.'

'Sure; and for you?' She turns back to Jem.

'I'm not that hungry . . . '

'Kenny hates it when people don't order food,' Mika says. 'You should get something.'

'Um . . . ' Jem casts his eyes over the laminated menu, which seems to have hundreds of items and minimal

description. 'You're getting pancakes, right? I'll get the, uh
. . . Hunky Dory?'

'Sure, coming right up.'

Tamara whisks back towards the kitchen while Mika
throws her jacket into the booth. Jem starts to stand
awkwardly, using the table as support, then realises she
isn't going to reciprocate a hug and sits back down.

'So . . . ' he says.

'It's really you, huh?'

'And it's really you.'

Her fingers drum the tabletop for a moment.

'Tell me something else. Something only you could know.'

Jem thinks. In their messages, they have exchanged details
– what they were wearing, the story of the tree, the story
of the market – as though they were spies exchanging
codewords to prove they were who they said they were.
Jem remembers the tree now, the whole thing dredged from
the post-accident sinkhole in his memory.

'You said you'd travelled, what was it? "From the Eastern
Ocean all the way to . . . to . . . "'

'The Kingdom of The Three Sovereigns. I looked it up.
Basically means China, or whatever China was five thousand
years ago.' She picks up the menu and scans it. 'You said
the Hunky Dory?'

'Yeah; should I not have?'

'No,' she smirks. 'I admire a bold orderer.'

Jem feels a jolt of irritation. It's a relief, in a way, to be
irritated. It's easier than feeling anxious or awestruck at
the physical manifestation of the woman from his dreams.
She is exactly the same – pale eyes; reddish hair; slight
crease between her brows from frowning. There is a scar
on her right jawline, small but too wide to be a cut. A

burn, perhaps. She takes out a lip balm – cherry flavour – and smears some on. He looks away.

There is something almost unbearable about her. It's like sensory overload – too bright, too hot, too loud – except for a sense Jem never knew he had. He is scared that, if he perceives her too clearly, he will be overwhelmed.

Mika, in turn, is surveying Jem – brows very straight, very serious; dark eyelashes; tawny-brown skin, freckled at the cheeks. There is something asymmetrical about his smile, but she's not sure if she finds it sexy or irritating. His lips are full, almost feminine. Or perhaps she just remembers how he looked in that last dream. He had looked the same, really, but unmistakably a woman. She imagines dressing him up in her clothes.

Yes, Mika decides, she has a crush on Jem. She suspected it. That was half the reason for arranging this meeting. But Mika knows that a crush is just a lack of information. If Jem has a certain mystique to him now, it's only because he is a low-resolution image. A grainy JPEG of a person. The surest remedy is to find out more about him. Once she fills in the blanks, her mind will stop populating them with more exciting things.

They sit in silence for a moment, comparing each other to their memories.

'This is . . . ' she starts.

'Weird, right? I mean, I think it's weird. Maybe you—'

'You think I've done this before?

'I'm not saying—'

'Because I didn't ask for this to happen.'

'Look,' he spreads his hands on the table. 'Maybe we're getting off on the wrong foot.'

She sits back in the booth but says nothing, so Jem continues.

'Maybe we should get to know each other a little.'

Mika is tempted to agree, the faster to fill in the blanks. But now Jem is suggesting it, she feels a contrary urge not to please him.

'Why should we?'

'I just think, if we're going to have these dreams—'

'I'm not planning on having any more.'

Jem frowns. 'Aren't you curious?'

'This is my life! This—' she slaps the Formica table for effect. 'This is what's real. I don't want to have weird dreams where I'm someone else. And, no offence, but I don't need to be dreaming about some stranger every night.'

'Not every night . . . '

'But you *are* a stranger.'

He takes a deep breath. 'That's what I'm saying – maybe if we got to know each other a bit better—'

'Then I wouldn't mind you popping into my head every night?'

'I work for a bank. I have three brothers,' he says, ignoring her. 'All older and . . . and they're all more successful than me.'

Mika looks like he's made a bad smell.

'Why are you telling me this? Why should I care that your brothers are more successful than you?'

Jem has listened to a self-improvement podcast which explained that sharing vulnerabilities can help to build trust with new people, but does not say this.

'How about you? Do you have any siblings?'

Mika just stares at him, arms folded. He sighs, rubs his eyes with finger and thumb. When he looks again, she's staring out of the window. She speaks again, her voice smaller.

'What happened to you, after you left me in the market?'

Jem thinks hard to remember.

'I went to get beeswax, then back to work . . . '

'And after that?'

'I don't know,' he shakes his head. 'I just went on with my life, I suppose. Woke up not long after that. After you'd gone the dream, the memory, whatever it was – it just petered out.'

'It was the same for me,' she sighs. 'I remember walking through the market, with smoke in my eyes . . . but the moment you were gone, everything became hazy, like a normal dream.'

'I looked some of it up,' he says, getting his phone out.

'Looked what up?'

'Well, I remembered stuff. The shape of the writing I was doing.'

'The writing?'

He shows her the screen and she looks at the pictures of clay tablets. The symbols are strange, scratchy.

'Akkadian . . . can you read it now?'

'No,' he laughs. 'I thought it'd be great if I could. I'd be a genius! But I look at them and . . . nothing.'

'Nothing at all?'

He shakes his head. 'It's funny, but I still remember that life. I remember what it felt like to be that person.'

'To be a woman?'

'Sort of . . . ' He looks bashful. 'But all of it, you know? It was like finding a book from childhood that I'd totally forgotten. Only, when I started to read it, I knew every word. How could I have forgotten?'

'I feel the same . . . '

'Do you think they're memories?' he asks, but at that moment Tamara reappears with their order. Jem surveys the plate, trying to decide if he's ordered something sweet or savoury. The pancakes, stacked five high, have chorizo, corn and cheese in the recipe, but over the top is drizzled something syrupy. Mika is already tucking into her more traditional fare of banana and pecan.

'Try it – it's really good.'

Grudgingly Jem takes a bite, trying to get as little of the syrup on his fork as possible, but she's right – the pancakes are delicious. The stuff on top is marmalade sauce.

'Kenny is my kind of chef; he improvises.'

'You like to cook?' Jem latches onto this scrap of information.

'It's my job,' she shrugs, peeved to have let something slip. 'Sometimes I enjoy doing it, but mostly I just do it for the money. Like a prostitute, right?'

Jem says nothing. She feels suddenly sorry for him – why is she giving him a hard time?

'Only child.'

'Huh?'

'You asked if I have any siblings,' she says slowly. 'I don't. Just my dad, and he's a thousand miles away.'

'Oh . . . cool.'

'"Cool?"'

'I mean . . . thanks. For telling me. Has your dad lived abroad long?'

'His whole life. He was born abroad . . . like me?'

It takes Jem a moment to work this out; Mika rolls her eyes so hard she thinks she might lose consciousness.

'Oh! You're not— I mean, I wouldn't have guessed! You seem like you've lived here all your life.'

'I have an accent.'

'Sure but, I don't know, you speak English better than most English people.'

'I grew up watching American TV and learned English in school. I've always been good at languages.'

He goes back to eating his pancakes to hide his embarrassment. She watches him, as though she's trying to figure something out.

'What do you think?'

'About the pancakes?'

'About the dreams.'

'Oh, I dunno, they seem . . . more like memories than dreams. More vivid. Like I was reliving past lives. Not that I believe in that sort of thing.'

'Me neither. But that's not what I mean.'

'No?'

'Well, if it was a memory, why *that* memory?'

'We were both in it . . . '

She shakes her head, but has nothing else to offer. He knows what she means. It feels as if the dream should have meant something, but sitting here with Mika he can't think what it should be.

'You were better looking, in the dream,' she squints at him.

'Are you always this nice to people?'

'I'm very nice.'

'You sure seem it.'

'Listen – I didn't ask to be stuck in some kind of dream arrangement with a banker who I never met in my life.'

94

'I'm not a banker!'

'So now I'm expected to meet up with you and make small talk because our brains got tangled up in something I don't even understand.'

She drops her fork on the plate with a clatter.

'Look, it was interesting to meet you, but I think I'm done here.'

'You're leaving?'

'I have stuff to do.'

'Oh . . . okay.'

He looks crestfallen, and for a moment she thinks of changing her mind. There's no mistaking her attraction to him. It feels magnetic, electric, oh-so-tempting. If he were anyone else, she would just enjoy it while it lasted. But he isn't anyone, and she can't trust this dizzy, horny-teenager feeling. Her hormones blow in like summer showers, then are gone. She doesn't want her metaphysics any more tangled up with Jem's than it already is. It's enough being pregnant.

Instead, she takes time finishing her juice. He pretends not to be watching, sipping green tea and checking his phone, but every few seconds his eyes will dart to her face and away again, as though trying to make the most of the time remaining. Around the world, one hundred and thirty-four divorces are finalised. At last she grabs her jacket and wriggles out of the booth. Jem stands, unsure of what etiquette demands. They shake hands.

'It was nice to meet you,' she says, more formally than she intended.

'And you,' Jem nods. 'Maybe we could—'

'No offence, but I hope there is no more "we".'

He frowns down at his chest. There are no words for

what he wants to say, so he says nothing. How can things be stranger here, in the waking world, than they were in the dream? He watches as Mika puts some money down on the table and waves goodbye to the waitress. She leaves. He sits back down in the booth and forces himself not to turn around to watch her walk away.

Reaching over, he breaks off a piece of her uneaten pancake and sees that the stick of cherry lip balm has rolled under the rim of her plate. He thinks about running after her with it. Instead he looks to see if the waitress is watching before pocketing it.

'Behind. You okay, Mika?'

The noise of the kitchen is deafening as they enter the pre-theatre rush, the biggest bottleneck of the day. Everyone turns up at the same time and everyone wants their food in a hurry. Suzy speaks directly into Mika's ear. She's carrying a platter of raw pastry cases, bound for the oven. Mika is leaning on her workstation with both hands, head bowed.

'I'm just a bit . . . ' she takes a few deep breaths through her mouth, trying not to smell the red wine reduction bubbling in front of her. In the back of her mind she knows that James is in today, and while he's not actually helping in the kitchen, he could appear at any moment.

'I'm fine.' She straightens up.

'Great to hear it.' Suzy bustles off to the ovens.

Mika curses under her breath, then returns to slicing near-perfect baby carrots into near-perfect halves, keeping an eye on the simmering pan. Around her the other chefs work automatically, dicing, stripping and mixing. Usually, she thinks of the kitchen as a machine, taking raw ingredients in at the back and pushing plates of food out the front. Today, she can't stop thinking about how many violent verbs there are in cooking – to beat, batter, bruise, cut, chop, crush, crack, flay, pulverise, pound, scrape, shred, slice, skewer, skin, scald, tear and whip.

She looks up.

There's a billow of steam on one side, the orange-blue flash of flambé on the other. She's never felt so much like she's looking at a vision of hell. Each of the chefs is a demon, specialising in their own form of torture. What comes in and what goes out isn't the point – it's the punishment that matters.

Deep breath.

She'll be fine; these moments come and go. With the nausea comes a swell of anxiety – most of the time she can ignore what's happening to her body; now she can't.

Technically, the restaurant should give her maternity leave. Then again, James is a tyrannical dipsomaniac, and their contracts are full of intentionally vague phrasing. She renegotiated several clauses when she started, but maternity rights weren't her priority. She hasn't told him yet, will wait until the first scan, but she knows it won't go well. James doesn't employ cheap immigrant labour so they can go off and have babies.

Even if she *did* get paid for the time off, what happens after that? Her wages aren't bad, but rent eats up a third. She has no spare money for childcare, let alone the endless lists of 'Essential Buys For Newborns' she's read online. She has her Plan B, of course, but that was never designed to include a baby. Her fingers tremble as she takes the knife to another tiny carrot. The nausea rises again.

Deep breath.

The kitchen is loud but there is mercifully little chat. Like most good kitchens, the chefs are focussed on making whatever they're making, and talk is limited to calling orders. SINE doesn't make the best food in London, but it specialises in making food that *looks* amazing. If people are going to pay a hundred pounds per plate, they want to take some photos for the social meeds. Scallops are presented in the shell. Sprigs of uncooked herbs accompany roast meats to the table. Mika thinks you can tell a diner's personality by how they arrange their inedible leftovers.

Olly is up to his elbows in suds, scrubbing a pan. She watches him for a moment, happily bobbing his head to the music on his two-hundred-pound wireless ear buds. She wishes she could broadcast her nausea straight into his head. She hasn't told him yet, hasn't refunded the money he sent to her account for the abortion. Out of the corner of her eye she sees Suzy returning and grabs her.

'Do you know how to do this? I'm gonna puke.'

Suzy takes a look at the food, then at her. Mika feels like she must be the colour of those raw pastries.

'Get some air. I've seen you do this a bazillion times.'

She turns, untying her apron, and tries to walk to the door at a dignified pace. Halfway there she breaks into a run, throwing the apron vaguely in the direction of the laundry bin. She punches through the door to the alley behind the restaurant and vomits over a pallet of eggshells.

The door clicks shut behind her. She stands, hands pressed to the sweating brickwork, focussing on each breath as though she might forget how it's done. A minute passes. She straightens up, walks a little way down the alley, and perches on a box of empty olive oil cartons. The cardboard crumples under her weight, but holds.

She rests her head back on the wall, not caring that the alley stinks, not caring how unhygienic it is, not caring that James might notice she's gone. She closes her eyes and, for a short while, the rushing in her ears drowns out every other sound. London is muted. Slowly, she comes back to herself.

She takes her phone out and dials a number without knowing why. One thousand miles away, a phone is ringing. She has dialled the number so many times, but only now does she picture the old-fashioned rotary ringing behind the restaurant bar. She thinks of the optics trembling a little from the clattering of the bell, thinks of her father trudging his well-worn groove, thinks of him gripping the pillar next to the ice bucket before lifting the receiver.

Click.

'*Ahoj?*'

Her father's voice is thinned by distance. He sounds old. How long since she called? She replies in her first language, stiff but comfortable, like an old shoe she hasn't worn in some time.

'Hey, Dad.'

'Mika? Is that you?'

'Yeah, it's me. How are you?'

There is a pause.

'What are you calling for, at this time?'

She hears his suspicion. Her father is a gentle man. A little distant perhaps, but interested and forgiving. Still, he runs a restaurant. He knows how to get angry when needed. She takes a deep breath to force the words out.

'You're going to be a grandfather.'

There is silence for a moment as he unpacks the words. Mika is an only child; there's no mistaking her meaning.

'That's . . . ' His voice hovers, like a bird of prey about to descend. 'That's wonderful!'

She's so stunned, she says nothing.

'I'm so happy for you, Mika. Oh Cub, that's brilliant news! A baby . . . '

Does she hear tears? They talk about the due date (January sometime, she hasn't had the scan yet), about the scan (didn't have them when your mother was pregnant with you), about whether she'll find out the sex (not sure). More hesitantly, he asks:

'The father—?'

'He's not . . . I mean, we're not really . . . '

'Forget I asked. You're enough parent for any child, Cub.'

'Dad, don't.'

'Your mother would be proud.'

Would she? Mika supposes he knows better than she does.

'When will you be coming back?'

'Coming back? Where?'

'Home, of course. You're not going to have a baby over there, are you? Isn't your visa running out any day?'

'I've got a little time left,' she hears herself say. The visa ran out six months ago. She had been planning to leave, but then the money from her mother's estate had come through, and she'd hatched her plan . . .

'Still, you can't stay there forever.'

She can hear her father smoothing down his flannel shirt, as he always does when he's anxious.

'I'd better hang up – the kitchen will be wondering where I've gone.'

'Yes, but—'

'I'll let you know when I've made plans, okay?'

'Yes, of course. Love you, Cub.'

'You too, Dad. Bye.'

Mika usually hangs up first, but this time she just listens to the quiet for a moment, until she hears the receiver clatter down and the line goes dead. She is suddenly aware of the noise beyond the alley. The beeping and honking, the roaring and shouting and drilling and hammering. She puts her hands on her belly. It's too soft to see any difference there, but she thinks she can feel it. She cradles the swelling silence. A silence promising noise, but silence nonetheless, small and vulnerable amid the clamour.

Let's relax our grip on the present moment, for it was only our attention that slowed it down. Feel the silken rope slipping, the seconds speeding into minutes, into hours, into days. Perhaps this is what death is like – eternity's starry ribbon fluttering through your hands. But let's not go so far. Hold tight again. June has almost passed, the days becoming mostly dry, mostly warm. The longest day has come and gone and, imperceptibly, the increase of darkness has begun.

Each morning, Jem wakes early to his alarm and sits in the chilly air of disappointment. He did not dream of her. Why should he have? Those two dreams were a fluke. Why the sense of expectation? Why does he feel as though he's been stood up? He gets up, measures his portion of breakfast muesli, adds a scoop of flaxseed, eats it with a black coffee while repeating along to a recording of morning affirmations on his phone.

I am happy . . .

'I am happy.'

I am worthy . . .
'I am worthy.'
I am loved . . .
'I am loved.'

He has returned with little pomp to his job at the bank, processing account closures for deceased customers. The process is so familiar, it's as though he never stepped away from it. He visits Emily and takes her to the cinema. She asks him about the accident, but seems confused about the answers he gives, as though he's talking about something else entirely. He tries to learn more about her, but she's evasive. Maybe that's just how seven-year-olds talk. He remembers a time, not so long ago, when he knew everything there was to know about Emily's life. Now she's a stranger. Sometimes he worries that Emily believes he chose for things to be this way. That he didn't want to be in her life. But, if she thinks that, she doesn't say so.

If he thinks at all about the adventure that he promised himself in the hospital, it is with a sense of failure.

Mika works more days than not and makes no decisions. She imagines that, if she waits, a fairy godmother will appear and tell her what to do.

Neither of them entirely forgets the dreams they shared, but with each passing day they are less able to recall the shape of the other's face. They don't dream together, but that doesn't mean they don't dream *of* each other. Mika appears as a background extra in one of Jem's dreams, selling newspapers; Jem is on the TV in Mika's dream, presenting the news. These little echoes ripple until morning, when all are forgotten.

Around the world, people are fighting. In boxing rings, fencing pistes and MMA cages, they are squaring up. In ritualised combat, where the swords are blunt. In street warfare, with guns and knives. In liquor-store brawls, where the bottles being stolen become weapons of convenience. In riots and revolutions, squaring up against police. Throwing Molotov cocktails, being hit by water cannons. People are kicking, punching, stabbing, shooting, garrotting, bludgeoning, manning drones, pulling the trigger, arming the detonator, lighting the fuse.

People are killing.

People are dying.

On opposite sides of the Thames, Mika and Jem get ready to sleep. They brush teeth, put on pyjamas, fetch glasses of water. Outside it's a balmy 18 degrees, humidity 63 per cent, storm clouds rolling in from the east.

They sleep.

9

PERSONS REPRESENTED

MIKA, a Christian wine merchant
JEM, a Roman bureaucrat
CONDEMNED MEN of Tarraco (The Chorus)
A GLADIATOR

Place and time – the cells under the amphitheatre of Tarraco, around midday, on a day of celebration for the emperor's birthday. Mika reaches out to light his incense from the lamp which flickers before the mural of Nemesis, before which condemned men pray before entering the arena.

> ### MIKA
> *Will not my hands be still, to light*
> *A final taper on this earth,*
> *To burn for me when I am gone*
> *And raise my prayer above this cell?*

I light it not for Nemesis,
Who Romans call to take revenge.
There is no shrine here for my God;
I know my God forgiveth all.

I have no faith in Nemesis,
Not even as a demon sent
to tempt the minds of wicked men.
She is an idol, false and base.
Yet by the flickering of this lamp,
The painted creases of her robe
Blow in a breeze I cannot feel.
Her dark eyes follow as I wait
For the flame to accept my final
     offering.
The incense is cheap, the smoke is acrid,
But this is all I have to give.

JEM approaches and shoves MIKA back from the altar.

JEM
Move away.

MIKA
I am just—

JEM
You are not the only man condemned
Who wants to say his final prayers.

CONDEMNED MEN

He grits his teeth
And sideways looks.
At once he feels
As though he's falling.
Sweetness tastes
And music hears
Though neither come
From this dark place.

See how they look
From man to man.
Is this life,
So close to death?
To look into
Another's eyes
And see a little
Of his past?

They speak in unison.

MIKA

I am done—

JEM

I am sorry—

MIKA walks away to the furthest corner of the cell.

MIKA

I close my eyes against this scene,
The easier to pretend it is

Nothing but a sour dream.
But the arena's sounds and smells
Intrude upon my other senses.
Distantly I hear the crowd,
Like ocean's roar behind a hill;
The air is thick with sweating bodies,
Unclean straw, piss and shit.

I do not know how I will die.
I have visited the arena once before,
In company I could not refuse.
I have seen men set upon by bears,
By leopards, boars, and famished lions.
Then, a maddened heifer tossed
Two female martyrs in the air
And trampled them before the crowd.
Perhaps it will be one of these,
Or all of these, or none of them.
Will my death have teeth, or claws?
Will my death be quick and sharp,
Or slow and crushing on my chest?
Somewhere, not so far away,
My death is breathing this same air,
Listening to the same crowd roar,
Waiting for our moment together.

JEM approaches, MIKA opens his eyes.

JEM
I am sorry, for before.
I should not have rushed you, friend.

MIKA

It is no trouble.

JEM starts to laugh.

MIKA

What did I say to amuse you so?

JEM

'It is no trouble . . . '
Politeness in this impolite place
Took me by surprise.

MIKA laughs also.

MIKA

Strange, to share a joke with you,
When soon enough we won't exist.

JEM

Yes . . .
Still, I am sorry, friend.
It was not right of me, to force
You from the altar at a time like this.

MIKA

It is not my altar anyway.

JEM

No, I can tell. To own the truth
I never had cause to pray to Nemesis.

I paid her homage, in a roundabout
  way.
But . . .

MIKA

You had no cause to call on her.

JEM

So it would seem.
An unblemished life, until this day,
An unpicked peach upon the branch.

MIKA

What were you, before you were this?

JEM

A local administrator. Nothing exalted.
I audited the surplus grain.
One day there was less grain than
  expected.

MIKA

Stolen?

JEM

In a manner of speaking, yes.
I am sure I know who did it, but
His tracks are covered far too well.
He made it look like I alone
Could have changed the city's records.
He will benefit from my removal.

CONDEMNED MEN

See his smile,
But see it waver
Like the midday heat.
Jem is beautiful,
Mika sees.
He wants to kiss
The Roman's jaw,
To see if it will soften.

JEM

What about you? What brings you here?
They are rounding Christians up again?

MIKA

As you said, in a manner of speaking—
I understand a child was killed.

JEM draws back a little; MIKA puts his hands up.

MIKA

It was nothing to do with me.
I had not arrived in Tarraco when
They say this awful thing took place.
But I came the morning after,
With my cart of wines to sell.
They arrested me as a stranger.
Of course, I am a Christian.

They look to the middle of the room where an elderly man is practising with a sword, lunging and slashing at an invisible foe.

MIKA

His footwork does not look too bad,
And yet the effort winds him so.

JEM

Of course, it is not a real sword.
It is carved from a single piece of
  wood,
Blackened with grease and metal
  powder.
There is no edge to it, no point.
No point at all . . .

MIKA

Yes, but could you bear to tell him?
I wish I still believed in tomorrow.

JEM

Do you have a family, friend?

MIKA

A wife, two daughters, God be praised.
But they are very far away.
I hope that word of my arrest
Never makes the journey back to them.

JEM

My family know of this all too well.
They condemned me, to save
  themselves.
I wonder if my wife is watching,
Or my daughter . . .

MIKA reaches out and touches JEM'S face.

JEM
You said you just arrived in town?

MIKA
Four nights ago.

JEM
I feel as though we've met before.

MIKA
I thought the same thing when I saw
*   you.*
A swooping feeling just as though
I had missed a step in the dark.

JEM
Have you visited the city before?

MIKA
I have not travelled to Hispania
*   before.*
Perhaps we met some other place.
Have you been to Rome, perhaps—?

JEM
I have never left here, all my days . . .
Ah!

MIKA
What is it?

JEM
Truly, my days were all spent here.

CONDEMNED MEN
They try to grasp at
Something close.
It's on the tip
Of both their tongues.
An idea or
A memory.
A sound, a smell,
A name, a touch.

JEM
I suppose we have familiar faces.

Enter GLADIATOR, a secutor with his heavy helmet
and shield.

CONDEMNED MEN
He opens the door
And stands well back
Waiting for
Our last rebellion.
But none of us had
Such a thought.

GLADIATOR
Time to go!
Get up, come on!

The other men shuffle out of the room, one by one, prodded by the gladiator. Some of them hold the fake swords, but mostly they do not bother. MIKA gets up and starts to follow the others, then sees that JEM is not moving.

MIKA

Come, friend.

JEM does not respond.

MIKA

Come; let us see this through together.

GLADIATOR

Hey, you two!
Follow them, or die where you stand.
You know it is all the same to me.

MIKA holds his hand out to JEM, who takes it. MIKA gasps.

MIKA

Oh!
Suddenly, I remember you.
Everything I was trying to recall.
It is not one thing – it is everything.
A forest floor strewn with wild figs;
Clouds of blue smoke from bundled
    leaves;
Cups of spiced milk by the well;
Plucking notes from a tortoiseshell lyre!

114

Strange vistas unfold before my eyes,
Memories from other times,
Memories from other lives.

JEM
It's you.

MIKA
And you.

The GLADIATOR approaches, idly swinging his sword.

GLADIATOR
Alright, lovebirds; time to go.

Together they walk, still holding hands.

CONDEMNED MEN
There is weeping,
There is pleading,
Attempts at bargaining.
But those two
Barely hear it.
They hold hands,
A stranger's hand,
And yet it's not
A stranger's hand
At all.

MIKA
I wish we had more time to talk,
To recount the memories that we share,

To make new memories, together.
But there is no time – this is the end,
When all is said and all is done.
What words have I to sum up all
The words we will not have time to say?
There around the tunnel's bend
Is daylight and the crowd's full roar.
His hand round mine tightens as
We step beneath our final sun.
His dark eyes shine like topaz stone;
Topaz stone, flecked with gold.

JEM
If we meet again—

A rasp of war trumpets cuts him off.

CONDEMNED MEN
The crowds curve up
Into the sky;
We stumble out
Into the sun.
There is laughter
There is jeering;
A thousand eyes
See our frailty.
The guards retreat;
The gates are closed.

MIKA
If we meet again, my friend,
I pray we remember sooner.

I pray we do not waste time
By not remembering the past we share.

JEM opens his mouth to reply, just as the gates at the other end of the amphitheatre open up. The crowd roars.

July

10

Let's fast forward through most of July. Seen from space, north Africa blushes terracotta red. Drought, intensified by climate change, parches the land. Grey blots trickle down the continent like raindrops – troops of elephants in search of sustenance. A crack in the Arctic ice sheet widens, and an iceberg the size of Greater London steams into the ocean. The Okovango delta, approaching its seasonal peak, spreads like a silver fan. Hold on, almost there. Press play . . . *now*.

The screen is dark, with white writing at the top.

St Thomas' UH	C003728	33Y	GA 12w3d
Prosound F75	ZIELINSKA MIKA	64%	25Hz

'Are you ready?'

'Yes.'

Mika peers at the screen with her name on it, trying to understand the rest of the jargon. She's laid on her back in a dimly lit room, but that's where the romance ends. She's got tissue paper tucked into her pants, a lot of clear goo on her belly, and is desperate for a wee.

'Here we go,' the woman says matter-of-factly, putting down the bottle of ultrasound gel. 'Now I'll start my measurements. I'll explain what we're looking at as I go along . . . '

The sonographer presses the wand at a different angle into her belly, hard enough to be uncomfortable.

'Hm, playing hard to get . . . '

Mika expected this to be delicate, the wand ghosting over her like she was a precious vase that couldn't be opened for fear of breaking its contents. Instead, she feels like a package whose barcode won't scan. None of this feels magical or exciting. Like the ritual of the pregnancy test, there are too many trivial things to distract her. Before the appointment she drank two pints of water, as they asked her to, and now she's sloshing around like a waterbed. The room is too chilly for somewhere she's supposed to lie half-dressed for ten minutes.

At least she came alone. They kept saying it would be nice to have the father, or a family member, or even just a friend to accompany her. It's as though they're worried about her state of mind. Mika supposes that some women might be unhinged by the reality of new life growing inside them. In fact, she couldn't have brought Olly, because she still hasn't told him she's keeping the baby. She couldn't bring her father because he's a thousand miles away. She thought about bringing Suzy, but Suzy does think she's lost her mind.

She's biting her lip in frustration when the little screen in front of her flickers. It's just black and white, with details of her name and age at the top. Grey shapes move across the void as the wand shifts on her belly. Suddenly, something appears.

'Ah, there you are!' the sonographer chirps.

Mika opens her mouth, but someone's stolen the words. She doesn't know what it is about the image. It doesn't, after all, look much like a child. She can see a head, a torso, but the rest is hard to make out. Perhaps it's the way the picture looks all fuzzy, like it's beamed back from the surface of the moon in 1969. The baby feels close and distant at the same time, floating weightlessly in its capsule.

'The CRL is within the expected range,' the sonographer says, using the space-jargon of mission control. Mika would know what she was talking about, if she'd been paying attention. Every so often the woman moves the wand, and the image will warp and disappear, replaced by a new viewpoint. Pulses of sound strobe over the silence in her belly.

'That's fine . . . '

The sonographer is drawing lines on the computer, taking measurements of the foetus. The skull, the brain, two arms, two legs, a heart, stomach, bowel, pelvis and bladder – each is sized up and found acceptable. The mission is viable; proceed to stage two.

Appointment done, the first thing she does is go to the bathroom. Then she has to wait for the results of her scan to be typed up and presented to her. The baby has tested negative for two syndromes she's never heard of. Mika asks if she can take a picture of the screen, but that's not allowed. If she wants a picture, she has to buy one. A machine down the hall dispenses tokens. She buys three for three pounds each and waits to receive her prints.

At last they release her. She sits on a wall outside the

hospital, with a bundle of papers certifying her baby is perfectly normal and three black and white photos that make her stomach swoop every time she looks at them.

'Great, great – I'll see you then. Yeah. Yeah! Ha ha ha!'

James Conroy rip-snorts into his phone and drifts out of the kitchen. Mika watches without turning her head. She has been noting his comings and goings all afternoon, like a hunter tracking a dangerous animal. It is important she times this right, because she won't get a second chance. Punishment or reward depends on where James is in his day – emotionally, financially and chemically. She doesn't want to get trampled.

On the other hand, she mustn't be overcautious. Wait for the perfect moment and you'll wait forever. He is in a good mood, has sunk a couple of dry martinis, just got off the phone to a friend/associate/drug dealer, and is off to be lord of his domain for ninety minutes before rush hour. Mika, in turn, has nothing she needs to cook.

She wipes her hands, makes a moment of eye contact with Suzy that means both 'this is it' and 'cover for me', and walks to James's office. The silence comes with her. She finds James fully reclined in his leather chair, feet up on the desk next to a pile of invoices weighed down by a wheel of Pecorino Romano. She has a moment of wanting to turn back. He is too relaxed, like a cat exposing its stomach, yet will scratch you if you try to pet it. But he has spotted her. Too late to turn back.

'Mika, pull up a pew!'

She steps inside but does not sit. She makes sure to leave the door ajar. His eyes flick to it and his smile crystallises.

'What can I do you for?'

It's not that she's scared of James, as a person. Most times of day, he could be blown down by a strong gust of wind. No – it's everything that's behind James she's afraid of. The State, the statutes, the status quo.

'I have some news . . . '

He eyes her for a second, sighs, and swings his legs off the table.

'I had a feeling this was coming.'

'You did?'

'Who is it, eh?'

'Who . . . ?' For a moment she thinks he's asking after the father.

'Is it Charles? Or Vinnie? Tell me you're not going to work for Vincenzo. What's he offered you?'

'I've not—'

'Because look, I'm not going to double your wages to hold onto you. There are other chefs in London, you know. Ha ha!'

It's unclear to Mika what the joke is.

'No, I—'

'But you *are* good, Mika, I'll give you that. And I can't be bothered to train someone else up, right now. I can give you, let's see . . . five percent?'

She can't quite believe she's being offered a pay rise. Briefly she considers taking it and pretending nothing's the matter for another month or two. She could wear thick sweaters . . .

'I'm pregnant.'

There is a wink of light as James raises his hand to the desk and his signet ring catches the fluorescent light. He says, very quietly:

'And?'

'Well, I know there's not much in our contracts about maternity leave, but—'

She is stopped by a bark of laughter.

'We don't *do* maternity leave. What do you think this is, Google?'

She takes a breath, mentally digging her feet in.

'UK law states—'

'Fuck UK law. You're not a UK citizen, Mika. Your visa expired months ago, am I right?'

His voice is getting louder; she wonders if they can hear him in the kitchen.

'Even undocumented migrants have maternity rights when—'

'Ha! "Undocumented migrants". Is that what we're calling you now? You're. An. Illegal. Immigrant. Mika. I don't dob you in because we have an unspoken understanding – you take my money and ask for nothing extra, *comprende*?'

She realises her fists are balled and forces them to open.

'You knowingly broke the law,' she says, quietly. 'Don't lecture me about illegalities.'

'Are you recording this?' he says, standing suddenly. She's seen him like this before, taking a paranoid turn. It never goes anywhere good. 'Are you wearing a wire? Show me your phone.'

'I'm not recording this, James.' (Why *isn't* she recording this?) 'I just want to know what your position is.'

'My position is, you can get an abortion and stay, because I'm feeling generous. Otherwise, you can fuck off!'

He's yelling now, his face going pink. They stand off for a second.

'Under my contract I'm due severance pay of—'

'Under your contract you're supposed to give two weeks' notice.'

'If this went to tribunal—'

'Then they'd fucking arrest you, wouldn't they? You and your illegal sprog, and stick you both in a detention centre before they fly you off to Rwanda.'

Mika can hear people coming from the kitchen now. Suzy appears in the corridor, followed by Danny, the porter. She feels a little safer – Danny is six foot five and hates James's guts. Behind Danny she spots Olly, wide-eyed with fear. She hasn't told him yet about keeping the baby, but perhaps he has some inkling of what's going on.

'All I'm asking for—'

'You're in no position to ask for anything!' James bellows, spittle flying onto her cheek. 'You've no fucking rights here, yeah? You're not a British citizen, so stop pretending you have some kind of bargaining position. If you dob me in then you're dobbing yourself in, and your friends here, too.'

Danny moves forward, not coming between them but positioning himself if the need arose. James's eyes flicker to his face and see no loyalty there. Quietly, Danny says to her:

'Do you wanna go, Mika?'

She swallows but her throat is dry. She just nods, and then Danny puts one hand on her shoulder and leads her back through the kitchen.

'That's right, fuck off!'

She doesn't cry. She passes everyone in the kitchen, the people she has happily worked with these past few months of their lives. They watch her. The ones she talked to every day. The ones she knows are in the same situation as she is. They watch her, to see what happens next.

'Do you have much in your locker?' Danny speaks low, his hand still on her shoulder.

'A few bits.'

'I'll bring them out to you; okay?'

'Thanks. Oh, um, the combination is three-nine-four.'

'Got it.'

Suzy walks alongside her but says nothing. Mika knows she can't afford to lose this job. Not now, when she's so close to signing the papers on the flat. But she walks alongside. Behind them, getting closer, James is following.

'The fucking nerve of you people, as though I'm some kind of NGO. As though this is a fucking soup kitchen!'

He gets closer; too close. Danny lets go of her shoulder and turns around. James stops in his tracks.

'Mika is leaving,' Danny says.

James looks at him for a moment, then nods.

'Good. Make sure you scrape all her shit out of the locker.'

With this he stomps back to his office. They all watch him go. Danny brings her rucksack, open so she can see everything stuffed in it – the herbal teas, sanitary products, deodorant, change of clothes, cheap sunglasses, promotional knickknacks from Soho, Duracell electric fan, Gatorade water bottle, Budweiser playing cards. Strange how these objects find a way into your life without you inviting them, piggybacking on your life like so many barnacles on a whale.

She zips the bag up. Nobody knows what to say, and she's keen to head them off. Orders are still coming in, meals need to be cooked, and they're down one member of staff.

'Bye guys.'

Before anyone can reply she pushes through the swing door. The night is warm and smells of rotten vegetables. The lock latches behind her; she keeps walking. Still she doesn't cry. Crying is not something Mika does, she doesn't know why. It's as though her creator forgot to plumb her eyes in before clocking off and sending the invoice. Instead, that drip-drip-drip of emotion falls inside, like water over coffee, percolating something dark and strong and bitter.

She spends the next hour in a café bar on Beak Street, drinking an overpriced virgin cocktail. She wouldn't have a proper drink even if she could; she needs to stay clear-headed. Thankfully, she's planned this moment in advance. She knows three things:

1) After the drama, James will want to score. His addiction keeps a regular schedule, but turbulent emotions are smoothed over with a hit. He will double his order so that he has some for now, some for later.

2) Once he's made the call (thinking he's being subtle) it takes an hour before pick-up is ready.

3) Wherever he goes to make the transaction, he walks this way, down Beak Street. Vitali, their old bottle washer, followed him this far one night before losing his nerve.

Mika doesn't need to know exactly where James goes, she just needs to know he's on his way. She's sitting at a table near the window, so she has a good view of the street. If anything it's too good – she doesn't want James to spot her. She thinks about putting her sunglasses on, but decides it would draw more attention. She pulls on the jumper she had in her locker, even though the bar is sweltering. There is a hen party behind her, and she tries to concentrate over the shrieks and jostling.

An hour and a half has passed, and she's about to give

up, when she sees a figure striding down the street. The man is the right build, but is hunched and keeping his head down. She has to look longer than she would like to be sure. James raises his head to dodge around a man dressed as Darth Vader. Mika spins around so that her back is to the window.

'Oh heya, mystery lady!' One of the hens shoves a jug of Blue Lagoon in her face. 'You joining the party?'

'Just on my way out, actually.'

'Suit yourself!'

Shrieks of laughter behind her as she pushes her way to the toilets. It's even hotter in here and smells awful, but there is a stall free. She relieves herself, because she's been busting for the last hour, then gets her phone out.

'Hello? Police, please.'

She takes a winding way back to SINE, avoiding any road that James might take. She could play it safe and hear the outcome second-hand from Suzy. But where's the fun in that? It's harder to find a place to sit, this time – there is a pub across the road, but the windows are frosted at street level. She settles for standing in a shady doorway. Of course, nothing might come of her call. It depends how busy they are tonight. Mika admitted that she didn't think James had a previous record for drug offences, and said she wasn't willing to give a statement. They may decide her tip is bullshit, another time waster.

She thinks all of this through for twenty minutes, until the police car rolls up. There are no lights or sirens. Is it too soon? She's not sure that James has returned yet, because he will use the back entrance. Mika fights the urge to run away, suddenly afraid of the creature she has summoned.

She watches a man and a woman get out and make their way into the restaurant. She sees the diners at the front tables look up, their gaze following the police as they walk to the back of the restaurant, then return to their meals. There is an agonising wait – a minute becomes five, becomes ten. There is no commotion. The diners chat and take pictures of their food, the way they always do.

Leaves skirl around her feet. Not autumn leaves, but summer leaves from city-sick trees. Eczematic leaves. Tobacco-brown leaves, dried and cured by petrol emissions.

She looks up.

The diners aren't taking pictures of their meals any more. They're not chatting. Everyone is looking backwards, into the restaurant. All their eyes are fixed on the same thing, one magnet in a room full of compasses.

Mika presses herself further into the shadows, not caring how awful the doorway smells. Then she sees him, all spotlit by the restaurant's Instagram-friendly lighting. James Conroy is being led out through his own restaurant in handcuffs. His jacket is off, and the buttons at the top of his shirt are torn off, as though there has been a struggle. Ordinary possession probably wouldn't have warranted this kind of performance, but James buys in bulk, and Mika *might* have implied on the phone that he was distributing.

People are taking pictures now. Oh yes. This will get so many more likes than the wagyu and yuzu nigiri. This might even be worth a few quid, if they message the right newsroom. James keeps his head down, so she cannot see his expression, but she watches as the police pilot him out of the front door and into the waiting car. She watches as the car pulls away and people go back to their meals. She feels her phone buzzing in her pocket. Several messages from Suzy appear all at once:

What the fuck just happened?

Did you do this?

What happens now?

Mika puts the phone away and walks in the direction of the Tube.

11

A night passes.

Humankind has existed now for three hundred thousand years. There have been, in that time, one hundred and seventeen billion people. Threaded together like beads on a string, these lives last almost four trillion years. For one tenth of that time, we have been hunter gatherers. For sixty percent, agriculturalists. One point five billion of those years have been spent having sex, another two hundred and fifty million giving birth. Twenty percent of our time was spent raising children.

Mika wakes with the sense that yesterday was not an ordinary day. One by one she sets out yesterday's events, like readying the ingredients for a meal she would never wish to eat. There is the moment of telling James and there is James's reaction. There is staking him out in the cocktail bar and seeing him in the street. There is phoning the police and watching the arrest.

Taking out her phone she searches for James's name and finds that, while his arrest hasn't yet appeared in the papers, the news is filtering through social media. The story multiplies and mutates, like a virus. Relayed by different people it gains new interpretations – middle-class drug use, the demons of the catering industry, white privilege. There are messages of sympathy and offers of help, but these are soon neutralised by testimonies of poor treatment from old employees.

James isn't so famous that it will be a huge story, but he appeared on *Saturday Kitchen* once, and the restaurant has a certain notoriety. By tomorrow morning, she is certain, people up and down the country will be reading about him over their breakfasts. She feels sick and satisfied at the same time. She knows that her revenge may have consequences for her colleagues. Her old colleagues. She was not a white knight, galloping in to save them, by getting their boss arrested.

But there's no use in regret.

She takes the memories, takes her feelings, and makes something of them. The narrative does not appeal to her; its flavours are not natural companions. Never mind – it is done. Plate it up. Send it out. There are more important things to be getting on with. She hands in her résumé to a few places; talks to a few people she knows. She takes her Category D driving test and passes with flying colours. She starts a master list of things to buy for the baby.

A week passes.

On Monday she spends time out west, where her Plan B is slowly taking shape. Time gets away from her and she only leaves when the owner kicks her out. By the time she's on the last Tube home the tiredness has caught up with her. Her whole body aches. As she's walking up the hill, she thinks only of getting inside, a cool shower, a pack of instant noodles, bed. She hopes Yanni is serving a customer, because she can't be bothered to have a conversation with another human being. It's only when she gets close enough to see the sign outside Yanni's shop that she spots the white van.

Immigration Enforcement.

She stops in her tracks but doesn't turn around. It's possible, of course, that this is a coincidence. It's possible that they are here to talk to Yanni about Ajay, who helps out on weekends. It's possible that they're here for no one in particular – that they're just parked up right in front of her flat a week after she had a blazing row with her boss who threatened to have her deported.

She turns and walks back the way she came.

She doesn't look over her shoulder.

Jem is at work, staring at his computer screen. He should not be here. Not that it's forbidden, exactly. Parts of the building are used through the night. But everyone else in his department has left. Far away in the open-plan space, a cleaner is emptying the bins. He can't hear any of the sound they're making. It's swallowed up by the padded desk-dividers, the air-conditioned white noise.

Why is he still here?

He's not working. As each one of his colleagues left, Jem told them he was a bit behind. He was just going to stay another five minutes. Just going to finish this last customer's transition from a living account holder to a dead one. There is a scan of a death certificate open on the screen, but he has already transferred the relevant details into the system. Name and surname. Date and place of death. Name and surname of informant. Cause of death. Spontaneous subarachnoid haemorrhage. Just one of a dozen he's worked on today. Just one of thirty-four thousand three hundred and twenty he's worked on in the last eleven years.

As soon as his last colleague left, Jem stopped pretending to work. For the last hour and a half he's just been sitting at his desk. He should get up, go home. What's stopping him? What's for him here when he could be at home? He tries to tempt himself. He'll order takeout. He'll pick up a bottle of wine on the way back. He'll rent a movie.

But no.

He's hanging on to work like a man dangling over a precipice. He's hanging on to work because he knows that, if he lets go, he's not coming back. He gets his phone out and opens the message chain which has been dormant since his meeting with Mika at Hoban's. They did not get in touch after the third dream. Jem thought about it, but decided that he couldn't bear another cold shoulder.

From the breast pocket of his suit jacket he takes out a stick of cherry lip balm, removes the lid and takes a deep breath of its sweet, heady perfume.

Now he types a quick message, sends it before he has time to regret it, puts the phone in his pocket and shudders as though he's swallowed something bitter. He looks around the room. Time to go. He opens the word processor on his computer, types out a brief but polite resignation letter, sends it to the printer and finds an envelope. He leaves the letter propped up on his line manager's keyboard. He looks up and sees the cleaner watching him from across the room. He waves, and the cleaner waves back.

After eleven years, Jem walks out.

A crowd of revellers jostle past Mika outside Camden Town, dressed as national stereotypes: a French woman with a baguette and a beret; a Mexican man in a poncho and pound-shop sombrero; a Chinese man in red robes and Fu Manchu moustache. For better or worse, Mika knows there is no easy costume for where she comes from. Rather, she is lumped into the general category of 'Eastern European'.

Mika is going through a list of places to stay in her head. Kenny will be in bed already. Suzy will be at work, filling in as head chef in her absence, and might not be in the mood to see her when she clocks off. That leaves a hotel which she can hardly afford. Her phone buzzes several times in quick succession. She takes it out and scrolls through the notifications.

Olly
Hey, I know you're probably not in the mood but
Maybe we should get a drink
Just lmk

Weird Guy
Hey, I know you said you didn't want to meet up again
but . . .

She opens Jem's message to read it in full.

. . . I'm central if you fancy getting a drink. Totally
understand if you'd rather not.

By the entrance to the Tube she pauses and looks again at the two messages – Olly's and Jem's. She types a quick reply and steps down to the muggy warmth of the Northern Line.

*

By the time Jem arrives at the Royal Festival Hall, Mika has found a table by the window. Outside, the South Bank is busy with foot traffic, people buying pints in plastic cups and food in paper trays. Buskers play, people laugh, cyclists yell at people to get out of the way, but it's all silenced by the plate glass. Inside it's quiet, low chatter and tasteful jazz. Mika uses her phone to find the name of the track. *'Stardust' – The Robert Mauchlen Allstars – Live from Ronnie Scott's.* Jem approaches the table cautiously, as though he might be interrupting.

'Hello again,' she says, forcing a smile. 'You're off your crutch.'

'Yeah, still getting used to walking without it. Can I get you a drink?'

'I'd take a fruit juice. Any kind, dealer's choice.'

'Oh . . . okay.' Jem pauses. 'You don't want wine, or something?'

'Did I not tell you last time? I can't.'

'Oh, I'm sorry.' Jem looks apologetic. 'Are you . . . recovering?'

'Sorry?'

'I mean, how long have you been, um, abstinent?'

Mika pauses, then starts to laugh.

'What? What did I say?'

'I'm *pregnant*,' she snorts. 'Not an alcoholic.'

'Oh. Oh! Sorry, I . . . '

'It's fine; I really thought I told you last time.'

'No, I don't think so.'

'Well . . . '

'Yes . . . I'll go and get that fruit juice.'

'Great.'

Mika watches him hurry off, still hobbling a bit. He's

shaking his head with embarrassment, talking to himself. She's smiling in spite of herself. It's not that Jem is the first person she would have chosen for this situation, but it's good to have someone else around. She was going mad with her own thoughts. She keeps thinking of the message from Yanni:

Nasty bloke hr asking q's about my upstairs neighbour. Told him to eat shit but u might want to stay away fr a bit

She knows she can't live there any more. She'll go back when it's safe and clear her stuff out.

'Orange juice is all they've got, is that okay?'

Jem appears and sets the drinks down. He's got himself a beer, and she feels vague irritation. He catches her looking.

'Sorry, I . . . it's been a bit of a weird day.'

She laughs a short laugh which she doesn't understand, then looks contrite.

'Tell me?'

'Well . . . I think I just quit my job.'

'You think?'

'Well, I did. I'm just not really sure why I did. I just felt like I wouldn't be able to make myself go in tomorrow. So I wrote a letter and left it on my boss's desk.'

Jem smiles nervously. He clearly thinks he's been wild and crazy, and Mika is taken by the irrational urge to burst his bubble.

'Funny coincidence – I also left my job.'

'Really?'

'Just last week.'

'How'd that happen?'

'Well,' she smiles. 'I told my boss that I was pregnant, which didn't go well. He got very angry. Threatened me. So I left work, waited until I knew my boss was going out to buy drugs – which he does quite a lot, you see – and then I called the police.'

Jem's mouth is hanging open, the beer undrunk.

'And then . . . ?'

'And then I waited around until they turned up. Saw them take him out.'

'Oh. Wow.'

'Yeah.'

'Is everything okay now?'

'Well, that's the thing.' She leans back. This is the delicate moment. 'I don't feel entirely safe, going back to my flat.'

'You don't?'

'No, because my boss had my address on record. And I think he might be feeling vindictive. He's not a very nice man, and he has some . . . unsavoury connections.'

'Oh . . . '

None of this is untrue, it's just a matter of interpretation. Of course, she's leaving out the bit about her visa and the immigration van. That would just complicate things. She can practically see the neurons firing behind his eyes. Come on, Jem, you can do it.

'Do you need somewhere to stay?'

Bingo!

'I mean, if you're offering? It would just be for tonight; I'm sure I'll be able to find somewhere new to stay tomorrow.'

Jem nods his head. He looks somewhere between disappointed and nervous.

'You're welcome to come back to mine.'

140

'If you're sure?'

'No, of course. It's not a big place, but I can sleep on the sofa.'

She almost tells him that she'll take the sofa, but to hell with it. She deserves a real bed.

'Thank you. But you know, this isn't a date.'

'No, of course.'

'But I'm very grateful.'

'It's no trouble, honestly.'

They stumble into silence like a finishing line. The main order of business out of the way, the tension goes out of the meeting. From where they're sitting, Jem can just see the lights of boats passing on the river. Sunset is turning the Thames bronze and gold. Another sort of sunset is happening in Jem's brain, casting everything in shadow, making each light a remote point in space. To be so close to Mika – yet so distant – is a form of pain he's just discovering. He says:

'That last dream . . . '

Mika looks up. It's not that she had forgotten it. There hasn't been a day she hasn't thought about it. Rather, she had forgotten that it had anything to do with why they were meeting. She has started, unconsciously, to think of the dreams as occasional symptoms of pregnancy. Everything about pregnancy is strange; the centre of her seems to have become molten, like the centre of the Earth, and the magnetic fields thrown out by that flowing metal make her think and act in strange ways, pull her in every compass direction.

She says:

'Weird one, huh?'

'I looked it up, the next day.'

'Looked up what?'

'Tarraco. The Roman name for modern-day Tarragona, in Spain. There are still the ruins of an amphitheatre there.' He woke from that dream trembling with fear and desire. Fear for the death he had just died; desire for the person he had shared his death with.

'It's so weird,' she shakes her head. 'This doesn't just happen to people.'

'I dunno,' Jem says. 'My dad used to tell a story about a girl he met on holiday when he was a teenager. It was a campsite abroad, and they didn't speak a word of each other's language, but he said he knew her. Just . . . knew they had met before, knew each other so well. They spent all day together, doing stuff. He said it was the weirdest feeling, but he knew she felt the same way.'

'What's that got to do with dreams?'

'Nothing, really. I just mean, maybe weird things happen to people all the time and they don't tell anyone. I mean, who would believe us?'

Mika thinks about this but looks unconvinced.

'If weird things happen to people all the time, surely they would be more likely to believe them rather than less?' she says.

'Do you think we're special?' he asks.

'In what way?'

'I dunno. I mean . . . the dreams, finding each other over and over again. Seems pretty special.'

She pulls a face. 'I don't think so. Probably everybody is like that, if you go back.'

'Really?'

'Yeah, like, if you're from Britain – if you have British heritage, I mean – you're related to everyone who was alive in Britain a thousand years ago. Every single person.'

142

'What? That can't be right.'

'It is. There weren't that many people then, compared to now. All of them are your great-however-many-times grandmas and granddads and cousins-whatever-removed. That's just how it works.'

'Still though, the way we keep meeting. I mean, the way our *ancestors* keep meeting . . . '

'Is just chance. Any two people in the world would be the same, if you looked back at every time their ancestors met.'

'How do you know all this stuff?'

'The internet is a great thing, Jem.'

'I'll give it a try sometime.'

'Hm.' She grins at her drink. 'What's your dad like?'

'Dead, for the past five years.'

'Shit, sorry.'

'It's okay. I didn't know him that well, really.' Jem looks out of the window. 'He left when I was fifteen. Divorced my mum, emigrated to Spain, married another woman. I hadn't seen him since I was a teenager. What's the matter?'

Mika looks like she's bitten down on a cardamom pod.

'I *hate* parents who run away.'

'Your parents . . . '

'My dad is fine. Runs a restaurant. Nice guy. Made sure I had a proper childhood, even though he was working all the time. Makes model boats and sails them on the lake.'

'But your mum . . . ?'

'Disappeared when I was little. Didn't leave a message, didn't bother to say goodbye. She's dead now, so I won't even get to tell her how angry I am.'

'I'm sorry.'

'It's fine.' She shakes her head. 'But yeah, parents who leave – fuck 'em.'

Jem thinks of Emily, and resolves not to mention her to Mika, at least for the time being. The whole truth might exonerate him, but then again it might not. He isn't certain of what Mika will think of anything he has to say. He enjoys it, infuriating as it is. Best to err on the side of caution, until they know each other better. If they ever get that far.

'I'm going to have another, if you fancy one?'

'Still going on this, thanks.'

Jem stands, then seems to freeze. Mika watches him for a moment, until it becomes clear that something is wrong.

'Jem? Hello?'

He doesn't respond, just carries on staring straight ahead. She stands up and steps in front of him.

'Hey, Jem. You okay?'

He looks at her, hazily.

'Hm?'

Gingerly she puts one hand on his arm, takes his hand with the other, and guides him back down into his chair. She holds onto his hand on the table top, looking around for someone to call over, but Jem seems to be coming round.

'Mika?'

'Yeah, it's me. Are you okay?'

'Yeah, just . . . where are we?'

'South Bank. Royal Festival Hall. Do you remember . . . ?'

'Yeah . . . of course.' He nods slowly, as though trying not to shake his head around too much. 'Sorry, I'll be fine in a mo.'

She realises her hand is still holding his and lets go. Her

144

cheeks are flushed. That magnetic feeling is back, stronger than ever, swirling around the two of them. Mika can feel every part of herself aligning in Jem's direction, and it takes an effort to pull away.

'Headrush?'

'No, I just sort of . . . went away.'

'Has it happened before?'

'A couple of times,' he nods. 'This one wasn't so bad. I just seem to disappear, then I come back.'

'Have you seen anyone about it?'

'No, I thought maybe it would go away on its own.'

'Do you want some water?'

'No, it's fine, just give me a moment. It's just been, since the accident—'

'Accident?'

'Didn't I tell you? I was hit by a car.'

'Oh, god; I thought you'd just broken your leg.'

'A bit worse than that. But the leg was the last thing to heal up. Anyway, I'm fine now, apart from . . . But it was a close thing, they told me. Internal bleeding. Fifty-fifty chance of pulling through.'

'Jesus . . . '

'It's funny,' he says, still looking half in a dream. 'But I had this sort of vision when I was in hospital. An out-of-body experience, I guess. Life and death arguing over which one of them got to keep me. And it was like I was making this bargain with life.

'What was the bargain?'

'I said . . . ' He seems suddenly shy. 'I said, "Just let me have an adventure. Just one adventure, and I'll be happy." Bit daft really, but there you go.'

'What did you offer?'

'Hm?'

'If you're making a bargain, you offer something. So, if you were asking for an adventure, what did you offer in return?'

Jem thinks for a moment, his face darkening.

'I don't know . . . '

She changes the subject.

'How long ago was this?'

'April 1st,' he smiles ruefully. 'April Fool's Day, right?'

She sees the coincidence. She has the feeling of being trapped in some great mechanism, the turning wheel of the year, and wants to say something that will break its spell. But when she looks at Jem he is looking off, embarrassment written on his features. She feels a pang of something sharp enough to make her gasp. He looks up.

'You okay?'

'Yeah . . . just pregnancy pains.'

'Sorry.'

'Don't be – you didn't do this to me.'

Jem looks vaguely flustered by this. Mika asks:

'The last dream, did it remind you of your accident? Thinking you were going to die?'

'Maybe, a bit. But it was different. In the dream, I knew I was going to die. No bargains, no take-backs. But also . . . you were there.'

Mika says nothing.

'It wasn't the same, because we were holding hands. It wasn't so bad to die, holding someone's hand.'

They both stare out at the river for ten seconds. Forty-eight thousand new stars are created and a further three hundred explode. She says:

'Look, if you don't mind . . . '

146

'Shall we go?'

'Yeah, let's.'

They stand, and she resists the urge to reach out and support him. He doesn't need it, he's fine. They walk, side by side but not too close, as though if they accidentally touched something bad would happen.

By the time they arrive at Jem's flat, they have settled into something like a comfortable silence. There is nothing much to say, and they are both tired. It isn't unpleasant, this silence. It occurs to Mika that Jem might be good at being quiet in the way that Olly isn't. Yet when they step through his front door, Mika feels the tension she would at entering a stranger's space. Suddenly it feels like the end of a date, or a random hook-up.

'Here we go,' he smiles apologetically. 'It's not much, but . . . '

'But?'

'Well, it's not much.'

She wanders down the narrow hallway until she comes into the open-plan kitchen/living room area.

'It's very . . . tidy.'

'The layout, or my housekeeping?'

'Both.'

'Can I get you a drink? Something to eat?'

'What do you have?'

'Not much . . . '

'I could make an omelette?'

'No eggs, I'm afraid.'

'I'd love some toast?'

'Ah, no bread either.'

'You have a four-slice toaster!' Mika rolls her eyes. 'So

what food *do* you have in this godforsaken bachelor pad?'

Jem thinks about offering her his high-protein granola with low-fat yoghurt, but decides against it.

'There's a shop downstairs – let me get a few bits.'

'Are you sure?'

'Yeah, of course. Back in a mo.'

'Get some jam, please. I'll pay you back.'

'What kind?'

'The cheap kind.'

Jem disappears from the flat and she is alone. Mika resists the urge to go rooting around, and instead makes herself a decaf tea from a box she finds in the cupboard. She runs through a mental list of things she wants to do to Jem when he returns, and one by one she discounts them as Very Bad Ideas. By the time it's brewed, Jem is back, decanting hastily bought eggs, bread, jam and spreadable butter.

'Are you going to have some?'

'Uh, sure.'

Mika rips into the bread and pops four slices down in the toaster. Then she opens the pot of cheap strawberry jam, cracks the lid and inhales deeply, eyes closed.

'Ah! Don't you love the smell of strawberry jam? Like childhood in a jar.'

She opens her eyes to see Jem is staring at her with an expression like hunger. They both look away quickly, him to refill the kettle, her to the glowing filaments in the toaster. A minute later the toast pops up and she spreads all four slices with butter.

'Do you want jam?'

'No, I'm fine thanks.'

'Suit yourself.'

Jem looks at the toast for a moment, mouth watering like a child at a sweet shop window.

'Oh, go on then.'

She smiles without looking sideways at him.

'Do you often deny yourself jam?'

'That was my nickname, when I was little.'

'What, Jam?'

'Because people mispronounced my name, but also on account of me liking it so much. I kept trying to take the jar to hide it in my bed.'

'Here you go.' She hands him the plate. 'My nickname was Cub. Bet you can't guess why.'

He bites into the toast – pillowy, sweet and salty – and thinks about it.

'Because you look like a fox?'

'I *what?*' Her eyebrows shoot up.

'That wasn't— I mean, I don't mean—' he flusters. 'Your hair is reddish. And your face comes to a point . . . '

Mika thinks that Jem would be blushing if his skin were lighter. She likes it when he's flustered, she realises. She thinks of other ways to make him squirm and stops before she starts blushing too.

'No, when I was little my face was round and pudgy, like a potato.'

'Oh.'

'I was called Cub because one day I found a badger hole . . . what do you call it in English?'

'A warren, maybe? No, a sett.'

'Well, I found a badger sett in the woods. Big hole, yes? And I'd read too much *Alice in Wonderland* or *Wind in the Willows*, because I thought it would be a great adventure to climb down there and meet the badgers.'

'And you did?'

'Got about as far in as my waist,' she nods. 'Then I was stuck.'

'No!'

'Couldn't use my arms for much, as they were squeezed down the tunnel. And my little legs were just flapping around outside the hole. Dad found me eventually, and pulled me out. He always said that I wanted to be one of the badger cubs.'

They stand and eat their toast for a minute, each wrapped in their own thoughts. There is an unspoken intimacy to all of it. An eating-toast intimacy. A being-together-in-silence intimacy. A middle-of-the-night intimacy. Mika wonders what would happen if she asked Jem to bed. Jem wonders what would happen if he moved a little closer, put his hand on her hip . . .

'I wonder if we'll have another dream,' she says.

'Hm?' He drags his thoughts back to the present. 'I suppose we might.'

'I know I said I didn't want to have them any more, but . . . '

'You're having second thoughts?'

'I dunno,' she shrugs. 'It's a bit like watching half a movie. I want to know how it ends. I want know who else we were.'

He thinks about this for a moment. It all sounds so different to the conversation they had in Hoban's. He wonders if the dream of the amphitheatre changed her mind.

'We're not really those people in the dream, are we?' he says. 'I mean . . . we're us.'

Mika shrugs.

'Who's to say?'

'I thought you didn't believe in souls, reincarnation, all that stuff?'

'I don't, but . . . I dunno, it'll sound weird.'

'No, go on.'

She puts her plate down, takes out her phone, scrolls for a minute, then shows him a photo. A photo of a photo, in fact – the colours of the image are oversaturated, and there is a film of dust over the two faces.

'Is that . . . ?'

'Me and my mother.'

Jem looks closer at the image. A woman – late twenties, towering blond perm – is carrying a girl of maybe four or five on one hip. The girl is wearing a sundress with Donald Duck emblazoned on the front. The girl – Mika – is ignoring the camera in favour of a half-melted ice cream which she is trying to manoeuvre into her mouth. A Guy Fawkes beard of melted vanilla is evidence of her previous attempts. The woman is smiling, but Jem can't help but feel there's something distant in her expression, as though she's looking at something behind the camera.

'You look just like her.'

'People say so; I can't see it. This is one of the only photos I have of her. Anyway, that's not the point. Tell me – is that me?'

She points to the girl in the sundress.

'Huh? You just *said* it was.'

'But why is she me? I don't remember the day this picture was taken. I don't remember what happened next – whether I dropped the ice cream or gave some to my mother to try. Apart from having this picture to show you, nothing about it seems to belong to "me".'

Jem peers at the image again.

'But you are the same person. You've grown up, you've changed, but, well, I mean, it's no one else, is it?'

'Okay, so there's this chain, yes? This perfect chain of events which links me to her. The chain links my body back to her body. So in some sense you might say her body *is* my body.'

'Erm . . . right.' Jem frowns.

'Even though all the atoms that made up that little girl are gone from the body I have now. And maybe that's all that identity is. Just that chain, linking us back, moment to moment into the past.'

'Yes . . . ' Jem says, growing in certainty.

'But if that's the case,' Mika smiles, pulling the rug out from under him once more, 'what does that say about birth?'

'I . . . don't follow.'

'Isn't that part of the chain too? Isn't there an unbroken chain of physical events, leading back to the point of my birth, when I was joined with – effectively the same being as – my mother?'

'Er . . . '

'And isn't there the same chain, leading back before she was born? And my grandmother, and my great grandmother? All the way back to the earliest humans? Why am I the little girl in the picture, but not them?'

'Because . . . '

Jem searches for the difference, and he's sure there is one, but the more he tries to grasp it the more it slips through his fingers. Eventually, he starts to laugh. He laughs and laughs.

'What's so funny?' she asks.

'I don't know,' he says, wiping tears from his eyes. 'I don't know!'

But he does know, sort of. It's the same reason you laugh at a joke, or at being tickled, or even when someone tells you that something awful happened to your cat. It's because he is surprised. It's as though Mika has surprised him with reality, and the only thing to do is laugh. After a minute, Mika starts to laugh too. It's contagious, this laughter, each of them making the other laugh more and more. Jem is bent over the worktop, and Mika doubles up, putting her hand on his shoulder without thinking. Reflexively he puts his own hand on top of it.

They stop laughing.

Jem straightens up. Her hand is still on his shoulder, and his hand on top of hers. For a moment they look into each other's eyes, and they are closer together than either of them thought. Mika looks into his dark, amber-flecked eyes and remembers them from the dream.

They draw apart.

'I should sleep . . . ' she says.

'Yeah, me too. I'll just tidy up in here first.'

'No, please, let me.'

'Um, yeah, okay. I'll sort the bedroom out for you.'

Jem hurries off to the linen cupboard, then to his bedroom. Mika can have the single bed; he will sleep on the sofa. His eye is drawn to the bedside table, where there's a school picture of Emily taken a couple of years ago. He looks at his daughter for a moment, looking back at him, then takes the frame and hides it in his wardrobe. He tells himself that it's too complicated a story to tell right now. But really, it's Mika's own words playing on repeat in his head – 'parents who leave – fuck 'em.' Whether he chose it or not, Jem is still a parent who left. He takes a deep breath and walks back to the kitchen.

Around the world, people are flirting. The air is heady with hormones. People are looking, sizing each other up, making eye contact. At swimming pools and beaches, they parade in swimsuits and trunks. They are dressed in beads and metal collars and bright fabrics, headdresses and piercings and face paint, lining up the way their parents lined up. At bars lit in neon blue and neon pink, they look sideways at each other, ordering drinks.

And they dance – of course they dance!

They dance to music in the streets, alone or in pairs, while chicken fries on a hot plate. They dance at other people's weddings, where everything is high-spirited, silly, not to be taken seriously. They dance in rooftop gardens, overlooked by chimney pots and old television aerials. They dance in converted cellars, where the music tries to vibrate the buttons off their shirts and blouses.

In separate beds, Mika and Jem sleep.

12

She walked the weald   on a weft of needles;
Sea of the animals;   Ymir's flesh.
The air was made heady   with the incense of
    conifers,
Skirts brushing flowers,   wild garlic and ferns.
Already Jem smelled   the peat smoke of home.
In a bolt of old cloth   she was carrying
    mushrooms,
their golden-brown tops   like milk-glazed bread.
Cresting the hill she   sighted their homestead,
a squat pile of stones   with straw-thatched roof,
so covered with moss   it looked not manmade.
Chalk-white smoke   rising through branches
reluctant to join   the awning of cloud-halls.
Chickens were pecking   the well-trodden dirt.
Jem walked faster   back to her hearth-ship,
smelling now clearly   the stew in the pot.
Next to the cottage   breaking wood on a stump
Mika raised high   his sharp tree-splitter.

Mika wore trousers,   since ere they came there.
He took all his skirts   and gave them to Jem.
When a trader first asked   whether Mika wore
    trousers
because 'she thought   that she was a man',
Mika had asked him –   'is that why *you* wear
    them?'
That made Jem smile;   she wouldn't dare say
    that.

A crack sounded   as he sundered the wood;
Then two thuds   as the halves met the floor.
Straightening up,   Mika sighted Jem coming,
smiled at her,   then went back to chopping.
Jem opened the door   and entered the cottage.
Inside was dark;   lamps were for nighttime
when weaving was done,   and stories were told.
But the weald was always   a hall of shadows.
The air in the cottage   was the air of a
    storehouse,
musty with turnips,   sweet with apples,
tangy with haunches   of mutton and goat.
Sometimes Jem felt   like a stored thing herself.
The stew in the pot,   chicken and barley,
made the air so savoury,   you'd grow plump from
    breathing.
They were both plump   from good living there.

Jem set to cleaning   the mushrooms in water,
breaking them up   and into the stew.
Mika came in,   wiping his hands,
poured out horn-froth   from the earthen jug.

Jem said nothing,   but this was usual.
They spent so much time   in each other's
    company,
Silence was natural,   a comfortable thing.
Sometimes speaking   felt like a failing,
so eloquent was   the silence between them.
Other times, in bed,   often when late,
when the year-counter rode   high in the heavens,
the two would talk   'til their mouths ran dry;
then they would open   a bottle of honey-wave
from their own hives   summer stored
and take turns drinking   under the furs.

There was more understanding   in their silence
than in a young man's   lamb-bleating.
When she felt Mika   appearing behind her
as she stirred the pot,   Jem was startled.
Mika's lips met the crook   of her soft neck,
at the place he knew   unlocked her.
His hands went around   Jem's broad waist,
smoothing her skirt   over her thighs.
Jem felt the warmth   of desire in her belly.
'Mika, I'm cooking—'   'The *stew* is cooking,
so now it doesn't   need your hands.'
Jem turned around,   brushing crumbs from her
    fingers.
And took his face   in both her hands.

Jem never tired   of coming together.
There were some days   she didn't want it,
like a favourite dish   she had no appetite for.
But a dish so savoury,   so delicious!

It was never long ere   she wanted her fill again.
They both had husbands   before this place.
Jem's husband died;   Mika's ran away.
Neither had felt   this way for their husbands.
They had got on   with being wives:
'necklace-sleighs;   ribbon-yearners'.
They raised children,   they were dutiful.
That was before   they found each other,
Jem becoming a wife   for the second time,
Mika becoming a husband   for the first.

Carefully, he took up   the hem of her skirts;
Jem felt his rough hands   running over her
     thighs.
She reached down and   undid his trousers.
There were soft places   everywhere in the cottage –
cushioned alcoves   and their curtained bed,
where she led him   and laid him down.

They lay there at night   and talked about
     memories.
The strange memories   they both shared,
from times before   either were born,
remembering until   their mouths ran dry
and they opened   the bottle of honey-wave.
Sometimes they talked   of those other lives,
those brief bodies   they once called home.
And sometimes they lay   and made no sound.

August

13

The heavens turn like a backdrop, from azure to inky blue, and all the stars are done in silver paint. The world is rearranged by unlit stagehands – the cleaners, the lorry drivers, the security guards and shelf-stackers – ready for a new scene to play out.

Time passes; sun raises the curtain.

Mika wakes early, and for the first four and a half seconds does not know where she is. A probe on an alien planet, she scans her surroundings. It is dark, but from the reflected sounds of her breathing she is in a small room. The pillow and duvet covers are soft, bobbled cotton. She breathes in and recognises unfamiliar washing powder, body spray, and below them, concealed, the smell of another human being. Not unpleasant. There is a faint ticking from a bedside clock, which she would never allow in her own room. All these readings are processed near instantaneously, and her coordinates provided by the onboard database:

Jem's flat.

She doesn't startle, but her body tenses. Reaching out,

she does not find another body in the bed next to her, but rather the edge of the bed. Jem sleeps in a single, yes; how strange. Rising, she feels the floor with her feet. It is soft carpet, and does not creak under her. These flats are all concrete, under the soft furnishings. They do not talk like old buildings.

She remembers the dream.

Something like a blush spreads down the length of her body. She remembers clearly the yearning, still keen in her belly, but now she is ashamed of it. This feeling isn't hers to feel. Is it? No – it belongs to someone else. In the dream she slipped out of her skin. Now she is back, and wants nothing more than to slip away from the scene of the crime.

She makes her way out into the hallway and through to the living room. It is lighter in here, and it occurs to her that there was a blackout blind in the bedroom. There is Jem, on the sofa, under a blanket. One arm trails down, fingers brushing the floor. He looks different in sleep. Less guarded, less nervous. More like the person from her dream. And there is that yearning again, although now it is for something less tangible. A feeling she had so naturally in the dream, which seems alien to her now she's awake.

The feeling of being home.

She looks around the room and frowns. She's sure he said he had been living here for a few years, yet it looks as though he just moved in. Perhaps she is just remembering the crowded cottage they shared, but there is a sterility to this place, all straight lines and inoffensive neutrals. In his rumpled blanket, Jem looks as though he's broken into a show home for somewhere to sleep.

She wants to wake him up.

She wants to make them something for breakfast.

She wants to spend the day here, wallowing in their mutual unemployment; she knows he would let her.

Jem stirs a little, his mouth moving as though he is saying something in his dream. Quietly, she turns and pads back into the hallway, slips into her socks and trainers. She gets her rucksack from the bedroom and unplugs her phone from the spare charger he lent her. After a moment she unplugs the charger and puts it into her bag. She lets herself out into the hallway. It is as clean and sterile as the apartment itself. She stands for a moment until the door clicks shut at her back. Checking her phone, she opens a message from Tamara:

dad says come by and talk

She looks back at Jem's door for two, three, four seconds, then walks on.

'Mika! Get in here, let me see you.'

'Hey, Kenny.'

She shuffles into the kitchen. He doesn't turn away from the hot plate but waves her over with a spatula. Several things are cooking at once – bacon, pancakes, a hash of different things cemented together by egg. Kenny is wearing his always-outfit of black T-shirt, athletic headband holding up his shock of grey hair, and a white apron cinching his generous waist. He works the contents of the hot plate, always moving, never in a rush. He glances sideways at her and drawls in his Bronx accent:

'You look like shit.'

'Thanks.'

'Come for the food, stay for the bonhomie. Pass the cabbage.'

She hands him a dented metal bowl and he sprinkles shredded savoy into something which might be huevos rancheros.

'May I ask why?'

'Why I look like shit? Or why I'm here?'

'I assumed one would lead to the other. Oh, but first, can you scrub up? I need someone to do the prep. Billy was meant to be here half a fuckin' hour ago.'

She goes to the sink and washes her hands, then goes back.

'Do I need an apron?'

'Only if you're precious about that raggedy T-shirt. Chop those carrots. Nice and fine, if you please. Now – talk.'

She proceeds to tell him the story from start to finish: the pregnancy, telling James, getting fired, calling the police, all the way up to the Home Office van turning up on her doorstep. She's on safe ground here; Kenny is an ex-pat New York hippie and doesn't believe in borders. She doesn't mention Jem. While talking she finishes the carrots, shreds half a pound of cold chicken and peels three hard-boiled eggs. Kenny listens and says nothing until she's done.

'Where did you stay last night?'

'A friend's.'

'Hm.'

'Anyway, I'm not expecting you to—'

'Could you do five American pancakes while I go to the freezer? The mixture's already in the thing. Chocolate chips are on the side.'

'If you're sure?'

'I trust you not to fuck it up!' he calls over his shoulder.

Frowning, Mika steps up to the hot plate and picks up the 'thing' – a metal funnel with a handle and a trigger to open the nozzle. She dumps five dollops of sizzling batter onto the hot plate. Before bubbles can form on the surface, she sprinkles chocolate chips onto each of them. Kenny reappears with a plastic tub labelled 'boiled potatoes' which contains chilli. He eyes her work, nods wordlessly.

'I can give you Tuesday through to Saturday,' he says, flipping the pancakes. 'Bright and early up to mid-afternoon. Sound okay?'

It takes her a moment to catch up.

'Yes, that would be—'

'I get fucking grumpy some days, though. Just eff-why-eye. Is that going to be a problem?'

'Not at all.'

'Hm. You need a room?'

'Kenny, you don't have to—'

'We got a free room on the second floor. It's pretty big. Mostly used for storage at the moment but there's a double bed in there, if you don't mind sharing it with the pickles.'

'Rent?'

'Fuck rent.' He shakes his head. 'If you work here, you can stay here. And I'll pay you cash in hand.'

'You're an angel, Kenny.'

'You think? Those bible bashers are in for a nasty surprise when they get to heaven.'

He laughs at his own joke; Mika feels dizzy with relief.

'You want me to—?'

'Start now? No, you can start tomorrow. Tamara is sick of helping me and waiting tables at the same time. She'll be glad I've got someone else to help out. Go upstairs, find your room. You got anything to move in?'

'No, I . . . ' Mika frowns. 'Only what I've got with me.'
Kenny plates up the pancakes, shaking his head.

'You need someone to go and pick your stuff up?'

'No, no. I'll just wait a day or two before going back.'

She suddenly feels tearful. But Mika doesn't cry; everyone knows that. She hugs Kenny from behind and hastens out of the kitchen. Past the back room where they keep the chest freezers, she goes up the creaking stairs until she gets to the second floor. The decor up here is faded grey, the carpets worn down to nothing in the middle, and every once-straight line, from the floor to the walls to the ceiling, has become a curve.

She wanders one way down the hall, finding bedrooms and a small living room, then goes the other way. At the furthest end she finds the storeroom, with its stacked tins of cooking oil, bottles of lemon juice and gallon tubs of mayonnaise. She goes in and closes the door. There, as promised, is a bed. She moves some boxes and removes the blanket serving as a dust sheet. The covers underneath are soft, bobbled cotton, like Jem's sheets.

She gets under the duvet fully clothed. The sheets are musty and a little damp, but the mattress and pillow are comfortable. She closes her eyes and listens to the sound of London beyond the window, a muted rumble which is almost white noise. For a few minutes the bed warms up around her, but she doesn't warm with it. Then, like a knob of butter in a frying pan, she melts away and is gone.

Jem wakes late. By the time he finds his bed empty, it has lost all trace of Mika's warmth. He does not bend to smell the sheets; he has some self-respect. Still, it's a shame she has gone; it would have been nice to have someone around to take his mind off the order of the day. The reminder has already popped up on his phone:

Emily.

He measures his breakfast muesli, adds flaxseed, washes it down with black coffee. He puts the morning affirmations on.

I am happy . . .

'I am happy.'

I am worthy . . .

'I am worthy.'

I am loved . . .

'I . . . '

He trails off, then reaches out and stops the voice before it carries on. He stands, waiting for his bad leg to straighten out. It aches, as though in warning. But he takes his wallet and keys from the table and leaves the flat. He gets the bus and rides it for eleven minutes. It should take longer, he thinks, for how far away Emily feels, as though she's in another city altogether. As though distance in London is measured in people rather than miles. All those individual worlds, laid side by side, making an infinity. In the countryside it would be nothing to go and see her.

He stands before a house on a leafy street. Mid-terrace, Edwardian, red brick with the details painted white. The door is cherry red, with a geometric stained-glass window. There is a pear tree in a terracotta pot to one side of it, with ribbons still tied to its branches from Easter. Jem has never been inside the house, but he can see into the living room from the doorstep. Original fireplace with painted tiles, large gilt mirror on the chimney breast, shelves to either side with books and family photographs, a faux-fur rug over the parquet, on which a few plastic toys stand out garishly.

Before he can ring the bell, the door opens. It is Sarah. Dark hair pulled back in a ponytail, dark brows drawn together in a frown, dark eyes never quite meeting his. At this moment, she is looking at his chin, or perhaps his shirt collar.

'Hello.'

'Hi, Sarah. I'm here for—'

'I know why you're here. Why else would you be here?'

She sounds flustered rather than angry, as though he is adding to an already stressful time, though from inside the house he hears a child's laughter and a man's voice raised in jest. Pop music is playing, but he doesn't know the song.

'Well, I . . . '

'Yes, fine, wait there.'

She closes the door on him and he waits, trying not to be nervous. A woman walks by with a dog that looks like a teddy bear. He says good morning, but she doesn't say anything and hurries on.

He doesn't feel like Emily's father when he comes here. He feels like another child, asking permission for her to come out and play. Not that they do anything which could be called 'play'. He will take her somewhere – to the cinema or to a restaurant – and they will pass the time in each other's company. Cinema is best, he thinks, because someone else is doing the talking. He will look over at her in the dark, barely turning his head, and watch her face, lit up by the screen.

He hears voices and can see movement behind the stained glass, and finally the door opens, revealing Emily. For a moment his mouth goes dry, but then he says:

'Hey Ems. I love your dress!'

She frowns a little, and he regrets saying it. She is wearing a purple dress with sequins at the hem, a light denim jacket and a rucksack.

'Hello, Jem.'

The sound of his own name, spoken with the same formality as a work colleague, briefly halts Jem. Trying not to show emotion, he asks:

'How's school been?'

Emily looks down at her sneakers; Sarah flashes a warning look. Don't ask about school, he thinks. Sarah says:

'Where are you going?'

'I don't know, I thought I would let—'

'You don't *know?*'

'I thought I would let Emily decide.'

'Surely you have some ideas? You can't expect a seven-year-old to plan your day for you.'

'I didn't say I have no ideas, I said—'

'You don't need to take that tone with me.'

'Everything alright?'

A man in a hipster cardigan – the owner of the voice – appears behind Sarah at the door and puts a hand on her shoulder.

'It's fine, Dean.'

Dean smiles, but Jem is reminded of how chimpanzees smile to show aggression. He reaches a broad hand out at Jem.

'Nice to see you, Jeremy.'

'And you, Dean.'

Jem's face betrays nothing as his hand is squeezed like a lemon. He has always felt that there is something of the stock image about Dean, as though Sarah bought him online. 'New husband, highly successful, antagonistic to old partner with plausible deniability etc., good with kids, hobbies inc. upcycling and Nordic knitwear. RRP £666.'

'Anyway, we should get going.'

Emily looks suddenly uncertain, and Jem is worried she will turn back. Sarah is wringing her hands as though she cannot bear to see her daughter leave in his company. Jem has more parental rights than he exercises, but tries to avoid provoking Sarah's anxiety. Sarah doesn't call it anxiety. She says she is 'concerned for Emily's safety', as though being around Jem at all is a dangerous activity. She will send dozens of messages in the time he is with his daughter, 'just checking in'. If he doesn't reply, she starts calling. Having Emily over to stay for the night has never been an option; Sarah wouldn't be able to sleep.

Emily turns and gives Sarah and Dean a quick hug around the legs, before stepping up to him.

'Let's go,' she says.

He resists the urge to take her hand. They walk down the garden path and up the road, and it's only when they have gone halfway to the top of the tree-lined road that he hears the red door closing behind them.

'So . . . what *do* you want to do?' he asks, trying to sound jokey, matey, super casual.

'You told Mummy you had ideas.'

'I *do* have ideas, but I want to hear what you think first. Maybe there's something you've wanted to do for a—'

'You said you were hit by a car.'

Emily stops and he stops too.

'Yes. I mean, I was. We talked about this last time, remember?'

'But you were fine . . . '

He's not sure if it's a question. He's not sure how long Emily has been thinking about this.

'Yes, I am.'

'But if you were fine, why didn't you visit, or call me on the telephone?'

He says nothing.

'You weren't really fine, were you?'

Jem takes a deep breath.

'No. But I am now.'

They stand and stare at each other for a moment, then the moment is gone and they walk on. Jem blinks hard several times and clears his throat.

'So, what do you want to do?'

'Nothing.'

'You know, when you were little, your favourite book was *Mr Autumn's Busy Day.* You asked me to read it over and over. Do you remember that? He walked down the high street and stopped in every shop. First, he had a cup of tea in the café. Then he had a haircut at the barber's . . . '

'When I was little,' Emily says, 'my favourite book was *The Very Hungry Caterpillar.*'

'Oh,' Jem says. 'Yes, right.'

They walk a bit further, up to the main road. The cars and buses come close to the pavement here, and he wants to hold her hand more than ever, but resists.

'Well, there's a showing of the *Minions* film at—'

'I've seen it.'

'It's the new one.'

'I've seen it. Last week, with Da— with Dean.'

She glances sideways to see if he noticed her slip of the tongue. He has never minded her called him 'Jem', but calling Dean 'Dad' is something new. He tries very hard to seem as though he didn't hear it.

'Well, a café then.'

Emily nods. 'I brought a book to read.'

'Oh.'

'It's in my backpack.'

'Right. Good.'

14

It's early lunchtime at Hoban's. Not the busiest time of day but approaching it. People at the tables are talking, and what they mostly talk about is what they believe. What TV show everyone should be watching. Which of their colleagues is a piece of shit. What the one true god wants us to do. Around the world there are 2.3 billion Christians, 1.9 billion Muslims, a billion Hindus, a billion atheists. There are Jews, Zoroastrians, Sikhs, Rastafarians, Buddhists and neo-Pagans. There are free-market economists, Keynesians and Marxists. There are existentialists, stoics and rationalists. There are people who believe in paleo diets, Atkins diets, intermittent fasting diets. There are people who believe we are living in a simulation. There are people who believe the royal family are lizards. There are people who believe they are the second coming of Christ.

Many of these beliefs overlap into neat categories, but really there are as many belief systems as there are people. 7.8 billion and counting, and it's only lunchtime.

'Hey Mika, there's a guy out front asking if he can talk to you.'

Mika is mixing pancake batter with Kenny at the hot plate. She feels a flutter in her stomach which might be excitement or dyspepsia. She thinks of dark eyes with flecks of gold.

'Tuna melt with extra cheese.' She slides a plate towards Tamara. 'What's he look like?'

Tamara looks over her shoulder.

'Tall glass of water, blond hair, expensive shirt. You hire a solicitor?'

'Ah, no; that's my friend Olly.'

Her hand instinctively goes to her pregnancy bump. In the last month it has become more noticeable. People ask her when she is due.

'Has he ordered anything?' Kenny asks.

'Not yet.'

'Tell him to order or get the fuck out.'

Tamara says nothing as she whisks the tuna melt away to its destiny.

'You wanna go see him?' Kenny says without looking away from the grill.

'I . . . no, it's fine. He should have let me know he'd be coming.'

'I can handle things for five minutes.'

'We're busy.'

'If people don't like waiting, they can complain.'

'You're not paying me to—'

Kenny slaps his spatula down hard on the hot plate.

'Are you wanting an excuse not to see this guy, Mika? Cause I can do that, but I'd appreciate you being upfront with me.'

'No, it's . . . it would be good to see him, actually. Just for five.'

'Great.'

She shrugs off her apron, washes the flecks of batter from her arms, and pushes through the swing door. Beyond it the café is loud with chatter, and a golden oldies radio station playing through speakers in the ceiling.

Mika sees Olly being hectored by Tamara and smiles. She has missed that look of puppyish bewilderment. Since the night she was fired, she hasn't seen anyone from her old work, not even Suzy. They exchanged a few messages, in which time Mika discovered that James had been released by the police but hadn't returned. That was the last she heard. Suzy is clearly in two minds about her – sympathetic and angry.

Tamara weaves past on her way back to the kitchen. Without stopping, she says:

'He's cute, in a dopey sort of way.'

Olly spots Mika and his face lights up; he waves her over. His blond, angelic radiance is only enhanced by the billowing folds of pink vinyl booth; he might have been painted on the ceiling of the Sistine Chapel, napkin dispenser and all. God passing the ketchup to man. He rises to embrace her but she slides into the seat opposite him before he has the chance.

'You know I'm working, Olly?'

'Oh sorry, I, um . . . '

He looks unusually flustered. She's not sure why he's here, but she can see this isn't how he planned on it going.

'It's okay; I've got five minutes. How's things? How's work?'

'Oh, well . . . James hasn't returned yet.'

'Still? And the restaurant?'

'We've kept it running. All of us. Though a lot of it was Suzy. She was in early next day, figuring out how to contact the suppliers, calling up James's accountant to make sure payroll was still running, everything. Since then, we all just got on with it.'

'A ship without a captain,' she says.

'I guess it always was,' he shrugs. 'Anyway, business was booming in the days after you— I mean, after James's arrest. I guess people wanted to see if he would reappear. We just carried on. After two weeks we got a call from his accountant to say he'd checked himself into rehab in the Cotswolds.'

'Wow.'

'Yeah, it's been a bit weird. How are you? How is it working . . . here?'

He looks around, and she can tell he doesn't have the highest opinion of Hoban's. It's not haute cuisine; it should be beneath her. His snobbery is misplaced, she thinks, because Kenny would never allow Olly anywhere near his kitchen, and a lot of the food tastes better than anything they made at SINE.

'Yeah, it's good thanks.'

'Good, good . . . '

He wants to say something, but can't quite bring himself to. He glances down at her midriff, then back up. She takes it as a cue.

'I'm still pregnant, yes.'

'I thought—'

'That I was getting rid of it? Me too.'

'Suzy told me you were keeping it, but I wasn't sure. So that's it? You're having a baby? Our baby?'

'I . . . yes. I'll refund your money, for the—'

'Keep it,' he cuts her off. 'Use it to buy some . . . I don't know, nappies? Baby things.'

He smiles that charming, innocent smile. Ridiculous, she thinks. She paid Olly the courtesy of letting him know she wasn't keeping the baby, but it had barely occurred to her he might want to know he was becoming a father.

'What made you change your mind?'

She shrugs; there's no point in trying to put it into words.

'And, you're living . . . ?'

'Here, upstairs.'

'Suzy said you had to move out because . . . '

He clears his throat.

'Because the Home Office want to deport me,' she says, quietly. 'You don't have to tiptoe around it, Olly. My visa ran out, I didn't tell them I hadn't left, that's the whole story. James ratted me out when he fired me.'

'Right, right . . . ' Olly has a far-away expression, as though he's doing a difficult sum in his head. Then, apparently reaching a figure which he finds acceptable, he reaches into his coat pocket and starts rummaging. Tamara appears at the same moment with a cup of coffee and one of the sweet potato brownies that Kenny is especially proud of. Olly pulls out a little box. A box upholstered in red velvet. Tamara's eyes go wide before he's even opened it. The lid hinges back to reveal a diamond of such dazzling ferocity that, catching the light, it makes Mika wince.

'I know this is out of the blue, but . . . Mika, will you marry me?'

The brownie drops off its plate and onto the table with a dull thud. Nobody seems to notice. Tamara half turns to go, then turns back.

'I'll let Dad know you'll be needing five more minutes.'

Mika opens her mouth to protest, but Tamara is already gone.

'Olly . . . '

'I know, I know. This is crazy. But just think about it for a moment. You're having my baby. *We're* having a baby. And unless we're married, you can't stay in this country—'

'I don't want to stay in this country. Not forever!'

'But where would you go? If they catch you, you might end up giving birth in one of those awful detention centres. You might get sent who-knows-where.'

She shakes her head.

'I'm not going to get caught. When the baby is born, I'll be on my way.'

'Where to?'

She shakes her head at the question – not important. Her plans are her own. The point is, the point . . .

'I'll give up cooking,' he says. Mika forces herself not to laugh at how serious his expression is. 'My dad always wanted me to inherit the family business. I'd start off in a lower-level position, but we'd still have enough money for a nice house, lots of family holidays. You wouldn't be stuck here; we could go wherever.'

She scoffs.

'Olly, you're talking about us as a family – we're not a family! We hardly know each other!'

'I know that I'm—' he starts, but doesn't finish, deeming whatever he was going to say unwise. 'I'm not asking for us to be a family. Not if you don't want to. I'm just asking you to give me a chance. Because I care about you, and I care about our child. I want to give you the best chance that I can.'

He puts the box with the ring down on the table between them. She has never seen this side of him before. Strange for him to suddenly be serious, when he's saying such ridiculous things. But she sees herself in him. The way he pursues what he wants with such certainty, the way people do when they've seen how life can change in a moment.

'I can't, Olly. I . . . '

'I'm not asking you to make a decision right now.'

'Who said I needed to make a decision?'

'Take some time.'

'Olly, this is *crazy.*'

'Yeah, I know. But think about it.'

The more she thinks about it, the crazier it seems. But they're both keenly aware of the fact that she hasn't said no. She leans back and looks out at the street. A police officer walks in their direction. The officer isn't looking at her, but Mika still finds herself drawing in, turning her face away from the glass.

'Olly—'

'I could give us a nice home, Mika.' He ploughs on, trying to pre-empt her arguments. 'I could give our baby a nice home. You would have freedom to do stuff, travel, go back to work if you wanted to. We could hire a nanny.'

Mika can't seem to say anything.

'I know you think I'm an idiot.'

'Olly—'

'And I *am* an idiot. There was too much money around when I was a kid; I never worried about being smart. But you – you're the most amazing person I've ever met. You decide to do things, and then you just do them. You're clever and funny and . . . '

179

He trails off. She doesn't rise to the compliment, and waits for him to find his train of thought.

'I don't want you giving up everything you've worked for, just because of me . . . '

'It's still my choice, Olly.'

'I know that. But I don't want your choices to be limited because of something I did. If it weren't for me, none of this would be happening.'

The argument is disingenuous, she knows. Olly is trying to tie her into something by dramatising his guilt. And what is he trying to tie her into anyway? Citizenship, or a relationship? It seems ridiculous to have one without the other.

'I should get back to the kitchen . . . '

'Of course. I think I'll go too. Seems a bit weird to sit out here after that kind of conversation.'

He laughs, and she laughs too. It is awkward but not awful. They stand together. He takes out his wallet and puts a twenty-pound note down.

'It was good to see you, Mika.'

He thinks, for a second, about going in for a hug, then just touches her lightly on the arm and turns away. She watches him go, realising only now that several pairs of eyes are on her. She reaches down to pick up the twenty he left for the untouched coffee and brownie and sees the ring, still winking from its silk cushion.

'Now then, Mr Adjaye, what seems to be the trouble?'

Jem settles himself into the doctor's chair. The door, which is on a closing mechanism, clicks shut behind him. He forces himself to take a deep breath; since hospital the smell of disinfectant has made his heart race.

'Well, I've been having these funny turns . . . '

'Funny ha ha or funny peculiar?' the GP asks, then laughs at his own joke. Doctor Dawson Griggs is in his late sixties and always carries his head slightly to one side. The lobes of his ears sag down, as though they have grown larger on account of all the listening he does. Doctor Griggs has been Jem's GP for at least ten years, and was their family GP, back when Jem still had a family. Considering himself a discreet man, the doctor does not mention this change in Jem's circumstances.

'Sort of blackouts, actually.'

'Blackouts? That sounds serious. Have you been drinking more than usual? Doing anything you shouldn't have?'

'No, but my accident—'

'Ah yes, your accident . . . ' The doctor scrolls through some notes on his computer. 'And when you say blackouts, what are we talking about? You wake up on the floor? Or overstay past your stop on the Northern Line? Because I'm afraid to say the latter is a rather common ailment.'

Doctor Griggs laughs again; Jem gulps hard several times to calm himself.

'It's not like . . . I mean, I don't wake up anywhere.'

'But you fall? Lose your balance?'

'It's more like, one minute I'm one place and the next minute I'm somewhere else, and I have no idea how I got there.'

Doctor Griggs smiles an easy, patronising smile.

'Happens to the best of us, Jem. Especially as we get older. The number of times I've walked into the kitchen and thought – why on Earth am I here?'

'But I mean, I really just disappear. It's like I left my body for a minute.'

'Have you ever come to any harm during one of these "blackouts"?'

'No, but—'

'Any other symptoms? Headaches, say, or flashing lights?'

'No . . . '

'I think it's perfectly normal to worry about declining mental agility as we get older—'

'I'm really worried about it,' Jem says, as a last-ditch attempt. 'Isn't there a possibility . . . after my accident . . . wouldn't it be possible to have a scan or something?'

Doctor Griggs looks serious for the first time.

'You see Jem, the hospitals get very grumpy with us if we refer patients to them who don't meet the criteria for certain procedures and investigations.'

'Of course, but—'

'MRI scanners don't come cheap, you know, and there are long lists of patients with very serious conditions – cancer and so forth – who need those scans as a matter of priority.'

Jem sighs, nods.

'Of course . . . '

'So, what we'll do – I'll give you a quick check-up here to make sure that nothing's amiss. That should give you some peace of mind, shouldn't it?'

'Yes, of course. Thank you, doctor.'

Jem submits to the disinterested attentions of Doctor Griggs, who in due course pronounces him in perfect health.

'Of course, if you're concerned that these anxieties might start to affect you in your personal life, we can explore the pharmacological route.'

Jem is too busy wondering what is meant by 'personal life' to properly consider the proposal. Surely all his life is personal to him? Or is this a veiled reference to something?

To his love life? Does the doctor think he's having trouble getting it up? He says:

'Whatever you think best.'

Doctor Griggs regards him for a moment, like a tailor sizing up a client to fit him for a suit. He types for a moment on the computer, then the printer whirrs to life. The doctor whips out the slip of pale green, makes the necessary marks, tears off the carbon paper and hands Jem his copy.

'Only when you feel the need, and no more than four in a day. Give the instructions a proper read, all that.'

'Yes, thank you . . . '

Jem allows himself to be ushered out of the surgery and walks to the pharmacy where he gets his prescriptions. There he waits for five minutes, breathing in the thick fug of camphor, menthol, ivory soap, cough drops, barley sugars and medicated insoles until he is even more in a trance than before. He is handed a little blue box of pills, small enough to put in his jacket pocket, and floats onto the street.

The air is very warm. He hasn't been sleeping well, in the heat and humidity, these past few weeks. After a while, it's as though the undreamt dreams force themselves into the waking world. He keeps seeing Mika's face wherever he goes, as though she is under the surface of everything, waiting for him to peel back the layers of the street, the buildings, the sky, to find her there, to let her out. He hasn't contacted her since she spent the night at his flat, not since before the dream of the cottage.

He walks to the nearest pub and gets himself a pint of lager, with which he drinks down two of the pills. It's only after he's done it, reading the leaflet from the box, that he sees that you should be careful mixing them with alcohol. *Alprazolam is used to treat anxiety and panic disorder.*

Alprazolam is in a class of medications called benzodiaze-pines. It works by decreasing abnormal excitement in the brain . . . Ah well, too late to do anything about it now. He finishes the pint, by the end of which he's forgotten about the careful-with-alcohol thing. Then he goes to the bar and orders another pint.

What happens next is that events in Jem's head and events outside Jem's head are no longer running in sync, like one movie at half speed and another at double. He sinks ever deeper into his thoughts, while everything around him smears by like traffic seen through a rainy window. Does he get another drink? He's not sure, but he certainly has a drink. Does he leave the pub? Yes, it seems he has left the pub, and is somewhere else altogether, on a bus. Where is the bus going? What is his stop? Never mind about that – return to the inner movie, the one that makes you feel good.

The inner movie is nonlinear, non-narrative, more of a montage of moments, a loop which repeats but changes each time. Sun on auburn hair; pale fingers holding knife and fork over a plate of pancakes, arms crossed in a wool jumper. Looking through a window at the South Bank; sitting in a circle of chairs; a booth in a Soho café.

It is this last place that he lingers on, though he cannot say why. Perhaps because it has a personal connection to Mika, whereas the others did not. If he knew what bands she liked, he would listen to them now. If he knew what her favourite food was, he'd eat it (though eating seems vaguely unwise).

At one point he is aware of having his phone in his hands, his thumbs typing something, searching, but then the phone goes away and he forgets about it. He allows the outer movie to play out, because in truth there is nothing he can do to stop it. So it is with little surprise that he turns up at the door to Hoban's, that same Soho café where he met Mika. It makes as much sense as anything.

He goes inside, to the steam and noise. It is very warm in here – warmer even than outside – and for a moment his head swims. He thinks he might faint. But the same magnetic force that pulled him across town to this point pulls him upright now, like a puppeteer regaining interest, and he makes his way over to the same booth where they sat before. Content with having reached this place, this physical representation of his inner movie, he slumps down, then down again, putting his feet up on the seat opposite and resting his head on the vinyl seat-back.

Time passes.

It might be a minute or half an hour. Synchronising clocks between the inner and outer worlds is quite impossible at this stage. However long it has been, the end of this passage of time is marked by the midriff of a waitress appearing by the table.

'Sir? Hello?'

He doesn't remember her saying anything before these words. He looks up, and up, several miles to the waitress's summit. There is ice on her upper slopes. Spontaneously, he remembers her name.

'Tamara!'

She frowns, then her eyes narrow.

'Have we met?'

'The tea! I was a tea man.'

It is only now that he is saying things out loud that Jem realises quite how absurdly impaired he is. He remembers a similar feeling after having his wisdom teeth removed, the anaesthetic making his mouth feel like it belonged to someone else. Nevertheless, something like recognition breaks over Tamara's face.

'You're Mika's friend?'

He doesn't answer the question.

'I'll have . . . I'll have . . . thehunkydorypleess.'

'You're drunk.'

'No,' Jem shakes his head. 'Nonononononono. V'only had two. Mebbe three.'

'I don't think you need pancakes.'

'I do.' He nods his head vigorously, then stops, feeling the contents of his skull spinning round like a magic eight ball. He sees the message floating up behind his eyes:

OUTLOOK

NOT SO

GOOD

'Do you want to see Mika?' she asks.

Not imagining this to be a genuine offer, but more of a general question, Jem answers effusively:

'Yes. God, yes! I've been missing her so much, you know?'

Tamara hovers for a moment more then disappears. Jem assumes she has gone to get his pancakes. A minute later she returns, and he looks up to thank her. Except it's not Tamara.

His eyes go wide and he makes a hurried attempt to sit up, which seems to get him nowhere.

'Mika, I . . . '

'Why are you here?' She looks annoyed, impatient.

'M'sorry, I . . . '

'Tamara said you wanted to see me.'

He silently curses Tamara, as one might curse a genie in the Arabian Nights who has taken your wish too literally.

186

'I didn't—'

'You don't want to see me?'

'I do, it's just . . . I . . . I mean . . . I . . . '

His mouth runs on, making less sense as he becomes more agitated. With a terrible flush of embarrassment he realises that his eyes are filling with tears. He looks down at his lap, blinks hard several times, wills himself to sober up. Suddenly Mika has sat down opposite, her expression changed to one of concern.

'Are you . . . okay?'

'I'm fine, just—'

'You're drunk?'

'Not drunk. Not really. Shouldn't have taken—' He shuts himself up before giving away the truth, but Mika has already cottoned on.

'Taken what? What did you take?'

He looks guiltily at her for a moment, but cannot meet her eye. He fumbles at his jacket pocket but finds his hand has grown three sizes. Mika comes over and gently takes the pill box out. Her body, so close that he can feel her warmth, makes his head swim.

'Oh Jem . . . ' she mutters. 'You really shouldn't drink with these. Who gave you them? Your doctor?'

Jem tries to reply but can no longer locate his mouth. He knows it's in the general area of his face, but the face, as an area, is pretty crowded, not like the wide-open plains of his stomach or back. There are eyes and ears and nose, not to mention all those muscles for pulling expressions, and he finds himself quite lost between all of them, like a stage hand searching for the right rope to raise the scenery.

Mika looks at him for a moment in silence before suddenly disappearing. Jem looks around for a moment but can't see her anywhere in the café. He is bereft. Was she really there at all, or did he imagine her? Other people are looking at him so he closes his eyes and sinks further down. He must sleep for a moment, because he is jolted awake by a hand landing on his shoulder.

'Come on then, big guy—'

He opens his eyes to see a frog-like face, looming over him. Grey hair held back by a sweatband, unshaven grey stubble, grey eyebags – Jem startles back from this monochrome spectre, but the hand holds him in place. He is hauled up, out of the booth. Belatedly Jem realises he's being kicked out of the café and finds his mouth again.

'No – I ordered pancakes.'

'You're in no state for pancakes, buddy.'

'I'm fine, really . . . '

He struggles, but only succeeds in half-falling to the floor. His body is heavy as a wet dishcloth. Another hand catches him by his other arm, lifts him.

Mika.

He allows himself to be led. If she wants him to leave, he will leave. But instead of showing him to the door, they weave their way across the café floor to a dirty swing door. They push through and Jem just concentrates on keeping his feet moving underneath him.

They take him past the heat-belching kitchen, past a musty storeroom, up a flight of stairs, then another flight of stairs. Once or twice they stumble, stop to readjust, but in what seems like no time at all to Jem, he is brought into a quiet bedroom and eased down onto the bed. He closes his eyes. Mika and the frog man talk between themselves as though he's not there.

'Can he stay here for a bit?'

'Sure. He better not barf though; these are the guest covers.'

'I'm sure he'll be fine,' Mika says, though she doesn't sound sure. 'I'm just going to check on him every fifteen, to make sure he's still breathing.'

'Very wise,' the frog man replies. 'Those fuckin' pills are a liability, I'm telling you. Big Pharma wants us all hooked on their synthetic bullshit. Nature gives us all we need.'

'Sure, Kenny.'

'What's wrong with him, anyway? Apart from benzos and booze?'

'I dunno . . . I think he's having a hard time.'

'Yeah, but what kind of hard time?'

'A hard time of life, I guess.'

The frog man laughs, but not unkindly.

'Amen.'

Jem listens to them, and every time Mika speaks, he feels a little jolt of pleasure. Incapacitated as he is, he imagines her climbing into the bed next to him. As though he has found what he was looking for and can now rest, he falls into a dreamless sleep.

Around the world, people are kissing.

They kiss on the grass, in the sun. They kiss, with a bunch of flowers held between them, in airports and train stations. They kiss at the back of cinemas and music concerts – always at the back. They kiss in the line for the bus and on the top deck of the bus, and when they step off the bus they stop to kiss there too. They kiss, holding the pose for wedding photos and landmark selfies. They kiss, running hands through each other's hair and down each other's backs.

They kiss, until kissing is no longer enough.

Around the world, people are touching. People are grabbing. People are sucking and rubbing and riding. People are naked. People are clothed. People are doing it behind closed doors and in alleys behind the club and in orchards full of bees and sunlight and in caravans provided for conjugal visits and in eleventh-storey hotel rooms and against the bathroom wall and under three layers of blankets and in an empty house while their parents are away. People are doing it in twos and threes and fours. People are trying new positions, new partners, new personas. People are trying not to laugh, or cry, or cum. People are tipping over the edge.

People are going, going, gone.

15

Time passes.

Earth spirals through space and almost nobody pays this fact any attention. Midnight passes in London; a new day begins. Taking life expectancy into account, three hundred thousand humans are about to have the best day of their lives. Jem dreams of an infinite doctor's surgery, a labyrinth of rooms he's desperate to escape, except every time he finds an open window there are plants pushing in – vines, waxy banana leaves, orchids like colourful genitalia. If he could just find a door, he could get out to the jungle beyond.

He wakes up.

At least, he thinks he wakes up. He doesn't feel entirely as though he's been asleep. What time is it? He takes out his phone and squints at the time. He urgently needs to pee. He doesn't feel drunk or hung over, only as though someone else has taken his body for a joyride and left it sloppily parked on an unfamiliar street.

Mika . . .

He gets up more quickly than his head would like. He

fumbles for his shoes, which have been taken off his feet and placed carefully next to the bed. Out in the passage, everything is quiet. After some trial and error he finds the bathroom, which smells of Imperial Leather soap and Ajax powder. He relieves himself then inspects his face in the bathroom mirror, framed by gilded bamboo.

By the time he's downstairs, it's five past eight. He finds Mika sliding fried eggs out of a skillet at one of the café tables, where there are three places set. The chef – Kenny? – is sipping a cup of tea. He's wearing a faded black T-shirt, like the night before. Jem isn't sure if it's the same one or not. Everything feels dreamlike.

'Sit down.' Mika points to one of the chairs. 'You're just in time. We've got cereal, toast, and I can do you anything from a fried breakfast.'

'Scrambled eggs?'

'Of course. There's coffee in the pot, unless you want tea?'

'Coffee's great.'

Mika disappears back to the kitchen, and he's left with Kenny. Jem knows he should make conversation, but he's too fuddled by sleep and the closeness of the seating arrangement.

'You made it through the night.'

'Yes, um . . . thank you for letting me stay the night. I swear I don't make a habit of that sort of thing.'

'You're fine.' Kenny waves a meaty hand. 'We all fuck up sometimes, right? I don't believe in those fucking pills anyway.'

'No?'

'Nah. Whaddaya need them for, anyway?'

Jem shrugs. 'I don't know, to be honest. I told my

doctor . . . well, anyway, he seemed to think I was suffering from anxiety.'

'But *you* don't think that?'

'No, not really. Not the way he means it. It's more like . . . '

'Existential angst? Anxiety the way Jean-Paul Sartre meant it.'

'How did he mean it?'

'That you're free.'

'That doesn't sound so bad . . . '

'Are you kidding? You realise you're free, and it's fucking scary! It's terrifying to be free, because you can do anything. Found an orphanage or blow up a hospital – its all the same. You're free!'

'Oh . . . '

Jem didn't expect a philosophy lecture over breakfast, but recognises himself in what Kenny is saying.

'I almost died,' he says.

'What, last night? Mika wouldn't have let that happen. She was in and out every fifteen minutes.'

'She was? No, but I mean – I was hit by a car, earlier this year. Almost died in the operating theatre.'

'Shit.'

'And I was in the hospital, sort of in a trance, or a coma, and I asked the universe to save me. To save my life, right? I asked to stay alive long enough to have an adventure. And then, you know, my wish was granted.'

'That's heavy.'

'So I feel like – what now? How do I live up to not dying?'

'Wow.' Kenny chuckles, spearing a bit of bacon on his fork. 'That's some big stuff.'

'I know, right?'

'Maybe you need a different kind of medication.'

Kenny says it into his orange juice. Jem is about to ask what he means when Mika reappears with the coffee pot, a plate of scrambled eggs and toast, and a condiment caddy. They eat mostly in silence, with Mika and Kenny exchanging information as it occurs to them about the state of the kitchen – which supplies are running low, which appliances are on the fritz, which syrup dispenser has developed a leaky tap. Jem gets on with eating his eggs. They are buttery, cloud-soft and comforting, and he adds enough hot sauce to make his eyes water. By the time the plate is empty and the coffee drained, he feels fully awake. Kenny hauls himself up, collects their dirty plates and pads off to the kitchen.

'How are you feeling?' Mika asks.

'A little ashamed.'

'I meant: how's the hangover?'

'Oh . . . fine, I guess, though without a toothbrush my mouth feels pretty fuzzy.'

'I can ask Kenny if he's got a spare.'

'No, I've already been enough trouble. I'll get one when I'm out.'

She nods slowly; there is a space between them into which either one could step. Jem goes first.

'This is a cool place to live.' He gestures around at the pink banquette booths, the gold-framed mirrors, the swirling Formica galaxies on each table, the napkin dispensers advertising Coca Cola. The café looks like it was transplanted from New York.

'Yeah, I feel at home here. It doesn't belong, just like me.'

Jem isn't sure what she means by that, but his throat aches a little. He hears himself saying:

'Are you doing anything today?'

'I'm . . . not working.'

It doesn't answer the question, but Jem decides to be brave, to grab his existential freedom by the balls.

'If you fancy it, we could do something.'

'Buy you a toothbrush?'

'For starters.'

'Do you have something in mind?'

'Not really. Seems like it'll be a nice day. What do you fancy?'

'You're the one asking me on a date.'

Jem hesitates over her choice of words. She could sincerely mean they're going on a date. Or she could be using the word casually, safe in the knowledge that there is nothing between them and never will be.

'We could go to the park . . . or see if there's something on at the cinema. My treat.'

She considers him levelly for a few moments, then nods.

'Okay, sure. Do you need to get ready?'

'It's not like *I* have another outfit.'

'Give me ten minutes then.'

'Of course.'

Mika disappears. Jem pours another coffee, picks at the remains of the bacon plate. After a couple of minutes Kenny shuffles back to the table. He has something in his hand that Jem can't see.

'Thank you for breakfast. Can I give you something?'

'Nah, fuck it. Mika lives here; the eggs belong to her too. She's a good one, you know?'

'I know.'

'Here, I got you some alternative medication.'

Kenny slides something into the shadow of his breakfast plate. It's a sandwich bag, double wrapped around a dark substance.

'This is . . . ?'

'A cure for existential anxiety, if you're feeling brave. Take them all together, with a little orange juice. Go somewhere chilled. If it gets too much, drink something sugary.'

And with that he scuffs off again, before Jem can reject his offer. He takes the package and sniffs it. It has an earthy, musky, basement kind of smell. A dug-up-in-the-woods kind of smell. He sees Mika coming through the swing door and pockets it quickly. She has packed a bag and smells of coconut sun cream.

'You ready to go?'

'Yes.'

'Come on; let's find you a toothbrush.'

They step into the sunshine. It's a Soho sort of sunshine, trickling through the filter paper of pollution like so much morning coffee. But still – sunshine! It hits the backs of their necks as they walk and they both, separately, feel electricity shiver down their spines.

First Jem buys toothbrush, toothpaste and a roll-on deodorant. Mika buys menthol gum, paracetamol and a pack of tissues. As an afterthought, Jem buys a bottle of orange juice and a can of lemonade, but doesn't mention why. They stroll up to Oxford Street until they reach the big Primark, where Mika tells him there are public toilets. Jem goes up to the third floor and brushes his teeth in peace, while Mika picks out some cheap socks. Reunited, they walk west down Oxford Street as far as Mable Arch, and duck into Hyde Park.

Later, neither of them will recall suggesting where they go or what they do. The magnetic winds swirling around them pull them this way and that. It is only when they are within the park that Jem shows her the package that Kenny gave him.

'Oh, he gave you some of his "medicine?"' she smirks.

'What is it?'

'Magic mushrooms. Kenny grows them in the basement. Makes them into "tea" for trusted regulars.'

'Oh . . . he said they would cure my "existential anxiety".'

'That's Kenny. He's an old hippy. Are you going to take them?'

'No!' he says, rather too quickly. 'I mean, not right now, while we're out together.'

'It's okay,' she shrugs. 'Would be worth a few laughs.'

'Really?'

'Sure. And it's not like I can do *anything* fun any more. At least I could be an idiot vicariously.'

He thinks for a minute, chews his nails.

You wanted an adventure, he says to himself.

Yes, he replies, *like mountain climbing or caravanning. Not drugs in the park.*

Beggars can't be choosers, he replies.

'Well?' Mika asks.

'Okay.'

They find a quiet bench near the lake, and she keeps an eye out while he unwraps the sandwich bag. There is a faint smell of garlic and cumin which has nothing to do with the contents. Inside are roughly four grams of dried mushrooms, grey and brown, stained blue where they were picked. He takes one, places it on his tongue and chews.

'Ugh.'

'Don't chew, just swallow.'

'You've done this before?'

'I've done plenty of stuff; don't look so worried.'

Jem eats the rest more quickly, with swigs of orange juice. When he's done, he drains the bottle and shudders.

'Well done.' She pats him on the shoulder. 'That was very brave.'

'You're so patronising.'

'Lighten up.' She stands. 'You don't want the aliens in the seventh dimension to see you sulking.'

He gets to his feet and they walk on. The butterflies in his stomach are gone. It's as though, because he doesn't feel any different, he no longer believes the mushrooms will do anything. They walk around the Serpentine, talking about the time Mika almost won the Italian lottery. Then they talk about childhood, their favourite ice cream flavours (Jem: mint choc chip, Mika: mango sorbet) about why wanting to swim with dolphins is weird, about early rising versus late rising (Jem: early, Mika: late, when she gets to), and what they like to read (Jem: non-fiction, Mika: sci-fi, poetry). They tell each other their birthdays (Jem in November, Mika in February). It's the most date-like conversation they've ever had. Neither of them mentions the dreams.

They've gone full circuit when Jem notices a subtle shift in his head. It's not that anything looks different, just that everything looks interesting. He looks at the grass below and the folds of clouds above, wondering if they really are unusually beautiful, or whether he's imagining it. Mika notices he's gone quiet.

'Feeling okay?'

'I'm fine. What were you saying?'

They walk on, and he gets lost in the conversation for a while. He's not noticed before what a lovely voice Mika has, rounded and mellow, the very voice that her body would have, like the sound of a tuned instrument. And her accent, the words bubbling lyrically . . .

'Jem?'

'What?'

'You've not said anything for a minute. Were you listening?'

'Sure I was.'

'Then what did I just say?'

'Oh!' A goofy smile breaks over his face. 'I've no idea.'

Mika laughs. 'Man, you're high.'

'I am?'

'Come on.' She takes his hand. 'Let's find some grass to sit down on.'

They walk, but he struggles to hold the thread of conversation and walk at the same time. He keeps thinking he can see someone running just ahead of them, ducking behind each tree and bush before he can get a good look. He has the impossible belief that it is a younger version of himself, leading them on. They find a spot to sit. Mika opens her rucksack and pulls out a light blanket and spreads it on the grass. Jem sits, then lies down with a great sigh.

'Come down; join me.'

Mika smirks down at him for a second, then her sense of obligation kicks in. She manoeuvres her belly down.

'Ugh, sitting on the ground is a lot harder these days.'

'You should lie down instead.'

He feels satisfied with this logic. After a moment's hesitation she lies down next to him, and together they look at the sky. His eyes water. He listens to Mika's breathing slowing and deepening.

'Wow . . . '

'What can you see?' she asks, smiling.

'Clouds.'

'Well, yeah.'

'But they're . . . complicated.'

This is the best he can do to describe the geometric patterns which are growing through the clouds like crystals in sugar water. They are quiet for a while, just the wind ruffling their hair and the occasional call of a goose or swan breaking the silence. A bird flies over and lands in a nearby tree.

'Lesser spotted woodpecker,' he says.

'Was it?'

'It was.'

'How do you know?'

'I just do . . . ' he says, and almost leaves it at that. 'I like birdwatching.'

'I wouldn't have thought you were the type.' Mika is smirking as though she might say something unkind.

'My dad got me into it when I was very small. Bought me a pair of binoculars and one of those tiny books. *The Birds of the British Isles*. Of all the things he tried to get me to enjoy – football, action films, all that manly stuff – birdwatching was the only thing that really stuck.'

'Why do you like it?'

'Because . . . ' He searches for words for a moment. 'Because they're beautiful, I suppose. Beautiful and . . . and free.'

'Free?'

'They fly over boundaries, over whole continents. They

200

make their nests wherever they want to, halfway up cliffs and on the tops of lampposts. Birds don't have passports, they don't need to book a flight to go on holiday . . . '

The words tumble out of him, very free, then stop. He wonders where they came from. Mika is looking sideways at him, and her expression has changed. Seeing him look, she turns her face back to the sky and starts to hum a song. Slowly, Jem realises he knows the tune. He sings:

'I wish I knew how it would feel to be free . . . '

Mika smiles.

'You know it. When I was little it always made me cry.'

They are quiet for a moment, then Jem says:

'Life is weird.'

'Can't disagree.'

'Like, we could have been anyone. I *could* have been a bird. Or, I dunno, a fish!' He gets the giggles again.

'Well, I'm glad you're not a fish.'

'Me too. But it's reassuring, you know. The fish thing . . . '

He goes back to watching the glowing latticework of the clouds. He can feel her warmth at his side. If she just got a little closer . . .

'We never spoke, about that last dream,' she says, sounding drowsy.

'I know,' he says. 'I guess I didn't want to.'

'Why?'

Jem's thoughts are expanding outwards, like ink dropped in water, but his words are becoming sticky, hard to get past his front teeth. He concentrates and says:

'Because I didn't want to spoil it. I didn't want to prove it wrong.'

And, quite clumsily, he feels around on the grass until

his hand finds hers. For a moment she hesitates, her hand inert, then squeezes his hand once and doesn't pull away. Jem feels pleased with himself, though he's sure she's just humouring him so that he doesn't have a bad trip. Nevertheless they lie there, with their eyes closed, unremarkable among the other couples who have found their way to this open space. Children are playing; lovers are embracing; the world turns its face to the sun.

'I feel sleepy,' he says.

'You won't sleep though,' she says. 'Not while you're tripping.'

'No?'

'I don't think you can.'

'Oh. Probably for the best; those would be some strange dreams.'

'Yeah . . . '

A jet plane crosses the sky. Mika starts to hum a melody. Jem doesn't know the tune. It's soft, like a lullaby. The notes fill his head with little explosions of colour and meaning, and with each moment he gets a little drowsier. Mika's hand has ceased to feel separate, as though the sunlight has melted them together. He's about to say something, but the something never comes. He slips out of the present and into a tumbling sort of dream. At the same moment, Mika falls asleep, pulled down the same rabbit hole by Jem, who's still holding her hand.

They are falling back through the whorls of time, only much faster now. Powered by the psychic jet fuel of Kenny Hoban's Golden Hawaiians, Jem falls through the last few hundred years, pulling Mika with him. A moment later they are past the last few thousand years, catching nothing but glimpses of who they were. They pass their earliest dream, under the fig tree, and hurtle on, past the era of Homo sapiens, back further to the earliest common ancestor of humans and chimpanzees. Fur creeps over their chests, down their limbs, covering every part of their bodies . . .

Rain is falling in the jungle. Mika and Jem scavenge for nuts from a fallen tree, eyeing each other with mutual interest. Jem is about to make a move when he sees a pair of gold-green tiger eyes gleaming from the undergrowth, right behind Mika's head—

Further back, like salmon swimming upstream to the place of their birth. From two legs they hunch over and walk on four. They grow tails and claws. Mika transitions from a menstrual to an estrous cycle. Their noses flatten out as though pressed by a potter's thumb, each nostril facing sideways . . .

The plain is loud with shrieks. Mika and Jem throw rocks at each other. Their two packs are competing for territory, control of which allows them to swim and fish in the widest bend of the river. Each feels the hot blood pulsing in their necks. Jem snarls at Mika as a rock sails towards his head—

Further again, time in reverse, like a firework sinking down from the sky. They regain the ability to produce their own vitamin C – what a neat trick! They shrink again, their fur becoming lighter, their eyes swelling as they become nocturnal. Their teeth reshape themselves to eat fruit, seeds and insects . . .

Mika and Jem sniff at each other in the warm darkness, strangers passing in the night, circling, circling. There is a hush of wings above, sharp talons reaching out. They scatter, but by the time the owl has gone, they are far apart—

Further, further. They become cold blooded, egg-laying.

Their fur falls away, replaced by smooth skin, then scales. Their vision expands outwards at either end of the spectrum, like the curtains opening further at the start of a movie, to encompass infrared and ultraviolet wavelengths . . .

Mika and Jem bask on a slab of black, volcanic rock, close to the sea. The waves crash against the rocks and the spray leaps up, but they do not flinch. They eye each other with suspicion and lust—

Further! They grow smaller again, gain sharp teeth. They snap at millipedes and insects. Faster, faster. Their mouths widen, their small bodies becoming stocky as they take to the water, become amphibians. The sharp land-features of their bodies are softened by the water, legs becoming flippers, flippers becoming fins. They lose the ability to come onto the land . . .

Mika and Jem swim in a freshwater stream, racing away from a predator several times their size. It's after both of them, with rows of sharp teeth like a pike. Its jaws open, just behind them—

Further, how much further? Returning to the sea they become simplified again, retaining their jaws a little longer. Further, rubbing out revision after revision. What's under all these layers of paint? They have a sense of taste all over their bodies which will one day become the sense of touch. Keep going. Further, yes further. They become smooth sea cucumbers, worms, filter feeders just starting to figure out how life should work. The oceans are rich with oxygen and minerals, inviting experimentation. The whole of evolution is ahead of them, one grand adventure.

They are stripped back again and again. What is left? A sense of balance (but not hearing), rudimentary eyes (but not smell), a body (but no arms or legs, nothing to differentiate one part from another). Slowly, one by one, these features are erased. Mika and Jem, still travelling backwards but slowing now, are hazy concepts. They cannot see, or feel, or even reach out to grasp one another. They swim in a warm ocean, without any understanding of how large it might be. Two billion years in the past, half the life-age of the Earth, they stand at the dawn of sexual reproduction. Floating closer to one another, closer . . .

The film stops, freeze framed, at this moment, hovers for a moment, then starts to play again, in the right direction. A starburst of multicellular life. Connective tissue, mouths, symmetry . . . Forward, forward, picking up speed, like a comet that has reached the furthest point of its outer orbit, hurtling back to where it began . . .

Two billion years pass in the time it takes for one cell to divide into two. Mika and Jem open their eyes on the grass. It is a late Wednesday morning in the early part of the twenty-first century. Weather fine, with highs of 22 and lows of 13, average humidity 62, light cloud rolling in from the southeast around teatime . . .

They turn to look at one another. They look for a long time, just looking and breathing, with their backs to the world.

'I . . . ' says Jem.

'We . . . ' says Mika.

And they both start to laugh. They laugh, and laugh, and laugh, until tears roll down their faces and fall to the earth.

The rest of the day is spent prosaically, though nothing feels prosaic any more. To Jem everything looks bright and alien. They get salt beef sandwiches from the

Ashkenazi-Jewish deli on Rupert Street, then go to a matinee showing of *True Romance* at the Prince Charles. He buys her a box of mint chocolates after she says they remind her of a brand she liked growing up. By the time they're out, they feel hungry again, and go to a buffet in Chinatown. Later, neither of them will remember saying anything in particular, though both of them will remember talking.

What they will each recall clearly are the details of the other's face. Jem will remember the triangle of small moles under Mika's jaw – one dark chocolate, two mocha – and how he had the urge to kiss them, each in turn. Mika will remember the particular way the corners of Jem's eyes crease when he laughs.

After the meal, they stand on Wardour Street. Chinatown is busy, raucous, full of revellers, sightseers, theatregoers, drunks, hen and stag parties, escorts and drug dealers. Rickshaws pedal by, flashing with fibre-optic lights. London is a swirl of colour going down the drain, the ozone smell of the funfair, the threatening laughter of carnival. There is a summer scent in the air, delicious and rancid, heady as perfume, intoxicating. For a moment, the doors to the universe are all wide open. Anything can happen in a moment like this. Sins will be forgiven, old enemies become friends, sadnesses wash away. Mika thinks of her double bed back at Hoban's. Jem thinks of his quiet apartment.

'Well . . . ' she says.

'Well . . . ' he echoes.

But what's the rush, after all? If they like each other, why spoil it by stretching the day beyond its limits? They are weary with pleasure, heavy with happiness. This morning they lived through all of human evolution and ate salt beef sandwiches. Maybe they can wait another day to go to bed together.

'I guess I should be getting home,' Jem says.

'Yes,' Mika nods slowly. 'Me too. But maybe we could . . . '

'Yes, soon.'

'That would be nice.'

And, just as it seems they're about to fly apart, she takes a step forward, goes up on her toes and kisses him on the lips.

It lasts a moment. Less than 0.001 per cent of their day. But a moment like this bends time to its gravity. For Jem it's like a pinball machine high score, a shiver of lights passing through his brain and down his body, a pure dopamine hit that makes his toes tingle. For Mika it is like silence. Everything else goes away. The lights and smells and noises of the street vanish, yes, but the nagging voices in her head fall silent as well. Strange – she hadn't noticed them until they were gone. She doesn't need to be somewhere else, doing something else, always moving on. She is where she needs to be.

It lasts a moment, then she hurries away into the neon-soaked night. Jem watches her go, as he watched her disappear into the jungle, over the plains, under the rocks, away into the ocean. In short, she is gone, but he knows he will see her again.

On his way home Jem buys twenty different greetings cards. Some are for particular birthdays; others have no occasion printed on them. Along with them he buys a present box, with a glittery holographic covering, and a roll of ribbon. When he gets home, he lays all of these out on the floor of his living room, then rummages around for his best pen. He wants something that will not fade over time. When he's found what he's looking for, he picks one of the non-specific cards at random. On the envelope he writes 'Start Here', then writes in the card:

Dear Emily,
You might wonder why I'm writing this. I wonder too. But if anything happens to me, I don't want to disappear from your life completely. I don't think time really matters, for this kind of thing. It might mean that I can't give you a hug on your 18th birthday. But it doesn't mean I'm not there. So I'm writing these messages so that, even if I'm not there the rest of the time, I can be with you for some special occasions. And I'll write a few messages that you can open whenever, just as you feel like it. I hope that sounds okay.

He reads the message so far, then adds –

And if you don't want to, you don't have to read any of them. Just ignore your silly old dad. But if this is the only card you read, know that I love you very much. More than anything. And I'll always be your dad, even if we're not together at the same time any more.
Big hugs,
Dad xxx

He reads it all through again. It's not quite what he meant to say, and one or two parts make him cringe, but he doesn't want to start again – he wants it to be real, as though he's speaking to her in real time. It's not his mortality that concerns him (though the blackouts are worrying). It's that, after this morning, everything seems fleeting. He has seen countless lives made and unmade. He doesn't want to go without leaving a message for his daughter.

He puts the card away in its envelope, then he puts it in the glittery box and starts the next card – Happy 8th Birthday.

Dear Emily . . .

Mika is walking down the alley to the back of Hoban's when her mobile starts ringing. She takes it out and sees Tamara is calling.

'Hey, what's up?'

'Oh hi, Frank.'

'What? Tamara it's me, Mika. Did you mean to call Frank?'

Frank is the guy who supplies them with fresh bread every morning. Frank and Kenny had a fight a week ago about him overcharging for his baguettes. Since then Mika has been buying them from the market herself.

'Yeah, hi Frank,' Tamara says. 'I was just wanting to check about the baguettes.'

'What's going on? Tamara? Look, I'm almost there; I'll see you in a mo.'

'Hm? No, probably best if you don't come round now, Frank. We've got someone in . . . '

Mika is pushing through the back door and freezes. She starts to walk back the way she came, but her path is blocked. A burly man in a dark blue polo shirt and stab-proof vest is in her way. At the same moment another man steps out of the door she was just about to come through. Same uniform, and now she sees the embroidered epaulets – a crown, a diamond, and *Immigration Enforcement* in white thread.

'Mika Zielinska?'

She thinks for a way out of this, but there's enough evidence in her pockets to prove who she is.

'Yes.'

The officers exchange a quick, celebratory look.

'Miss Zielinska, I am an Immigration Officer. I am arresting you on suspicion that you are a person liable to immigration detention. This is because I suspect you have overstayed your leave. This is not an arrest for a criminal offence. You are not free to leave. You are not entitled to free legal advice at this stage. Do you understand?'

'Yes.'

Kenny and Tamara have appeared at the door behind the officers, but Mika finds she cannot look at them – his fury, her sadness. She turns away, in the direction the officer leads her. There will be a van waiting for her nearby, she knows. The burly officer is sent to gather her possessions.

Jem goes to bed and puts out the lights. He thinks about messaging Mika but decides to play it cool until the morning. He finds himself smiling into the dark of his room. It has been a strange, wonderful day, but he is pleasantly exhausted. He closes his eyes and lets dreams and darkness take him.

Life Number Nine

I

Though he is old, Jem walks without a stick
Down ancient streets where other feet go quick.
In his arms he cradles half a loaf of bread;
His back, once straight, bends like a candle wick.

II

A cold wind blows and raises clouds of dust
While all around him business is discussed
Stonemasons sing from a collapsed upper floor
And Jem holds tightly to his still-warm crust.

III

Deep grooves have been carved in all the paving
    stones,
By rattling wagons carrying rattling bones.
A cart of Nile geese thunders past his shoulder;
He listens to the caged birds' frightened groans.

IV

A thousand crowded voices reach his ears –
A father's scolding and a mother's fears,
A lover telling of a wasted eve
And a thousand stories more he overhears.

V

You become accustomed to noise in a city so great;
Jem first remembers stepping through the gate
Arriving from the country as a boy,
On a wagon, like another piece of freight.

VI

He had watched as hedges became walls,
As flowery banks became market stalls
As ditches became kerbs and grass became dust
And the songs of birds became traders' calls.

VII

He well remembers being frightened, then,
Of the noise and smell of ten thousand men
All gathered in a single teeming place.
Yet he cannot imagine leaving the city again.

VIII

Now Jem is jostled by a passing chaise,
Which makes the old man lift his crooked gaze;
Passing nearby is a woman of his age.
Lit up golden by the sun's winter rays.

IX

Her hair is greying, underneath her veil,
But she stands as straight as a new-made nail;
Her sky-blue eyes remain unclouded
And her ringless hands are delicate and pale.

X

Jem looks away but is struck by knowing;
Remembrance through him like a vine is growing,
Twisting through the trellis of his agèd brain
And memory's sweetest fruits bestowing.

XI

He sees his life backwards, as though from a hill:
Closest is the cottage where their lives stood still
Then the arena, with beasts in the shadows
Furthest the fig tree, where they ate their fill.

XII

He spins around, searching for her face,
But among every example of the human race
He sees no sign of the woman that he knew –
She has vanished into the marketplace.

XIII

Jem calls out, but his cry turns no stranger's head.
In panic now he drops the loaf of bread;
The crowd like water flows the other way
But he pushes back the way she fled.

XIV

See how he forces his ancient legs to go,
Against the tide of the bodies' flow.
Was her shawl dyed red, or was it yellow?
Ash blows on the breeze like early flakes of snow.

XV

He sees a carter with his barrel of clean water,
A gaggle of children, a soldier with his daughter,
A sooty kitchen girl with a basket of fish,
And oxen being led off to the slaughter.

XVI

But nowhere is there any sign of her.
While all the memories of her still recur
Paint flakes in the breeze from a furrier's door,
Leaves tumble, and the city starts to blur.

XVII

He stands awhile, as time keeps bearing down;
He stands, an agèd man in an agèd town.
The blossom tumbles from a cherry tree.
Already he knows he will not see her around.

XIV

Not in this lifetime, however he may roam –
He missed his chance beneath heaven's dome.
The chance may come to another of his line;
Jem turns around, and walks back to his home.

September

16

The Earth spins on, bearing many secret cargoes.

In a cave on the Iberian Peninsula, wall paintings unseen for thirty thousand years bear the likeness of galloping horses, aurochs and deer, beside the crisp outlines of human hands. In an underwater trench off the coast of Sumatra, the remains of the Flor de la Mar, sunk in 1511, strew the seabed with the Sultan of Malacca's looted diamonds and gold. Under the loam of a Lincolnshire field, the first crown jewels of England lie where they fell from King John's baggage train.

There is more, of course, so much more – hidden rooms in pyramids, clay tablets unlocking lost languages, whole attics full of paintings by Renaissance masters, enough fossils of undiscovered dinosaurs to fill a city of museums. There are unplayed sonatas and dusty demo tapes and masterpieces on defunct hard drives. The Earth carries it all, the heaving swag of it, to its unknown destination, like a thief waiting for a reliable fence.

Jem wakes with a jolt, physically reaching out to the

departing phantom of Mika. He gasps like a man breaking the surface of the sea. It's fine, though, it's fine – that was just a dream. He lost her, back then, but in the present he knows where she lives, has her mobile number. She's not going anywhere, will not disappear into this vast city, so different and so similar to the other one. Better still, she wants to see him again.

Sunlight is streaming through his bedroom window. He forgot to wind down the blackout blind last night, or even draw the curtains. He finds the fact that this is unlike him delicious. He feels like a different person in all the right ways. It's too bright for him to open his eyes, so for now he just basks. The afterglow of yesterday surrounds him like an all-body halo. He turns the memories over, one by one, like trinkets bought in a holiday market. But those trinkets always turned to tat the next day, like fairy gold. These memories aren't like that – they shine brighter the more he examines them, burning with delirious pleasure.

After a while has passed, he gets up. He makes toast with the jam he bought for Mika, and drinks a strong coffee. He feels pleasantly fatigued, as though he went for a long run yesterday. All this done, he takes out his supplies and writes two more cards to Emily, one for her tenth birthday and one for her twenty-first.

He has decided not to do them in order. This way there will be a better spread. So that, whether he dies today or in fifty years, she will have something to read. Not that he feels, in this moment, as though he's going anywhere. He carries on the project, more out of a sense of wanting to finish what he has started. Perhaps he will give the cards to Emily anyway, and they will joke about his paranoia.

He thinks she will find the effort endearing, when she is old enough to understand it.

When the cards are written he places them both in the glittery box. He shaves, showers, and brushes his teeth. He gets dressed slowly, picking out a T-shirt which he hasn't worn for years. He looks in the mirror for a long time, as though daring himself to keep it on. He packs a bag full of groceries he bought last night, along with a good blanket. Then he goes out.

The sky is full of clouds like glossy meringues laid on a pale blue plate, the air warm. Perfect for what he has in mind. Jem walks twenty minutes to Hayes' Cars. He found the place on his phone. There he speaks to a young man in a suit, who makes him sign a sheaf of forms before giving him the keys to a cherry-red Alfa Romeo Spider S2.

Jem listens politely to a lot of car chat but doesn't really take it in. He's not a car guy. All he wanted was a car that looks like it was made for fun, and this one is just that – a top-down carved-out red lipstick, smearing its way down the road, making everyone turn to get a proper look.

He puts his picnic bag on the back seat and drives off the forecourt, following the roads back to Sarah and Emily's house. There he gets out and hesitates. He looks down at the T-shirt he's wearing. He wants to change out of it. He has gone too far. But no, it's too late now. Be brave. He goes and rings the bell. Sarah opens the door and he sees the moment her eyes widen.

'Jem . . . '

'Hey; is Emily ready to come out?'

'Why are you wearing—?'

'Hey Jem.' Emily appears at the door and dutifully starts to put her shoes on. As though his visit is a chore to be ticked off. But then her attention slides onto the gorgeous slice of red behind him.

'Is that *your* car?' she asks.

'For today it is.'

Sarah forgets about the T-shirt.

'You're taking her in that? Do you even know how to drive it?'

'It's just a car.'

'Is it safe? It looks old. Has it even got seatbelts?'

'Yes and yes.'

Jem isn't watching Sarah; he's watching his daughter's face. There's something there. Not excitement, exactly, but curiosity. She looks up at him, then back to the car.

'Where are we going?'

'Anywhere you like, but I thought we could go somewhere green; I've brought a picnic.'

She thinks for a moment, then nods.

'Okay.'

'Hang on,' Sarah says. 'Emily—'

'It's fine, Mum; I'll see you later.'

She walks down the steps with Jem. She doesn't hold his hand, but waits for him to open the passenger door to let her in. He helps her with the seatbelt, then goes around to the driver's side. Sarah is still standing anxiously in the doorway. He ignores her. If he looks in Sarah's eyes, he will see her version of himself mirrored back. Untrustworthy, careless and uncaring. For the first time in a long time, he doesn't believe in Sarah's assessment. Her version of the past is just that – her version.

The engine makes a deliciously loud roar that becomes a sustained purr. Jem eases the car down the road. For a moment he is less sure of himself, now that Emily is in the car with him, but the moment passes. He watches out of the corner of his eye as she fiddles with the dash controls, turning on the radio and flicking through stations until she finds something she likes – a pop song as brightly coloured as the car – and turns the volume up. The sun comes out from behind a cloud and they speed on, in wordless accord.

Mika wakes in a stale-smelling room. In one corner there is a toilet without a seat. She lies on a thin mattress resting on two plastic boxes. The rest of the room is bare, the floor covered in spongy plastic. Easy to wipe clean, though it is streaked with mud. She hopes it's mud. There is a small window, which has white plastic-covered bars on it. The blanket on the bed is thin, but the room is oppressively hot.

The flooring is beige, except for a square in the middle which is darker brown, cut in to replace a damaged section. Mika wonders how it was damaged. Did someone start a fire? How would you get the materials to start a fire in this place? Or maybe someone attacked the flooring with their cutlery as an act of rebellion. The only cutlery she has seen was made of plastic. Perhaps that's why.

After getting in the van with the immigration officers, Mika had watched through the window as London went by, wondering if she would see it again. They passed Leicester Square, onto Coventry Street, and she had gazed with absurd longing at the tourist shops – Money Exchange, Cigarettes Mini Store, Best of Britannia. If they deported her, she wouldn't be allowed back, even as a tourist.

They had driven west, in the direction of Heathrow. Even though she has read the legislation, Mika was seized by the fear they were going to put her straight on a plane. Instead, they went through the gates of an anonymous but well-secured building, with a flat facade of beige brick, peppered with tiny windows. All the windows were barred.

The officers got out and escorted her inside. She wasn't handcuffed, but there was no way she could run. The gates had closed behind the van; the building and car park were ringed around by a chain-link fence with barbed wire. Inside they had taken her to a sort of reception, where her details were taken more formally and another body search performed.

'Careful, please; I'm pregnant.'

'You're pregnant?'

'Yes.'

The officer on the desk – a large woman with very pink, swollen hands, had looked annoyed by this.

'You're sure? Not pushing your belly out for special treatment? We'll find out if you're lying.'

'I'm six months along; the due date is January 8th.'

The woman sighed and fetched another form. Mika read the name of the form and recognised it: IS.91RA. She felt a little reassured by this formality. A copy of this form would be sent immediately to the Home Office caseworker who would deal with her case. Mika felt more confident that she might be allowed to leave, at least in the short term.

When all the necessary paperwork had been completed, her possessions logged and taken into custody, Mika had been shown away from the reception desk, down several corridors which required key cards to open them. The corridors were white, very brightly lit, with yellow doors. Mika could not put her finger on what felt so sinister about the place. She doesn't believe in bad energy – a building is a building – but the place gave her the creeps. As they walked, she heard distant shouting, then banging. They walked through a different corridor and she heard a low moaning that might have been a person.

Finally, she was shown to a room with a table and two chairs. There was a window but it was small, and too high in the wall to see through. The room was very warm and reeked of disinfectant.

'What's happening?' she asked.

'You're to wait here,' the officer had told her. 'For someone to interview you.'

'But—'

The door had already shut, and she listened to the lock turning. A heavy lock for what seemed a slight door. This building was a prison pretending to be something else.

Time passed, and no one came. Mika was ready to quote the law. There are special rules for the detention of pregnant women, she was ready to say. There are procedures, time limits. But no one came. There was no clock in the room and they had taken her phone, so there was no way for her to know how long had passed, but she guessed an hour, then two. The plastic chair was uncomfortable, but the floor looked as though it would be sticky. She started to feel that she must have been forgotten, and went to try the door. It was still locked, so she tried calling.

'Hello? Is anybody there? I need—'

She almost called out that she needed the bathroom, which was true, but she didn't want to give them the satisfaction of taking her dignity. Instead, she called again:

'Hello? I need to see someone. I need to speak to a Home Office caseworker.'

She had gone on, for a while. No one came. Next, she

tried banging the door. When that didn't seem enough, she kicked it. Eventually she gave up and sat down. Her bladder was aching. She was thirsty. The oppressive heat was making her groggy and stupid. What time of day was it? There was still light outside the little window, but at this time of year the sky stays light until eight.

Another half hour seemed to pass, and she was facing the prospect of urinating on the floor like an animal, when finally there was noise in the corridor and the sound of the door being unlocked. It was a new officer, male, unshaven. Mika didn't say anything.

'Come on,' the officer said, loudly, as though coaxing an animal. 'We've got a room for you.'

'I need to see a Home Office caseworker,' she said. The officer had looked a little surprised.

'Why?'

'Because . . . ' Mika had floundered for a moment. 'Because the legislation—'

'We know the legislation here, miss. All the caseworkers are busy, so you'll be waiting until tomorrow.'

'Wait?'

'You're lucky. They're giving you a room to yourself on account of you being up the duff.'

'I'm staying overnight?'

The officer had laughed at that.

'Did you think you was here for a nice chat? Cup of tea? Come on now, let's be moving.'

She had walked through those bright-lit, sunless corridors, until they came to something which might have been a central space. Here the facade fell away – this was a prison, pure and simple. A large area over two floors, with a guard rail around the upper floor, all lined with anonymous doors. The middle of the room was filled with tables and chairs, all bolted to the floor – a dining area for the inmates, she guessed.

The officer led her up one of the metal staircases to the upper level, by the top of which he was breathing heavily, then took her down to a door which he unlocked.

'There you go; home sweet home. We'll be getting you out for dinner soon enough though so don't get too comfy.'

Mika stepped into the room, for there was little else to do. The door closed behind her, and that was it. She waited five minutes, out of fear that he would return, or that someone was watching through a peephole in the door, before relieving herself in the toilet, holding herself against the wall so as not to touch the bare porcelain. Then she had gone to the bed and rolled up the thin cover, propping it with the pillow to give her something to lean back against.

Finally, she had wept.

'Why are you wearing that T-shirt?'

Jem feels his breath catch at the question. They are walking through the woods at Box Hill. The car is parked further down. Jem is worried about leaving it, uncovered and out of his sight, but tries not to show it. He wants Emily to see how easy he is, how carefree. He wants her to see that he can be fun.

'I just like it,' he says. 'Why do you ask?'

Emily shrugs, not looking sideways.

'It was his favourite.'

'Yes,' he says. 'I wasn't sure if you'd remember that.'

She nods, slowly. 'He liked the picture of the boat on it. He shouted "boat, boat!" every time you wore it.'

The T-shirt is plain white, with a design printed on the front in black lines that are faded with age. It shows a lake below a mountain range, with an empty rowing boat moored on the shore. The boat's hull makes ripples on the surface of the lake. He can't remember where he got it from. Maybe it was a gift from Sarah, or a friend. He stopped wearing it four years ago.

'It's nice that you remember that.'

Emily says nothing in return, and Jem cringes at his words. What does 'nice' mean? And why would it be nice for Emily to remember her brother? There's nothing nice about it. There is only the memory, and everything that came after it.

They walk on, up a short rise where wooden planks have been sunk in the earth to form steps. The ground around them is covered by old leaves, tangled through by mossy tree roots. There are other people, up and down the path, but Jem feels more alone with his daughter than he can remember since she was a baby. Somewhere nearby, he hears the *thrup-thrup* of a woodpecker drilling a hole.

'How are things at school?'

Emily frowns but still says nothing. Jem feels sure he is losing her, and doesn't push further for fear of accelerating towards total silence. They come to the top of a rise and walk towards a window of sky, barred by trees. They walk through the trees, and Emily makes a small noise of delight. Below them the landscape is hazy, soft with clusters of deciduous trees, wide open in every direction.

They spread the blanket he has brought, and he unpacks the picnic – supermarket sandwiches, crisps and a can each of fizzy grapefruit. It's a lazy picnic, but the saving grace is the cake, which he baked last night. He hasn't baked for years, and had to buy a new loaf tin. The cake is the last thing in the bag, wrapped in cling film.

'Is that—?'

'Lemon drizzle. I don't know if it's still your favourite . . .'

'I quite like carrot cake now,' Emily says; Jem's heart sinks, then she says: 'This is still probably my *second* favourite though.'

They sit and eat a while in silence. The sun comes and goes but the air is warm and muggy. Little insects buzz around, dipping into the clumps of wildflowers that dot the field. Jem watches a tiny bird on the wing which may or may not be a willow tit. They're so rare, it's more likely to be a juvenile bird of a more common species, but today is the sort of day for believing in the uncommon and unlikely.

'I do have memories of him,' Emily says.

'Oh?'

'Five.'

'Five . . . memories?'

'Proper ones, I mean. Not just stuff that happened every day like having breakfast. Those aren't proper memories.'

Jem feels as though he's filling up with dark water. Any minute now it will brim out of him. The idea of Emily's memories being so few, and so carefully accounted for, is unbearable. He wants and desperately doesn't want to ask what the memories are. Eventually, the wanting wins out.

'What are they? Your memories.'

'First there's the T-shirt one,' Emily says matter-of-factly. '"Boat boat!"'

'Okay.'

'And then there's the time we went to the zoo, and we

went in the butterfly house, and that huge butterfly landed on his nose . . . '

'Oh—' Jem exhales softly. He has not remembered this for such a long time, but there the memory is, safely folded up in his brain.

'And he screamed and screamed! Wouldn't stop screaming. But then, when we got to the shop, he wanted all the butterfly things. The postcards, the toys. You got him the butterfly plushie.'

Jem laughs, and Emily smiles to have made him laugh.

'The next memory is sitting on the step with him, while you and Mum packed the car to go on holiday.'

'Which holiday?'

'Don't remember. I don't even remember the holiday, just the sitting on the step, waiting to go.'

'That's lovely . . . '

'And then there's when he was so cross with you for not letting him watch *Postman Pat* that he pulled down his nappy and did a wee in your shoes.'

They start to laugh, both at the same time. They laugh and laugh until the tears come. Jem is glad of the laughter, because it excuses the tears, which were coming anyway. He wipes his eyes.

'What's the last one?'

Emily pauses, and the smile fades from her face.

'The last one . . . isn't a very happy one.'

A cloud passes over the sun, and the colours of the landscape change, as though an artist has mixed in blues and purples with the greens and golds. There's a word for that, Jem thinks, or a phrase. When nature mirrors your feelings. Perfect failure, something like that.

'You don't have to tell me.'

'No, I won't,' Emily nods.

They sit a while in silence, looking at the landscape. The cloud passes over them, the sun comes out, and they watch as the shadow chases down the hill, swooping over other people.

'Can we have some cake now?'

Later, they walk down the hill. They don't talk much, but it is a happy sort of silence. Halfway down, her hand reaches out to find his, and he blinks a few times before squeezing it back. As they're getting into the car – still mercifully there and untouched – he spots an early sycamore seed which has tumbled down onto his seat. Full of a new belief in omens, Jem places the samara carefully in his wallet.

'It's not been great . . . ' Emily says, and Jem is briefly concerned that she's talking about today. 'At school, I mean. You asked, before.'

'Oh. I'm sorry . . . '

'I posted some things online. Geeky things about what I was reading. And some girls from my class made fun of me. I took it all down, but . . . '

She trails off. Jem isn't sure what to say. He is so out of practice with this kind of everyday, proper parenting. The kind of parenting where it feels as though someone has handed you a pocket watch with the back taken off, all the delicate springs and bearings exposed.

'I'm sorry; that's awful.'

Emily nods slowly, her eyebrows tenting together in the middle. Jem takes a chance, reaches his arm out and hugs her to him. She doesn't resist. He doesn't say anything, or offer any advice.

'Thanks for telling me.'

She nods into his chest, then pulls away.

'Shall we go?'

'Yeah, let's.'

While Emily buckles herself in, he quickly checks his phone, but there are no messages or missed calls from Mika. For a moment he worries, remembering the dream, the figure disappearing into the crowds. Then he makes himself relax – it's nothing, don't be paranoid – and guns the engine to life.

17

A night passes.

Two hundred and nineteen billion emails are sent. Six hundred thousand new websites are created. Four billion likes are given on social media. There are one hundred and ninety-four billion Google searches, twenty-four million of which are for pornography. Fifty-eight billion WhatsApp messages are sent. Information crackles around the planet and through its skies, completely invisible. Humans walk through a library of information, every second, without ever knowing it.

Six million and sixty thousand tonnes of cargo will be transported today. Shipping containers of bananas, flat-pack wardrobes and trainers will cross time zones and international borders freely. Around the world, eleven and a half million people are in prison.

A rap at the door tells Mika it's time for breakfast. She gets up and straightens the covers. She's not sure why; there's not much else to do. She feels no excitement for the meal, after what they served last night. It had been some sort of 'British' fare – stew and mashed potato, or possibly a deconstructed shepherd's pie – but so awful (the mash watery and metallic, the stew boiled to a pulp) as though to make the food part of their punishment. The Worst of British.

She had eaten it, because there was nothing else. She had thought of the child inside her, felt its still-feeble kicks. The people around her had eaten it too, without wincing or pulling a face, so she knew this meal was no aberration. She had watched their faces as she ate, though none of them looked back at her. Some talked among themselves, where they spoke the same language, while one or two others spoke to themselves, in a low monologue, as though keeping themselves company. From these snatches of language Mika pieced together nationalities – Iranian, Iraqi, Syrian, Albanian, Vietnamese. One woman spoke in English about her homeland, Eritrea. She heard another conversation in Polish – a language she knows – but didn't try to join in.

There is a clunk as a key is pressed into the lock of her door. Against hope, she imagines it will be her Home Office caseworker, with a sheaf of papers and a flustered look of apology. But it is yet another officer (how many work here?) with eyes still bloodshot from the night before.

'Come on: out.'

She shuffles out into the clamour of the main hall, with the smell of breakfast already turning her stomach.

It is sometime after lunch when Mika is fetched from her cell and taken to another anonymous room somewhere else in the building. On the other side of the table is a man who, finally, is a Home Office caseworker. An officer stands by the door. As though she might attack this man. As though she's a criminal. They greet each other and shake hands, and sit on either side of the table. It feels like an interview for a job she doesn't want.

'The legislation—' Mika begins, but is silenced by the caseworker's hand in the air as he reads through her notes. She sits and waits, clenching and unclenching her fists. After a long minute, he says:

'You came here on a visa which has now expired. Agreed?'

'Yes, but—'

Again, the hand in the air. The caseworker looks relieved by her admission, as though it will save him a lot of work. The bags under his eyes are pale purple, like ripening plums.

'Miss Zielinska, we have a few things to run through here, details to take, but let me cut to the chase – you need to leave the country. You don't have what we call "leave to remain".'

'Are you deporting me?'

She is surprised by how small her voice sounds.

'You seem like a bright young woman, so I'll be upfront with you. I'm not supposed to, but it'll save both of us time. So long as you don't give me any reason in this interview to believe you're going to abscond, you can leave here today.'

'Oh . . . ' she breathes a shaky sigh.

'So – let's run through the paperwork, and hopefully we'll have you out of here in an hour or so. Then you'll have a set number of days to leave the country. You'll need to stay in touch with me and respond to any requests from the Home Office. Is that acceptable?'

He looks at her levelly. She knows he's not doing this

by the book. The officer by the door probably knows it too. The caseworker is cutting corners, saving time, and wants her to play along.

'Yes, that's fine.'

He nods quickly and takes his pen out.

Time passes.

Jem sends thirteen messages, starting off casual, then joke-concerned, then openly concerned. When the last message has gone unread for two hours, he tries calling, and hears the automated message:

'The number you have called is currently unavailable.'

It has been four days since they lay together in the park, with the world at their backs. He tries to think through the possible explanations. Her phone has broken. She lost her job at the café and hasn't been able to charge her phone. He misread everything about the other day and she doesn't want to see him any more.

He paces around his flat, until the leg that was broken in the accident starts to ache. He calls one more time, then leaves the flat and gets on the Tube. By the time he reaches Hoban's, it's the middle of the afternoon. Thunder clouds are curdling from the milky sky. He pushes through the door and stands, waiting for Tamara to spot him. Two of the tables are occupied, and everyone stares at him, but he doesn't sit down. He can barely resist the urge to push through into the kitchen. He expects he will see Mika there, dolloping pancake batter onto the hotplate. She will turn around and look confused and smile at his worry—

'Can I help you?'

The person in front of him isn't Tamara, but a boy a

few years older with a lip piercing and a strong family resemblance.

'I'm here to see Mika.'

'You know her?'

'I haven't been able to get in touch for a few days.'

'You haven't heard?'

Jem's stomach twists.

'Heard what?'

The boy glances over his shoulder, towards the kitchen.

'Maybe you should talk to Dad . . . '

He leads Jem back into the heat and humidity of the kitchen. Kenny is practically idle – standing at the grill, watching some eggs while chopping up pre-fried bacon. He sees Jem and his eyes go wide.

'You!'

'Yeah, I—'

'Do you know where she is? Have you heard anything?'

'She's *missing*?'

Jem thinks back to saying goodbye, the busy street in Chinatown. Had something happened on the way back? Perhaps something happened as soon as he lost sight of her in the crowd. He thinks of muggings turned nasty, random stabbings, kidnap and rape.

'Some Home Office motherfuckers turned up here, arrested Mika before we had a chance to warn her; we haven't heard anything since then.'

Jem opens and shuts his mouth like a fish on land, but no words come out.

'You knew her visa had expired, right?'

'Visa?'

'We're all worried. To hear nothing seems wrong. I tried phoning up but they kept telling me I wasn't authorised to speak to anyone . . . Hey, are you okay? You've gone a funny colour. Do you want to sit down? I'll fix you something to eat if you—'

That's the last thing Jem hears. Quicker than the last time, the darkness sweeps in from either side of his vision like black curtains.

Time passes, with Jem quite unaware of it. This is how it was before you were born; this is how it will be after you die. Life goes on – the births and the deaths, the coming togethers and the falling aparts, the rememberings and forgettings, the single flower of the universe with its infinite petals, always blooming and always wilting away. When Jem wakes, he has no idea how long he's been asleep. It could have been five minutes or five millennia. He has been outside of life, not asleep but beyond it.

He takes stock of the information his rebooted senses are sending to him. He is on his back, somewhere not especially comfortable. The air is hot and bad-smelling and there seems to be no cover over him. There is background noise consisting of murmured voices, electronic beeps and footsteps on a plastic surface. Over that are louder, one-off noises – a distant cry of pain, a trilling mobile phone, a quartet of squeaky wheels as something like a trolley passes nearby.

The light is very bright, but Jem forces his eyes to open. They immediately start to water, but he turns his head to the side. Everything is sideways – people sitting on plastic chairs are stacked floor to ceiling, a person in medical scrubs spider-climbs the wall.

He is in hospital.

Or, at least, the waiting room of a hospital. Nobody

seems to be paying him any attention, so he's probably fine. Not dying, at least. The room is very busy. How did he get here? Jem reviews his memories, replaying the conversation with Kenny.

Oh.

Mika is gone. Perhaps forever. She may already be out of the country. Where would they have sent her? Would they send her home? Or would it be like that awful policy he'd half-read about? A shady deal with another country to take unwanted people, the same way they sent plastic recycling to sit in Chinese landfills.

He sits up.

The room does not spin; no dark curtain falls over his vision. His body is his own. He looks at his phone. Roughly four hours have passed since he was at Hoban's. This is terrifying and reassuring in different ways. He gets off the trolley he has been left on. A person in blue scrubs and face mask, seeing this, comes over.

'You should lie down, sir.'

'I'm fine.'

'You were unconscious.'

'It doesn't seem like anyone here was too concerned.'

'We're *extremely* busy. You're first in queue for the MRI—'

'How long have I been waiting here?'

'The patients most in need are seen first. Your vitals were stable. But that's not to say your condition isn't potentially—'

'Okay, but I'm leaving.'

'Sir, please—'

'Is there anything I need to do before I leave?'

'You . . . no. That's your choice. But I would ask you—'

Jem doesn't wait to hear what they say to him. He's already walking out, through the sliding doors, to the cooler air beyond. He uses his phone to order a taxi, rides it home and makes a visit to the supermarket on the ground level of his building. He buys a six-pack of lager, a bottle of vodka, a two-litre of lemonade, and a microwaveable sweet and sour chicken 'banquet' with three spring rolls. He goes up to his flat, puts the meal on to heat up, opens the first beer and starts writing a card to Emily.

He writes two cards before the meal pings, eats half of it with a second beer, then writes two more cards before his handwriting starts to get sloppy. He retreats to the sofa with the vodka and lemonade, pays £3.99 for a heist movie he has no interest in, and settles into the work of once more losing consciousness.

Later, seventy-two minutes into the movie ('tell me again. Tell me again how I've failed her; I'll blow your fucking brains out'), Jem staggers to the bathroom to urinate. While there, he fumbles his wallet out of his jeans pocket, looking for something without quite knowing why. He pulls out all the bank cards and receipts, shakes the wallet upside down. There it is – the sycamore seed tumbles free, but its fragile wing has been crushed. Instead of spiralling down, it falls to the tiles.

The rest of September passes, for Jem, without variation. His heart is not, in the words of the song, ringin' in the key his soul is singin'. The stars do not steal the night away. He buys more microwaveable meals that he can't bring himself to finish. More cheap alcohol with cheap mixers. He stops paying for movies (his savings are starting to look less fulsome than they did when he quit the bank), and subsists on a thin gruel of daytime TV. It's easier than choosing something to watch. He will fall asleep in the afternoon and wake up when it gets dark. He stays awake until the early hours of the morning, then takes a couple of over-the-counter sleeping pills.

The only real task he sets himself each day is to write a card for Emily. He does it mid-morning, when he's most awake, and takes his time over it. In some he does a little drawing, in others he attempts silly poems – limericks and doggerel. Writing the card is the best bit of his day. Perhaps that's why he only allows himself one. Go too fast and he'll run out of occasions.

Sometimes, he thinks of the bargain he made with the universe. He thinks of that word – 'adventure', and how he's betraying it. Mostly he thinks of Mika, like a song he can't get out of his head. He tells himself it's not heartbreak. It's sadness that she is gone, disappointment that their strange adventure is over, grief at the sudden loss of contact, worry over her safety. Heartbreak is for people in real relationships; he and Mika had no relationship.

And yet, and yet, and yet – the weight of it leaves him breathless. That's why he spends so much time trying to feel nothing. He's holding his breath underwater, waiting for the tsunami to pass.

He tries calling the Home Office. Then, when he gets nowhere with that, he tries calling the police, who refer him back to the Home Office. He calls up the posh restaurant she used to work at and asks if anyone there knows where she is, but the woman he speaks to seems suspicious of his motives, and says she can't help him. He drinks a lot and eats less and less.

Around the world, people are eating. People are spooning

food into each other's mouths. Children are sharing chocolate with their stuffed toys. People are eating spaghetti, hamburgers, cans of food substitute, rice noodles, cornbread with coffee. Porn stars are fellating bananas and lollypops, among other things. People are getting sandwiches from the trolley, ten kilometres in the air. Another four hundred kilometres above them, astronauts are eating peanut butter and jelly sandwiches (made with tortillas for fewer crumbs).

Around the world, people are starving.

Hollow-cheeked babies suckle at breasts which give no sustenance. Teens who can count every rib are waiting to see a doctor. Men, with arms outstretched, jostle closer to the aid truck where loaves of bread and bags of rice are being thrown into the crowd. People are lying in dark rooms with their hunger, waiting for it to end.

Jem sleeps.

18

Night fell over the palace.

When they had finished carousing in the marriage bed, Shahrazad once more asked the Shah Shahryar to see her sister, that they might spend her final hours together, and the Sultan assented.

'Tell me, O sister,' spoke Dunyazad, 'for the night is long and we cannot sleep, some story to while away the hours before the sad sunrise.'

'If our cultured King permits,' said Shahrazad, and the Shah Shahryar – who was restless, and dearly loved a tale – once more agreed. And without ado, Shahrazad began –

THE TALE OF THE KING AND THE BEDOUIN

It hath reached me, O auspicious King, that in past times, in the far history of the world, there was a Bedouin, a desert-wanderer, who went from place to place, trading goods in exchange for food and wine.

Now it so happened that one evening, the Bedouin was

sitting on a dune, eating a loaf of bread. The bread had been baked three days before, and the Bedouin softened it in his mouth with the watered-down wine from his goat-skin. His camel was resting a little way away, chewing at nothing in particular. The desert around him was as wide and flat as the unleavened bread in his hand. Still, the desert was beautiful to him at this time of day, with the heat of the day passed and night approaching. Soon it would become cooler, the sand a richer gold, the shadows stretching luxuriously.

Now the Bedouin had crossed the desert many times, and regarded his wandering as freedom. He saw and heard many things which the *ḥāḍir* – the settled people – were ignorant of. He heard the songs that the dunes sang in harmony when the wind blew. He saw the snakes and scorpions which live in dunes and do not come into the towns. He heard the eagle's cry from the heights.

'Maybe this is not freedom,' the Bedouin said to himself. 'Maybe it is only stretching out the walk between bed and grindstone.' But this is not what he knew in his heart.

The Bedouin was about to reach into his bag, to pull out the last piece of fruit he had for this journey – a date – when something caught his eye on the horizon. It was a wink of light, such as might catch your eye from a pool of water, or a drop of dew. Now the desert is full of light, but rarely does it wink. Desert light is broken into a million million grains, like the sand itself. Rarely does it condense into a droplet.

The Bedouin focussed all his attention on the horizon, and there it was again – a wink of light, pure as a raindrop. Then it was gone again. Then, there it was again. Another, and another! The Bedouin stood on his dune, feeling his feet slip a little under him. But there was nothing more to be seen, only the winks of light, cradled between two hills on the horizon.

Now, the Bedouin had travelled many days and nights in the desert, and his travels had made him both wary and wise. Or perhaps it is better to say his travels had taught him the wisdom of being wary. He knew he should walk away, not in the direction of the lights, but south. It was another day and a half until he reached the town which was his destination. He had enough water, wine and bread to last two days more, because he was prudent, and always planned for a longer journey. It was imprudent to take diversions. Still, those winks of light . . .

The Bedouin sat down again on his dune.

So it came to pass that, over the next hour, the winks of light grew in number until they filled the small valley, twinkling like a handful of gold at the bottom of a well. Slowly, the Bedouin's keen eyes were able to pick out shapes against the dunes. Certainly there were camels, and men on foot. Perhaps there were even horses.

Now, it was not such an uncommon thing to see other people in the desert, vast as it was, because the paths were well travelled. What was uncommon was the way the light shone off these people, or something they were carrying. Perhaps they were soldiers, the Bedouin thought, with spears and halberds. The Bedouin had seen the soldiers of many places, in all sorts of livery, shabby and grand. But if these were soldiers, he had never seen so many in one place. If this was an army, he was afraid of what it was riding towards.

He knew it would be wise to leave; if he stayed where he was, they would pass no more than forty paces from where he sat. He would be on display to all those mounted men. The Bedouin had heard stories of nomads being press-ganged into the service of foreign armies. He had heard stories of men being run through for sport. He had heard worse: the fates of men who stood their ground.

The Bedouin stood his ground.

By the time the heralds reached him, the Bedouin had realised what a vast procession this was. It stretched as far as he could see, and they were still coming. He imagined the procession stretching from horizon to horizon, and felt dizzy. They walked three abreast, holding sand-stained banners. They wore brocade and Persian silks – rich blues, greens and pinks – which looked alien to the desert, like flowers from the coast. Behind them, riders on horseback carried trumpets and drums. If any noticed the Bedouin, they did not seem to care about the desert-dweller, crouched on a dune. He looked no different to them than a fennec fox, a wild thing staring back with wild eyes.

After the riders came slaves (for, although they too were dressed in Persian silk, the Bedouin knew a slave when he saw one), each bearing a golden staff. The staffs twisted like coiling snakes, and ended at the top with different shapes – a globe, a crown, a fish, a horse, a hand. Though the slaves were muscular young men, and the staffs were slender, still they seemed to concentrate on holding them. The muscles in their arms bulged, as though they were carrying real weight. It seemed impossible, the Bedouin thought, but the staffs gave every appearance of being solid gold.

There were hundreds of men. At regular intervals there were soldiers on horseback, with boots to their knees, resting one hand on the pommel of their swords. They were the only ones to eye the Bedouin.

Behind the slaves carrying staffs came the slaves carrying plates. Each plate was loaded with gold bars. Behind them came the camels, with saddlebags whose contents pulled heavily for objects so small – more gold. Gold to be carried, gold to be worn, gold ground to dust. Even if only a tiny fraction of it was real, the Bedouin knew he was staring at more wealth than he had seen in his lifetime. A thousand lifetimes! Where were these men from, heaven? Or perhaps they were djinn? They looked mortal enough: their hands were calloused, their dark skin was slick with sweat. It seemed as though all the wealth of the Earth had risen up to march somewhere else.

There were women too, their heads covered, their silks wound round with chains of gold, their wrists and ankles clinking with bracelets that might be manacles. The Bedouin smelled perfumes on the breeze – rose water, opopanax, myrrh – mixing into a single, heady fug. Proving the procession was no ghostly apparition were baggage trains of food and drink, of firewood and charcoal, rolled fabric and tent poles. There was a blacksmith and his attendants. There were water carriers with their barrels. There were physicians with their boxes of herbs and oils, saws and sickles dangling from their belts.

After many hundreds of men and women, camels and horses had passed him by, the Bedouin sank into a strange lethargy. It may seem strange that such a spectacle could make a man bored, but he was. The soft tramping through the sand of so many feet was soporific. The blaze of wealth numbed him, made him feel that nothing mattered, not even his own life. Night was falling. The glittering on the horizon faded, as though the procession was carrying the sun's stolen gold into the night. At last they stopped coming, and the Bedouin could see the end of the procession approaching.

It was then that he saw her.

One of the women from the procession, wrapped in the same silks and chains as the others, broke step. His eye was drawn to her, the only variation in the endless monotony. She stumbled once, regained her footing, then stumbled again and fell. She was at the outside of the column, so they barely had to move around her, and the procession kept marching. She lay on the sand, propped on her elbows but unable to raise her head.

The Bedouin watched, waiting for the mounted men to offer help, but they seemed not to see. It was as though no one dared break step. The woman tried to rise again, pushing herself up a little, but her hands slipped in the sand.

He knew he should not do it.

He knew he should not.

If it had been foolish to stay put in the first place, it was doubly foolish to get closer.

The Bedouin stood, feeling his legs ache after so long sitting. With a soothing word to his camel, he started down the dune, towards the fallen woman. He approached slowly, his hands raised to his chest. Like many nomads, the Bedouin carried a sword for self-defence, but he didn't want anybody thinking he might use it. He should have left it with the baggage, but it was too late for that. Now he saw eyes turning towards him – he was no longer a part of the desert scenery. He was a threat. Nevertheless, nobody stepped out of line. He got close, enough that the sound of feet marching in unison and metal jangling filled his ears like the ocean.

He stooped down to the woman.

'Are you alright?'

He asked it in his native tongue, which was common enough to the peoples of the desert, but the woman did not understand him. She kept her head down, her face covered by her hood, one cheek pressed to the sand. The Bedouin repeated the question in several languages, some of which he knew well, some of which he knew only enough to trade in. Out of desperation he tried a Manding language, and she murmured in response:

'Thirsty . . . '

'I have watered wine if you would like it?'

The woman nodded feebly. The procession marched on above them; it was now a rank of slaves bearing yoked baskets. The Bedouin could not see what the baskets were filled with, but it seemed likely they were more gold. He took out his goatskin of watered-down wine.

'You'll need to roll over.'

With great effort the woman did so, rolling onto her back.

'May I?'

The Bedouin gestured to the veil the woman was wearing and the woman nodded once again. Tentatively, knowing he risked the wrath of the army at his shoulder, he pulled back the veil.

The strangest, sharpest feeling came upon him then, an alloy of homesickness and homecoming, nostalgia and new beginnings. He remembered everything. Or at least, everything was there to be remembered, as though, from the horizon of his brain, an army was marching towards him, bearing endless memories. But whose memories? His own, he supposed, but from long ago, when he wore a different body. His ancestors, yes, but also himself. In the woman's eyes, the Bedouin saw an expression matching his own. He said:

'Jem?'

The woman opened her mouth, but no sound came from her dry throat. The Bedouin saw the desperation in her eyes and remembered.

'I'm sorry – here.'

He brought the goatskin of wine to her cracked lips and watched as she drank like a babe at the teat. In that long moment, he sorted through his treasure trove of memories, his lost inheritance. It seemed to him far greater than the wealth of gold before him. The Bedouin remembered the woman's eyes, the irises soft brown, the lashes very dark, the way they sloped down so finely that she always looked melancholy, even when smiling. He remembered she was not always a woman, just as he was not always a man.

The jumble of their past lives, folded back and forth like a paper fan so that they sat next to one another, bewildering him. Looking into her eyes, the Bedouin remembered places he had not been, people he had not met. When the woman had finished drinking, there was nothing left in the goatskin, but the Bedouin did not care.

'Do you want more? On my camel . . . '

'I should leave you some.'

'Do you remember also?'

'Yes.'

There was no need for them to elaborate, for they both understood. Their lives were a fretted filigree, intertwined.

'I can't believe I found you,' the Bedouin said.

'I can't believe I was lost.'

'How long has it been?'

'A marketplace. Where was it? A place I have never been, in this lifetime.'

'But I don't remember seeing you there?'

'You didn't; I saw you in the crowds but you kept walking. By the time I remembered, you had already gone.'

The lovers – for that is what they were, in the great scheme of things – stared at each other in silence for a while, as though neither dared to look away lest the object of their gaze disappeared like a phantom. The sky was getting darker now; some of the passing figures lit torches. He asked her:

'What is all this? Where have you come from?'

'You don't know?'

'I've not heard.'

'We came from Timbuktu. Our merciful lord, Mansa Musa, son of Kanku, is making his pilgrimage to Mecca.'

'A pilgrimage? I thought you had looted a city.'

'This is money for giving away. Only a fraction of his wealth. They say he is the wealthiest man in the world.'

The Bedouin believed it.

'Can you get up?'

'I don't know . . . I feel weak. I wish I'd never come on this journey, but I had no choice. I miss my home.'

The Bedouin wanted to take her away from this, to carry her up the dune and put her on his camel and find a way back to Timbuktu. He could not imagine what his life would be there, could not imagine married life, just as a man who has lived all his life in the desert cannot imagine the ocean.

He knew that if he tried to help her away from the procession, he would be stopped. It would not look well for him, a desert-wanderer, to be carrying this noblewoman away from her people. Besides, there was gold on her ankles and wrists. Men do not become wealthy by allowing their wealth to get up and walk away. She asked him:

'What do we do?'

'I don't know . . . perhaps we can wait until they've passed?'

No sooner had the Bedouin said it than a cry went up from somewhere in the procession, and the cry carried back, and back again to someone else. For a second, the Bedouin thought they would get away with it. Nothing happened.

Horns blared.

It started as one or two, then it was picked up by other horns in the procession, a message spreading both ways down the line, until the desert air rang with a single wail. And as the sound hit each pair of ears, that person stopped. Tens of thousands of feet stood still. The horns fell silent. Nobody spoke. Only the animals made their noises, groaning and whinnying, stamping at the ground, desperate to rest. Above them, the Milky Way unfurled its banner.

Now the Bedouin heard voices, the voices who were permitted to speak. From somewhere in the procession there was the sound of bodies dismounting, thudding onto the soft sand, and footsteps coming in their direction. Through the crowd he saw a man, very splendidly dressed, flanked by soldiers who in other company would have looked like kings. At his side, he heard the woman softly cry out. Hastily, she pulled down her veil.

'What is the meaning of this?'

The man stood before the Bedouin. Under all his finery he was very slender, his skin very dark, with high cheek-bones and eyes bloodshot from the sun and sand. The Bedouin knew, without being told, that this was the king she had spoken of; this was the man for whom this procession was assembled.

'My lord . . . '

'Bow your head!' one of the soldiers barked at him, putting his hand to his sword.

The Bedouin did so, arranging himself on the sand in supplication.

'Apologies, my lord; I am only a trader of these parts, I have no manners. But I saw this lady fall and wished to help her.'

'Is this true?'

The king looked sanguine, faintly amused. The Bedouin thought that such a man must be bored after so long travelling. Such a man must be used to every kind of entertainment, and unused to keeping himself company on a long journey. The woman spoke, very quietly.

'My lord, it is true. I fell because I was lightheaded, and this man . . . ' She hesitated, unsure of how to refer to him as a stranger. 'This man gave me water to drink and asked nothing in return.'

Mansa Musa thought for a second, then nodded. Two soldiers stepped forward and helped her to her feet. She stood unsteadily. The Bedouin was thinking fast. He no longer cared about being careful; all he wanted was to escape with her. If he could not escape with her, he would have to join her on this march across the world. The king – she had said he was the wealthiest man in the world – spoke again.

'I am grateful for the kindness you have shown. Allah looks favourably upon those who help the needy. You shall have your skin of water replenished, of course.'

'Thank you, my lord.'

'Is there anything else you desire?'

The Bedouin found he was trembling.

'I have seen your great wealth, my lord, and it is like nothing else under the sun . . . '

He paused as long as he dared, glancing at the face of the king. Mansa Musa did not look angry but disappointed; he had hoped this nomad would show him something different.

'But I do not wish for a reward in gold, my lord, nor to delay any further your holy pilgrimage.'

'If not gold, then what?'

'My lord, might I join you? I am adept at surviving in the desert, and I have my own camel. I only wish to travel with you on your hajj, that I might give thanks.'

'You are of the prophet's faith?'

The Bedouin could not say yes, for fear of being found a liar.

'I have heard much, and wish to convert, my lord.'

The king seemed to consider for a moment, turning the idea over, yes or no, like a coin. The woman waited behind him, watching the Bedouin with dark eyes. The king was going to say yes, he could see it on his face. Mansa Musa opened his mouth to speak when a man came up behind him. He spoke to the king:

'My lord . . . '

'What is it?'

'A report just back from one of the advance riders, which you may wish to read . . . '

'Hand it here.'

Mansa Musa read for a moment. Nobody said anything. He huffed a little at whatever was written and snapped the wax tablet shut.

'Get ready to march again; we should go further before we stop. Load her onto one of the wagons so she may rest.'

The soldiers started to lead her away; the king turned.

'My lord—?' the Bedouin called out, trying not to sound desperate. Mansa Musa turned back.

'Ah, yes . . . I do not require any more riders in my retinue, let alone those whose trust is not yet earned. I'm sure you understand. Have this for your trouble—'

The king took a gold ring from his finger and handed it over. It was more wealth than the Bedouin had possessed in his lifetime, yet it seemed to him quite worthless.

'Maybe you will use it to buy enlightenment. Go well, traveller.'

The Bedouin dared not argue. He did not wish to know what would happen if he spurned the king's benevolence. He watched as the woman disappeared into the crowd, craning to look over her shoulder. They were still watching him, all those assembled people, out of the corners of their eyes. The horns blared again, the sound spread both ways down the line, and sixty thousand people picked up their feet and went back to marching. The Bedouin stepped back and watched as Mansa Musa rode by, high on a black stallion.

He could not see her.

He watched as the procession moved on. It was only when the last of them had gone past – a standard bearer with a set grimace – that he remembered his goatskin was still empty. He dared not try to join the procession, for fear of the soldiers turning against him. The best he could do was go to the nearest town, trade what he had for water and food, and follow on behind. Sooner or later, he thought, he would catch up with the pilgrimage. This the Bedouin promised himself – he would find her. He would follow wherever she went. One way or another, they would be together.

'I will not trade the gold ring,' he swore aloud. 'I will save it, keep it safe. One day it shall be her wedding ring.'

At this point Shahrazad, seeing the first sunbeam touch the minarets of the Sultan's palace, left off her story once more.

'What a strange tale this is,' said Dunyazad.

'Indeed it is,' said Shahrazad. 'But it is nothing to what shall follow, if my lord will spare my life until the coming night.'

'By Allah,' the Sultan said to himself, 'I shall not kill her until I have heard the whole of the tale.'

So he went forth into his court, and the shroud they had made for Shahrazad went another day unused. When night came, the Sultan once more joined her in the marriage bed, and when they had caroused, and Dunyazad had been called for, she continued her tale—

October

19

The new month begins with showers, sluicing down the sun-sticky pavements and extinguishing summer barbecues. From space, Earth shows her scars without pride or shame. There is the old wound torn through California, above the San Andreas fault. There is Uluru, eroded into a lone island of rock by 500 million years of wind and weather. There are newer changes, not all destructive. In the South Pacific, over a matter of weeks, two previously separate islands are joined by an underwater eruption. A ring-tailed possum, who has lived all her life on one island, puts a tentative foot on the bridge of black rock, wondering where it might lead.

It's past midday, and Jem has just woken on the sofa, still groggy from the effects of the sleeping pills. He will take his time, find his way to the coffee machine before settling into the morning talk shows. Vaguely he remembers a dream, some hours ago, which was unlike the others. He reaches out to his phone, so that he can put something mindless on the TV, which is still on, scrolling through a

screensaver selection of beautiful landscapes – Grand
Canyon, snow-capped mountain, rice field . . .

There is a message on his phone.

In the last two weeks he has received barely any messages.
Lucas is away on holiday in Gran Canaria with his young
family. His brothers are too busy to notice anything out of
the ordinary with him. His mother doesn't do messages. He
ignores her, each time she calls, then sends a message to say
he is busy but keeping well. He no longer has work getting
in touch. After that it's just companies selling him stuff.

His eyes are blurry, even after blinking a few times, so
he puts the phone down and gets up. He goes to the bathroom, relieves himself, splashes cold water on his face. The
world comes into focus a little, and he looks at himself in
the mirror. How long since he looked at his own reflection?
The face in the mirror belongs to a stranger. This man is
thinner than Jem, his cheeks hollow, dark bags under the
eyes, stubble greying near the chin.

Ugly.

He turns away.

Back in the kitchen, he makes himself a large coffee, but
the machine beeps angrily at him – OUT OF BEANS. Jem
refreshes the beans from a bag in the cupboard. He presses
the button again, but the machine beeps in a different way
– OVERFLOW TRAY FULL. He removes the tray, spilling
some of the brownish water on his socks, and tips it into
the sink. Third time a charm, the machine whirrs into
action, grinding, boiling and percolating. Within thirty-eight
seconds, he is presented with a double-tall extra-strength
coffee. He goes to add milk, but the stuff in the fridge
smells bad, so he adds a little water from the tap and drinks
the coffee like medicine.

He goes back to the sofa and picks up his phone, ready to zone out to something that might be a property show, or an auction show, or a cookery show – it doesn't matter, because he's not really watching. The TV is just a mental screensaver, preventing certain recurring images from burning their shapes permanently into his imagination. He has forgotten about the message, and the notification is dismissed as he unlocks the phone.

He puts on BBC One, which is in the middle of a gardening show. He feels a vague sense of relief at the sounds, the movement, the immediate predictability of the format. Something niggles at the back of his mind, and he wonders if he left something in the kitchen. He cannot remember. The coffee hasn't had much of an effect yet, and his eyes start to droop. On the edge of sleep, he hears a familiar voice.

Let's go buy you a toothbrush . . .

Jem opens his eyes. There was a message. A message! He looks at his phone again, unlocks it, goes to the messages. His heart sinks – it's not from Mika, but an unknown number. Probably a money-off deal for takeaway pizza, or his internet provider trying to sell him a more expensive package. He is about to close the app when he catches the start of the message –

Hey, guess who? Want . . .

He scrabbles to open the message and reads the whole thing.

Hey, guess who? Want to meet up?

Without realising it, Jem has stood up. His heart is racing, and it's nothing to do with the coffee. He turns one way, then another, then sits down quickly. Fingers shaking, he manages to type –

Mika? Where are you?

He waits, listening to the blood pounding in his ears, A moment later a location comes through.

Meet here in an hour and a half?

Quickly he checks the postcode. The address is in West London. It will take at least an hour to get to on public transport, but he doesn't dare to suggest a later time. Quickly, he types –

I'll be there.

An hour and twenty-three minutes later, Jem is stepping off the Tube in another part of London. The air is different here. Having spent the last three weeks almost entirely confined to his apartment, this sudden acceleration leaves his head spinning. He is showered and shaved, but his neck is damp with sweat and the good shirt he chose to wear feels stiff and starchy on his skin, which has worn nothing but soft pyjamas for a fortnight.

On the journey he has read the Wikipedia page for Mansa Musa, and learned that he made his pilgrimage in 1324. Jem wants to go and edit some details on the entry, but of course he has no evidence to back up his version. He looked at a map of the 2,700-mile route that Musa's caravan took, passing by the pyramids of Giza and on through Cairo. He read an account of how Musa's return journey was struck by catastrophe: 'by the time they had reached Suez, many of the Malian pilgrims had died of cold, starvation, or bandit raids, and they had lost many of their supplies.'

He feels queasy. Many times in the last two weeks, he has thought about how he would feel better if he only went outside, but now that he is outside, he realises he was wrong. The only safety is indoors, the only comfort is in his own home. He craves the certainty of his sofa, his microwave, his coffee maker with its own particular needs, so easily satisfied.

It is starting to rain a little, and he has no umbrella. He follows the directions that his phone gives him. After a ten-minute walk, he stands at the gates of an industrial park. He pauses, assuming that he has got something wrong, but the postcode he put into the map is the one Mika gave him. If that even was Mika . . .

He walks on, past a timber warehouse, another which sells plumbing goods, another dedicated to tiling. He makes a right turn, past a Royal Mail sorting depot, until he comes to a garage. A large blue and white sign proclaims it to be an MOT test centre, approved by the vehicle inspectorate. The building is made of corrugated metal, patched with newer sections here and there where the older sheets have rusted away.

Through a large opening which seems more like a mouth than a door, Jem can see a car suspended on a platform, racks of tyres, a machine with lots of black hoses snaking off it. But the garage is huge, and this is just what he can see from the door – it goes back further, much further, into darkness. The only person he can see is a man in oil-stained overalls, who is taking something apart on a bench.

He almost turns back.

Either Mika has made a mistake in her message, or this is some kind of practical joke, sending him to a random corner of London to force him to leave his flat. For a paranoid moment he thinks of his deserted apartment and worries about it. What if someone is breaking in while he is here? He hesitates, turns to leave. If he can get a Tube quickly, he can be back in his flat within an hour, and put this ordeal behind him.

'Can I help you?'

It's the man from the garage, shouting over. Jem turns back.

'I just . . . I think I'm in the wrong place.'

'Oh yeah?'

'I was looking for someone – Mika?'

And if Jem had blinked, he would have missed it. Because the man doesn't say anything, doesn't invite him closer, doesn't confirm or deny. He couldn't say exactly what it is, except that one moment the man is open and the next moment he is shut.

'I'm a friend. She sent me this address. If I've got the wrong place—'

'I didn't catch your name,' the man cuts him off.

'Jem.'

The man scans the estate behind Jem, as though he hasn't heard. Then he says, more quietly:

'You could come inside, take a look around.'

Jem hesitates for a second. He doesn't know this man, and there is menace in his tone, the promise of violence if certain conditions are not met. But it is no more than a hesitation, and there is no real question about him going inside. He steps into the fluorescent-lit grease-smelling space.

The man doesn't move.

'Go back,' he says, and for a moment Jem thinks he is being asked to leave, before the man points deeper into the garage. Back there, Jem is vaguely aware of a vast, hanger-like space, but it is unlit except for grubby skylights, high up. There are shadowy forms, but nothing much he can make out.

'Go back as far as you can, until you get to the left corner.'

'And . . . ?'

'Go on,' the man says, without moving. 'And behave yourself.'

Jem walks into the gloom. He passes a Fiat Panda up on bricks, a row of half-disassembled scooters, a minibus missing half the panelling on one side. Other vehicles are less identifiable, just a chassis, a rough framework, a pile of disconnected parts, like bones in the desert. The room is a graveyard.

No, not a graveyard, because here everything is being broken down and reassembled. A place of transformations, then, a shared chrysalis. Something hopeful. The air is musty with chemicals leaching out of rubber seals and engine blocks, stale from being repeatedly heated and cooled by the sun beating down on corrugated metal. There are paths among the wrecked vehicles, wide enough for a truck, so it must be possible that some of these vehicles will one day drive out into the sun, return to the road, regain their freedom. But, for now, they are stuck in this shadowy limbo, awaiting metamorphosis.

He goes further back, listening to his own footsteps. The

floor is bare concrete, gritty and streaked with oil. The wrecks are bigger back here – a flatbed truck, a white van with a single patch of navy blue, a ruined ice cream van which hasn't seen summer for twenty years, inexpertly painted with the likenesses of Mickey Mouse, Donald Duck, and Sonic the Hedgehog. There is no sign of anyone else, nor any sound.

Jem feels uneasy. The wrecks appear to him as symbols of never-leaving. It is like one of those dreams where you can walk and walk and never find your way out. He imagines wandering through the labyrinth of broken transport until he starves to death, adding his broken parts to the pile.

There is a noise.

He cannot say what it is, or place where it came from. It might just be the sound of a wrecked hulk settling. That probably happens a lot in here, he thinks, just the odd creak as the vehicles settle. He walks on, quieter this time, careful of the sound his feet make. There it is again – a creak, and now he can hear something else, a low humming. To begin with it might just be the sound of machinery, a droning generator or a murmuring transformer. And yet, the harder he listens, the more the noise resolves into a tune. He knows this tune, has heard it before, though it takes him a moment to place – it's the melody that Mika hummed as they lay on the grass in St James's Park.

He looks around. Where can it be coming from? He seems to have reached the back corner on the left, where the man told him to go, but in front of him is nothing but a darkened shape, massive and half covered by tarpaulins. It takes him a moment to realise what he's looking at.

A bus.

A red London bus.

The doors of the bus are open. He walks towards them, following the sound of humming. But his foot must scuff on the floor, because now the humming stops. All sound has stopped, and he has a sudden, irrational fear that he has dispelled a ghost. He steps onto the bus, feeling it rock just a little under his weight, like a boat on water.

'Jem?'

Mika is crouching, with a wrench in one hand and a grease cloth in the other. Her face is streaked with grime but she looks otherwise intact, unhurt – herself.

'Mika—'

This is all Jem gets out before his throat is stoppered. He tries to speak again but there is a blockage. As though to bypass it, tears spring up in his eyes. Mika stands, frowning, throws the rag to the floor and wipes her hands on her belly.

'Are you okay?' she says.

His eyes are streaming now, like leaks in a pressurised system. Jem tries again to speak but cannot, and feels the tracks of tears running down his cheeks, gathering under his chin, falling to the dusty floor. Mika looks baffled for a second, takes one step, then another, and puts her arms around him. He feels a surge of warmth – from her body, yes, but also as though she is surrounding him.

He cries and cries, and does not try to speak for a while, though there are things he wants to say – 'Are you alright? Why are you here? Where have you been? I'm sorry, my tears are making your T-shirt soggy.' Mika has her own unasked questions but, since they all revolve around Jem's appearance, it seems rude to ask them. He's thinner than before, his cheeks hollowed, and his eyes were bloodshot before he started crying.

With each sob, a little more of the blockage in Jem's throat dissolves, until there is nothing left, and she is still holding him.

'Do you want to sit down?' she asks.

'Here?'

'Yes, come on – there's a place to sit further back.' She leads him back through the bus. 'It's a mess in here; I'm sorry.'

Jem wipes his eyes and looks around properly. The interior of the bus is indeed a mess, with loose packaging, unbolted sheets of metal, tools strewn around. But underneath all that is a space with a surprising level of order. The original seats from the bus have been removed, replaced by a kitchen. He can see a range with an oven, two hobs, a hot plate and a grill. There is a sink without a tap, open cupboards containing pans and colanders, and an extractor hood without a pipe connected. There are a couple of fridges under the work surface, and one of these has a red light glowing to show it's plugged in. At the back there is a table bolted to the floor in front of a padded bench.

'Sit, go on. Do you want something to drink? I was about to make a cup of tea.'

' . . . okay.'

Mika hauls a plastic bottle of water up to a kettle and sloshes some in.

'What is this?'

Mika looks around the space and laughs self-deprecatingly.

'This was my little project, before everything got . . . complicated. The bus used to be a travelling café. Lower deck kitchen, upper deck seating. It went all over. Did Glastonbury twelve years in a row.'

'Wow.'

'Anyway, the guy who owned it wanted to turn it into a mobile home. Keep the kitchen downstairs and turn the upstairs into somewhere to live. He got about half of the work done before he died.'

'And you—?'

'Saw the advert. I bought it off of Mungo, who had been doing the work for the old owner – you met Mungo, right? Anyway, he was selling it for not very much, though it was still all my savings. So he said, look, you can leave it here while you do it up; pay me to work on it and you can have the space for nothing. So that's what I've been doing. I only stayed so long because—'

She stops, looks a little abashed. It is the first time she has hinted at overstaying her visa.

'You were waiting to finish,' Jem breathes. 'And when the bus was done—'

'I was going to drive it down to Dover and see if it would fit on a ferry.'

'Will you be able to finish it?'

'I don't know. I've got some money that I saved up, and most of the materials are already bought. But I probably don't have enough time to fix it before the money runs out and . . .'

'You can't risk getting another job?'

The kettle rattles to the boil and clicks off. She looks away, pouring water into cups.

'Do you want milk?'

'If you have it. But Mika—'

'Jem, I—'

'Kenny said you were arrested.'

'Did he tell you why?'

'He said it was the Home Office. That they were going to deport you, because you'd overstayed. Is that . . . true?'

Mika looks him in the eye.

'Do you have a problem with that?'

'I . . . no.'

'That was a long pause,' she frowns. 'You're not one of those people, are you Jem? The "send them home" brigade?'

'No, god no. Well, I mean, I think there are controls for a reason—' Mika rolls her eyes a little. 'But I don't care if you overstayed. I just . . . '

'You just *what?*' she says, jabbing at him with the last word.

'I just . . . I didn't know.'

She says nothing.

'I didn't know where you were. I didn't know if you were safe. I didn't know if I was getting you back. And then there was that dream, watching you disappear over the horizon . . . '

He stops abruptly, realising how much he has said. Mika is frowning. She turns to take the tea bags out, then brings the cups over. With some effort, she squeezes herself into the space between table and bench, but keeps her distance.

'Do you want a biscuit? Oh, I must have finished them. Well . . . ' She runs her fingers through her hair, then pulls it all down so it covers her face. The hair is a little greasy.

'Are you okay, Mika?'

She sighs.

'When they took me to the detention centre, I thought they were going to deport me straight away. Even though that's not really allowed. But they change the law so often, just to see what they can get away with . . . In any case,

I knew I wouldn't be able to return. I thought I'd lost you too.'

Mika looks him in the eye. She feels as though no time has passed since that moment in Soho, where she went up on tiptoes to kiss him. Time must have passed though, because the Jem in front of her is smaller, greyer, impossibly older. She craves that same feeling of peace, when all her self-doubts fell silent. But she is worried. Worried that the moment is lost forever. This version of Jem looks too fragile to take anything away from him. She cannot ask him to solve her problems. Nothing has changed; everything has changed.

'They let you out though . . . ?' he says, hopefully.

'On immigration bail,' she nods.

'Are they letting you stay because of—?' He points to her pregnancy bump, but she shakes her head.

'I'm not far along enough for that. They gave me a couple of weeks to sort my stuff out and book a ticket to somewhere else.'

'Oh . . . ' Jem feels a crumpling inside himself. 'How long do you have left?'

Mika looks ruefully at him.

'I have a caseworker I'm supposed to be responding to whenever they call me, but . . . I threw my phone in a bin.'

'You—'

'I'm just glad they didn't make me wear an electronic tag. They probably should have done, but I made myself look so harmless, and I agreed with everything so quickly, they seemed to think they could trust me.'

'You're on the run!'

Mika laughs.

'Bit dramatic, Jem.'

'You're skipping bail!'

'*Immigration* bail, Jem. I didn't shoot the sheriff.'

'But what if they find you? Won't they—'

'I've been careful. Withdrew all my money so they can't trace my transactions. Dumped my phone. I've been staying different places. Besides, they're busy – they've got bigger fish to fry than one pregnant lady.'

'Are you . . . living here?' Jem doesn't keep the concern out of his voice.

'I mean, I sleep here. Mungo lets me use the garage bathroom. They've got a shower in there, for getting the grease off at the end of the day. And there's a little kitchen where I can microwave stuff. You should see upstairs. I've got a—'

'Mika, you can't live on a derelict bus when you're six months pregnant!'

She frowns. 'I can do what I like. It's fine here. Anyway, where do you *want* me to go?'

There is a moment. Perhaps there are a handful of such moments in every life, or maybe each life is full of them, more numerous than the seconds ticking by. The only difference is when we notice them, and they both notice this one. Jem knows that he could offer for Mika to stay at his flat. Mika knows that if Jem offered, she would say yes. The trouble with every possibility, of course, is that it's a doorway into a darkened room. There is no way of knowing where it will take you. So, Jem thinks – what if I drive her away by seeming too forward? And Mika thinks – what if he thinks I'm a freeloader?

The moment lengthens, hardening into a silence.

Mika makes a decision.

'I really like you, Jem.'

'I like you too . . . '

'I really like you, and that morning in the park, that day we spent together, I really enjoyed it. But I'm sorry . . . '

'Sorry?'

'I need someone who knows his own mind. I need someone who knows what they want.'

He feels the conversation slipping out from under his feet.

'Since when do *you* need someone? You've always seemed . . . '

'Like what?'

'Like, I don't know. Independent? Like you would always come and go as you pleased. I thought that was how you liked it.'

'What am I, a stray cat?'

'Maybe you are.' Jem rubs his eyes between finger and thumb. He knows that if he could just find the right way to say what he is thinking, everything would be well.

'Maybe you're right,' Mika says, bitterly. 'Maybe I don't need anybody. That sounds like me.'

'Okay?'

'But if I'm going to be with anybody, it needs to be someone who knows what they want. You don't have a job—'

'That's a problem now? I wasn't planning to sit around forever!'

She shakes her head so vigorously that the bus seems to shake a little in sympathy.

'But – but! You don't know what you want to do, do you Jem? Be honest. You don't know if you want to stay or go, don't know if you want to have a nine-to-five job or, I don't know . . . rent a garret overlooking the Eiffel Tower and paint watercolours!'

271

He laughs a bitter sort of laugh; he can taste the dregs from that bottle of cheap wine.

'I'm just working things out. I didn't know until now that that was such a problem for you.'

'It's not a problem,' she says. 'Not for me, anyway.'

That puts an end to the conversation, a granite capstone on the edifice of failed communication. Jem looks at the cup of tea she made him. It seems ungrateful not to drink it, when she has so little, but he doesn't think he can choke down anything. He stands.

'I should be going.'

'Okay.'

Does she look sad? Disappointed? He cannot read her any more, because he cannot read his own feelings. Before he came, he was so ready to tell her everything that he had felt over the last weeks, how he craved her like a drug, but now all those feelings are changed to something else, something corrosive inside him. He needs to get away; looks for a way to acquit himself.

'Can I give you some money?'

Mika scoffs.

'You don't need to take pity on me!'

'I'm just trying to be kind.'

'Well, good job.'

'What does that mean?'

Mika hauls herself to her feet. He wants to hold out his hand to help her, but resists. She says:

'Goodbye, Jem. It was nice seeing you again.'

He feels panic at her slipping away, perhaps forever.

'Will I be able to get in touch?'

'Why would you want to?'

'If we have another dream, I don't know . . . can we be friends?'

Mika looks as though she's about to argue, then relents.

'I don't have a phone right now; I used Mungo's to get in touch with you. But I still have my old email. I check it every few days.'

'Okay,' he agrees hastily. 'That would be great.'

She gives him the email and he notes it down in his phone, double-checking it with her.

'This is a real address, right?'

She folds her arms across her chest, as though to protect herself against his words.

'Do you think I hate you that much?'

'I didn't mean . . . '

'Goodbye, Jem.'

He stands there for a long moment, searching for a way out of this farewell. He had dreams like this, when he was a child. Dreams in which he had to say goodbye to his parents forever, for reasons that were never fully explained. He looks up at the bus, looking so shabby and forlorn under the tarpaulins.

'I could help . . . '

'What?'

'With the bus. I could help you with the bus.'

'You fix engines now? I thought you worked in a bank?

'I do . . . I did . . . But my dad, he was a builder. A lot of the time I would go and find him after school, at whatever job he was doing. And he would get me to do this or that. I wasn't really helping; he was trying to give me an apprenticeship. I learned how to do basic carpentry, wiring plugs, all kinds of things. This was when I was little, but . . . '

Mika frowns, looking past him at the grey warehouse.
'Why?'

'Why what?'

'Why would you want to help me?'

Jem carefully chooses his level of honesty.

'I've got nothing else to do at the moment, like you say.
It would be nice to have something to get me out of the
flat.'

She looks him in the eyes for a moment and he's certain
she is about to call him on his bullshit. But then she nods.

'I'll talk to Mungo – it's his garage. If he's okay with it,
I'll borrow his phone and send you another text.'

Jem smiles.

'I'll come by tomorrow?'

'If Mungo says it's okay.'

'Okay, cool . . . '

'This is a trial period. If you're making up all this stuff
about your dad being a builder—'

'I'll be good, I promise.'

Jem nods briskly and, not wanting to spoil the arrangement, puts one hand up in a wave.

'Bye, Mika. I'm sorry . . . for before.'

'Let's just forget it, yeah?'

'Friends?'

'Yeah, friends.'

She watches him turn and walk away, through the maze
of broken machines. She thinks of how all those cars and
vans and bikes were once new. Someone, presumably, felt
some excitement or pride at taking ownership of them,
fresh off the factory floor. Everything gets run down.
Everything breaks eventually. But some things get repaired.
Some things have another life, after the first one.

20

Jem has been gone for twenty minutes when Mika walks back through the garage to the front. In that time, Nike has earned seven hundred and thirty thousand US dollars. Workers at the Nike factory in Vietnam earned twenty-three cents each. World military spending was seventy-two million dollars, while people donated sixty-two million to charities. Twelve million Coca-Colas were consumed, seventy-two thousand lipsticks produced, and one thousand one hundred and sixty aeroplanes took off. There have been ninety-eight earthquakes and lightning has struck fifty-two thousand eight hundred and fifty-five times. The shutters are half-down and Mungo is cleaning his hands with a rag.

'Hey, Mika.'

'What did you think of him?'

'Hm,' Mungo thinks about it seriously. 'Seemed alright, I guess. Didn't get much of a look at him. Was he alright?'

'Yeah, I guess. He's going to be coming round more often, to help me with the bus. Is that okay?'

'So long as you're vouching for him.'

'Could I borrow your phone one more time? I need to make a quick call.'

'Knock yourself out.'

He hands over his scuffed Samsung with the cracked screen, and Mika retreats to the warehouse. She takes out the folded sheet of paper on which she had hastily noted down all the phone numbers she thought she might need. She types one in and dials. It rings three times before connecting. There's a lot of noise on the other end of the line.

'Hello? Who's this?'

'Olly, it's Mika.'

'I can't hear a thing. Hang on – I'll go outside.'

Mika hears a shouted dinner order and recognises Suzy's voice calling in response. She feels a pang of longing to be back in the kitchen at SINE, before everything got so complicated.

'Okay, it's quieter here,' Olly says. 'Who's this?'

'It's Mika.'

'It's . . . are you okay? I've not heard anything from you. I thought you were ignoring me. Were you ignoring me?'

'No . . . my phone broke and I lost all my numbers. Just got them back.'

'Oh, phew! I mean, sorry about your phone.'

'No big deal. I just . . . I thought I'd check in with you.'

'Is this your new number?'

'No, um, this is just a temporary number. I'll message you when I've got a permanent one.'

'Okay. Is this to . . . you know . . . '

'What?'

'Give me an answer? To my question?'

'Oh, um . . . no.'

276

'No?'

'I mean, I'm not saying "no". I just mean . . . I haven't decided yet.'

'Oh . . . '

Words seem to fail Olly. Mika can almost smell the alley where he's standing, the stale beer and the cats that use the back wall as a toilet. There is some noise on the line.

'How's work?'

'Dreadful. I was just about to pop out for a cigarette when you rang.'

'You never used to smoke.'

'I never used to do a lot of things,' Olly mutters.

He's probably going for world-weary pathos, but sounds more like a pubescent sixth-former playing Stanley in *A Streetcar Named Desire*. She looks up at the ceiling, high above, at the dirty skylights and the girders where a few pigeons have made their nests against Mungo's best efforts to evict them. She listens to the tobacco crackle as Olly draws on his cigarette.

'I don't like feeling guilty all the time,' he exhales.

'Then don't, Olly. You're not.'

'It's not that easy. Why don't you—'

'Make my mind up?'

God, she wishes she were there to snatch that cigarette out of his hand and smoke it down in one draw. She wants to go to the basement bar around the corner from SINE and order the biggest vodka tonic. She wants one stupid night out in Soho with Suzy, where she can say all the stupid things in her head out loud and hear how stupid they are and get them out of her system.

'Well, yeah,' he says, and she can hear the shrug in his voice. 'I know it's not easy, but—'

'Do you? Do you know? Because you make it sound like I'm dithering between getting the chicken or the fish. Life isn't a menu, Olly.'

'Isn't it?'

'I'm choosing between a million different things. A whole different life. Things that have consequences!'

'You can't keep me waiting forever.'

'It's not forever.'

'Waiting won't change anything.'

Mika's not so sure this is true. Everything keeps changing when she's not paying attention. She leans back against a battered transit van; he draws on the cigarette.

'I should be going,' she says.

'Huh?' He presses the receiver back to his ear.

'I need to go.'

'So, what? I should just go back to moping in the shadows, hoping you'll make your mind up someday?'

'God, you got melodramatic!'

'Hang on,' his tone changes abruptly. 'Just – can you just give me a deadline? Please? I don't want to be like this. Either way, I don't want to make you hate me.'

'Okay.'

'Okay?'

'By the end of the week. I'll make a decision by then, yes?'

' . . . okay.'

Jem appears early the next day, not long after Mungo has opened up for the day. He's wearing paint-spattered jeans and an old T-shirt, and has with him a selection box of biscuits and a pint of milk. Mika greets him at the door of the bus, still in the dressing gown she slept in, and Jem mock-salutes her.

'Reporting for duty.'

'Welcome to the war, soldier.'

He climbs aboard, the bus rocking gently under him.

'What can I do first?'

'Put the kettle on; I'll get changed.'

Over the next few hours, Jem takes a proper look at the bus. There's a lot to be fixed, and most of the jobs – if he knows how to do them all – are things he hasn't done since he was fifteen. Still, he wants to give the impression of competence. Together they draw up a list of jobs. The tasks fall into three categories: 1) get the bus on the road 2) make the kitchen usable and 3) make the bus an okay place to live. The first category is Mungo's domain, the second Mika's, so Jem picks some low hanging fruit from the third category. There's a toilet in a cupboard-like cubicle downstairs, and he sets to fixing the wonky seat.

Everything is slow at first – he has to go and ask Mungo for the tools he needs – but by mid-morning he's able to tick off his first task. Mika inspects the work.

'Not bad . . . '

'I chose something easy,' he admits.

'Well, keep working down the list and you'll get to the harder stuff, right?'

'Right.'

For lunch he buys fresh sandwiches from a local deli. Attracted by the flurry of activity, Mungo comes back to see what they're up to, and has a fresh look at the engine.

'This is the big push?' he asks, through the open back window. 'You'll want it running soon?'

'Maybe.'

'I'll put a bit more time into it, if you are. I've been leaving it while there was so much left to do.'

'Thanks. I can pay you, just let me know—'

He shakes his head.

'Nah, fuck it. You've given me enough. It'd be nice to see it drive out of here.'

By the end of the day, Jem has replaced the dodgy sealant on the front windows, reattached a loose railing on the stairs, and started cutting wood to make storage cabinets at the front of the top deck. Around dinner time, Mika comes and tells him to stop.

'Are you sure? I can keep going . . . '

She looks at him strangely for a moment.

'You've done loads. Besides, I can't fix you a hot meal yet. You should go home.'

'Can I come back tomorrow?'

Again she pauses for a moment.

'Sure.'

He leaves for the day, waving over his shoulder. At no point has Mika said thank you. She has said 'good job' and 'nice work', but not 'thank you'. He doesn't want her to. He doesn't want it to feel like he's doing her a favour. It feels like a favour to *him*, to be allowed to stay.

Over the next week, he settles into something like a routine. He wakes early and makes the journey across town to the garage. On his way he picks up a pint of milk and something for breakfast – croissants or toasted sandwiches, and a coffee for each of them. They sit at the table at the back of the bus and discuss what they did yesterday and what they'll do today. Mungo will come and go as time allows, leaving his apprentice, Jamaal, to mind the front of shop. He lends Mika a portable radio, so they often have music on, cycling through the limited stations she can tune in to. At the busiest times, all three of them are solving a different problem.

It's hard work, but he doesn't complain. He's not the one who's pregnant, after all. Sometimes he has moments of feeling lightheaded, and worries that he's going to have another blackout, but they never come. He decides he's just out of shape, but makes a doctor's appointment anyway. He asks politely to see someone other than Doctor Griggs. The receptionist makes no argument, and gives him a non-urgent appointment in a month and a half's time.

It feels exciting, Jem reflects, to be working on something real. He's not sure what 'real' means, except that his work in the bank wasn't 'real'. It's not that it didn't have real-world consequences. Next of kin had their deceased relative's monies made accessible to them. It's just that, if Jem hadn't done it, someone else would have. The great finance machine would have kept cranking out the same results. Whether he did it or not made no difference. But to fix a curtain rail, or a light switch, or a leaky tap – these things are real. It will be possible to shut out prying eyes, to light up the bedroom, to keep the water tank full overnight, because he did those jobs.

It's exciting in its own way that the bus is made to go. It's a vehicle, a business and a home rolled into one. He imagines that people who build ships must have a similar feeling; the sense of potential, the knowledge that their work will go on to have a life elsewhere. He does not think about the specifics of where the bus will go. He does not think about where Mika will drive, once it is finished.

Except . . .

Well, yes, he does imagine himself on the bus as it drives out of the garage. He imagines shielding his eyes as the sunlight sweeps over it for the first time. In his daydream it's always a bright day, when they roll it out of the garage. Not a cloud in the sky . . .

But that's all he imagines. No more. He doesn't dare to dream further down the road. Just get ready for that day, he tells himself, and see what happens.

Towards the end of the week they work more on the kitchen together. The jobs become bigger and more important. She fixes the fume hood on the range. He fixes the feed from the propane tank. Mungo fixes the external power supply hookup. The thirty-gallon wastewater tank is connected; the six-thousand-watt generator is fired up and, after adjustments to the circuit breakers, independently powers everything on the bus, from the lights to the fridge to the sockets in the bedroom. From seeming like a remote possibility, the idea that the bus might one day take to the road, even serve food to customers, becomes plausible.

'How're you feeling about it?' Mungo asks.

'It's weird . . . ' Mika shakes her head. 'I guess I wouldn't have bought it in the first place if I'd thought it couldn't happen. But still . . . '

Jem smiles and keeps his head down, fixing a loose bit of flooring.

They rest on the weekend. Mungo is busy with his actual work on Saturday, and Mika insists that Jem take a break. On Saturday he sits in his flat and watches videos about plumbing and carpentry, planning ahead. Mika sits in her half-formed kitchen. She cannot bring herself to do any more work, for now. The bus seems a quiet place, on her own. The more they have worked on it, the more it has come to feel like home. But now, without Jem here, that feeling is gone. She feels a yearning she can't admit to yet.

Around lunchtime she goes to the landline in Mungo's

office, dials Jem's number but doesn't press 'call'. She stares at the little screen for a minute, then puts the handset in the cradle and walks back through the empty garage.

On Sunday, Jem takes Emily to the British Museum. They peer through glass at Stone Age flints, clay tablets inscribed with Akkadian, Roman coins and pottery, the Sutton Hoo helmet, Arabic manuscripts from the Middle Ages on fine sheets of vellum. He couldn't explain what it all means to him, and doesn't try. It is enough to be here with Emily, looking at the past from the safety of the present. Afterwards they go to an ice-cream parlour and order giant sundaes. They find tall chairs by the window.

'How's school?'

'Good thanks. Better, you know?'

'That's good.'

Jem smiles sideways at her, but Emily keeps looking at the foot traffic outside. She plunges her spoon to the very bottom of the glass.

'You changed,' she says.

'I did?' Jem winces, sure he's about to be told off.

'Mum changed, when she met Derek. Not in a bad way. Well, sometimes in a really super cringey way. But you know, it was fine. I just *noticed* . . . '

She trails off, but Jem is pretty sure what he's being asked. He doesn't mind – he was wanting to bring up the subject sooner or later. It's only that he doesn't know the answer.

'I have changed, yeah. Is that okay?'

Emily looks at him now, spooning a large glob of half-melted mint choc chip into her mouth.

'Yeah, it's okay, Dad.'

283

Jem looks sideways at Emily for a moment, and makes a resolution to tell Mika about her. He knows they would get on. He has been stupid, to let it go on this long. He was just afraid, with Mika's dislike of absent parents, that it would spell the end of whatever they had. But things are different now. He can't keep hiding the truth. He wants Mika to know him as he is, even the ugly parts.

On Monday Jem returns, bright and early, to find that she has made scrambled eggs and toast using the propane-fuelled cooker. He puts the pains au chocolat he's bought to one side.

'It's starting to feel like a proper home,' he says, adding the hot sauce she bought from the shop.

'Yeah, though I'm still not using the wastewater tank, because it'd be a nightmare emptying it here. Still, it's starting to feel . . . possible.'

He nods, but says nothing. There is something different today about the way she is looking at him. She says:

'What will you do, when the bus is finished?'

His mouth is full of eggs and toast, and it seems to take an eternity to chew and swallow them. At last, he says:

'Nothing, really.'

'Think you'll look for a job?'

'Maybe.'

'But you don't have any plans?'

'No, I'm . . . free.'

That word, 'free', hangs in the air. It resonates, for a moment, like a ringing bell. He is free. She is free. What comes next is up to them. After a long moment, she starts to tidy up the plates.

'I should go and wash up. Mungo lets me use the garage kitchen.'

'Let me do it.'

'You sure?'

'You cooked; I'll clean.'

'Okay. Actually, do you mind if I borrow your phone? I need to make a quick call.'

'Sure, here you go.'

Jem unlocks the phone and hands it to her.

'Back in five.'

'See you.'

Mika waits until she can no longer hear Jem's footsteps outside before getting the sheet of paper out on which she has Olly's number. She's just starting to type it in when the phone starts ringing.

Calling: Sarah.

Mika is a little startled, but otherwise just waits for it to ring out. She doesn't know who Sarah might be. It might be anyone. Jem is the last person she would be suspicious of, so she feels no particular curiosity. If anything, that's why, when the same person starts calling a second time, she picks up – she will simply let this person know that Jem is out but will be back in five minutes, if it's anything urgent.

'Hello? This is—'

'Hello? Hello? Who is that? Jem?'

The voice on the other end of the line is brittle, rapid-fire.

'This is Jem's phone, but he's just gone for five minutes. Is it anything important?'

'Who is this?'

'I'm a friend. My name is Mika.'

'Oh, well . . . '

This Sarah woman sounds taken aback by the word 'friend'.

'Well, you can tell him that Emily has had a fall off her bike and has broken her arm.'

'Oh, I'm sorry to hear that . . . '

'Yes, well, she's fine. Just a fracture, actually. But she has an appointment at the hospital, so tell him next week's visit is cancelled.'

'I'm sorry?'

'I mean, if he wants to reschedule we can talk, but we already have quite a lot on the calendar, so—'

'Sorry, hang on . . . '

'Yes?'

Mika pauses, because whatever is coming, she feels every atom of her body coming to an abrupt stop, the top of the rollercoaster, the split second before the big dive, the eyes screwed shut, the screams.

'Who's Emily?'

'His daughter, of course.'

'Oh.'

'I thought you said you were his friend? Is he going to be back soon? Maybe I should talk to him myself, I . . . '

Sarah goes on speaking, but Mika is no longer listening. She says: 'I'll pass your message on' and hangs up.

Jem finishes cleaning the plates and cutlery in the tiny garage kitchen, dries them on a paper towel from the dispenser, then walks back to the bus. He knows the way through the maze automatically now, and his thoughts are all on the jobs he's going to do today. They need to properly check the plumbing, for a start, before they move on to the electrics. He's been thinking about what they could do for the sign on the outside, because that's the first thing customers will see—

'Sarah called.'

He looks up. Mika is stood in the doorway of the bus, holding his phone up. Her face is dark against the light behind her.

'Oh . . . '

'You have a wife?'

Jem feels the tilt, the sudden acceleration of the roller-coaster, the wind rushing in his hair.

'Ex-wife.'

'And I suppose Emily is your ex-daughter?'

A spasm of pain contorts Jem's face.

'I was going to tell you about Emily. I should have told you already. Lots of times I almost did. But I knew how you felt about absent parents and I—'

'Pretended you weren't one?'

'It's complicated.'

She rubs her eyes. 'This is so fucked up . . . '

'Mika, please—'

'Jem, you knew how I felt and you kept this from me. Not for a week or a month, but for half a year.'

'I can explain.'

'No.' She shakes her head. 'I don't want you to. I don't want to hear you explain it away. Just go, please.'

'Mika—'

'Just *go!*' her voice catches with anger and frustration.

He stands there, unable to move forwards or back. Mika steps down from the bus towards him. She comes so close he flinches.

'Here's your phone. Now go.'

He turns away. Without looking back, he walks down the path between the wrecked vehicles. The hangar is as silent as ever, but it's a different kind of silence now – not

menacing but empty. The silence of everything being said
and done. The silence of the universe when the last sun
fizzles out. He doesn't turn around, but he thinks that Mika
is watching him go from the door of the bus. With every
step, he has the visceral feeling of leaving his home behind,
forever. He walks through the twilit maze until he comes
to the front of the garage, where Mungo is inspecting the
inside of a manifold.

'You off, Jem?'

He says nothing in reply. Outside the rain has stopped,
the clouds have parted, and all that's left is the thin, unre-
lenting sunlight of the rest of his life.

Mika waits on the bus for a long time, until both cups of
tea have achieved thermal equilibrium with their environment. At last she goes upstairs, feeling the bus rock
underneath her. It smells of cut pinewood up here, and the
floor is gritty with sawdust. It's still far from complete, but
the shape of a living space is there, with the bedroom
separated by sliding doors at the back, the shower cubicle
on one side, the toilet and sink on the other. The rest of
the space, roughly one third left over, is free. She imagined
having a sofa at the front, so she could park up anywhere,
on the edge of a cliff if she wanted to, then sit and watch
the sun set.

What a stupid dream.

She goes back to the half-finished bedroom and gets
changed out of her grease-stained T-shirt and jeans, into
her only clean dress, a white babydoll with lace at the hem
and neckline. She cleans her face and armpits with baby
wipes, then puts on deodorant, perfume, and make up. She
doesn't want to be too obvious, but it can't hurt to look

good. Her hair is bad, but she has a can of dry shampoo with a little left and uses it all now.

When she is done there is no mirror to look in, so she steps out of the bedroom and walks downstairs and off the bus. She looks back, feeling as though she should lock up, but at the moment there's no way to even close the doors. She walks out of the garage, saying goodbye to Mungo, who does not ask her about Jem. She walks to the Tube, feeling a little better to be out in the open.

She feels as though she's making a mistake.

She feels as though she's doing the right thing.

She cannot decide which version of events is true, but wonders if it might be possible that they both are. Perhaps that's what being a parent is like, because you're no longer deciding for one person only. You have to choose, knowing that the choice itself is a coin flip, wrong decision, right decision, wrong decision, right decision, tumbling through the air toward an unknown landing.

By the time she reaches her destination, Jem is already back in his flat, with a week's worth of low-calorie microwave meals, a litre bottle of cheap vodka and some cans of slimline tonic. But she's not to know this. If she imagines Jem at all, he is frozen in the moment of leaving.

She steps up to the door of a townhouse in an expensive borough. She knows it is only rented accommodation, but it's unlike any rental place she's ever known. She got the address from Suzy. There is a single, hexagonal brass handle in the middle of the door, and a heavy brass knocker, like something out of a Victorian novel. She knocks three times and waits.

There is every chance that no one is in. There is every chance that he is at work. There is every chance—

The door opens.

'Mika?'

'Hi, Olly.'

Time passes.

And passes.

And passes.

It is almost the end of the month. The weather is changing, but hasn't yet settled into autumn. Hot and cold breezes refuse to mix, making dust devils that skirl across empty car parks, picking up rubbish and throwing it down in a temper. Everything is restless, arbitrary, unsatisfactory, broken, yearning, asymmetrical, grouchy, lethargic, hyperactive, done in, burned out, used up. Nobody seems to know what to do about any of it, except perhaps to wait for the new month. Maybe that will bring a solution. Maybe not. Only time will tell.

Around the world, people are sick.

Waterborne bacteria, insect-borne viruses, airborne pollution. Autoimmune diseases. Genetic diseases. Old age. Again those cells, doing things too small to see. Cells under attack by foreign invaders. Cells under attack from their own kind. Cells going rogue, breaking the system. People have a sniffle. People have cancer. People are listening to the voices in their heads. People are taking the day off work. People are living their last day. People are dying.

And time?

Time passes.

21

DRAMATIS PERSONAE

MIKA, a penniless playwright
MELANCHOLY, an airy spirit
MISTRESS CUSHAWAY, a landlady

•

Act V, Scene IV

MELANCHOLY

Hark! A banging from the chamber door,
Bolted within, and Mika lies abed.
The sheets are greasy, dust carpets the floor,
Frost covers the glass in its latticework of
    lead.
Though winter rubs herself against the panes,
Like a stray cat searching for a homely place,
Unlit the fire lies, Mika abstains

And languishes in sister Poverty's cold
   embrace.
See him shuffle to his writing table!
Here is where he spends his every windfall –
Here is fresh paper, ready for a fable
A good brass pen, and finest ink of oak gall.
The Mistress bangs again in all her rage
Rattling the bars of Mika's self-made cage!

    MISTRESS CUSHAWAY *(from off)*
I know you are in there, sir! I hear you
   moving about!

    MIKA *(to himself)*
I dip the pen and let it drink its fill,
Tap away the dark excess, and then
Suspend its point above a virgin page
Like a Damoclean sword to fall,
Daring it to drip before a word is writ.
If it blots this unspoiled paper then
I shall write naught and soon return to bed.
But see – it stays its venom. Against my will,
I find my place. It is a new beginning,
Or moreover a middle. Thus I write –

MIKA speaks aloud as he writes.

NOMAD in the desert.

NOMAD
For thirty days and nights my weary course
Has sailed through desiccated waves and troughs

No detail to regale the wand'ring eye
Save dunes, the burnished sun, the sky . . .

That couplet rhyme was not mine intention,
And I must find a better word for 'sky' . . .

More banging from the door.

MISTRESS CUSHAWAY
I can hear your pen a-scratching, damn you,
  sir!
You cannot stay in there forever – I shall have
  what's due!

MELANCHOLY
See Mika sigh, his concentration broken.
He puts down the pen, another tale untold.

MIKA
Outside my window, all of London steams
Like a herd of cattle out in the winter cold.
Snow edges all the brown-backed buildings
  white.
Across the way a woman from the bawdy
  house
Opens the casement with plume of billowing
  vapour.
I saw a trick once at the Rose just so, for
  Faustus,
When Mephistopheles from Hell appeared,
And once again when Faust was dragged
  below.

Joe Heap

See, she tips the water from her bath:
Watch as the twisting column fumes and
    seethes
Like angels falling through the frigid air . . .

It has been so long ere I felt warm;
The tips of my fingers now are dull and
    numb.
At length, my landlady wears herself out . . .

MISTRESS CUSHAWAY
(Departing with a final cry)
    You cannot stay in there forever, sir!

MELANCHOLY
He listens to her depart, then takes the pen.
The desert fragment broken on the page,
Withered like fruit on a storm-snapped
    branch.
Now Mika cannot find the rest, although
The scene still plays out in his troubled
    mind –
The nomad, the desert, the pilgrims of Afric,
The woman falling on the golden sands.
But the fragment is a bird that shall not fly.
He crumples the paper into his palm, and
Throws it aside to start a different theme:

MIKA
LOVERS ONE and TWO in the forest

294

Life Number Nine

LOVER ONE
A tree has stood upon this sacred spot
Since ere my people came upon this fertile land
And see: the figs are ripe as Eden's crop;
Let's take our fill and rest ourselves awhile.

LOVER TWO
My sisters are not far from here I know,
Seeking out honeycomb and . . .

And? I cannot find the word that follows.
I have tried this scene a hundred ways or
     more,
And each new time it falters like the rest.

He tears the paper up and scatters the pieces.

It has always been thus, whene'er this season
     comes,
When the days shrink down and darkness
     falls.
That darkness of spirit descends on me also,
Mirroring the turning of the wheel.
And, in darkness, these scenes play out again –
The desert, the city, the arena, the forest.
I know not whence these dreams of mine may
     come,
Yet they torment my waking, ceaselessly.
They are fragments of a pirate's treasure map
Which never can I piece into a chart.
So I write them down each time, in my own
     way,

Into poetry, plays, histories and fables.
In writing them down, I free myself awhile,
Yet the peace I win lasts only for a day.
The dreams return, and I am never free.
I write them down again, and each one
   chimes
A note, the threnody of a distant bell –
Gone . . . Gone . . . Gone . . .

It has been this way, since first I came of age,
But this time it is worse, for in my soul,
I know this winter is the last I'll see . . .

MELANCHOLY
His words sound the fanfare of my triumph!

MIKA
The room is strewn with paper –
My poetry and prose among the fragments.
Fragments, all.
Will anything I have written last?
It seems a thought most improbable.
The landlady's words come back to me:
'I shall have what is due'.
Indeed you shall, indeed . . .

MIKA takes up the razor from his washbowl

MELANCHOLY
Everything I've said 'tis true
As I have shown this day to you.
All Mika's efforts are o'erthrown

His life and death are now mine own.
See! As he cuts through life's cold bands
With razor's edge and his own hands,
Released now from his memories' spell
In some other place to dwell.
Do not begrudge that he is free
For one day you may hope to be!

Exit MELANCHOLY, still singing.
MIKA dies.

November

22

Time passes.

Seen from the edge of space, Earth is a patchwork of patterns. Some are made by natural forces, some by animals, others by humankind. Coral reefs edge tropical coastlines with lace. In West Africa, a ring of concentric circles is formed and reformed by erupting magma. In the salt desert of Iran, abstract swirls are all that remain of an ancient ocean. In California, the whorls of grapevines like green fingerprints. In Ukraine, the ordered gold rectangles of wheat fields. And in deserts the world over, the endless ordered dots created by circular sprinklers.

Jem stays in his flat, writing cards to Emily. He does his best not to think about what has happened, using tried-and-tested techniques. It can't last, he knows. Soon enough he will need to make a decision, as to whether he's going to get his life together or throw it away. His birthday comes and goes like any other day. He gets three cards – from his mother, his eldest brother and Emily – plus a text from Lucas. It's no matter.

Emily is with her mother and stepdad for Bonfire Night, but Jem gets tickets for a display in Wimbledon Park the day before. They sip hot chocolate and gaze up at the colourful explosions, which are in time with music playing over the speakers. Emily's mittened hand grips his hand when the bigger rockets go off. Walking back through the dark crowds, she hugs close to him. If she notices anything wrong with Jem she doesn't say, and for a few hours he forgets his unhappiness.

Mika stays in a rented house, where the bedsheets are changed every three days by a cleaner. She looks Filipino; Mika wonders whether she has her visa in order but doesn't ask. She has an en suite bedroom; the walk-in shower is bigger than her old bed. She sleeps alone, but she knows this cannot last. The weather becomes mild, the evenings cold.

Jem senses he has missed a dream. That one should have happened, and didn't. Whether Mika had the dream without him, he isn't sure. Perhaps she will go on to have those dreams with someone else. Perhaps it is just a dropped beat in the rhythm. There's no way of knowing.

He buys fresh fruit and vegetables, and makes himself eat something at each mealtime. He stops taking the sleeping pills, and suffers through a week of wakeful nights. He forces himself to go out for short walks, to a local café or down the canal, and writes about what he saw in the cards to Emily. He goes for a haircut, wincing every time the buzzers come close to his ears. In the evenings he sits with the TV off, and listens to the silence.

Three weeks after Mika told him to leave, he opens an email which he has drafted and redrafted several times, without putting a name in the address bar. Deleting everything, he writes:

I'm sorry for before.
I just want to explain.
Hope you're doing okay.
   Jem x

He stares at it for a minute, deletes the kiss after his name, then presses send. He isn't waiting for a reply, but is still sitting at his laptop four minutes later when a new message notification pops up.

Want to meet up?
I have news.
   Mika.

Jem finds the pub, after a little searching, down an alley off Fleet Street. A barrel-shaped sign hangs over the doorway.

Ye Olde Cheshire Cheese
Rebuilt 1667

He pushes through the door, into the smell of beer and sawdust. It is very dark. He goes first into one room to look around, finding a bar with a few men standing around it, and orders himself a pint.

'I was wondering . . . ' he says, to the barman.

'Yeah?'

'The sign outside says "rebuilt 1667". Why was it rebuilt?'

The barman gives him a wry smile. 'Ever heard of the Great Fire of London?'

'Ah.'

'You go downstairs though, to the cellars – all that's the old stuff. Older even than the pub. Thirteenth-century monastery.'

'Thanks, I'll take a look.'

He goes through to the next room, a dining area with wood panelling so dark it seems to absorb what little light that struggles through the windows. Over in a corner, under a louring portrait of Doctor Johnson, is Mika. She sees him approaching and makes a face which is not exactly a smile.

'Can I get you a drink?'

'I've got one.'

'Ah, well . . . '

The seat next to hers bears a brass plaque which reads: *This was the seat most frequently occupied by Charles Dickens*. Over Mika's seat, below the portrait, another plaque reads: *The Favourite Seat of Dr Samuel Johnson*.

'I wonder what they talked about,' Jem says.

'Hm?'

'Doctor Johnson and Charles Dickens. What do you think they talked about?'

'Given that Johnson died almost ninety years before Dickens was born, not a lot.'

'Oh . . . '

They sit in silence. Mika is satisfied to have got this jab in, first thing, but cannot quite let go of the idea of a conversation between the two men, those giants of English literature. Can a conversation be carried on with the dead? With the not-yet-living? She imagines the two of them, side by side, with their steak and kidney puddings, separated only by a hundred years.

'How are you?' Jem ventures.

'Fine. And you?'

He's about to offer a standard British platitude – not bad, muddling along, can't complain – but suddenly they all ring hollow. So he musters as much emotional honesty as his upbringing allows:

'Not great.'

'Am I supposed to feel sorry for you?'

'No, I'm . . . just saying.'

He sips his beer; she sips her orange juice. At last, he asks:

'You said you had a dream here?'

'I lived upstairs. Shakespeare's time.'

'I would have liked to see that one.'

No you wouldn't, Mika thinks. He says:

'Do you think it means something, that I wasn't in the dream?'

'I don't make the rules, but . . . '

She shrugs, as though to say 'isn't it obvious?' They have uncoupled. Whatever force held them together has now released them. Their dreams will slowly drift apart, like astronomical bodies, never to come together again. They sit in silence. That seems to be what they're best at now. They can sit next to each other and say nothing for ages. Their lack of communication is prodigious. Mika wonders if there's a Guinness World Record for two people not saying anything to one another. They should enter. Eventually, Jem says:

'How's the baby?'

She shakes her head.

'You said in your message that you wanted to explain.'

'I did.' He nods. 'I do.'

'Then explain.'

'Right . . . okay . . . '

Jem clears his throat, blinks a few times, like a man who's about to step on stage, or into the dock.

'Me and Sarah were childhood sweethearts. Started going out in sixth form, but we were friends before that. We got married just out of school. Both our parents told us we should wait but . . . well, we were in love.'

He pauses for a second, but Mika doesn't react to any of this.

'I got a job at the bank; she got a job as a teaching assistant. We had two kids. Emily was the youngest and, um . . . '

For a moment, Jem seems to forget the name of his elder child. Mika frowns.

'And Jack was the eldest. He was eight years old . . . '

Jem swallows hard. With that single use of the past tense, Mika feels herself grow cold. The baby kicks inside her. She says:

'Tell me.'

'Sarah was gone on a course. She was training to be the school's welfare officer. It was the perfect job for her . . . ' He smiles. 'Anyway, so, Sarah was away for the night. I got the kids home from school, made dinner, did bath time and stories. And Jack . . . he was a bit under the weather, you know? A bit grumpy and quiet. But it was Friday, so no school in the morning. He had a bit of a fever so I gave him Calpol, but there was nothing else, no rash . . . He had his milk and brushed his teeth and went to bed.'

Jem's not looking at Mika; he's looking at the grain of the wood on the table, but she can't take her eyes from him. His whole body is tensed in supreme effort.

'Usually I'd go in and give him a hug and say "I love you". But that night, Emily was upset about something. I can't remember what, something at school, something that was on her mind. So I . . . I didn't.'

Mika doesn't want to stop him, because she's not sure he could start again, so she resists the urge to reach out and put her hand on his.

'I checked him after Emily was down, and he was asleep. I could hear him, breathing deeply. So then I went downstairs, put on the telly and sent a message to Sarah. I didn't mention that Jack had a fever. I didn't want to worry her. And then, in the morning . . . '

Tears, which have been pooling in his eyes, fall with a blink. Mika is unfrozen. She takes out a balled-up tissue and hands it to him.

'Thanks. Anyway, in the morning, he didn't get up. He liked a lie-in on weekends, so I didn't wake him. But by the time it was getting on for ten, I thought, better get him up. I'd made pancakes. So I went into his room and he was . . . '

Jem takes a breath. All there is in the silence of the dining room is that shuddering breath.

'Meningococcal septicaemia, is what they said. They said it would have been very quick . . . '

'I'm so sorry.'

Jem looks at her, blearily. It's not that he forgot she was there, more that he forgot she was able to speak, not just an audience to his performance.

'Sarah was . . . broken. And for the first few days, she said nothing to me. But, after the funeral, she told me I had to leave. She blamed me for what happened to Jack. Said I should have taken him to hospital, that I should have told her he had a fever. Wouldn't believe me when I said I checked him for a rash . . . '

'That's . . . awful.'

Jem shrugs. 'It was hard for both of us. I think she felt guilty, for not having been there.'

'But still—'

'Anyway, I did what she said. I wasn't coping well, and didn't feel up for a fight. I moved into a hotel, then a flat. We did all the stuff you need to do to get a divorce. I was very depressed, I suppose. I thought a lot about how I should, um, follow Jack.'

Mika puts her hand on his and squeezes, tight enough that it hurts a little.

'In the end, I checked myself into care. Because I knew, if I didn't get help, I wasn't going to be able to resist. It helped me get back on my feet, but Sarah used it as a way of proving that I wasn't a fit parent. Had my visiting rights reduced for Emily. I see her more now, most weeks, but for a while I barely knew her . . . '

Mika lets his hand go, because if she holds on, she might break something. She looks at Jem and sees a man who has been broken, and put himself back together, piece by little piece.

'What was he like?'

'Jack?' Jem looks surprised by the question, then breaks into a smile. 'He was very big – long arms and legs, a bit gangly – and very funny. He loved making people laugh. He collected fossils. He played the violin really, *really* badly.'

Mika laughs, and that makes Jem laugh too.

'Thanks for telling me about him.'

'Thanks for asking. No one ever does.'

'Your family?'

'No. I think they have this idea that it would upset me.

After the funeral, they would look sad when I walked into the room, but they wouldn't actually *mention* him.'

'Have they ever, since?'

'No, I don't think so. To be honest, except for the therapist in the place I stayed at, I've not talked to anyone about him since it happened.'

'That must be lonely.'

'Yes . . . ' Jem teeters on the edge of saying something. 'What?'

'The thing I've never talked about, to anyone, is the life I had before. One minute I was in that life and the next minute I wasn't. And I had that life all planned out, you know? A whole life. Very traditional. The marriage, the house, the kids. Such a cliché. Getting old together. And if it were anything else that ended that fantasy, I might see it as a good thing, you know? If I'd – I don't know – if I'd lost my job and decided to become a professional mountain climber, I'd be able to put a positive spin on it. "It's good that I lost my job, because it stopped me from living out someone else's idea of happy-ever-after." But he's not . . . '

Jem's voice cracks, and he swallows a few times before going on.

'Jack's not here. He's gone. He died. And I can't make that into a positive thing. If good things happen to me, that's fine, I suppose. But I can't ever think "maybe things are better this way", because that's saying that things are better without him. And they never . . . they never . . . '

He starts to cry in earnest, the sort of crying that precludes talking. He dips his head and his shoulders heave with sobs. Mika hesitates, looks around the empty room for someone to tell her what to do, to give her permission. Fuck it. She reaches out and wraps her arms around him. They stay like that for a minute. The barman pops his head in to look for empty glasses, then beats a quick retreat. Eventually Jem runs out of tears, and she lets him go.

'I shouldn't have kept them from you . . . '

'No,' she says. 'You really shouldn't have. You let me down, Jem. It hurt.'

'Yeah . . . '

'But thank you for being honest with me now.'

He waits, holding his breath. She says:

'So, if you'd like to be friends . . . '

'I would. I'd really like to be friends.'

'Okay then. We are.'

He does not say how he feels, and that's just as well. Friends is infinitely better than strangers. They sit in silence for a long minute, readjusting their expectations of what comes next. Jem searches for something to move the conversation on.

'You said you had news?'

Mika blinks.

'Oh . . . I did, didn't I?'

'Everything okay?'

'Yes, it's just . . . ' She reaches down, into her bag, and takes out a square of card. 'To be honest, I was expecting to be in a bad mood with you . . . '

She hands the card over. It is printed with golden letters that sink into the plush card. Jem reads:

Life Number Nine

Claude Lambert

invites you to celebrate the marriage
of his son

Oliver Lambert to Mika Zielinska

on 30th October at 2.30 p.m. until late

Venue: The Crypt at St Paul's,
Warwick Lane, London

followed by champagne, dinner and dancing

R.S.V.P.
by 25th October

Jem blinks several times, as though his eyes are blurry and the letters on the card might rearrange to form different words, different dates, different names. Mika is getting married in a week's time to a man he has never heard of. He thinks of the caravan moving off through the desert, of the crowded street, of blue smoke disappearing into the forest. He opens his mouth and says:
'Congratulations!'

Time passes.

Jem returns home and cannot, for a moment, place the smell that is hanging on his clothes. A particular perfume, a certain shampoo, and something beyond those changeable things which is out of reach. He takes off his jumper and breathes in Mika's scent. He isn't proud any more. He feels the need of her like an ache in his stomach. Like a hunger.

He gets into bed with his clothes on, all the day's sadnesses weighing him down like sandbags on a hot air

311

balloon. He makes an effort to let them go, to untie them one by one so that he might drift up and bump against the ceiling, but the knots are hard and unyielding. He waits, instead, for sleep to take him, though it is only mid-afternoon. He is ready to lose a few hours of his life to that ordinary sort of time-travel. He would Rip Van Winkle his way through the next week, the next month, even to the end of the year, if he were able. The weight of the present is crushing him.

Mika goes back to the house she's sharing with Olly. She puts on a nature documentary about urban foxes and tries very hard not to think about several things. She tries not to think about how nervous sending out wedding invitations makes her. How nervous going out in the street makes her, when she knows the Home Office is still looking for her. She isn't sure whether the paperwork for the marriage will get flagged, but from what she can find online, it seems things aren't that joined up. If they're quick, they'll get away with it. She'll be allowed to stay.

Most of all, she tries not to think about Jem, and especially not the way his expression melted and hardened into a smile when she handed him the invitation. Neither of them sends a message to the other for the five days between their meeting in the Cheshire Cheese and the pre-wedding drinks Jem has agreed to go to. When they see each other, Jem is wearing the same rictus smile, as though he hasn't been able to stop since they last met.

'You made it!'

He tenses up when Mika throws her arms around him. The bar is small but the music is loud. His entrance is noticed by everyone already there. He had been hoping for somewhere bigger, more anonymous, where he might be able to stay on the sidelines and watch. Instead, he looks around and recognises Tamara and Kenny Hoban, and the girl from the lucid dreaming workshop whose name he doesn't know. Apart from them there are three men, all a little younger than him. Any one of them might be Oliver Lambert – they all look alike, standing in a blond triangle as though to protect themselves from the rest. Each nurses a pint of fizzy beer. There are tiny spotlights in the ceiling with coloured gels, and the light they cast makes every face look grotesque.

'Of course I came!' He points his smile at her. 'Can I get you another orange juice?'

'I've already had about seven of them,' she shouts over the music.

'Nice place . . . '

'Olly's choice. You've met Suzy before?'

The woman shakes his hand for a little too long, looking at his face as though she's trying to find something there.

'You're Jem?'

'That's me.'

'How's the leg?'

'Much better, thank you.'

He is about to ask Suzy how she knows Mika when she smiles briskly and walks past him to the toilets. Mika looks at him for a moment, wearing an awkward smile of her own. He's not sure whether she's pleased he came or was only offering out of politeness. For a moment he thinks she is about to introduce him to her fiancé, then she says:

'Are you going to get a drink?'

'I guess I should.'

'I'll come with you.'

They go through to the other room, which is larger and

has sport on TVs. Different segments of the bar's population are facing in one direction or another, towards the screen of their choice. There is a faint smell of urine. They go and wait for the overworked bartender to get to them. Jem is rifling through his mind for an appropriate thing to say, but he seems to have lost the facility for natural conversation. Mika keeps looking around, as though she's worried who might be watching her.

'Thank you for coming,' she says, staring straight over his shoulder. 'I don't have a lot of people to invite . . . '

'It's nice to be here,' he says, wondering what on earth those words mean in this context. She looks at him as though to acknowledge that this is not true.

'It's all a bit sudden, I know.'

'It did surprise me a little.'

'We wanted to do things quickly.'

'Well, you certainly are. Doing things quickly, I mean.'

'Yes . . . ' She unconsciously adjusts the ring on her finger. 'You can understand why. Though Olly's father was difficult to convince.'

'Is he—'

'For you, sir?' the bartender interrupts.

'Gin and tonic, please. A double.'

'And for the lady?'

'Nothing for me.' Mika pats her belly.

The bartender scoops ice into a glass and takes it to the optics. They stand awkwardly for a second.

'You were saying?' She clears her throat.

'Is he – Oliver – the father?'

'He – Olly – is the father, yes.'

'Ah, right, makes sense.'

'What makes sense?'

'I just mean . . . it's nothing, I was just trying to understand.'

'What is there to understand?' she asks, scowling a little. Jem opens his mouth to reply.

'There you are, sir. Seven pounds eighty.'

Mika slips away as he's getting his wallet out. Jem watches her go. Perhaps he should follow her, but what would that achieve? He drinks down half the G&T in a long gulp, then orders another and drinks the rest. By the time his second drink has arrived and he's made it back to the side room, both Mika and Suzy are missing. Kenny is explaining something to two of the blonds, in a tone which might be enthusiastic or angry. The remaining blond, broken out of his protective triangle, approaches him, smiling insipidly.

'Hi, you must be Jeff? I'm Olly.' He gives a surprisingly firm handshake.

'It's Jem. Nice to meet you. Congratulations.' Jem does his best to sound sincere, but it rings hollow to him.

'How do you know Mika?'

'We . . . I guess we met at a lucid dreaming workshop.'

'Ha! That's very Mika.'

'Is it? I don't think it was really her thing.'

'Well, you two must have hit it off.'

'She hated me,' Jem says. 'She told me to go away.'

Olly frowns at him, trying to work something out. It looks like hard work. Jem isn't sure why he's being so contradictory, only that Oliver Lambert's whole demeanour puts his teeth on edge. He can smell the public-school entitlement coming off him like aftershave.

'What is it that you do?' Jem asks.

'Well, I used to work in the catering industry. That's how

we met –' (smug emphasis on that word 'we') '– but I've since gone on to take a senior position at Lambert BevCo. The drinks company.'

'Family business, is it?'

'It's . . . ' Olly's smile cranks up another notch to mask his irritation. 'My father's company. What was it you said you do?'

'I didn't.' Jem finds himself pulling his shoulders back. 'I'm in-between jobs right now. Taking a break.'

'Were you doing something very . . . *taxing* before?'

At this moment Mika and Suzy reappear. He thinks Mika looks a little flushed, but it could be his imagination. She comes and stands with Olly, and they hold hands, but this is the closest thing to intimacy Jem has seen. They smile at each other, but he wonders if he's the only one who can see the disparity there. One smile is honest, open – the smile of someone who thinks they have won the lottery. The other is the smile of someone who is giving nothing away.

He drinks some more.

Time passes.

The various sports on the TVs around the bar reach their conclusions. There are winners and losers, and the boundaries between the two camps are satisfyingly clear, in a way that they rarely are in real life. The punters go home elated or despondent. All in all, a satisfactory evening.

The rest of the pre-wedding drinks go off without incident. Mika returns with Olly to their rented house. She looks out of the taxi window all the way back, watching London pass by, its colours strangely muted, as though seen through mist. He chats about details of the wedding arrangements, and she responds with her thoughts, but her mind is elsewhere. Jem had talked with Kenny for a long time, which had kept Kenny from winding up Olly's friends any more with his socialist utopias. It was considerate of him, really. She remembers the apologetic look on his face when he left; she had felt she should be apologising to him.

'Will you come?' she had asked.

'To what?'

'To the wedding, I mean.'

'Oh, I wasn't sure whether—'

'It's a small guest list; it would mean . . . what I mean is, it would be nice if you could make it. Apart from Kenny, Tamara and Suzy, I've only got a distant cousin coming. Too short notice for my dad. Olly's got this huge family . . . '

His dark eyes had held hers for a moment, then he had nodded.

'Of course I'll be there.'

She had been so glad when he said it. Now she feels bad. Why does she want him there anyway? To remind him of what he could have won? Is she that awful? At least she gave him the present that she'd brought in her bag.

'What's this?'

'I missed your birthday, didn't I?'

'You really didn't need to,' he had muttered. 'Should I open it now?'

'No, no . . . open it later.'

Back in his flat, Jem tears into the red crepe paper and takes out a coffee table book. *Ornithographies* by Xavi Bou. He flips through the glossy pictures before reading the introduction, and at first he doesn't understand what he's looking at. Pictures of the sky, certainly, but with strange shapes – dark waves and tentacles and things that look like undulating soundwaves. Then it clicks – each picture is a time-lapse photograph of birds, revealing the shapes their flight makes. He looks at the labyrinthine shapes, the charcoal smudges and crisp ink-stokes. It's like seeing in four dimensions – height and depth and width and time. He flips back to the title page, where Mika has scrawled a dedication:

Jem – saw this and thought of you x

23

The next week passes for Mika in a pot pourri-scented blur. She thinks about all the weeks she has lived. She thinks about the roughly four thousand weeks she will hopefully live in total, and the twenty-four hundred weeks she has left. She reads an article entitled 'Making the Most of Your Time', which tells her that, if each of those remaining weeks were a 2 mm diamond, they would take up less than half a tablespoon. Suddenly Mika's remaining weeks seem impossibly small, impossibly precious.

And yet, here she is.

She is fitted for a dress with Suzy for company, but no one is there as she picks out the set menu for the reception, or the flowers for the arch under which she will be married. She feels no excitement for any of these things, but that doesn't matter – she never expected to get married, never saw the appeal anyway. Why should she be excited now? Each night she climbs under freshly laundered sheets and sleeps quickly, as though her mind is glad to be relieved of its duties for a few hours of unconsciousness.

When she wakes up on the day of the wedding, she is almost surprised. Some part of her had assumed the universe would intervene, that the Home Office would raid the house, that Olly's father would discover the truth about her immigration status, that St Paul's cathedral would collapse in a freak earthquake. She goes through the morning routine alone, because Olly is staying at his parents' house. She tries not to think too much about her in-laws to be. She can tell they're not happy with the wedding, but are surprisingly traditional when it comes to getting a girl pregnant. In spite of their reservations, they are eager to be grandparents. The thought of those strangers holding her baby occurs to Mika every time they meet, and she finds herself involuntarily hugging her bump.

By the time she gets to the venue, Tamara and Suzy are already there, in their midnight-blue bridesmaid dresses, doing each other's makeup. Mika isn't sure they'd be getting on without their shared job. Before any of the guests arrive, she wanders through the crypt. She has already seen inside the chapel where she will be married. Only about thirty couples get married in St Paul's every year. They're allowed to use the chapel because Olly's father is an OBE, and can request it for his children's weddings. There are heraldic banners hanging from the ceiling. The altar is very white, with a huge crucifix atop it. Mika isn't sure how Jesus would feel about the stunt she's pulling.

She walks through the vaulted crypt. She walks past the grand tombs of Admiral Nelson and The Duke of Wellington. She finds the memorials to William Blake, Florence Nightingale and Lawrence of Arabia. She stares for a while at the bust of George Washington, which stares resolutely back. It seems like an odd place to have a wedding, she thinks, surrounded by all this death. But maybe that's what a wedding is – a reminder that this is the choice you're making, the big choice, till death do you part.

'Oh, hey. It is Mika, isn't it?'

She spins around. Her thoughts were too far removed to notice the woman walking up behind her.

'Yes, um . . . '

'It's me, your cousin Jillian? But everyone calls me Nova.'

The woman is petite, her skin light brown, her hair very dark. Mika isn't sure what she expected her distant cousin to look like. They have met once, at a family gathering, when they were both too young to make much of one another. Mika has a faint memory of a girl a few years older than her, wearing dark glasses, sitting on top of the piano and singing songs to the room. They embrace. If Nova feels awkward, she shows no sign of it.

'What an amazing venue! I've never been down here. Don't you have to be a royal or something to get married here?'

'Well—'

'Oh, and I love your dress! The sparkly bits – so cool.'

'I . . . um . . . ' Mika looks down at the dress, seeing it as though for the first time. She had just picked the first one that fit.

'My wife Kate wore something a bit like that for our wedding. I wore a tux, because why wouldn't you, amiright? But it did have some sequins.'

'I . . . '

Mika finds herself lost for words. Nova is looking at her with such unabashed enthusiasm, she's finding it hard to take. When Tamara or Suzy are enthusiastic with her, it's a put-on, the way you're enthusiastic with a child to get them to do something they don't really want to do. Nova doesn't know anything except that her cousin is getting married, and has no reason to think Mika is anything other than excited to be here.

'Mika?'

'I'm . . . um . . . '

Mika is blinking very hard, trying to force the tears back inside. She has proper makeup on, she can't—

'Are you okay?'

Nova is peering at her closely, trying to work something out. She used to be blind, until she had an operation. It's something of a family legend, how she learned to see as an adult. Mika wonders what her face looks like to someone who didn't see a face until the age of thirty-two.

'You're crying.'

'No, I'm . . . fine . . . '

Her voice definitely does not sound fine.

Nova finds a tissue in her purse and hands it to her. Mika dabs her eyes, trying her best to preserve the mascara. They look at each other levelly for a moment, and whatever it is that Nova sees, she seems to understand.

'Do you wanna take a walk? Look at the dead people?'

'Yes, please.'

Jem cannot stop staring at his surroundings. It's the sort of place he's only ever seen on TV, for royal weddings and funerals. Rather than the usual rows of pews facing the front of the chapel, there are two rows of chairs facing inwards down either side. He's sat about halfway down, between Kenny and some relation of Oliver Lambert. He feels exposed. Across the way he sees the decoy blonds from the bar, and more men and women who clearly share a genetic link with Olly. Between them, nothing but polished marble.

He remembers once being taken to a play 'in the round' by Sarah, and found he could not relax for the whole performance for fear that the actors were going to call him up on stage to play a part. Kenny shifts awkwardly in his seat. He has put on a double-breasted suit with huge lapels which clearly hasn't been worn since the Seventies.

'What d'ya reckon?' Kenny says.

'Sorry?'

'Do you think the catering here is going to be good, or dogshit? I can't decide.'

The relation on Jem's right-hand side makes a noise of distaste, but Kenny doesn't seem to hear.

'On the one hand, clearly they've got money for the best. On the other hand, rich people don't know good food for shit.'

Jem is saved from replying as music starts up – a string quartet playing something classical. Olly is fidgeting by the altar, with a best man who is so similar he might as well be a stunt double. The air is syrupy sweet with the garlands of freesia and gypsophila tied to each chair. All heads turn to watch, as Tamara and Suzy walk down the aisle in matching blue, bearing more flowers, which they place on the altar before taking their seats. Then there is an expectant pause.

Jem knows he shouldn't have come. Now that he's sat here, he realises he cannot bear the thought of seeing Mika in a wedding dress. But he is here, and he will have to look and smile and seem happy, because he is on display. The pause lengthens. There is murmuring among the gathered relations. Then a small woman who Jem doesn't recognise steps into the entrance that everybody has been watching.

'Hi guys,' Nova says. 'I'm afraid there's been a change of plan.'

Jem takes his time leaving. It's only twelve minutes from Blackfriars to Catford; he'll be home in no time. He thinks if he's alone right now he might lose his mind. Since the woman – Mika's cousin, apparently – announced that the wedding is off, all hell has broken loose. There have been a lot of raised voices and recriminations echoing around the vaulted ceiling. Kenny has been particularly vocal in defending Mika's honour, and the rights of women in general to choose their destiny.

Jem hasn't spoken to anyone, though he considered going over and giving his condolences to Oliver Lambert, whose button-hole rose already seems to have wilted. He has collapsed in one of the chairs, and is being fed whisky from an uncle's hip flask. Jem feels sorry for him, but Oliver wouldn't want a kind word from him now. He lets himself out. Nobody stops him. The crypt smells of cooking meats – beef and salmon and something gamey – and he wonders vaguely who will be eating it all. He hopes it won't go to waste.

Eventually he finds his way above ground. The sunlight is pale, and it must have rained recently because the pavements shine like platinum. He finds a pub not far from the cathedral which is practically empty, orders himself a pint of bitter, a whisky chaser and a plate of sausage and mash. When the food is done, he has another whisky and feels, if not better, then at least well enough sedated to cope with the next few hours. He keeps wondering where Mika is. Will she have gone back to the garage, to the half-finished bus? Or back to Hoban's, despite the risk? Or is she nowhere

– just floating around, looking for a home? He imagines her sleeping rough and feels cold.

Finally he pays the bill and hauls himself to his feet. Outside the sky threatens rain, but he doesn't rush. By the time he reaches Blackfriars it's spitting. He rides the train to Catford, and when he gets off the drizzle has become a downpour. He doesn't have an umbrella, and there's no point in running – he's going to get wet either way. He moves his phone to the inner pocket of his suit jacket and plods on, keeping his head down.

Within five minutes he is at his apartment, and considers going to the supermarket, to buy something for dinner. But no, he will check what he has in. He can have a hot shower and—

'Hey.'

He stops, still standing in the rain. Under the awning which covers the entrance stands Mika. She is changed out of her wedding dress into jeans and a hoodie. She holds a carrier bag of clothes, but that's all.

'Mika . . . '

'You're getting wet,' she says, smiling at the understatement – he's already soaked.

'You're here.'

'Uh huh.'

'Have you been—'

'Waiting long? Half an hour. Did you go somewhere after I ran away from my wedding, or did they have the reception anyway?'

She's making jokes, but there is a look of such eggshell fragility to her smile, he cannot bear to laugh.

'I went for a drink. I thought you . . . '

'Were gone?'

At last he moves quickly. Mika flinches, as though he might be coming towards her, but he just goes to dial in the code for the door release, and holds it open for her.

'Come in, please.'

She follows him. A lift takes them up to the third floor. It's cramped. He can smell Mika's perfume, and the half-can of spray she has in her hair. She can smell the wet wool of his suit and the fabric softener he uses on his shirts. The lift doors open and they walk out together. The corridor is narrow, and Jem concentrates on not blundering into her. It would be so much easier to reach out, take her hand, but he doesn't dare. He unlocks the door to his flat. The air in here smells a little stale, but if Mika notices she doesn't say anything. They stand for a second, looking at each other. Jem clears his throat.

'Can I get you something? A cup of tea?'

She shakes her head.

'How about this – I'll get us both a cup of tea. You go get changed, maybe have a shower?'

'Okay.'

He turns around in a daze, then calls back:

'Mugs are in the—'

'Cupboard above the kettle; I remember!'

Jem goes to the bathroom. He doesn't want to leave Mika in case she disappears again. He can't work out what this means. He'll just have to keep living and find out. Closing the door behind him, he starts the shower and strips out of his clothes. The water is too hot but he doesn't turn it down. It wakes him up, makes him feel something.

When he's done, he gets out, takes one of the bath towels which are neatly rolled in the airing cupboard and wraps it around his waist. He should have brought fresh clothes with him, but it's no good now. He gives his teeth a brush to get rid of his whisky breath. He goes out, intending to go to his bedroom before finding Mika in the kitchen. But, when he steps into the bedroom, she's already there, sitting on the bed.

'Oh—'

'Just milk, yeah?'

'Um, yeah . . . '

He sits down in the chair opposite the bed, picks up the cup of tea and holds it for protection.

'Is this okay?' she asks.

'It's fine.'

'Fine?'

'No, not "fine" . . . ' he shakes his head. 'Have you noticed yet that I'm not good with words?'

She says nothing, just watches him, so he says:

'I'm glad you're here. And you can stay as long as you want.'

She looks into her cup, smiling.

'Thanks.'

'Are you . . . okay? About the wedding, I mean.'

'Well, I feel like I might be a bad person. Like, the worst person in the world. Olly didn't deserve that.'

It's Jem's turn to wait and say nothing.

'But I didn't deserve it either, so . . . '

'What will you do now?'

'I haven't really thought that far ahead. Is that okay?'

'Sure . . . ' Jem's smile looks a little forced.

They are quiet for another moment. Outside, a V of geese flies past, silhouetted against the pale purple clouds.

'I should—' Jem begins.

'You look ridiculous on that chair,' she cuts him off.

'Oh, really? Should I—'

'What I mean is, you should come sit on the bed.'

He blinks a couple of times, stands up too quickly, and catches himself on the edge of the bed. Mika crawls a little further up, towards the pillow end, and pats the space next to her. He sits down, keeping hold of the towel. Mika hooks her arm around his neck and pulls him into a kiss. He makes a surprised *oh!* For a moment, Mika feels as though he's going to pull away, but the moment passes. He brings his hand up to her cheek. She says:

'Am I taking advantage?'

'I hope so.'

Laughing, she makes space on the outside of the bed. After some wriggling, they're lying on their sides next to each other. This would be easier, except her baby bump is doing its best to push them apart. They kiss for a few minutes, and the only other sound is the ticking from his bedside clock and the faint rumble from the trains outside. Jem is a good kisser, Mika thinks. Still, he's a little too respectful of her personal space, and she takes his hand and places it under her T-shirt.

A few minutes pass. Everything is quiet, and Mika is starting to believe that all the best things in life happen in the silence.

Then, Jem pulls back.

'I don't want to spoil anything, but . . . '

'What does this mean?'

'Uh huh.'

They look at each other for a moment. This close, she can see the flecks of gold and green in his dark eyes. He can count the freckles that cross the bridge of her nose.

'All I know,' she says, 'is that whenever we're together,

I feel like I'm home. And I never feel like I'm home.' She closes her eyes, which makes it easier to talk. 'So at first, I wasn't sure I liked the feeling. It was too . . . domestic. I was worried that, if I gave in to it, I'd be stuck in one place forever.'

Jem says nothing; she resists the urge to open her eyes and look at his expression.

'But every time you went away, I felt lost . . . '

He puts his forehead against hers and kisses her. After a moment she kisses back, pressing her face against his as though she wants to leave an imprint, as though she wants them both to leave an imprint on the other, something that can't be rubbed out or hidden. Jem feels, perhaps for the first time, like he's no longer trying to catch up. Time and place fall away – it might be that he has found her in the crowded street, or returned to find her in the market place, or that their paths have crossed again in the jungle, her mouth still sticky with stolen honey. He wonders – did all of those reunions happen, or none of them? Is this the first time? Then she slips her hand inside the towel, and he forgets everything else for the time being.

Time passes.

They stay in for the first few days. He goes and buys food from lists which she has written. When he can't get what he's looking for in the supermarket downstairs, she accompanies him to the local grocers, showing him how to pick out the best stuff. Then they go home and cook together, stews and roasts and tagines that take a long time to cook, while they do other things. At night he lets her have the single bed and sleeps on the floor, except sometimes she can't sleep and pulls him up, under the covers.

They spend their days being a couple, doing couple things. It's all so ordinary, and ordinary is nothing of the sort. So they go to the cinema and eat popcorn. They visit the Museum of London and point at bones and clay pots and Roman coins. They go to an Ethiopian restaurant near St Pancras and eat their food off giant pancakes. To anyone else it would be a syrupy montage, but to Mika and Jem it's everything. It's poetry. It's the thing on the other side of music. It's heat and light and shelter.

It's true that neither of them quite relaxes, when they're out in public. Mika has no idea how the Home Office would track her, after she ditched her phone, withdrew her savings and stashed them on the bus. Nevertheless, if a waiter approaches the table too quickly, or a tourist asks them to take a picture, both of them startle.

At the end of the first week, they are lying together in the bed at the back of the bus. Jem is on his back, Mika is on her side, which is more comfortable, tracing shapes on his chest to try and tickle him.

'It's weird to think this bed will be somewhere else soon,' he says.

'What do you mean?'

'I mean, I'm used to my beds staying in the same place. Unless I move house.'

'Mm, I guess,' she says. 'You know what I saw in a documentary?'

'What?'

'Earth – the planet, I mean – isn't just spinning around the same bit of space over and over.'

'No?'

'It's moving. The whole galaxy is moving. Really fast. Like, a kajillion metres per second, I dunno. So, if Earth was leaving a line behind it, like one of those skywriting planes, you wouldn't see a circle, you'd see a spiral.'

'Like the book you gave me – the shape of the birds' flight.'

'Yes, like that.'

'But what's it got to do with this bed?'

'It's already moving,' she shrugs. 'Everything is. Always has been. You'll never stand on the same spot twice.'

He thinks about this for a minute, trying to ignore her finger, which is really starting to tickle now, ghosting over his sternum.

'It's all relative though, right? Relative to the garage we're staying still.'

'Sure. Relative to one another, too. We're not going anywhere.'

She traces, very gently, the crescent under his right pectoral.

'It'll be nice though,' Jem says, screwing his eyes shut. 'When you can look out of that window and see a field, or the sea, or whatever. I'm jealous.'

She stops tracing.

'What do you mean?'

Jem opens his eyes.

'I mean, it'll be nice, when you can—'

'No, not that. What do you mean "I'm jealous?"'

'Just that . . . well, it'll be nice.'

'Do you not want to come with me? I know that soon it won't just be me, but . . . '

He turns his dark eyes towards her, very serious.

'I do. I want to come with you. Very much. But I always assumed . . . '

'Assumed what?'

331

'In the dreams, you were always leaving. And I was always staying put.'

'Not always. There was the cottage.'

'Mostly though. So I thought – why would real life be any different?'

She screws her eyes up and laughs.

'What? What did I say?'

'You're just a heart-breaking individual, Jem. Like an orphaned puppy.'

'I don't think that's a compliment.'

'Of course you can come with me, if that's something you'd like. You have a passport, right?'

'I do.'

'Well, we might run into some trouble, what with your country's messy divorce from the EU . . . '

'It's *my* country now, is it?'

'But we'll figure it out. The nice thing about being on wheels is you can always move on.'

Jem considers it for a moment. The open road. Selling pancakes from a converted double decker. Going from country to country with a newborn baby. It would mean leaving Emily behind for longer periods, but maybe at some point Emily could join them on the adventure, when the school holidays allowed. It seems absurd, yes, but then so does love. And, as he thinks that word, he finds he cannot keep it inside.

'I love you,' he says.

Mika holds his gaze for a moment, not in a hesitating way, but only to give his statement its time and space.

'And I love you,' she replies.

*

They go shopping together. Between them, they're running low on savings, but the bus is almost ready. They buy the items that Mika hasn't already got from her newborn baby list – a collapsible crib, a sling, a steriliser tub and tablets, a huge number of sleep suits, vests and muslins. Jem is surprised by how much of this he remembers from first time around, and makes his own suggestions.

He spends time adapting the bus for the baby – installing a stair gate that won't be needed for at least another year, attaching soft corners to anywhere a child might bump its head, building compartments into the bedroom storage for nappy changing supplies. Mungo cuts out and welds a frame into the driver's compartment so that a baby seat can be strapped in.

When they're not out, they split their time between the bus and Jem's flat. He's arranged for an estate agent to come around so it can be valued and put on the market. He doesn't own much to get rid of – slowly his clothes migrate to the bus, and he takes a couple of boxes to charity shops on the high street. They keep his good coffee maker but sell the TV. His Bluetooth speaker goes to the bus, but his games console goes on eBay.

'What's that?' Mika asks.

It's late afternoon, and the sun is slanting in through the front windows. They've been clearing the kitchen, selecting pans and knives which are good enough for the bus. Mika is pointing to the sparkly box.

'Oh,' Jem laughs apologetically. 'Take a look if you like. You'll think I'm weird.'

She takes the lid off the box and leafs through the cards. They're all different shapes and sizes. Most of the envelopes are white, but some are pastel blue, pink, or purple. A few are deep red or green. Jem knows those are the Christmas ones. She reads the messages written on them. 'To Emily, for your 13th Birthday', 'To Emily, for when you leave home', and 'To Emily, for any time you need it'.

'They're all to her . . . '

'It's a funny thing but, after my accident, I felt like I wasn't going to be around for very long. Or, at least, I couldn't rely on it. So I wanted Emily to have some messages from me, even if I wasn't around any more.'

Mika is running her hand gently over the sheaf of envelopes. There must be close to a hundred.

'You okay?' he asks.

'What are you going to do with it?' She blinks hard.

'I dunno. It seems a bit silly now.'

'It's not.'

'Well, I guess I'll take it with me. There's no point in her having it if I'm still around, sending her messages.'

Mika puts the cardboard lid back on the box, presses it down gently with both hands. Then she stands up and hugs him so tight it knocks the air out of him.

'Are you—'

'Okay? Yes.'

'Good.'

'Now, come to bed.'

'Um, okay then.'

Afterwards, they doze in late sunlight. Mika puts her head on Jem's chest, and at length his breathing changes until it's clear that he's asleep. She thinks about waking him up, because there is still plenty to be done. But Mika is drowsy too, and a ten-minute nap can't hurt.

Around the world, 386,206 mothers are waiting to give birth. Running hands over the taut skin of their stomachs.

Arching into the backache which never quite goes away. Taking deep breaths which become shallower each day. Feeling the flutters of change which seem too faint to mean anything so profound. Around the world, mothers are in labour. In water baths, mothers on operating tables, mothers in beds at hospital or at home. Mothers in refugee camps, in the backs of cars going 70mph on the freeway, in birthing huts of mud and reed with the family gathering outside. Mothers with partners, mothers with friends, mothers with mothers holding their hand. Mothers with nobody.

Mika closes her eyes.

24

UNTITLED

1. FADE-IN

CLOSE-SHOT of a young pair of hands shuffling
a deck of souvenir playing cards, with the
words TARRAGONA / TARRACO printed on the
back, encircling a Roman gladiator . . .
Then we hear the warm crackle of a vinyl
record . . . Cat Steven's 'Oh Very Young'.

TITLE: 1974

2. EXT. PITCH 142 — DAY

MIKA (14) is sitting with her back against a
palm tree, shuffling the cards, wearing

336

oversized sunglasses. A tent and campervan can be seen in the background. It is morning. The sun isn't high yet, the wind lazy. Starlings fly between palm and poplar trees.

(Mika's dialogue is in Czech, with subtitles)

> MIKA (V.O.)
> When I look back on that summer, I think of it in terms of objects – the stubby bottles of beer the adults drank; the stacks of board games we played each evening; magazines and boiled sweets bought from service stations; 8-track cassettes to play in the van – T-Rex, Olympic, Bowie – and the deck of cards I bought . . .

3. EXT. PLAYA BARA CAMPSITE

While she talks, we see all the campsite has to offer in a glossy montage. A huge swimming pool with slides . . . a crazy golf course, tennis courts . . . three 'Gottlieb' American pinball machines, lighting up frantically . . . a souvenir shop full of pool floats, racy calendars and cigarette multipacks.

                    MIKA (V.O.)
My family kept coming back to this
campsite, in southern Spain, for
years. We would drive up in two
campervans with tents, folding chairs
and cooler boxes.

That morning, I was bored, but I
didn't mind. I liked the feeling of
boredom, because it was so easy to
fix. Everyone there was on holiday,
from the adults to my cousins.
Nobody had work or school or chores
to do. Everyone was ready for fun.
So it was nice to be a little bored,
the same way a rich person must
wonder which Rolls-Royce they'll
drive to the shops.

I thought: this is what heaven must
be like.

        4. EXT. BETWEEN PITCHES

WIDE-SHOT showing MIKA'S pitch and the pitch
opposite. She is watching the new people at
pitch 143 go about their morning routine.
They have a car and an old-looking tent,
khaki coloured, army surplus. A man and a
woman are boiling water on a paraffin stove
to make cups of tea.

5. EXT. THE OPPOSITE PITCH

> MIKA (V.O.)
>
> They arrived late the day before,
> while we were out having dinner at
> the beachside restaurant. British
> number plates – I was good at
> spotting them. I was just thinking
> about changing into my swimsuit to
> go to the pool . . .

A boy steps out of the tent.

ZOOM-IN on Mika's face as she pulls down her
sunglasses. A look of realisation – *Oh!* –
and she fumbles the glasses, dropping them.
MID SHOT of JEM (14). His hair is cut short,
he wears a baggy T-shirt and shorts. He
looks sleep-rumpled and dazzled by the light.

> MIKA (V.O.)
>
> For a moment, I thought this was how
> love at first sight felt. But it was
> more than that. I had never seen him
> before, but at the same time I'd
> seen him a thousand times. As I
> watched him, rubbing sleep from his
> eyes, I felt the memories coming
> back to me, one after the other,
> until I had them all in my hands,
> shuffling through them.

CLOSE SHOT of her hands shuffling the cards
and laying them out in the dirt, but the
usual suits have changed, instead showing JEM
in a variety of different costumes. We see
him as a caveman, a scribe, a Roman
bureaucrat, an old woman in the woods . . .

> COUSIN #1
> Mika, you want a game of tennis?

> MIKA
> Hm? Oh, no . . . you go ahead.

> COUSIN #1
> You okay? You were miles 'away.

> COUSIN #2
> She's probably getting her period.
> (He makes retching noises)

> MIKA
> Fuck off, loser.

> MIKA'S MOTHER
> Mika, don't speak to your cousin
> that way.

She watches as JEM eats a bacon sandwich and
finishes his tea. He doesn't glance her way,
in the shade of the palm tree. His parents
talk to each other and ignore him.
Eventually, just as Mika is thinking she

will be waiting all day, the man and woman leave with their shopping bags. Mika watches them walk down the dirt track.

FULL SHOT of JEM sitting in a deckchair to the right of frame, reading a magazine. MIKA appears, left of shot, standing hesitantly. Only after a moment does he look up. He stops. His eyes widen. After the shock comes a more complex expression, and Mika realises he's having the same moment she just had.

                    JEM
     It's you! I don't understand but, I
     remember . . .

                    MIKA
     I'm sorry, I don't speak English.

                    JEM
     Huh? Oh, um . . . how about Spanish?

                    MIKA
     Spanish? Did you say Spanish? No,
     but I know a little French . . .

JEM shakes his head - no French.

                    MIKA
     Shit, if only I'd taken English at
     school. Not that I'm any good at
     French. But if I'd known . . .

JEM
What? What are you saying?

A beat.

MIKA
Shall we go for a walk?

JEM looks helpless, so she holds out her hand. He stands, hesitates, then takes it. From silence, an explosion of sound - 10cc's 'The Things We Do for Love'.

6. EXT. PLAYA BARA CAMPSITE

MIKA takes JEM around the campsite like it's the Garden of Eden. That's how it looks to Jem, who has never ventured far beyond Croydon. The campsite is so filled with trees, they might be in the woods, were it not for the lines of washing strung between caravans. There are fat cycads that look like they've been there since the dinosaurs; towering palm trees, many of which are so elderly that they have been fitted with iron braces to stop their tops from snapping off; crooked pines. Everywhere are tanned, smiling people on their way to the pool or restaurant.

LONG ZOOM OUT to EXTREME WIDE SHOT – they walk down a path while above, a flock of swallows twist and swoop.

7. EXT. CAMPSITE GATES

They walk out to the road in front of the campsite, where there is a famous Roman archway. Once it stood astride the Via Augusta, leading into Tarragona, or Tarraco, as the Romans knew it. Now the two halves of the road part around it. Mika and Jem put their hands on the 2,000-year-old stone, each remembering the last time they passed under it, neither able to express their memory to the other. In FLASHBACK we see them waiting in the cells of the amphitheatre, waiting to die.

8. EXT. PITCH 142

They return to their families for lunch, to let them know they are okay. They eat separately, feet apart. CLOSE-UPS on both their faces, looking across at one another. EXTREME CLOSE-UPS on their eyes and mouths. From their looks it is clear – words or no, everything is wonderful.

343

9. EXT. THE BEACH

They watch the waves. MIKA buys them both an ice cream. JEM points out a flock of starlings eating crumbs outside a café, and both of them smile as though they are an old couple and this is a joke of theirs. After that JEM points to every bird they see, saying its name in English – sparrow, hooded crow, sandpiper – and she repeats them back like magic words from the Arabian Nights that will open the door on to a new, secret life.

10. INT. BEACH CAFÉ – LATER

They play card games while drinking tall glasses of Coca-Cola. They share a cigarette JEM stole from his father.

11. INT. CAMPSITE REC ROOM

JEM plays pinball, egged on by MIKA.

12. EXT. THE BEACH

MEDIUM SHOT as they walk down the beach, holding hands.

MIKA
(Wonderingly) A perfect day . . . My
first perfect day.

JEM
What does that mean? 'Perfect day?'
Can you point to it?

JEM mimes pointing; she laughs at him.

MIKA
You're cute when you're being stupid.

13. INT. CAMPSITE RESTAURANT — EVENING

Dinnertime. We see them with their families,
looking at each other across the courtyard.
MIKA sees JEM'S parents frowning at her, but
doesn't care, except for his sake. Let them
look.

JEM'S parents pay the bill and leave first.
MIKA watches him go.

SLOW PULL BACK from MIKA, who sits unmoving
in the middle of the frame, faintly smiling.
Everything around her is SPED UP – her
cousins order an endless parade of drinks
and desserts, the adults get drinks and
light cigarettes, the cousins start arm
wrestling, a glass of wine is spilled.

14. EXT. PITCH 142 — NIGHT

They return to their tent. MIKA looks, but there are no lights from JEM'S tent, nor any sign of them around.

15. EXT. UNDER CAMPER VAN AWNING — LATER

MIKA is playing poker with her family. The pot is gummy sweets and small change. She sees JEM emerge from his tent, eyes widening. He comes over to them all, in his pyjamas, with a washbag in one hand and a postcard in the other, which he hands to her.

CLOSE SHOT on the postcard in her hand. On the back JEM has written his name and address.

CLOSE UP on JEM'S face. He smiles in an apologetic way that says — 'just in case'. CLOSE UP on MIKA'S face. She understands without having to be told — in the memories they have rediscovered, there are many disappointments.

Task complete, JEM raises one hand in goodbye and slopes off towards the shower block.

                    MIKA'S FATHER
Who is that boy?

                       MIKA
I just met him today . . . He's
nice.

                     COUSIN #2
He's 'nice' . . .

COUSIN #2 makes a blow-job gesture with his
hand and tongue which earns him a swat on
the ear. Mika pays no mind. She tucks the
postcard under her leg, to look at when
nobody else is around.

        16. INT. MIKA'S TENT — EARLY NEXT
                     MORNING

Sun, stained orange by the canvas, falls
over MIKA'S face and wakes her. She opens
her eyes wide, with little sign of
sleepiness. Within a moment she is up, out
of her sleeping bag, unzipping the tent flap.

           17. EXT. PITCH 142

MEDIUM SHOT of MIKA emerging from the tent,
smiling broadly. We see her face fall in
dismay, but for a moment we can't see why.

WIDE SHOT of the pitch where JEM'S tent was
the day before. There is no sign of the car
or the khaki tent. They have packed up and
left before the dawn. MIKA looks around,
thinking she must have made a mistake. She
is looking at the wrong spot. But no, she
hasn't been turned around in the night. He
is gone.

She runs across the track, looking around in
case they have moved. She's breathing very
fast. She turns left, then right, then a
thought occurs to her - in FLASHBACK we see
the postcard.

18. INT. MIKA'S TENT

She goes to the tent and starts to rummage.
She looks in her rucksack first, then inside
her sleeping bag. She searches the floor
inside the tent, but finds nothing.

                    MIKA
     (Muttering) Where is it? I know it
     was here . . .

19. EXT. PITCH 142

THE FOLLOWING IN RAPID MONTAGE – as the morning goes on and her family wake up one by one, Mika searches again and again. When her cousins wake, she interrogates them fiercely. All to no avail – the postcard is gone. JEM is gone, with no trace of him left behind.

20. EXT. PLAYA BARA CAMPSITE

We see MIKA walking alone through the campsite, along the same route she took with JEM the day before. She goes to the shop, then beyond, in the direction of the beach, out of the campsite gates.

21. EXT. ROAD BEHIND CAMPSITE

MIKA walks down the road, which runs parallel between the camp and the beach. There's nothing special about this place. It looks a bit grubby. We see the campsite bins behind the wire fence. But –

FLASHBACK to the day before. MIKA and JEM stop here, returning from the beach, under the fig tree which stoops over the fence. They stand close, conspiratorial.

BACK TO PRESENT – MIKA walks over to the tree. She looks up at the leaves blowing in the breeze, wondering what signs they are making, wondering what stories are being told without her knowing she is part of them. It is late in the season. The figs are overripe, almost rotten. Many have already fallen to the floor to be trampled by passing flip-flops.

          (MIKA V.O)
We stopped there. Mutual understanding. The figs tasted strange to us both, with our twentieth-century palates. Wild and rank and heady. And then . . .

FLASHBACK to them stood under the tree, their lips dark with juice. Their eyes lock. They kiss, not knowing it will be the only time. Passionate but chaste. At the moment their lips touch, we hear the first piano note of Warren Zevon's 'Accidentally Like a Martyr'.

BACK TO PRESENT – MIKA picks a fig up from the ground and eats it. She grabs several more from the tree and eats them too, hardly bothering to chew. The juices run down her chin, mingling with her tears. As Zevon sings about making mad/shadow/random/abandoned love, we see a fast-cut montage of FLASHBACKS to her different memories – prehistoric, Roman, Elizabethan, etc. . . .

She eats another fig, and another, then her gorge rises.

WIDE SHOT – MIKA turns away from the tree, heaves once, twice, and vomits into the dust. CLOSE-UP on her face – she feels a bitter sort of relief.

It is done.

22. EXT. CAMPSITE GATES

MIKA walks back towards the campsite. People are shuffling to the shop, with canvas bags over their shoulders. Final WIDE SHOT as she walks into the shop to buy the morning bread.

END

December

25

They wake together, after the dream. It has never been this way, this relief so soon after the disappointments of the night. They have slept through the night and crossed the border into a new month. In those nine hours, the universe has expanded 479,000 kilometres, and it feels like it – like there is more space for everything. Like the world is spacious and full of light. Breathe in, breathe out. *Ah!* Mika finds that there are tears still drying on her cheek. They speak in unison:

'Did you—?'

'Was that—?'

They stop, take stock. She rolls onto her back, her hand finding his.

'That was our parents, wasn't it?' she says.

'I think so. I remember my dad telling that story, a couple of times when he'd had a drink. And I never really understood it. It was like a fairytale without a proper ending.'

'He didn't tell you about all the other memories though?'

'No, he just said they knew each other. Like they'd always

known each other. I thought he was just being romantic, over the top. I thought he was drunk.'

'And that was my mum . . . ' Mika says, frowning.

'That must be weird.'

'I haven't seen her since I was little. To see her life before she had me, to see my grandparents there . . . yeah, it was weird.'

'They both left,' Jem said, realising something for the first time. 'Both of them left us and moved away. Do you think—?'

'That they were searching for one another? Maybe. Still doesn't make it okay.'

'No, it doesn't. It's weird though, I always thought of the dreams as long-ago ancestors, people we could never have met. To see our parents . . . '

'Makes it real?'

'Yeah, I guess. Makes me realise that we're next in the chain.'

They are both silent for a while after that, as the world rearranges itself around them. After a long while has passed, she says:

'That's the last one.'

'What do you mean?'

'As in, we're up to date. The dreams have always been coming forward in time, closer to us. Those were our parents. There's nothing more to see after that. Just us.'

'Oh . . . I guess so. Just us.'

'That's okay though, right?' she says.

'Of course. Why?'

'I don't know, I'm just being paranoid. It's been an adventure, hasn't it?'

'It has,' Jem nods to himself, realising at the same

moment that his hospital-bed wish has been granted in full. It's been an adventure. Yes, there were times where he didn't leave the flat and ate nothing but microwave meals for days. But that was part of it too. He thinks of lying on the grass, still remembering the dawn of time. He thinks of driving his daughter in an open-top car. He seems to have become someone different to who he was, nine months ago.

'So, you know, I'm just worried that, now it's over, you might not want to . . . '

'See you any more? God, no . . . this is the adventure, Mika. Me and you. Whether it was ten thousand years ago or right now. This is the adventure. So let's keep having it.'

She takes a deep breath.

'Okay, yeah. Deal.'

It is December in London. Over Oxford Street the angelic arrays of Christmas lights are lit. In a thousand grubby windows across the city, pound-store fairy lights are strung up to flicker into the dark. It's dark a lot at this time of year, approaching the solstice. That turning point where it feels as though the day might go on getting shorter and shorter, until there's no light left.

Mika misses the warmth. She dreams of driving somewhere hot, but Jem doesn't mind the British winter. It's different, with someone to share it with. It's different, when the dark and the cold are drawing you closer to someone else.

The bus gets cold, but Jem says this is no bad thing – it's a good test of what it'll be like on the road. He buys a roll of insulation from a homeware store on the business estate and spends a day packing the cavities between the walls and panelling in the bedroom. Downstairs, Mika tests the kitchen and herself by making gingerbread.

The next day is Saturday, and it's time for Jem's visit to Emily. He's tempted to ask Mika along, but decides he should casually mention her to his daughter first, before making introductions. He takes Emily to Hoban's, where they are doted on by Tamara and Kenny, who invites them back into the kitchen. Tamara shows her how everything works, and gets her to make a batch of pancakes, while Kenny quietly interrogates Jem about everything that's happened since the wedding.

When it's time to go, Emily is gifted a bag of all the decorations Kenny puts in the ice cream sundaes – paper parasols and palm trees, flamingos, pineapples, tinsel pom-poms. She grins from ear to ear. When Jem is dropping her off at Sarah's, she turns on the doorstep and hugs him around the neck. It's a little tight, but Jem doesn't mind.

'Thanks, Dad.'

'What for?'

'For taking me to my new favourite place.'

'Oh, well . . . I'm glad you liked it.'

'Love you.'

'Love you too.'

She runs off down the hall. He straightens up. Sarah is looking at him.

'You changed,' she says.

'I guess.'

They look at each other for a long moment, two children who grew up.

'See you next time,' he says.

*

Jem stops to pick up a loaf of bread on the way back. The light is fading as he lets himself onto the bus. The kitchen is quiet. He calls:

'Hello?'

There is no response. He feels the beginnings of panic. Then, from upstairs, a faint reply:

'Up here.'

He breathes in and out, then climbs the stairs, still holding the loaf of supermarket bread. Mika is sat on the bed, with her hospital-ready bag next to her.

'Hey, how's it going?'

'It's . . . going.'

He frowns, puzzled by her tone. Then his eyes widen.

'Are you . . . is it . . . ?'

Mika puts one hand up. A cramp is building in the centre of her, bit by bit. It could be a regular cramp, nothing to get excited about. But, with each gathering second it becomes clearer. There's a reason they call it a contraction – she feels as though her insides are compressing down to the smallest possible point, into a core of wood or stone that presses heavily on her pelvis. Then, gracelessly, it's over, and she gasps a little air.

She looks up at Jem.

'Showtime.'

Immediately he's dumped the bread on the floor, is turning this way and that. It's comical and, for a moment, free of pain and flooded with relief, she smiles placidly at him while he dithers.

'What should I do?' he looks at her for guidance.

'It's fine. Mungo is going to lend us a car. He's bringing it back here now.'

'Oh.'

'I mean . . . '

Mika is about to say exactly what she means, but suddenly her throat closes up. Before she knows it, she's crying.

'What's the matter?'

'Nothing . . . stupid hormones . . . '

'Are you sure?'

Jem sits next to her and puts his hand on hers. Disarmed, she tells him a version of the truth –

'I just thought we'd get more time. It's a fortnight to my due date. I thought we could have Christmas. Watch shitty movies and eat cheap chocolate. I thought we wouldn't have to . . . '

Jem looks at her for a moment, trying to work something out.

'Wouldn't have to what?'

'I don't know. It's easy, when it's just the two of us. Informal.'

'You want things to be . . . informal?'

'Yes. No. I mean . . . '

'I'm not asking you to marry me.'

'No, I know. It's not that. I just . . . I'm scared that you might change your mind. When it's time to go. When you're leaving your quiet life behind for a noisy one.'

Jem stands up and turns away. He paces up and down the top deck a couple of times. Mika doesn't realise she's holding her breath until another contraction knocks it out of her. Finally, just as her insides are unknotting, he turns back and looks right into her eyes.

'I don't want a quiet life,' he says, 'if it doesn't have you in it.'

'You mean that?'

'I do; is that still what *you* want?'

'I want . . . ' Mika isn't sure what to say, but a contraction is starting to gather, so she needs to say something quickly. 'I want a life with you, Jem. A whole life. I want to dance in sweaty clubs with you, while twenty-year-olds point at us because we're so old. And I want to wake up in the morning and hear you banging around in the kitchen to bring me breakfast in bed. I want to hear you shouting at my child – *our* child – for being such a little shit. So, if that's not something you're up for, I need to know—'

The contraction grips her, and she can only groan the last drawn-out syllable. Jem waits for it to pass.

'I am,' he says at last. 'I'm up for it.'

'On a trial basis, yeah?'

'On a trial basis.'

Mika starts to laugh. She takes his face in her hands and kisses him, but she can tell his mind is on other things. There is the honk of a horn from outside the bus – Mungo is here with the car.

'Shouldn't we . . . ?'

'Alright, alright . . . want to tag along for the messy bit?'

It's the most elegant way she can think of asking the question, and elegance has never been her strong suit. Jem looks fixedly at her face for a moment, then nods quickly.

'Yes,' he says through a dry throat. 'Of course. Mika . . . ?'

He's cut off by her sharp inhalation. Another row of stitches is pulling tight around her insides.

'It can wait, Jem. Just get me to the car?'

Together they hobble down to the door, then out to the garage. Mungo goes and opens the passenger door.

'Are you going?' Mungo asks Jem.

'I am.'

'You okay to drive? I should really be minding the garage.'

'Are you sure? I'm not on your insurance.'

'Just one of you get in, for God's sake,' Mika shouts, 'before I give birth in a garage.'

'That would be very Christmassy . . . ' Jem mutters, sliding into the driver's seat and taking stock of the controls. He puts the car into gear, and they trundle through the garage, out into the dwindling sunlight. Mika is just coming out of another contraction, relief spreading through her like a warm glow.

'Right, here we go . . . ' Jem mutters to himself. He's gripping the wheel so hard his knuckles have gone white.

'Jem . . . '

'Just need to adjust my—'

'Jem!'

'What?' He looks at her, alarmed. 'What's wrong?'

She places her finger on his lips and, after a beat, he understands. For a moment they say nothing at all. For a moment, they sit in perfect quiet, and the world beyond is a frozen wave. The rest of their noisy life waits for them to begin.

All the rooms on the labour ward are busy when they arrive, and Mika has to wait in a bed on the antenatal ward. A woman in the next bed is listening to an action movie without headphones, and the sound of gunfire punctuates the more distant screams and moans from the ward. Jem fetches drinks and fans her face when she's hot. After an hour a room becomes free, and they move through.

'Make yourselves comfy,' the midwife says, as though the room is a venue they've hired. 'Play around with the lights, put some music on if you want to, as long as it's not too loud.'

'Thank you,' Jem says, stiffly.

'No need to worry,' she pats him on the arm. 'There's a little kitchen next door if you want to make tea or toast. All free on the NHS!'

The midwife hooks Mika up to a machine which measures her contractions, then she's gone, and for a few moments they are alone.

'You ready for this?' she asks.

'You don't need to worry about me.'

'Good, I won't.'

'Do you need anything?'

'You know, I probably won't want it by the time it's here, but since she mentioned toast . . . '

'I'll go find it.' He gets up. Just before he leaves, he turns back and looks at her in the bed.

'You okay?'

'Yeah,' he nods. 'Just trying to fix this in my memory, you know? Like taking a picture. Anyway, back in a mo.'

He goes out into the corridor and looks around, disorientated. There are so many doors in this place. Where did the nurse say the little kitchen was again? He walks one way, through some double doors, then down another corridor and out into the reception area. The nurse on the desk looks up from her paperwork.

'Okay there, sir?'

'Oh, yes . . . ' he frowns. Why did he come this way again? 'I just thought I'd pop out for some fresh air.'

The nurse smiles slightly and presses a button to unlock the main doors. Jem walks into the cold air. It's a cloudless night, very clear. The stars are unusually bright, for London. He looks up at his breath curling into the darkness. He thinks of the conversation with Mika, about how Earth is tumbling through space. He can believe it, looking at a sky like this. A sky with depth. He feels himself tumbling through the star fields.

And then he really is tumbling.

Before he knows what has happened, Jem is lying on the floor. Something strange is happening inside his head. Or rather, it's as though his head has split open like an overripe fig, and what was inside him is now leaking out. The feeling is familiar, but it takes a moment to remember. Ah yes, the night of the accident, in hospital, while life and death arbitrated. He struck a deal with the universe then, and the deal is done.

'Are you alright? Sir? Can you . . . ? Hang on, I'll get help.'

It's fine, Jem thinks. He's only fallen over. He'll get himself up in a minute. Above him, the stars get a little closer with every second. The first person reappears with someone else – the nurse from reception, who Jem now recognises as one of Mika's friends from the jungle – the one with the bundle of smoking leaves. How did he not recognise her before?

More faces are peering down at him now. There's Porus the beeswax merchant; the woman from the Fleet Street bawdy house; the centurion from the arena, wrapped up in a puffer jacket. Mansa Musa approaches, dressed in a parking inspector's uniform.

'Is he . . . ?'

'They're coming with a stretcher.'

'Should we . . . ?'

More faces now, impossibly more, crowding his vision – as many faces as there are stars hurtling towards him, and every one of them he knows, every one he has met countless times before. There is one face missing though, and he searches for that face in the crowd, the way he has searched for it a thousand times before.

'Hello,' he says, though he's not sure anyone can hear him. 'Tell her . . . tell her . . . '

And time passes.

26

It has been ten minutes. Eighteen thousand stars have exploded. Another two million stars have been created. Back on the labour ward, Mika has been joined by two more midwives, plus a doctor and two other people who are hovering nearby. Through clenched teeth she asks:

'Where's Jem?'

'I don't know, love,' the main midwife says. 'Just focus on this.'

'It would be easier to focus if I knew where he was.'

The doctor turns to one of the women hovering near the door.

'Would you just pop out and see where this lady's husband—'

'Not my husband.'

'Where this lady's . . . friend is.'

The woman departs. Mika is lost in the waves of pain crashing over her, but she notices the woman return after a couple of minutes and whisper something to the doctor. His expression doesn't change, and he says nothing.

'What's going on?' she asks. 'Where is he?'

Nobody answers; she shouts:

'Where *is* he?'

'Miss Zielinska, I'm sorry. Your friend had a fall outside, but he's being looked after now.'

'A fall? Why was he outside? Is he going to be *oh*—!'

The last syllable is drawn out as pain slices through the middle of her. For the time being, she forgets about Jem.

All over the world, women are going into labour. All over the world, they are waiting, feeling the pains which seem like a forewarning of the pain to come, the pain of separation. For a while, it seems like it will never come. Then, all at once, the moment. The moment of parting and the moment of meeting for the first time. The moment of one life, splitting in two. The moment of a life forgetting its past so it might have a future. For some, the cold slap of air, an unfamiliar medium. For some, born into water, a moment of respite, a moment in limbo, gazing up through cloudy liquid at a world which is still muffled in sight and sound.

And yes, there is blood, and bodily fluids, and screaming. Nobody said life was going to be pretty. But the mothers and babies, fresh-swaddled and reunited, look like nothing so much, to the people who gaze in at them, as gods.

Mika looks down at her baby, but it's not the baby she cares about right now.

'Will you take it for me?'

She tries to hand the baby boy to the midwife.

'Are you alright, dear?'

'Please, just take it. I need to get up. I need to go and find him.'

They turn their eyes to the doctor, who seems to have

authority over this situation. He steps up to the head of the bed. Mika sees his expression, and knows what he's going to say before he says it. After the empty feeling of giving birth, a second emptying takes place. She has never felt so hollow, so alone, so scared.

'I'm sorry . . . '

After a suitable time has elapsed, Mika and her baby are transferred to the postnatal ward. Although neither of them are suffering complications from the birth, they are given a private room. It's very hot on the ward. Mika supposes this is for the babies, to make it feel like they're still in the womb, but she feels as though she's slowly being stifled.

She can't look at the baby.

The nurses bring her food and drink but she can't touch any of it, and eventually they take it away again. The baby cries and she doesn't go to it. A nurse comes to try and teach her how to breastfeed, but Mika won't let the baby come near her, and soon enough a bottle of formula milk is produced for the child to suck on. Mika watches the nurse bobbing her son around the room with no particular emotion either way. Another woman appears, a therapist of some sort, and tries to talk to her about Jem, but Mika dismisses her just as quickly. A lot happens around her in the space of the next few hours, but Mika is barely aware of it. The baby sleeps but Mika cannot close her eyes. The ward is always half lit, and she sinks into a similar state, neither fully awake nor truly asleep. She is wrung out and bleached of colour.

Jem is gone.

A brain haemorrhage, they said. Very sudden. Probably a weakness, caused by his accident, which had gone unnoticed. Not unnoticed by Jem, she wants to shout, but does not. This is not the same doctor. There is no point. It would change nothing.

He is gone.

He is gone, and she is the one left behind. This is not a dream she will wake from. There is no time travel that will get her out of this. She is stuck in the present, like a fly on flypaper, and Jem is gone.

Morning comes and Mika watches the sun rise through her window. She is aware of people looking in. Some of this is concern for the baby, she knows. Some of it is concern for her, after what happened. And then, she thinks, there is something else. There are muttered conversations about her records, getting 'in touch' with someone whose name she doesn't catch. She hears something that might be an argument between a doctor and one of the senior midwives, outside the room. The midwife briefly raises her voice, and Mika hears:

'—that's not for *you* to decide.'

But they go back to whispering, and slowly drift away.

The baby wakes and starts to cry. She's surprised by how loud it is. It seems strange that something so small can make so much noise. After a while a nurse or a midwife – she's not sure of the difference – comes in and picks the baby up, rocks it until it calms down. Mika sees a raw-pink leg sticking out of the swaddling and winces. Her child's skin looks peeled; his limbs look as though you could snap them off like chicken wings.

Within ten minutes the baby has its nappy changed, is given more formula milk, is burped. Replaced in his plastic cot, he lies peacefully, staring at the ceiling and making no noise. Mika watches in a detached sort of way, then goes back to staring at the shape of her body under the sheets. Her whole body is sore, which seems unfair. It's as though someone picked her up and twisted her body like a wet rag. The nurse looks at her for a moment, seems to be about to say something, then leaves.

Time passes.

It always did, yet Mika did not feel it pass this way, like something abrasive, as though the sand falling through the hourglass of time is scouring her. She ignores breakfast first, then a midmorning snack, then lunch. At lunch a nurse pleads with her to eat something, anything, even just to have the little carton of pasteurised apple juice, but Mika shakes her head. The nurse takes the tray away but leaves the juice and plastic-wrapped coconut cake on her bedside table.

There are regular checks on her and the baby. Notes are taken. It all seems satisfactory. At one point the baby starts to cry and she realises she's leaking through her bra. A midwife persuades her to pump some of the milk, and Mika does it sullenly, as though it's a punishment for not trying to breastfeed.

It is early afternoon when someone comes in and closes the door. Mika looks up. It's the midwife she saw having that argument with the doctor. She pulls a blind over the window in the door.

'Mika . . . ?'

She says nothing, but looks levelly at the woman.

'Look, Mika, I know you're not feeling good right now. I don't blame you. And maybe I shouldn't be telling you this . . . '

She looks over her shoulder, at the shut door.

'They're coming for you. The immigration people. Do you know what I'm talking about?'

'Yes.'

It's the first thing Mika has said in hours. Her voice is strange, misshapen.

'I tried to stop it happening, but . . . '

'Now?'

'I think so; I don't know.'

Mika takes a deep breath. Come on – you need to wake up from this. Just wake up for a bit, and then you can go back to it. This was always the plan. Get out as soon as possible. Coming to hospital for the birth was always the risky bit. It was only a matter of time before some public-spirited bastard phoned the hotline.

'What do I need to do?'

'Well . . . ' the midwife frets for a moment, then snaps into professional mode. 'There's paperwork, but I'll do what needs to be done with that. I'm not going to let you go without giving your baby a final check-up, and we'll give you some of the formula he's been drinking. Are you okay for supplies otherwise?'

'Yes.'

'Sure now?'

'Yes, I promise.'

'Do you have somewhere to go?'

'I . . . yes.'

'Don't tell anyone I helped you with this, alright? They'll probably find out anyway, but . . . '

'I won't say a word, I swear.'

The midwife nods, seeming to convince herself.

'Alright. You get yourself ready, I'll get him ready. We can't go out the front door because there'll be questions down there. There's a way out the back. Do you need me to call you a taxi?'

'Yes, please. Thank you, I can't—'

'Don't, it's fine. Oh, hang on.'

She takes out a pen, tears a bit of paper from Mika's notes and scrawls a telephone number.

'You'll get in touch with me, when you're out? To let me know you're okay?'

'I will.'

'Come on then, up you get.'

Mika wills her legs to move. Slowly she swings herself out of the bed and lands softly, then waits for a moment to see if her legs will support her. Her body takes a minute to readjust to gravity, as though everything inside her is still in a semi-liquid state. She stands, and her legs only tremble a little. She goes to her bag, finds the jeans she changed out of when she arrived and pulls them on. Getting socks and shoes on is more of a challenge, but within five minutes she's ready to go. The midwife has done her checks and calls her over.

'You have something to wrap him in?'

'There's an outfit . . . '

'In the bag? Let me get it.'

'End pocket.'

The midwife pulls out several tiny items of clothing and proceeds to wrap the baby – hat, mittens, fleecy vest. Mika is amazed by the speed with which she does it. The baby doesn't complain. The final thing is a padded pram coat which is printed to look like a spacesuit. Her breath catches – Jem picked it off the rack at the store, held it up to her with a look of such childlike glee that she hadn't been able to say no.

'Are you ready?'

'I think so.'

'Can you take baby? Then I can bring your bag.'

'Um . . . okay.'

Mika takes the baby handed to her, holds him in an imitation of how the midwife was holding him. It's fine, really, when he's so padded out like this. She might be holding anything. Just another piece of luggage.

'Alright, come on. Keep your head down and keep moving.'

The midwife lets herself out of the room, and doesn't look back at Mika as she starts to walk down the ward. They get to the end of one corridor, turn left, and pass a nurses' station.

'Angela—?'

'Hey, Holly. Just taking Miss Zielinska to another room.'

'I didn't see anything about that. Let me just check . . . '

They keep moving. Mika's heart is beating fast, but it's a weak sort of beat, as though this excitement might wear it out. She concentrates on Angela's feet walking the plastic floor ahead of her. The midwife puts a key that she's already got in her hand to a locked door.

'Through here.'

Mika steps into a stairwell that smells of bleach and damp. Angela picks up her bag and jogs down the stairs. Mika can't follow so quickly, but does her best. The baby makes it difficult to see where she's putting her feet. At the foot of the stairs they proceed into a stockroom full of a fleet of mops in wheelie buckets. She feels sick. From there they go through one locked door, then another, out to an empty lot.

'I have to leave you here,' Angela says, looking at her phone.

'Okay.'

'The taxi is around the front. I told him Trafalgar Square, but you can give him the real address. Go that way and follow the building around. Registration ends SMR. Good luck.'

Mika finds a way to hold the baby with one hand, takes the bag with the other and starts to move. She's already out of breath by the corner but doesn't slow down. Behind her she hears the door close and the key turning in the lock. Around the front of the labour ward there are a couple of cars waiting outside the building. A pregnant woman is getting out of one. The other is a taxi but has the wrong registration. She looks wildly around and sees another car driving further up, towards the main hospital building. She starts to sprint again. She would wave if she had a hand free, but the driver must spot her, because he stops now and gets out. He looks alarmed as she approaches.

'Slow down! Is okay – I help. Bag?'

Wild-eyed, Mika just nods. The driver takes her bag, lugs it into the boot, and goes to open the back door for her.

'I have no car seat . . . '

For a moment she has no idea what he's talking about, then remembers the baby.

'It's fine; I'll hold it.'

The driver looks dubious but nods. She gets in and he closes the door behind her. In the struggle to get the seat belt around them both, the baby squeals once. She looks down and sees its dark eyes looking up at her.

'I'm sorry . . . '

It's the first thing she's said to her child. It seems

appropriate. She's about to say something else when the driver opens his door and swings into the seat.

'Where you go?'

Mika gives him the address for Hoban's. It's not the safest place, but she can't face the garage right now. At least she'll have Kenny and Tamara to help her. The taxi drives up towards the main building, where she knows Jem's body is lying in a cold room. The taxi driver asks her some friendly question or another, but she doesn't hear it. They follow a roundabout and come back down the way they came. As they pass the labour ward, she sees a man out front who seems to be looking for someone, and a white van pulling up. Mika puts her head down as though she's looking at her baby.

She spends the next week in the spare room at Hoban's. It's a risk, but what's the alternative? She is sore and tired and cannot sleep without having nightmares. She feels leaky with tears and blood and milk; she can't hold things in any more. She learns to look after the baby, but doesn't feel any easier in its company. It's as though it was switched with someone else's child without her noticing, but her body knows the difference. She still cares about it being okay, the way she would about any motherless child. But whatever you're supposed to feel, whatever a 'maternal instinct' is, she lacks it.

So she learns to change nappies, to feed and burp it, to bob it around while singing songs. She gets better at pumping and bottle feeding, but never puts it to her breast. Then, when it is asleep, she will stare at it, willing herself to feel something other than failure. In spite of Kenny's urging that it might be a good idea, she doesn't give the baby a name. It doesn't feel like she has the right to do that.

Christmas comes and goes. In the middle of the night, when she can't get back to sleep after a feed, she looks up how to give up a child for adoption. She has heard of women walking into hospitals and leaving their baby in the reception. She fantasises about what it would feel like to walk out. Morning comes and she's still awake when there comes a gentle knock at the door.

'Come in.'

'Morning, lodger,' Kenny whispers, appearing around the door with a tray.

'It's okay, Kenny – he's awake.'

'Well good morning, little buddy.'

The baby turns its head in the approximate direction of Kenny's voice as he puts the tray on the bed. It's chocolate chip pancakes and fresh orange juice. Kenny has been making Mika all kinds of things to tempt her. She tries a little of everything to be polite, but still has no appetite. Kenny is standing over the cot – which he went and picked up with a load of other stuff from the bus – blowing raspberries and pulling faces. The baby doesn't laugh or seem surprised, but is very attentive to it all. Mika thinks he probably appreciates the show of interest, and immediately feels bad.

'What d'you think you'll do today?'

'You're looking at it.'

Kenny nods slowly. He hasn't objected to her moping around the place, contributing nothing. She thinks every morning that he'll kick her out, or at least insist she makes a plan. But each morning he just leaves the tray. This morning, however, he lingers.

'I found out. About Jem.'

Her eyes dart up from the patch of bedspread she had been considering.

'When?'

'Tomorrow. New Year's Eve, eh? A crematorium down Catford way. Open invitation.'

'Oh.'

'Could be risky though, if the Home Office goons made the connection between you two. Still, we can babysit if you want. Think you'll go?'

Mika says nothing.

It's snowing when she arrives, ten minutes late. Not heavy snow. Not the kind that will settle. It skirls from the grey, dancing over the gravel drive, then disappears. There's a hearse sitting outside the chapel but it's already empty. She goes inside, carrying the package with her.

' . . . I'm told he was a devoted worker, and several of his colleagues are with us here today . . . '

The pews are a third full, all down the front. She takes a seat near the door and tries to work out who everybody is from the backs of their heads. That must be his mother there, with the hat and gauzy veil. Then his three brothers next to her, with their wives and older children in the row behind. There are a cluster on the other side who must be the colleagues from the bank, and a man sitting alone who might be a friend. Behind them is a woman sitting very upright, as though she's holding herself together, with a little girl next to her. The girl is maybe eight years old and is looking fixedly down at her shoes. Mika feels her stomach swoop as she recognises Jem's daughter.

The minister, or celebrant, or whatever he is, drones on

in an uninspired way about Jem's interests and hobbies. Some of it sounds unlikely to Mika, such as his love for craft beers, as though someone has made it up to fill space. Still, in the short time since Jem died, Mika has reflected on how little she knew about him. She had just assumed there would be more time to find out, so why rush? Birdwatching is never mentioned. She wonders, for a moment, if she might not have come to the wrong ceremony.

They play a piece of sad classical music, without claiming it had any particular relevance to Jem. His mother breaks down and is comforted by a brother. Mika thinks about leaving, but the sight of Emily, staring at her shoes, makes her stay. There are readings and a eulogy from one of the brothers, which is fond but vague. Mika doesn't know if Jem's spirit is anywhere any more, but it's certainly not in this room. The casket lies there, sealed and inert. Mika wants to go up and prise it open, just to prove he's really dead.

'We'd like to finish with a piece of music that Jem really loved when he was younger. If you'd like to stand, as he makes his final journey . . . '

They stand.

The music starts, and for a moment Mika almost laughs. For the first time – something true, something that belongs to Jem.

I wish I knew how it would feel to be free . . .

Nina Simone rings out loud and clear through the chapel, and when she sings about wishing she could fly like a bird, the curtains behind the casket part and it rolls into darkness.

When they walk out, the snow has stopped and the sky is lighter. Mika catches up with Sarah and Emily, who are standing a little way apart from everyone else.

'Hello . . . '

'Um, yes?' Sarah instinctively moves a little, so that she's in-between Mika and Emily.

'Sorry, you don't know me. I was a friend of Jem's. Of your dad.'

Emily looks up at her.

'That's very nice,' Sarah says. 'It was nice meeting you, but we have to—'

'I have something from him, for you.'

'For . . . me?' Emily says.

'It's not a gift he wanted to give you. But he had a feeling . . . no, that's not right. He had no idea. But he said to me that, after his accident, he hated the idea of you growing up without him. So he made you this.'

She hands her the box, which she has wrapped in brown paper to keep it nice. Sarah looks as though she's about to block her for a moment, but Emily is quick to reach out and take it.

'Can I . . . ?'

'Please.'

Emily tears off the drab paper, revealing the sparkly holographic box underneath, and takes off the lid. The three of them look at the trove of cards. Emily picks one out at random. On the front, in his particular handwriting, it says: *To Emily, to be opened on your 13th birthday.*

Sarah and Mika exchange a look.

'He never said . . . '

'No, I only found out by chance.'

'That silly man,' Sarah says, not unkindly. 'He was . . . he was . . . '

'I know,' Mika nods.

*

She calls a taxi on the phone she borrowed from Tamara, and it drops her back in Soho. The pubs and clubs are bloated with New Year's Eve revellers and Mika thinks about getting drunk. Properly shitfaced. She could do that now, if she wanted to. Blot everything out for a few hours. But what would be the point? Reality would bleed back with dawn and a crying baby.

She goes back to the room above Hoban's. The baby seems indifferent. Another round of nappy changes, feeds, singing while patting his back. Often, he cries and wakes again when she puts him down, as though he would prefer not to be parted from her, or at least from her warmth. But she persists, feeding him again, rocking him around the little room, putting him back in the cot. She does it as many times as needed to get him off her.

She lies in the dark. At length sleep comes, but it's an uncomfortable kind of sleep. She tosses and turns, trapped in repeating loops of the labour ward, the funeral, the morgue she never visited. She dreams of the casket, rolling into darkness like a spaceship.

All around the world, bodies are in motion. Bodies are on rollercoasters, on Air Force-funded centrifuges, flying off the sides of mountains and suspension bridges. Bodies are canoeing down river rapids and waterfalls, surfing on rolling waves, riding 200cc engines through rush hour traffic. People are being flung into the air like the fireworks celebrating the advent of the new year.

What is this love of motion – motion for motion's sake? Do we yearn to know what it would be like to be a bird on the wing, a fish racing downstream, a planet tumbling through space? Does it just feel good? Or does it remind us of the truth – that we are never standing still, even when it feels as though we are? That to be alive is to be always tumbling, head over heels.

Mika is tossed by nightmares, and doesn't wake for midnight. But then, like diving beneath a stormy ocean, she reaches calmer currents and allows them to drag her into the deeps.

27

<f.o.>: locate_configFile
<f.o.>: main: using log level 511
<f.o.>: connected to 'MSVPimlico/B771'

. . .

xRui Hofoen
~ **Mika, you awake? It's time.**
~ **No? Seriously?**
~ **Okay, 'Wake up, Mika.'**
[Beginning *Wake-Up 3*, moderate urgency]
>> *Heartrate 64bpm*
>> *Heartrate 68bpm*
>> *Heartrate 71bpm*
[Wake complete, *Wake-Up 3* deactivated]
[Beginning *Pep-Up 7*, 40Hz]

[*AI diarist* engaged]

\>> Mika swings her legs out of her bunk.

\>> She sits, waiting for the Pep-Up sequence to boost her cortical levels of dopamine and norepinephrine.

\>> It's a long time since she talked to anyone except the ship's small crew in person, and she wants to be at her best.

\>> She stands, goes to the sink and brushes her teeth.

[Check *Morning News*]

Top Stories

1) CNX Presenter Tells Boss 'Everyone Knows'

2) Black Friday Deals Not to Miss

3) Six Dead in Supply Ship Attack

x*Rui Hofoen*

~ You up?

~ Yeah, I'm coming. How long?

~ Just under an hour.

~ Okay – there in two.

\>> Mika gets into her overalls.

\>> Leaving her room, she walks down the corridor until she reaches the bridge of Pimlico, looking through the narrow forward windows at the approaching star.

\>> The star is the brightest object ahead of them, but still only has a magnitude of -1.4 at this distance. It would look like any other star, except for the occasional flicker as the ribs of the Dyson sphere collecting its energy get in the way.

\>> Over the next ten minutes, the star grows steadily in size. Without any change to its background, the star looks as though it's inflating, a balloon filled with light.

\>> The ship's accountant, Rui Hofoen, comes and stands next to her, peering through the scratched glass.

>> 'Seventeen years since I've been back,' they nod at the approaching star. 'How 'bout you?'

>> 'Never,' Mika shrugs. 'I've never been back.'

>> 'What? How old are you?'

>> '127. I know it's weird. But I was born on one of the Spica orbitals and both my parents were born on ships so . . . I dunno. It didn't seem like anything special, I guess?'

>> Rui shakes their head, laughing.

>> 'Maybe you'll change your mind when you see it.'

>> 'Yeah, maybe . . . '

>> As though on cue, something comes between them and the star, partially eclipsing it. Mika feels a swoop in her stomach.

[*AI diarist* override]

[Personal Note]

It's the way you feel when you see a famous work of art, or pass by a celebrity . . . Meaningless really. Just a silhouette, but it's my first glimpse of Earth.

[Uploading hi-res sensory stream to *MSVPimlico/B771*]

@vrx.009281

[*AI diarist* reengaged]

>> Over the next few minutes they swing around to the sunlit side of the planet. A shudder passes through the MSV Pimlico as their deceleration, which has been happening since the outer reaches of the solar system, finally brings them to a stop.

>> They hover. At least, it feels as though they are hovering. Rather, they're moving sideways very fast, perfectly matching the spin of the planet. Behind her the senior navigator asks for permission to land.

>> 'This is ship registration beta-seven-seven-one-four

dash epsilon-nine two-seven, requesting permission to land.'

>> 'Copy that, beta-seven-seven-one. Confirm your cargo.'

>> These communications are a formality; everything important has already been agreed by computers. The mining ship will unload its cargo of star metal and reload the same amount of rubbish to be fired into the nearest star.

>> 'Helium, iridium, platinum, lithium . . . '

>> Mika stares through the window.

>> Mika stares through the window.

>> Mika

[Personal Note]

Set reminder: install a better AI narrator. One that doesn't get on your tits so much. See if there's a Black Friday deal. Mind you, they say AI narrators are getting it all from your own brain. If it's annoying me, it's probably just that I find myself annoying.

[Reminder set, tomorrow at 13:00:00]

Of course, Earth is exactly how I expected it to look. I've seen it on screens bigger and clearer than this narrow window, with its four layers of glass. Swirling clouds and shimmering oceans – check. Mountains, deserts and forests – check. Marks of human activity, cities and megastructures etched across the continents – check. It's not the beauty of it. I've seen ringworlds and orbitals that were bigger and more beautiful. Not to mention all the uninhabitable places I've seen – all kinds of stars, planets, asteroids and gas clouds.

It's just that, you know . . .

This is it.

Earth.

The place that people who have never been here still call 'Home', with a capital H. The place I come from, even though I've never breathed its air. Actually, that's not quite true. For my eighteenth birthday my girlfriend got me a jar of 'Earth Air' she bought online. God knows if it was real, but I opened it up and breathed it in, like I was huffing glue, while my girlfriend filmed and laughed. I wish I had that video. I wish I had a sense stream to play back. It sucks that I didn't get my NeuraNet put in until I was twenty-one.

Anyway, I don't want to be like the tourists who come here to gawp at 'the pale blue dot' and get all misty eyed.

But . . .

>> 'Okay, we're good to go,' the navigator addresses the room. 'Starting our descent.'

>> There is a slight jolt as they move towards the planet. Mika has no particular role in the descent unless something goes wrong, so she stays at the window.

>> After a minute the position of the ship relative to the planet changes, so she goes to the lower deck of the bridge and looks through a blister on the underside of the ship's nose.

>> Everything through the window gets bigger, until the windows are filled by blue ocean and white cloud. There is no fiery halo as they descend, the way it would have been for the first brave men returning from space.

[Personal Note]

Fucking pretentious software.

>> She watches as they zero in on a landmass surrounded by water. She watches as the land grows and

the water shrinks, until all she can see is land. A glittering mineral sheen of glass buildings, shot through with veins of green that must be tree-lined avenues.

>> Unlike the orbitals she has visited, everything seems cramped. An irregular grey rectangle widens in their view, then takes it up entirely.

>> A whirring sound vibrates through the ship as the massive landing gear emerges. The space port flickers with landing lights, and she catches her first glimpse of another human being, just a stick figure in a high-viz jacket, waving a flag. Around her the ship groans, as its massive bulk comes under the effects of Earth's gravity.

>> The ground comes closer, then a series of impacts sound through the ship as each of its eight legs makes contact with the surface. The engine sounds die down, until all she can hear is creaking metal.

>> 'Home . . . ' she whispers.

xSouth Terminal 7

~ **Welcome to Earth!**

~ **Local time is 16:09:03**

~ **Please read attached information for new arrivals**

~ **@welcome.info.packge/0032**

~ **Enjoy our new range of perfumes, courtesy of**

[Messages dismissed]

• •

<f.o.>: locate_configFile
<f.o.>: LogSearchAhead 2hrs 16mins
<f.o.>: main: using log level 511
<f.o.>: connected to 'South_Terminal_Free3'

>> It's a couple of hours after touchdown that Mika actually leaves the ship. The automated systems to

unload the ship take time to set up and calibrate with the ground crew.

>> At last, she walks with half the crew down the jetwalk to the terminal, pulling a suitcase behind her.

>> There are adverts for local landmarks (the Tower, the New Houses of Parliament, St Paul's) and products (chocolate, jewellery, drugs).

>> As they step through into the terminal, the doors swish open and an automated voice says 'Welcome to South London Spaceport, and welcome to Earth, the cradle of humanity.'

>> 'So *cheesy*,' grimaces Y'ven, the ship's doctor.

>> 'Ha, yeah,' Mika laughs, but her heart's not in it.

>> She feels strange. It's probably something to do with the differences in gravity.

[Uploading image bundle to *South_Terminal_Free3*] @imx.0234442

>> At length she goes through passport control and her luggage is checked for anything that should be in quarantine. It feels strange to be leaving the ship behind. The ship is her home, but no one is allowed to stay on board when the cargo is unloaded. Pimlico hasn't always been her ship, and she's left it plenty of times before on orbitals, but it feels weird to be checking into a hotel across town when her comfy bed is sitting in the spaceport.

• •

: LogSearchAhead 00519

>> From the terminal the crew ride a Tube train north and step into the grey drizzle of Soho.

[location found @152783.92110]

>> 'The cradle of humanity,' Rui quips, shielding their face from the rain.

>> 'Shall we find a bar?' Y'ven asks.

>> They find a bar on Gerrard Street, with a booth by the window. Y'ven buys a round of spiced wine, served in tankards. Very traditional. They drink and laugh, and have the same sorts of conversations they have on the ship, only a little more high-spirited.

>> Mika is aware of her crewmates eyeing the room, searching for anyone to chat up. They're only here for a long weekend, then it's back on the ship. Sowing wild oats is an imperative, but she's not interested.

I didn't say that.

>> 'You know what,' she says to Rui, 'I'm not feeling so great. I think I might go check in.'

>> 'Want me to come with?'

>> 'No, stay, have fun. Put a notch on someone else's bedpost.'

>> 'I'll do my best, lieutenant.'

>> 'Anything to get out of a round, eh Mika?' Y'ven nudges her in the ribs from the other side.

>> 'Yeah, yeah . . . '

>> After a minute of good-spirited mockery, she extricates herself and leaves the bar, suitcase in tow.

[Search Location: 'Vivaldi Hotel']

[Vivaldi Hotel, Soho, London @152783.92237]

>> *Three minutes' walk.*

>> A glowing line appears on the ground which only she can see, leading the way.

>> She looks up into the rain to see the shapes of the buildings looming over her. Unlike the orbitals she has been on, the architecture seems an odd jumble of styles,

new and old and very old. Some of it, she can't tell whether it's real or not. Surely there aren't buildings with wooden beams like that? But the patchwork quality is charming in its own way. The air smells strange to her.

>> She finds the hotel, a tower of dark glass.

>> After a minute at the check-in desk, she goes to an elevator, which takes her to the eleventh floor.

>> Her room is small, even by ship standards, but well kept. The view out over the rainy city – waves of light and shadow rolling in from the west – makes her feel strange again, so she presses the button to close the curtains.

>> She lies down on the bed, thinking she might doze.

[Beginning *Sleep 1*]

[Beginning *Sleep 5*]

>> Despite setting her NeuraNet to Sleep Mode, the feeling never comes. She gets up, goes to the bathroom and splashes some water on her face.

>> Perhaps she will get a drink after all.

>> The hotel bar is on the fourteenth floor. She rides the lift up and steps into a wide space lined with dark marble. Tall windows give a panoramic view of the sunset which has uncovered itself on the horizon.

>> The room is lined with pot plants, some of them trained onto frames so that they trail over the heads of the drinkers. There is a low hum of conversation and piano music, which at first Mika thinks is piped in, before noticing a figure sitting at a baby grand piano in the corner.

>> She finds a table next to a window but not too close to the piano. There is a patch to scan on the table,

and the menu appears before her eyes. She scans through until she sees the caipirinha.

[Order: 'caipirinha']

xVivaldi Bar

~ Your order has been accepted

>> Mika watches the sunset for two minutes.

>> Her drink arrives.

>> The lime juice makes her jaw clench.

>> 'Mika?'

>> She looks up at the sound of her name.

>> The piano has stopped playing.

>> A man in a crisp suit is standing over her.

[Search identity]

[Facial scanning complete]

[No match found]

>> *Heartrate: 88bpm*

>> *Heartrate: 91bpm*

>> *Heartrate: 97bpm*

>> Mika stands.

>> Unexpectedly, she throws her arms around the man.

>> It's as though they've known each other all their lives. Tears spring from Mika's eyes, unbidden and unexplained.

>> 'Jem . . . '

>> It takes a moment for her memories to catch up with the present.

>> Mika feels a wave of memories breaking over her.

>> No, not like that. Not a wave. Wave.

>> Like the surface of her memories breaking open. Splitting, like an over-ripe fig. Bursting rotten, bursting sweet. As though . . .

>> As though . . .
>> As though . . .
>>asthoughmemoriesareburstingthroughthebursting
rottenburstingsweetmemoriesfigtreeandconveniently
skippingoverthreehundredyearsofmemoriesarebursting
rottenburstingsweetfiiiiiiiiiiiiiiiiiiiiiiiiiiiiiiiiiiiiiiiiiiiiii . . .
[*AI diarist* has stopped responding]
[Do you want to wait?]
[*AI diarist* ended]
[Uploading hi-res sensory stream to *Vivaldi_Bar_0982*]
@vrx.009282
>> 'I went to your funeral.'
>> 'I died . . . '
>> 'Are you working here?'
>> 'The piano. Did you—?'
>> 'Yes, I heard; very nice.'
>> 'And you—?'
>> 'Visiting. First time on Earth.'
>> 'Oh . . . '
>> 'Will you sit?"
>> 'Yes.'
[Unknown User *239/F329K2n2* wishes to message you]
[Message accepted]
xUnknown
~ **What is happening?**
   ~ **I don't know.**
   ~ **It's like friction.**
~ **Friction?**
   ~ **Between 'me' a minute ago and 'me' now.**
~ **Yes. I don't know where to start.**
   ~ **Let's see . . .**
[Personal note]

The whole thing was a dream. All of life, a dream . . .
[End Log]

Thank you for viewing.
This transcript ©NeuraNet.

Epilogue

28

Mika wakes in her bed in the upstairs of Hoban's. It's early morning, still dark. The first morning of a new year. It takes her a minute to remember where she is, and when. She remembers a version of London several hundred years in the future. She remembers looking down at Earth from space. She remembers looking up and seeing a familiar face.

The baby is asleep; she can tell by its breathing. She gets out of bed and goes to look at the shadow-shape of it. Its head is tilted back. With her eyes she traces the flick of the baby's nose, the brushstrokes of its open mouth. She stares for a long time, as the baby sleeps, working something out. It's not a maternal instinct that she's feeling, but a survival instinct.

She saw Jem again. They had a conversation. The memory of it glows inside her, but she knows it will not sustain her on its own. She wants more. And for there to be more, she has to look after the baby. She has to make sure she continues into the future to meet Jem. It's not a noble reason to start caring about her child, but who cares if the result is the same? If you've lost your car keys you can still hotwire it.

In half-darkness she packs her things, then the baby's supplies. When this is mostly done, she moves the baby to the bed. He stirs but doesn't wake. She collapses the travel cot and puts it inside its own bag. Finally, she changes the baby's nappy. He wakes this time, and cries a little until she puts him to her breast. He doesn't seem to know what to do for a moment, but he's startled enough to stop crying, and for a couple of minutes they struggle to work it out between them.

At last, he latches, and sucks for ten minutes until the effort wears him out and he sleeps again. Mika puts on the baby sling she's only once got out of the packaging and straps it on, fumbling in the dark, then gets the baby into it. Again he stirs, then finds a comfortable position against her chest and sleeps again.

She tries to be quiet, getting out of the room and down the stairs, but it's impossible with the baby strapped to her and the unwieldy luggage. Still, nobody seems to stir. Kenny snores, and Tamara sleeps with earplugs in to block it out. Mika gets down to the café. Everything is dark and quiet. The ghost-smells of food hang in the air. She turns on enough lights to find an order pad and pencil:

Thank you for everything.
I'll be back sometime.
Mika x

She tears it off to stick up, then thinks of one more thing to say:

You saved us.

She pins it up with the other note, thinking about who the 'us' is that she's referring to. From the kitchen she takes the formula milk the baby has been drinking, then steals a large carton of apple juice and some stale croissants. Kenny will forgive her, in time.

In time, in time, in time.

Time to go – she lets herself out of the back door, using the key Kenny gave her, then wraps it in a tissue and posts it back through. Soho is dark and mostly deserted as she walks to the Tube. A street sweeper whirrs along, close to the pavement, gathering yesterday's wrappers, bottle tops and spent firework casings. A couple of drunks in sequinned outfits progress slowly, propped against one another. A homeless man sleeps in a doorway and does not stir. They ride the Tube west, with men in hi-vis jackets and steel-toe-capped boots. Mika thinks about the buildings they are on their way to build, and whether they will still be standing in three hundred years' time. They are quiet when they get on, sleep-groggy or hungover, but by the time they get off at Vauxhall, they're chatting away.

All around the world, people are talking. To each other, first thing in the morning. To strangers on the way to work. On phone calls and video calls which criss-cross the globe. Into microphones. Whispered words, a hand cupped around an ear. Vocal cords across the world are vibrating. The air is vibrating. Millions of microphones are carrying the words through ticket booth plexiglass, into Millions of Homes All Over America, over airport PA systems, into recordings which will never be played back. People are singing. People are chanting. People raise their voices alone, or with another, or with a whole crowd.

People are saying their last words.

People are saying their first words.

When Mika arrives, the garage is shut up and dark, but she knows a way to let herself in using the side door. By the time Mungo arrives to raise the big shutters, she has fed and changed the baby in the little kitchen, has put all their stuff on the bus, and strapped the baby car seat into the rack by the driver's seat. While Mungo makes her a coffee, she books them onto a late afternoon ferry from Dover, using a new bank account she set up online. She has tested the bus's electrics, secured everything in the kitchen inside the lockable cupboards, and fastened everything down on the upper deck.

Everywhere she turns, Jem's handiwork looks back at her. She moves quickly, not dwelling. For a long minute she had stared at a splat of paint on an upstairs window, where she had tickled him while he painted the ceiling.

'Look what you made me do!' he had shouted, not seeing the funny side.

'Lighten up,' she had replied, 'it'll scrape off easy when it's dried. Now, back to work, chop chop!'

She runs her fingers over the dried paint, feeling the ridges from the brush. Then the baby cries, startling her, and she gets back to work. When everything is done, Mungo reappears.

'You sure you're ready?'

'Do I look ready?' she quips.

'You look – and don't take this the wrong way – unhinged. You've never driven it, now you're taking it out with a baby onboard.'

'I've got my licence.'

'But it's your first time with this bus.'

She smiles a don't-fuck-me smile.

'Can I get my bus out of this garage, please Mungo? I thought you wanted that?'

He looks at the baby on her shoulder.

'What are you going to do? Like, I get that the bus is a home and a business, and that's great. But what about when he needs to go to school?'

'I'll homeschool him.'

'What about making friends?'

'There are other kids who travel with their parents. And kids make new friends every day.'

'What about when he needs to see a doctor?'

'I'll work it out.'

'What about—'

'Mungo!' she yells, and hears her voice bounce around the hangar. She takes a moment to breathe. 'Look, I haven't got it all worked out. I'm not saying it's not crazy. But the world is crazy, fitting people into little boxes labelled "French" or "Chinese" or "Asylum Seeker". It's borders and passports that are weird, not me. It'll take some working out, but I'll manage.'

He frowns, still looking for the objection that will cut through.

'And you know what?' she says. 'It'll be *fun!* Because it's fun not knowing what you're doing. It's fun, flying by the seat of your pants.'

He looks at her face, and seems to give up.

'I'll make sure you've got a clear path.'

'That's it? I'm good to go?'

He nods; she hugs him.

'Thanks, Mungo; you've been amazing.'

'Mika, I'm not good at the soppy stuff. But, you know, I'm really sorry . . . '

He trails off, looking awkward.

'It's okay,' she says. 'I'm sorry Jem's not here too. But maybe I'll catch up with him, on the road.'

Mungo looks briefly misty-eyed before turning away. Over his shoulder he calls:

'The door will need raising a bit more than I usually have it. Gimme five.'

'Okay.'

She turns back to the bus.

'O-kay,' she repeats to herself. 'Okay, okay, oookay . . . '

She gets onto the bus and carefully places the baby into the car seat next to the driver's seat. She's held him so little, she's still unsure of how best to manoeuvre him. But she straps him in as tightly as she dares, then tucks a blanket over to keep him warm. Then she swings herself into the driver's seat, buckles herself in and places her hands on the wheel. Her stomach is in knots.

'Come on, Mika . . . '

She guns the ignition. Behind her, the engine shudders then roars. The vibrations travel down the length of the bus, up her spine. She breathes in short gasps. Putting the bus in gear, she releases the handbrake. Very slowly, she eases up the clutch and for the first time feels the engine bite. The huge bulk of the bus is under her control. In time, she knows, it will come to feel like an extension of her own body. For now, she'll settle for not crashing.

She eases it out of the spot where it's parked, onto the wide path between the wrecked, half-dismantled vehicles. There's not a lot of light in the hangar, so she turns on her headlights. There's a tight turn at the corner, then another turn to line up with the exit, then it's a clear run. Ahead, she can see the sky getting light. Mungo stands to one side, watching with barely concealed apprehension.

She eases the bus forward. It's too much to wind her window down, so she just waves at Mungo, who raises one hand and holds it there, like a salute. Then they're out, under the doorway. Early morning light washes over the bus, and for a moment she's dazzled.

They pull out, over the forecourt and onto the road. The sky is foaming pink and gold and purple. Another day is in the offing. Earth continues to shoot into deep space, orbiting a star which is just coming into view for Mika and her son. Somewhere not far from here, she knows, Jem's daughter will be waking up. She adjusts the sun-shield and checks her mirrors. When she looks down, the baby is squinting up uncertainly at her.

'I should warn you,' she says, 'I don't really know what I'm doing. There's every chance we'll get picked up by immigration at Dover.'

The baby frowns at her. It's just gas, she knows, but he looks as though he's having second thoughts about his mother.

'But I'll work it out. We'll work it out, together. You're going to go to the stars. Well, not you, exactly, but sort of . . . it's complicated.'

Lulled by the rumble of the engine, the baby closes his eyes. Mika looks at him for a moment more, puts the bus in gear and eases it forward.

Across London the average temperature is five degrees, light winds from the east, skies clear with no rain predicted. On her sixth-floor balcony in Lambeth, Keira Abdullahi has stepped into the chill air to watch the birds. Not a murmuration of starlings this time, but a group of eight – no, nine – crows, circling up into the bright air. Keira remembers those questions which came to her before, half a year ago: how did we get here? Where are we going? Is this all an accident?

She is seven years old now, not six, but she still doesn't know the answers. Still, as she watches the circling crows she sees – for a moment – the shape they are making with their flight. An arabesque on the paperwhite sky. She cannot read the meaning of the symbol, more complex than the calligraphy on the cover of her father's Qur'an. For a moment time ceases to exist. No, it does not cease – it happens all at once, all together. Everything she lost – the Minnie Mouse wristwatch, the pack of glitter pens, her grandfather – is still there, right where she left it. Keira looks at the secret design for a moment more, then shivers. The morning is cold. She goes inside to eat her Coco Pops.

In a bedroom a few miles away, Emily takes the sparkly box Mika gave her and places it in her lap. She cannot do this every day. For all the cards in the box, it would last less than a year if she opened one every morning. Besides, most of the envelopes are marked with a particular occasion – her first heartbreak, her wedding day, the birth of a child. Emily doesn't know if she will ever do those things, or if she even wants to do all of them. Still, it's comforting to know that Jem will be there if she ever does.

Today, however, feels like a special day. She cannot say why. Carefully, she takes the lid off the box and sets it to one side. Her fingers dance over the stiff envelopes, until she finds one that looks appropriate.

Whenever you need it.

She takes out the blue envelope, closes the box, and tears open the paper. The card inside is a watercolour of three swallows swooping over a pastoral landscape. She pauses for a second before opening the card. The message is written over both sides:

Dear Emily,
What to tell you about today? I went to the shop
and bought some bread and milk. On the way back
I saw that a pipe had burst under the high street,
and water was welling up from cracks in the
tarmac. I made a vegetable soup for dinner and
froze half for another day.
That's about it, I think . . .
I wonder when you will read this card? I don't
have a particular occasion in mind. I'll write 'read
whenever' on this one. You might be nine or ninety-
nine. Come to think of it, how old am I? Am I a
robot now? Do you remember to charge my
batteries every day?
Do you know what though, there's that cliché
people always repeat – today is the first day of the
rest of your life. And like a lot of clichés, it
happens to be true. Today is the very beginning of
the rest of your life, and that truth doesn't change
with age.
Oh, and I'll always love you. That won't change
either.
Go and enjoy the rest of it, my love.
xx

Emily sits with the card for a minute after she had stopped reading. Then she folds it into its envelope and puts it back in the box. Her mother is calling from downstairs. There are pancakes with chocolate chips in them. Kenny wrote them his recipe. Emily leaves her room.

And then?

Time passes.

Acknowledgements

Suzie Dooré and Jo Thompson at Borough; Laura Macdougall and Olivia Davies at United Agents; DC Calum Ker, who helped me with the police bits; Alex Mauchlen and Chris Wynne, for the sofa and the Guinness; Alexandra Metaxa, who read me Antigone in the original Greek; Alice, Sam and Ewan – thank you.